CONTRACTS

THE KING & SLATER SERIES BOOK TWO

MATT ROGERS

Join the Reader's Group and get a free 200-page book by Matt Rogers!

Sign up for a free copy of '**HARD IMPACT**'.

Experience King's most dangerous mission — action-packed insanity in the heart of the Amazon Rainforest.

No spam guaranteed.

Just click here.

BOOKS BY MATT ROGERS

THE JASON KING SERIES

Isolated (Book 1)

Imprisoned (Book 2)

Reloaded (Book 3)

Betrayed (Book 4)

Corrupted (Book 5)

Hunted (Book 6)

THE JASON KING FILES

Cartel (Book 1)

Warrior (Book 2)

Savages (Book 3)

THE WILL SLATER SERIES

Wolf (Book 1)

Lion (Book 2)

Bear (Book 3)

Lynx (Book 4)

Bull (Book 5)

Hawk (Book 6)

THE KING & SLATER SERIES

Weapons (Book 1)

Contracts (Book 2)

BLACK FORCE SHORTS

PROLOGUE

1

Nepal

Aidan Parker hadn't come here expecting sweltering heat.

It contrasted with the brochures, the word of mouth: hell, it even clashed with a simple Google search. Type "Nepal" into any internet browser and you'd come away convinced the only danger besides altitude sickness was the potential for hypothermia. Sure, the mountains were coming eventually. They were headed for Gokyo Ri, a snow-capped peak in the Khumbu region offering staggering views of Everest and the surrounding Himalayas. Temperatures plummeted at altitudes above thirteen thousand feet, but they weren't anywhere near those heights yet.

They were low.

And it was hot.

In truth, it wasn't that bad if you stayed still. Maybe low seventies if you checked the weather app on your phone. But for the past few days they'd been trekking, and trekking in Nepal involved excruciating ascents and descents in equal measure, which, complete with the sun beating down on the back of your neck, meant perspiring like there was no tomorrow. And when you started sweating one hundred feet into a five hundred foot rise in elevation, there was little chance of it stopping anytime soon.

But that was only half the reason Parker's pores were working overtime.

His fourteen-year-old daughter, Raya, had deemed the trip the perfect opportunity to air years' worth of grievances.

'Did you even hear what I said?' she said as they reached the top of a steep hill.

Parker paused for breath, sucking in air as he hunched over. 'Hold on, Raya. Please...'

'You're not that winded,' she said. 'Stop making excuses.'

'You've been running track for, what, three years now? I'm not on your level. Work keeps me—'

'Yes,' she said. 'Exactly, Dad. That's what I was saying. Thanks for bringing it up on your own. Work keeps you—?'

Parker's heart rate settled and he said, 'Busy.'

'Understatement of the century.'

Parker flashed a glance over his shoulder. Sure enough, the rest of the party was in tow. It was, of course, a deliberate effort to hang back on their part. Both bodyguards had passed the request onto the Nepali guide and porter, so all four of them were a couple of hundred feet behind, ascending the mountain at a snail's pace. It gave Parker breathing room to muster retorts to his daughter's insults without having to deal with the added pressure of an uncomfortable audience, listening to everything that came out of their mouths.

He said, 'That's what this trip is about, Raya.'

'No,' she said, 'it's not. This trip is about you feeling less guilty, so when we get back home you can say, "But, honey, don't you remember Nepal?" every time I complain about you not spending enough time with me.'

Parker threw his hands in the air — each clutching trekking poles — in exasperated fashion. 'So you're already writing it off? In that case, what am I supposed to do?'

'I don't know,' she said. 'Maybe find a job that doesn't need the presence of bodyguards whenever you step foot out of your office?'

'It's not like that.'

'What's it like, then, Dad?'

Parker wiped sweat off his brow to save it dripping into the dirt at their feet. 'You know I can't talk about my job as much as I'd like.'

'Which is bullshit.'

He frowned. 'It's not. And you're not going to speak to me like that. If you have problems with me, which you clearly do, you're going to convey them to me like an adult. You can't have it both ways. You're pretending you're not my daughter so you can insult me for giving this my best shot, so you're going to do that civilly instead of swearing at me every chance you get. Understood?'

He'd been on the back foot the whole trip, and she hadn't seen him riled up often.

It made her hesitate.

Raya said, 'Okay, Dad. Sorry. I didn't mean to swear.'

'And I didn't mean to bite like that.'

'I just...'

'What?'

'I think you do a good job,' she said. 'You know ... as a father. When you're around. So I'd like to see more of it. But that's tough when you're at work twenty-four-seven. And I can't talk to you about it because we're sitting in teahouses every night with your two bodyguards awkwardly hanging around, making shit conversation. Sorry for swearing.'

'It's okay,' Parker said. 'I get it. Can we talk about it tonight?'

'In front of Winston and Oscar? As usual?'

'No. We'll find somewhere private to talk. We're only a couple of hours from Kharikhola. I'm not in the shape I used to be. Can I just focus on the walk, please?'

She said, 'Can we talk on the descents?'

'Okay,' he compromised.

So they set off, an uneasy pairing, trailed by a convoy that was required to accompany Aidan Parker at all times thanks to his crucial role in the rarely-discussed black-operations sector of the U.S. government.

2

B ut Raya didn't know that.

She knew her dad worked for the government, and little else. He'd always kept it that way. Mostly because of the NDAs he was forced to sign every year, but also because there was seldom a heartwarming conversation that would come from openly discussing his job. He'd tried to imagine opening the floodgates, spilling the beans on what exactly he dealt with day in and day out, but he couldn't see it ever brightening the mood at the dinner table.

Not that they gathered round the dinner table all that often back home.

His marriage was disintegrating, in the same way that many marriages did. No vicious arguing. No real emotion at all. In fact, it was precisely the opposite of how divorces play out on television, but wasn't that the case most of the time? He and Catherine had been drifting for the better part of five years. Each day that passed without his presence, each night he stumbled through the door exhausted and depleted, sometimes after ten p.m. ... each of those instances drove another slight wedge through the ever-widening gap between them. And that seemed to be a regular occurrence these days.

Raya didn't know of her parents' marital problems, either. Parker had ensured it, and Catherine hadn't been jumping at the bit to enlighten her.

How exactly could they explain that they'd probably soon divorce for no real reason other than sheer lack of passion and interest?

Thankfully, Raya eased off on the verbal assault until they reached Kharikhola, a small town at the peak of one of the mountains. They strode in an hour or so before sundown, and Parker dropped his trekking poles into the dirt at the first sign of the nearest teahouse. It was much the same as the buildings they'd stayed in over the last few nights, made of stone and bright yellow wooden trim, with an open front door that faced the trail and a cohort of young Europeans clustered around a plastic table with Everest beers in their hands out front.

Parker took a moment to compose himself. He hadn't expected to have to exert himself so hard. His ankles throbbed, and his chest tightened with each breath, and overall he felt a decade older as he put his hands on his hips and flashed a relieved look at his daughter when she pulled to a halt beside him.

But she looked fine.

She said, 'Were you ready for this trip, Dad?'

He said, 'Yeah. I'll get used to it. This is day three. I'll be fine by day five.'

'You're not as thin as you used to be. Maybe you should have shed that before we came here.'

'Thanks, honey.'

She shrugged. 'Do you want the truth, or do you want me to bullshit?'

For a fleeting moment, he was seized by a flashback to the endless days he'd spent cooped up in a featureless office, coordinating the high-pressure, high-stress, high-intensity operations that his fellow countrymen routinely embarked on. He tried not to shiver.

He said, 'The truth always leads to the best results.'

Briefly, she smiled. 'That's the dad I know. So, you want the truth?'

'Sure.'

'You're getting fat. You're spending too much time at work. You're ageing three years for every year you spend on this planet. I don't want you to work as hard. I don't want you to drop dead. I want to spend time with you. I want you to have a life.'

Parker didn't retort.

He just stared at her.

He said, 'Thanks, sweetheart. I understand.'

'But are you going to fall straight back into the same routines when we get home?'

He paused. 'I'll do my best not to.'

'Your best?'

'I can't promise you anything. My job ... won't allow it.'

'Why don't you quit?'

'Because what I do is important.'

'Will you ever talk to me about it?'

He bowed his head. 'I can't.'

She almost yelled at him. Almost. He could sense the words catch at the corners of her lips, on their way out but snatched by the protective shield of common decency at the last moment. He knew what they'd be.

You fucking selfish prick. Why don't you care about your

family? How could your job be so important that it means you have to neglect the people you're supposed to care about the most?

He didn't answer.

There was nothing asked, but there might as well have been.

He knew, deep down, exactly what Raya thought of him.

Because he thought the same of himself.

You don't talk about your job under the guise of nobility but you don't have the foresight or the self-discipline to even keep yourself in shape.

The bodyguards, Winston and Oscar, made it to the top of the trailhead. They wordlessly glanced at the teahouse.

Then they looked back at the guide and the porter.

The guide, Sejun, spoke passable English. The porter, whose name they hadn't had the opportunity to memorise, didn't speak a word of English. What he could do incredibly well was carry close to half his bodyweight in luggage on his back. He had both Parker and Raya's North Face bags tied together with rope and draped across his upper back, which meant he'd been carrying close to fifty pounds for the entirety of the trek. He was a small, skinny man with wrinkles and bags under his eyes from a lifetime of hardship. But he didn't complain, let alone utter a word, as they reached the top. This was his job, and he was damn good at it.

Sejun turned to his clients.

'Not here,' he told Parker. 'This place sold out. No rooms. Maybe twenty minutes down road, okay?'

Parker sighed.

Raya shrugged.

It spoke to their respective fitness levels.

They trudged along the trail, jabbing their trekking poles into the loose dirt at any opportunity, grinding their aching bones together endlessly, on and on and on as it started getting darker.

3

There was no trouble.

They made it with plenty of time to spare before the sun fell and night swept over the mountains.

But Aidan Parker arrived exhausted to the bone.

He realised with staggering clarity that there was a world of difference between mental stress and physical stress. He thought he'd be prepared to handle anything Nepal could throw at him due to the chaos he handled on a daily basis in his small windowless office in Washington. But as he stumbled into the teahouse's communal area and sat down at a polished wooden bench and dropped his head to the table, he understood the depths the human body could plunge to when pushed to its limits.

Raya said, 'Are you faking it?'

Parker lifted his head. He felt cold and clammy. 'What?'

She was sitting across from him, looking no worse for wear, scrutinising him. 'Are you pretending? You know ... to get out of our talk?'

He nearly groaned. 'What talk, Raya?'

'I told you I'd hold off until we were here safe and sound.'

'Hold on. I need a moment.'

'Like always.'

'Raya,' he snapped.

The owner of the teahouse, a small squared-away Nepali man, tiptoed out of the kitchen. '*Namaste.*'

'*Namaste*,' Parker said.

Raya repeated the greeting.

Then the rest of the party arrived.

Winston, then Oscar, then Sejun, then the porter.

The two bodyguards conducted a rudimentary survey of the premises. It didn't take a great deal of effort. There was the communal area which doubled as a dining room, then the separate low building consisting entirely of sleeping quarters. Each room had rickety metal bed frames and thin mattresses and nothing else. Maybe blankets, if they were lucky, but they'd brought their own sleeping bags regardless.

They watched the porter drop their bags on the concrete patio in front of the bedrooms and trundle into the communal building. He sat separately, as was the custom. He seemed to prefer it. They'd tried to coax him over many times during their time together, but the guide had quietly informed them it was Nepali tradition to sit on a separate table to the clients. Anything else would be seen as intrusion.

Parker respected that.

He appreciated his alone time as much as the next man.

Now, Raya said, 'I feel like this is our only opportunity to talk.'

Parker raised an eyebrow. 'And why's that?'

'Winston and Oscar are sweeping the rooms. Soon they'll be here.'

'They could sit at another table if you want to talk privately.'

'"*We can't do that, sweetheart,*"' Raya said, impersonating her father from the night before. '"*We don't want to exclude them.*"'

Parker sighed. 'Look, if you really want me to...'

'I don't want you to *do* anything. Except think about what a vacation entails.'

'This is a little tougher than a regular vacation, don't you think?' he said, attempting a half-smile.

She scowled and turned away.

The joke fizzled out, dead on arrival.

Sejun sauntered over, sensing an opportunity in the silence, and said, 'The usual?'

'Yes, please,' Raya said.

Five minutes later, the teahouse owner brought out steaming mugs of masala tea. The spices and herbs had been added without restraint, which Parker appreciated. He liked the tang. He sipped gratefully at the drink until it was all but drained. Now that they'd stopped they were getting cold, and the spicy tea warmed his insides. He hunched over the tabletop and stared at his daughter.

'Let's talk,' he said.

She looked up at him. 'Oh, now you want to—?'

'Yes,' he said abruptly. 'Let's cover what we need to cover.'

'Why?'

'Because I'm in the mood now.'

She said, 'I already told you what I wanted to—'

'People depend on me,' Parker said.

A pause.

Raya said, 'Okay...'

'Do you understand what that means?'

'Of course.'

'My job is what you'd call high-stakes. I'm not supposed to tell you that, Raya, but I will. I handle very important matters every day. I know you're not an adult, but you want to be treated like one, so I'll do exactly that. Without me doing what I do, people will die. I'm not exaggerating. I take my job very seriously, but sometimes the schedule isn't as clear-cut as it seems and I need to stay back at the office. Sometimes it takes all night — you've seen that. And I don't want to stop because people rely on me to be very good at my job. I'm sorry if it's hurting you. It's hurting your mother, too. But I have a tough decision to make day in and day out — do I want to give my family my undivided attention, or do I want to protect the lives of my countrymen?'

Silence.

Deafening silence.

Raya sat back and chewed her bottom lip and intermittently sipped at her masala tea.

Then she said, 'Do you like what you do?'

He shrugged. 'It's hard to say.'

'Do you look forward to going to work?'

'I guess. Because I know that the only thing I'm good at is coordination. And my job involves a lot of that. And if I wasn't doing that, I'd know full well that I was letting people die.'

'But then isn't that just guilt?'

'I guess.'

'So you don't really enjoy it?'

He said, 'This isn't a conversation I wanted to have with my daughter.'

'Why?' she said. 'Because I'm young? Because you think I won't be able to understand?'

'No...'

'I'm nearly fifteen. I can hear this shit.'

'I know.'

'Then what is it?'

He said, 'I guess I just never wanted you to be in danger.'

'You think I'm in danger?'

'No,' he said, backtracking. But he gulped involuntarily. 'Just a hunch I've always had.'

She seemed to pick up on something. Something deeper in his eyes. Something ... caring.

She leant forward and said, 'Can we sleep in the same room tonight, Dad?'

He tensed up. 'Raya, you know—'

She held up a hand. 'If you need to spend that much time at your job, then I understand. But it doesn't need to carry over out here. We're alone on a mountain. And I don't like it when Oscar has to sleep on the other bed every night. Can't you make the bodyguards share a room? Just for once?'

It went against all his instincts.

But, he realised, sometimes you had to rebel.

For the sake of your family.

He shrugged and said, 'I could do that. Just for one night.'

'We'll be safe,' she said. 'I promise.'

The naivety of youth, he thought.

But he said, 'I know.'

She excused herself to go to the bathroom, and Parker ushered Winston and Oscar over to the table in her absence.

4

I t hadn't been easy.

They'd debated, and debated, and debated, and finally Parker brought the hammer down.

He'd said, 'Gentlemen — this job pays well, right?'

'Yes,' Winston said. 'But, Aidan, you know it's—'

'I *know*,' Parker hissed. 'But humour me, will you? What if this is the last night I ever have with my daughter? I'm going to grant her this one wish. I don't give a shit what rules I'm violating.'

'But how are we supposed to—?' Oscar started.

Parker held up a finger, silencing him. 'If you still want your jobs when we get back, you'll let this happen.'

'It changes our plans.'

'I know. But you're going to do it regardless, because I want time with my daughter, and quite frankly she's sick of the pair of you.'

Winston bristled, and Oscar didn't visibly react.

Then Oscar leant forward and said, 'We're doing everything you wanted from us. We're maintaining a respectable distance during the day. We're not getting involved in conversation. We're—'

'I know,' Parker said. 'But you're here. And that's all that matters to her. Cut me some slack.'

'You don't get to do that,' Oscar snapped. 'Not with your position. Not with what you demand of us when—'

Parker held up a hand, cutting him off again. 'I won't hear another word. I'm not kidding. We're in the middle of fucking nowhere. Both of you bunk down for the night in the same room and worry about what you need to worry about later. Not right now. Okay?'

Oscar glanced left, then glanced right, then opened his mouth to say something.

Parker just wordlessly shook his head.

The bodyguard threw his hands in the air in mock defeat. He slapped Winston on the back and shot out of his chair. 'We'll eat in our rooms.'

'Do they allow that?' Parker said.

'Do I give a shit?'

Winston sheepishly followed his co-worker, and the pair disappeared from the dining room.

Raya returned moments later.

'How'd that go?' she said.

Parker shook his head. 'You're lucky I love you.'

She paused, and stared at him. 'You don't say that often.'

'When I do, I mean it.'

A half-smile crossed her face. 'Love you too, Dad.'

They ate steamed vegetable momos and sipped at mushroom soup and drank more masala tea. Then Sejun and his porter waved goodnight, leaving them alone in the dimly-lit teahouse.

Raya cradled her mug in her hands and said, 'I'm really enjoying tonight.'

'I think Oscar might be mad at me in the morning.'

'Not Winston?'

'He didn't seem to take it so personally.'

'Why do you think that is?'

Parker shrugged. 'He can probably see the humanity in this.'

Raya half-scowled. 'It's a strange life, isn't it? Having to fight to get a single moment that seems ... I don't know ... normal.'

'Comes with the territory.'

She paused to mull over her thoughts, and finally said, 'Would you do it all over again?'

'What do you mean?'

'All of this. The constant protection and the fact that you're never able to see your family. Is it worth it?'

'I didn't really choose this. It sort of fell into my lap. I'm good at it.'

'Right.'

'Yes,' he said. 'I'd do it again. But I'd compartmentalise better.'

'You'd—?'

'I'd forget about my job when I walked out those doors every evening.'

'You don't do that?'

'It's hard not to think about things.'

'What do you do, exactly?'

A sad smile crept across Parker's face. 'Not tonight, Raya. One step at a time. There's only so much I can tell you at once.'

'Oh, well,' she said. 'At least we get to be alone like this.'

She looked over her shoulder, seemingly paranoid that one of the bodyguards would be watching. But there was no-one in sight. Just the cold wind trickling in through the open doorway.

She said, 'You going to be okay for the rest of the trip?'

'I'll be fine. I can feel my body adapting.'

'Can you?'

She smirked, and he did too.

'I feel lighter,' he said. 'Trust me.'

'Imagine the sort of shape you'll be in by the end.'

There was Wi-Fi at the teahouse, so Raya pulled up pictures of Gokyo Ri through Google Images and flicked through them. There was a twinkle in her eye. Parker watched his daughter gaze with wonderment at the screen.

She looked up at him and smiled. 'It's really going to be something, isn't it?'

He didn't respond.

Just thought long and hard about the direction his life had taken.

Maybe I should have spent more time with her, he thought.

He shrugged it off. There'd be plenty of opportunities in the future. He wasn't that old yet. If all went according to plan with his health, there'd be a few more decades to strengthen the bond. So he didn't write it off as an abysmal failure yet.

He checked his watch and said, 'Time for bed, I think.'

'For you or for me?'

'I'm going,' he said. 'It's an early start tomorrow. You can make up your own mind. You're not ten anymore, kid.'

She smiled. 'Don't worry. I'm coming.'

The room consisted of the same setup they'd seen half a dozen times so far along the trail. Single beds pushed to either wall, with a thin strip of stained carpet in between to rest their bags, their boots, and their trekking poles. Parker unfurled his sleeping bag and stripped off his salty hiking clothes. He changed into thermals, slipped into bed, and adjusted the hard thin pillow under his head.

Out of the corner of his eye, he noticed Raya mirroring his actions.

She turned the light out, and all that was left was the steady mountain wind battering the building. The foundations were thin, so the structure shook slightly with each gale.

But it held.

In the darkness, Parker said, 'You're right.'

Raya's voice floated across. 'About what?'

'Feels a whole lot better when it's less ... professional. I don't like Oscar sleeping in the room. Feels like he's always watching.'

'See? I think I can get you to cut loose a little more going forward.'

Parker smiled. 'Maybe.'

'Night, Dad.'

'Goodnight, Raya.'

'I love you.'

He hesitated.

Maybe it would all be okay. He couldn't be paranoid forever.

He said, 'You too.'

Then he rolled over and exhaustion took hold and, utterly spent, he drifted into the deepest sleep of his life.

5
_____

As soon as he woke up he knew something was dreadfully wrong.

The fog of deep sleep took a few moments to lift. Parker peeled one eye open, saw the faint tendrils of daylight snaking across the wooden ceiling, and lay on his back as his mind and body came back to reality. He shifted slightly in his sleeping bag, and his muscles groaned in protest. His ankles and knees were swollen from repetitive blunt impacts on the steep descents. He shimmied his arms out of the bag and stretched them over his head.

His chest was tight — that worried him.

Other than that, he figured he'd be okay.

It'd soon be time for breakfast.

He rolled over to wake up Raya.

She wasn't there.

The sleeping bag was open, zipped all the way down. The silence became more pronounced. Parker listened to the nothingness and stayed still for a beat. He kept listening. Figured she'd be using the drop toilet, or up early, tapping away at her smartphone in the communal building.

But that didn't make sense, because her bag was gone, too.

Maybe she'd packed early.

Unlikely.

The last few days had been a constant battle to get all her gear stowed away so they could set off on time and maintain some sort of coherent schedule. He didn't figure she'd had a total overhaul of her habits within twenty-four hours.

He looked at the bedroom door. It lay ajar, cracked open a few inches. Wind whistled in softly. Through the gap, he could see the door of the opposite room. Winston and Oscar's. It was firmly shut.

He unzipped his sleeping bag and clambered to his feet. His joints were stiff, and his muscles were sore, and his neck was tight. He cracked his neck left and right and padded across the thin carpet, feeling the concrete underfoot.

He didn't say a word.

He creaked the door open and stepped out into the tiny alcove separating the two bedrooms in this module. The drop toilet lay in a small room between them. The door was open, and it was unattended.

Leaving only the communal building.

Parker thought about letting Winston and Oscar rest, but instead he raised his hand and knocked sharply on their door. Three times, to let them know it was him.

No response.

He looked down at the entranceway. Winston's Scarpa hiking boots rested diagonally against the wall, caked in mud and dirt and grime.

Oscar's were gone.

The foundations of unease crept in. Parker's throat tightened, and he felt the sudden *thud* of each heartbeat in his chest.

He knocked again.

Silence.

He reached down and tried the handle.

Unlocked.

Hesitant, he pushed the door open.

Oscar was gone.

Winston was there.

His head had nearly been ripped off his shoulders.

He'd been strangled to death with a garrote. Parker would have recognised the handiwork anywhere. It might have taken a civilian minutes, if not hours, to work out what had happened, but Parker took one look at the pale corpse splayed across the bed with a deep red line of ruptured skin winding all the way around his clammy throat, and knew the cause of death immediately. Winston's mouth was open in a twisted grimace, and his bloodshot eyes had crimson stains around them. He'd struggled and strained so hard against the metal wire that his eyeballs had nearly popped out. The sockets had bled as he'd fought for his life with a silent scream in his throat. His hands were still clenched tight, having locked up as he died in unimaginable pain.

Parker sat down hard in the middle of the alcove.

His own mouth fell open.

No sound came out.

His lips flapped like a fish out of water.

His hands started to twitch imperceptibly.

He looked back into his own room.

No sign of Raya.

He looked forward.

No sign of Oscar.

Fighting back vomit, he clambered shakily to his feet

and stumbled out into the pre-dawn light. Steam billowed out of his mouth in clouds as he rasped for breath. Reality shimmered, like this wasn't really happening. But it was. His heart rate was dangerously high. He found a plastic table resting on the concrete patio and clutched it hard, stabilising himself as his legs nearly collapsed.

The trail was dead ahead.

It was quiet.

Movement sounded to his right, and he looked over. He was barely lucid. Like a zombie. He couldn't concentrate on anything. But through vision blurred by tears he saw Sejun, perched uncomfortably on a step, hands in his pockets. The guide seemed disoriented. Out of sorts. But he still noticed Parker's condition.

'Are you okay, Aidan?' Sejun said.

Parker didn't respond. He fought back an overwhelming wave of nausea.

Sejun said, 'Have you seen Mukta?'

'W-who?'

'The porter.'

'No.'

'He's not in his room. Very strange. I go looking.'

Parker raised a shaking finger and pointed at the bodyguards' window.

As if that would explain everything.

Sejun raised an eyebrow. 'What?'

Parker couldn't fight back the urge any longer.

He turned and vomited on the table, then collapsed from the shock.

PART I

6

_____

The civilian flight touched down at Tribhuvan International Airport to audible sighs of relief.

A particularly vicious bout of turbulence had plagued the passengers for the better part of the last hour, and they were relieved when the wheels found solid ground and coasted toward the terminal. The wails and sobs of children dissipated, replaced by the steady murmuring of nervous laughter.

Jason King and Will Slater barely noticed.

They sat side-by-side in economy class. Not exactly the norm for a pair worth well over four hundred million dollars, but sometimes allowances had to be made. The flights had been booked on an hour's notice, and the small first-class section aboard was sold out.

It was okay.

They could handle a little discomfort.

The leg room wasn't optimal. King was six-foot-three and two hundred and twenty pounds, and with most of it rippling sinewy muscle spread across a bullish broad-shoul-dered frame, he was practically squashed into the seat. He wore flexible denim jeans and a black leather jacket over a T-shirt. They fit him well, but he'd only selected them for the flight. The rest of his luggage was home to an arsenal of outdoor and cold-weather gear. The job demanded it.

Slater's frame wasn't far behind his colleague's. A couple of inches shorter, and maybe a dozen pounds lighter, but what he lacked in power he'd always made up for with sheer raw athleticism. He had a little more space to breathe in the economy seat, so he'd leant into the aisle and let King's massive fist take the left-hand armrest for the majority of the flight. Not that he had a choice in the matter.

But he didn't mind.

He had all he needed in his right hand.

He cradled the plastic cup and drained the last of the vodka as the plane taxied to the terminal. It hadn't taken much effort to convince the stewardess to fill it to the brim at the beginning of the flight and charge him five times over for the hassle. Mostly because he was willing to pay, but partly because of his charm. He wasn't entirely oblivious to that particular talent. He used it when necessary.

And sometimes when not.

King glanced over. 'Is that smart?'

Slater said nothing. Scrunched the cup up, put it in the seat pocket, closed his eyes. Felt the warm glow bathe his insides. When he opened them again, he was happy.

Didn't take much to make Will Slater happy.

He said, 'Didn't realise we were on the clock already.'

'You never know...'

Slater looked bemused. 'What — first time we're back at work for Uncle Sam and you think it's all going to kick off the moment we step off the plane?'

'I'm surprised that someone with your history instantly assumes it wouldn't.'

'We're finding a missing kid on a hiking trail. Something tells me we're not exactly going to stumble across an international conspiracy here. I'd say we'll be okay.'

King scratched at the five o'clock shadow coating his jawline. 'Why do I get the feeling you're not exactly thrilled about this one?'

Slater threw his hands up in the air in mock disbelief. 'I don't know, buddy. Rub a couple of brain cells together and you might figure it out before we're done here.'

King half-smiled. 'I forgot to ask — you ever been to Nepal?'

'First time.'

'Same.'

Slater looked over. 'Isn't that strange, given our ... extensive travels?'

King nodded. 'Feels like I've been everywhere but here.'

'Looking forward to it?'

'About as much as you are.'

'You don't seem as irritated as I am about this little endeavour.'

The seatbelt signs blinked off, and everyone in the cabin leapt to their feet in unison.

King and Slater stayed put. They savoured the sudden cacophony of noise. It allowed them some discretion to talk about sensitive matters.

King slapped Slater on the shoulder and said, 'Because I don't whine and bitch about everything I don't totally agree with.'

Slater said, 'I'm here, aren't I? You think this is whining?'

'Yes. I do.'

'What do you think I should do, then? Shut up and get on with it?'

'Took the words right out of my mouth.'

'You *really* think this is the best use of our talents?'

'I think whatever Violetta approaches us with is the best use of our talents. I assume it's been determined by people far smarter than us. That's the way it's worked our whole careers.'

'So we get left on the sidelines for months in anticipation of a job, and then our first op involves cleaning up the mess a pen-pusher left behind when he got too careless and got rid of his security detail so he could have some precious one-on-one time with his baby girl?'

The cabin was emptying out, and King didn't immediately respond. He got to his feet, encouraging Slater up too, and they collected their carry-on packs from the overhead compartment. Then they sauntered toward the exit doors, with Slater leading the way.

King leant forward, over one shoulder, and muttered, 'Say something like that again and I'll hit you in the mouth.'

Slater barely reacted, but King could sense the hairs on the back of his neck rising.

Before they reached the exit, Slater glanced over the same shoulder and said, 'I think you're forgetting the last two times we fought, brother.'

'With that much alcohol in you, you think it'll go the same way?'

Slater slowed his pace even more. 'Want to find out?'

'Keep walking,' King said. 'Don't do anything stupid.'

'You're the one that opened your mouth first.'

King wasn't having it. He reached out and planted a hand in the small of Slater's back and timed the momentum exactly right and gave the man a gentle shove. Slater almost tripped over his own feet and was slow to right himself, clutching the back of one of the economy seats to prevent himself going head over heels.

When he stood up, he kept facing forward, and half-sighed.

'You see?' King said. 'You've had more to drink than you think. Let's have this chat another time.'

'Just shut up until we get to the hotel.'

They made it to the stewardess, and both of them smiled and nodded and said, *'Namaste,'* as they passed by. Then they descended the exterior stairs, both brooding.

Slater muttered over his shoulder, 'Still got something you want to say?'

King dropped a hand on the same shoulder. 'You drink too much. It makes you too volatile, and you say things I know you don't mean. I understand there's some serious shit swimming around up there in that head of yours, but you need to cool off and deal with things rationally. How's that for a character analysis?'

Before Slater could respond, King thundered past, practically knocking him aside to join the stream of passengers making for the terminal.

He didn't look back.

He didn't have time to deal with Slater's bullshit.

7

———

They passed through immigration without
incident.

They weren't armed — granted, with the
weight of the U.S. government behind them and enough
time to negotiate a deal with the Nepali counterparts, they
might have been able to get permission to bring weapons
into the country. But time wasn't on their side, and rapid
progress had to be made, so improvisation was necessary.

Hence — no guns.

They collected their duffels from the baggage carousel
and slung them over their shoulders. There were no disas-
sembled automatic rifles, or switchblades, or, really,
anything that could be used to defend themselves. Just thermals and waterproof hiking pants and Gore-Tex jackets and
trekking boots. All top-of-the-line, because they weren't
about to scrimp and save when they knew they'd need to
make up time *fast*. The gear wasn't going to be much of a
factor — that's where their elite conditioning came into play
— but it couldn't hurt.

They didn't speak to each other as they ploughed their way out of the small terminal.

Slater certainly wasn't in the mood to talk.

He stewed silently, his mind racing faster than he could keep up with. Usually a drink or three subdued the constant chatter, but not today. Because they were on the move in a foreign country, surrounded by naive tourists and wizened locals alike. Technically on their first live operation together.

They made it out to the pick-up point and were bombarded by a horde of Nepali men practically fighting to help newcomers carry their bags to waiting vehicles.

Slater saw tourist after tourist get swept up in the madness, as helpers wrestled their bags off them, carried them five feet to the car, placed them aboard, and then aggressively demanded a tip for the trouble.

A gang of five men approached him as he stepped off the sidewalk.

'We help, sir,' one of them shouted, gesticulating at the duffel draped over his shoulder. 'We help.'

'No,' Slater said.

King watched from the sidelines.

Another Nepali man materialised — he was younger than thirty, with long black hair tied back, wearing a simple puffer jacket and dark grey jeans. He motioned to them both.

'Jason? Will?' he said.

'Yes,' King said.

'I'm Utsav. Your guide.'

'Great to meet you.'

'The car is this way.'

He led them through the horde, but the helpers had zeroed in on Slater. For reasons unbeknownst to either of them, they'd determined they could find success if they persevered. Little did they know how unlikely he was to agree.

One of them reached up and seized hold of his duffel, trying to tug it off his shoulder. 'I help, sir! Car there? You go! I take.'

Slater stopped dead in his tracks and his eyes turned to ice and he said, 'Take your hand off the bag.'

The atmosphere bristled. Sudden realisation spread across the Nepali man's face and he backed away like he'd been electrocuted. There was no palpable threat conveyed, but there might as well have been. Slater felt the cold dead blackness of his soul spread across his face, just for a moment. Only for a single second. But it was enough. There was something inhuman in his eyes and all the hustlers recognised it and backed off immediately. And then suddenly he was back to normal, smiling at them and brushing straight past, and he passed his duffel to Utsav and slipped into the back seat of a waiting four-wheel-drive.

The seats were tattered and smelled strange, but Slater didn't care. He'd dealt with worse conditions. The chatter in his brain fired up again, but truthfully that was when he felt most at ease.

King slotted into the rear seat beside him and slammed the door shut, and Utsav got in the passenger seat and nodded to the driver.

They weaved around the army of hustlers and plunged into the chaos of Kathmandu traffic.

8

K ing figured there was no use planning for the operation if they died on the way to the hotel.

And, by his estimation, they came close a dozen separate times within the first ten minutes of leaving the airport. Their driver leant on the horn like his life depended on it, and narrowly avoided clipping every motorcycle or vehicle that shot past.

King and Slater, both warriors with storied history in a secretive black-operations division of the U.S. government, held on for dear life.

Because death was death, no matter how it happened.

King's phone shrilled in his jacket pocket. He took one palm off the handle above the door and fished it out. He knew who it would be.

The screen read: VIOLETTA LAFLEUR.

He swiped a finger across the screen and said, 'Hey.'

'Hey,' she said back.

There was an awkward pause, and the driver took the opportunity to get as close as humanly possible to another head-on collision without actually going through with it.

Beside him, Slater swore.

'What was that?' Violetta said.

'Oh, it's nothing,' King said. 'I think we're going through our initiation into Nepal.'

From the passenger seat, Utsav laughed.

King's quip glossed over the discomfort emanating from both ends of the phone. Because this was uncharted territory for their relationship. It was King and Slater's first official contracted operation — at least, the first since they'd parted less than amicably from the government years earlier.

Violetta was their handler.

But to King, she was much more than that.

'Is this just business now?' he said, vocalising what they were both wondering.

'I think it has to be.'

'So we put everything else on hold until I get back?'

'Something like that.'

She paused, and he could sense her chewing her bottom lip, debating what to say.

He jumped in with, 'How are you?'

'Good. All things considered. Yourself?'

'Same boat.'

A pause.

Then an audible smile from the other end of the line.

'I don't know what to say,' she said. 'Acting professional is weird.'

'Same boat,' King repeated.

'Got any updates for me?'

'I was about to ask you the same thing. You didn't give us much to work with before we got on a plane.'

'That's getting put together. I'll brief you both tonight. For now — everything okay?'

'Will's not happy,' King said. 'He thinks you've misjudged the situation by sending us in. He doesn't think it's the right move. He wants an explanation.'

Slater bristled, but didn't say a word.

Violetta sighed and said, 'Are we going to run into this problem every time I give you two instructions? This is exactly what happened in New York.'

'We didn't know who you were in New York,' King said. 'Now we do. And he has his doubts.'

'Just Slater?' Violetta said. 'Or are you speaking for yourself, too?'

King half-smiled. 'You're a mind reader.'

'So you're not happy with this?'

'The way I see it — based on the information you've given us — we're being sent up a few mountains on a wild goose chase to look for a missing girl. Which is terrible, of course, but I'm not sure we're the right candidates for that. I think our skills are more selective. There's more relevant parties you could send to handle this that aren't … us.'

Slater threw his hands in the air and said, 'There we go. That's what I was trying to say.'

Violetta said, 'So you both feel this way?'

King said, 'I think Slater put it a little more bluntly. But, yes.'

'You had these same concerns last time. And what ended up happening there? You prevented the collapse of the entire country.'

'That's not what we're dealing with here.'

'No,' Violetta said. 'You're right. It's not exactly the same situation. But Aidan Parker has been critical to our operations for the majority of his career, and we owe the man a great debt for what he's achieved in the service of his country. I could rattle off his track record to you, but it'd take hours. He's been working diligently behind the scenes for a decade to streamline black operations and make sure our operatives are as safe in the field as they can possibly be. He's a genius in that regard. A tactical magician. Which is beside the point, because right now there's a fourteen-year-old girl in the hands of someone who probably knows they have an enormous amount of leverage.'

'You don't know that.'

'We have every reason to believe Oscar Perry is responsible for this.'

'The bodyguard?'

'Yes.'

'Why?'

'Who else would it be?' Violetta sighed. 'It's either him or the porter, and the porter's a thirty-eight-year-old illiterate Nepali man who's been working diligently with the trekking company to keep himself above the poverty line for the better part of three years. He has no knowledge of the clients besides first names — we confirmed this with the trekking company — and has had no behavioural issues for the entire time he's been in employment. By all accounts he's a quiet man with a physically brutal job. So do you think it's him, or do you think it's the man who knows full well what sort of bargaining power he can get with Raya Parker?'

'I don't know,' King said. 'And neither do you.'

'Are you getting all conspiratorial on me?'

'I don't like anything that seems too obvious.'

She said, 'Does it really matter? Either way, the kid's going through hell. I don't want to have to rattle off kidnap statistics to you, but I will if that's what it takes for you to take this seriously.'

'Humour me,' he said. 'I've got nowhere else to be.'

'Most of the time that there's a protection detail involved in a kidnap case, things get violent. That's been proven time and time again.'

'What do you mean?'

'Probably because of the added stressors,' she said. 'When it's a routine run-of-the-mill kidnapping, it's a lot easier to keep things under control. When it starts concerning police or private bodyguards, everything quickly goes south. It breaks the norm. It makes everything violent right off the bat, because usually force needs to be applied to break through the protection detail in the first place.'

'But if it's the private bodyguard himself doing the kidnapping?'

'That's incredibly rare.'

'So it's uncharted territory.'

'More or less.'

'I assume you'll be hitting us with the important details later tonight.'

'Yes. We're still compiling all the intel we have available. You'll be staying at the Dhanyawad Boutique Hotel in Kathmandu tonight, and then setting off in the morning to Phaplu.'

'That's where Parker is?'

'Yes. He's laying low with the guide from the trekking company. He's taking all the proper precautions, because his security detail is now non-existent.'

'If it's the porter,' King said, 'then should we trust the guide?'

'It's not the porter.'

'Glad to hear you're so confident.'

Violetta scowled. 'We'll speak later. I'm not giving you details just yet.'

'So we rendezvous with Parker tomorrow?'

'Yes,' she said. 'I'm trying to arrange a flight from Kathmandu to Phaplu. You'll meet him at one of the teahouses and do your best to reassure him before you set off.'

'That's not going to happen.'

'Excuse me?'

'We'll talk to him,' King said. 'But we won't be nice.'

Slater looked across and nodded.

Violetta said, 'May I ask why?'

'Because we're walking bullshit detectors,' King said. 'And I don't trust anyone involved in this.'

9

The SUV banked hard to the right and shot down a narrow dead-end alley choked with dust and rubble. It swerved around a beggar, avoided a collision with a departing rickshaw, and then coasted through a pair of half-open steel gates manned by a uniformed guard.

Necessary precautions for anything that constituted a luxury hotel in Kathmandu.

Slater didn't need luxury. He took one look at the three-storey building forming a U around the pleasant courtyard in the centre and shrugged. Acceptable. It'd do. He wasn't fussy.

His mind was elsewhere.

Staff in smart buttoned-up white shirts opened the car doors for them and collected their bags. They hurried around with the same urgency as the hustlers at the airport, but they were far less intrusive about it. It was included in the service. Slater slipped out of the vehicle, stretched his limbs, and glanced at King.

Who was staring down at his phone.

The screen read: Violetta LaFleur.

'You going to take that?' he said. 'Seems like she wants to talk again.'

King slipped it into his pocket. 'Not now.'

'Everything okay between you two?'

'Yeah,' King said. 'Just a weird dynamic. You know...'

Slater shrugged. 'I've never been in that sort of situation.'

'Ruby was...'

'*Was,*' Slater said. 'She's not around anymore. In case you didn't notice.'

King stared. 'I noticed.'

He left it there, and Slater was grateful. Sometimes they irritated the shit out of each other, but each knew their boundaries. He wasn't entirely over Ruby Nazarian. She'd been something unique in the midst of his monotonously violent existence, and he'd honestly thought it could have led to something permanent down the road. They just ... clicked. For the first time in a long time, he'd hoped to end the emotionless womanising and try something more stable.

But life's not a fairytale, and she'd bled out on the streets of San Francisco, fighting alongside Slater and King to prevent the worst mass shooting in history.

She'd died a hero.

Which meant nothing if she wasn't around to hear the praise heaped upon her.

King said, 'You okay?'

'Yeah,' Slater said, but he placed a hand on the side of the SUV to steady himself.

Utsav noticed, and dashed forward. 'Will, are you—?'

Slater held up the other hand, stopping him in his tracks. 'Fine, Utsav. Thank you.'

The guide nodded, sensing his presence wasn't desired, and melted into the background.

Slater battled down something very close to misery and steeled himself. Then he adjusted his jacket against the evening chill and followed King into the reception.

They were given a pair of simple two-bed rooms on the third floor. Utsav asked if they needed anything, and they both shook their heads. The guide knew the general gist of why they were here, but details had been kept sparse for obvious reasons. He knew not to push it. This wouldn't be an ordinary trek. They would need to set a pace that not even a seasoned Nepali guide could maintain, so he'd help them get to Phaplu and then see them off at the starting line.

It'd push Slater and King to their physical and mental limits, but they'd spent most of their careers operating on the outskirts of those limits, so what was a little more pain other than a simple inconvenience?

King disappeared into his own room with the muttered promise to meet in the courtyard an hour from now, and Slater trudged into his own quarters, alone with his thoughts.

Just the way he liked it.

There were miniature bottles of spirits in a bar fridge underneath the small desk.

He dumped his bags down, eyed the alcohol, then took out the two small bottles of whisky and emptied them into a plastic cup. He swirled the amber liquid around, sipped at it, and sat on the edge of the bed.

He should be apprehensive. There was foul play afoot in the mountains, and a violent kidnap involving murder and betrayal was nothing to scoff at. But that was the issue, and Slater knew King would be quietly grappling with the same problem. In small circles amidst the upper echelon of the U.S. government, they were considered the premier operatives in the country. The best of the best, and their orders were filtered accordingly. They were tasked with matters of the utmost priority, and this just *wasn't* that. In all likelihood it was the case of a bodyguard who got greedy and figured a remote inaccessible hiking trail would be the perfect location to stage such a risky stunt against his employer. That was bad, but it wasn't King-and-Slater business.

They were the last-minute cavalry, the stone-cold killers sent into a salvage a situation that had been deemed unsalvageable.

They didn't do this.

So he'd get drunk tonight. He was already halfway there, and the whisky helped him right along. That way he wouldn't need to mull over the details for hours on end, pensively wrapped up in his own thoughts until the doubts threatened to eat him alive. He'd just succumb to the pleasant dullness of the alcohol, and deal with the consequences in the morning.

He didn't realise he'd been sitting on the edge of the bed for close to an hour until he glanced up at the clock. He put down the empty cup, shook himself out of the semi-trance, and went downstairs.

King was there, in a change of clothes, sitting around one of the circular tables by the bar. He'd showered and shaved, and there was a pint of beer in front of him.

Slater felt strangely unclean as he joined his friend and closest ally.

King said, 'You realise there's showers here, right?'

'I'm a little distracted.'

'By the job?'

'Trying to distract myself *from* the job.'

'It's worrying you?'

'The fact that it doesn't worry me at all is worrying me.'

'Been there,' King said.

'You talked to Violetta?'

'Briefly.'

'What'd she say?'

'There's works at the airport preventing us from getting a flight to Phaplu. Looks like we'll be in a jeep all day tomorrow.'

'How long's that going to take?'

'Around ten hours if we make good time.'

'Bumpy ride?'

'I'd bet on it.'

'Did she tell you anything else?'

'No. She's still putting the report together. She wants to hit us with all the information at once instead of drip-feeding it to us. We'll have all the time in the world to get the details tomorrow.'

'You really think Parker's up to something?'

'I don't know him,' King said. 'I'm not ruling anything out.'

Slater shrugged.

King motioned to the beer. 'You want one?'

'Better not.'

Slater could sense eyes on him. Boring into him. Drilling deep.

King said, 'Been hitting the minibar?'

Slater drummed his fingers on the table, and didn't answer. Then he lifted his blurry gaze to meet King's. 'Do you think I have a problem? Be honest. I want to know.'

King looked at him in the same way. Drilling deep.

He said, 'No.'

Slater kept tapping his fingers. 'I'm starting to think I might.'

'Given what we do, I'd say it's understandable. I'm starting to think *I'm* the one with the problem for having a grip on it.'

Slater nodded. 'Do you think about what we've done? What we've been through?'

'All the time.'

'Does it affect you?'

'How wouldn't it?'

'I always thought you were the shining example of how to deal with this life.'

'I'm the shining example of how to mask your problems,' King said. 'I wouldn't claim to be much more than that.'

They sat back and watched the scene around them. There were groups of tourists dotted across the tables, laughing and drinking and eating, eagerly anticipating the beginning of their various treks. There was nervous excitement in the air. Slater could understand why. Live an ordinary life with an ordinary office job and the prospect of hiking through Nepal seems exotic, extravagant, otherworldly, mysterious. Live a life like his own, or like King's, and hiking through Nepal seems banal.

He wondered which group had the issue.

He thought he knew the answer.

These people were enjoying themselves.

He was restless and miserable, questioning every aspect of the operation.

He nodded goodnight to King, got up, and went to bed.

10

The next morning, Utsav ushered them into an off-road jeep built to handle the treacherous roads between Kathmandu and Phaplu.

Weak light had crept into the sky, but it was still practically dark. They'd set their alarms for four-thirty in anticipation of heading off at five. Downstairs, they'd wolfed eggs and bacon and sausage and spinach into their mouths to fuel them up for the day, and downed a couple of coffees each to get the juices flowing.

King knew the reasoning behind Violetta keeping information at bay, but he didn't like it one bit. He stewed silently over breakfast, until Slater finally piped up when they clambered into the jeep.

'Now you're the quiet one.'

King looked across. 'What do you mean?'

'What else would I mean?'

'What do you want me to be talking about?'

Slater pointed an accusatory finger in King's face. 'You're acting how I was last night. Did I pass my bad mood onto you?'

King didn't respond as Utsav got in the passenger seat and nodded to the driver, a thirty-something Nepali man with wrinkly skin weathered by years of exposure to the outdoors. The guy backed out through the steel gates, and they plunged back into the relentless traffic.

King said, 'Headphones on, Utsav.'

It was an already-established request, passed on by whichever bureaucrat in the government had liaised with the guide and his trekking company. Utsav fished a pair of noise-cancelling headphones out of the footwell and slipped them over his ears. Even from the rear seats, King could hear the music blaring.

He tapped Utsav on the shoulder, and pointed surreptitiously to the driver.

Utsav shook an open hand back and forth across his own throat.

No English.

King nodded, then turned to Slater and said, 'Remember all those problems we had in New York with the way information was passed along? I guess I'm not satisfied with that just yet.'

Slater said, 'Then we both have the same issues. I hate this. I hate that there's probably a dozen things she's not telling us that aren't yet important, but might give us a better idea about why we've been sent all the way out here.'

'I just don't want to sound like a broken record when I complain about it.'

'They think we're too dumb to take in information piece by piece. That's what it comes down to. They want to hit us with all the intel at once.'

'I'll give her a call,' King said.

He dialled, and she answered almost immediately.

'Yes?'

'We're en route to Phaplu.'

'Good. It's going to be a long ride.'

'I think we can handle that.'

There was an uneasy pause.

The driver gunned it around a convoy of mopeds and shot into an enormous intersection, where motorists and drivers roared around the wide dirt track in an eternal chaotic spiral. Then they were on a new road, flooring it through the outskirts of Kathmandu, where the old multi-storey buildings were spaced a little further apart, and the endless grocery stores sporting signs for Tuborg beer and Pepsi weren't jammed up end to end.

Violetta said, 'Got something on your mind?'

'We want details. Now. Same deal as New York.'

She seemed to relent. 'What do you need to know?'

'Everything you've got.'

'That'd take too long.'

'Did you miss the part where we're in the car for the next ten hours?'

She said, 'I was about to tell you that we're still working on an intelligence briefing, but that's not what you want to hear, is it?'

'Give me something, Violetta. This is our lives here. We need to know.'

She told him what little information they had to work with.

11

S later sat in quiet patience as King listened.

For a few beats, he tried to make out what the tinny voice emanating from the phone's speaker was saying. But amidst the blare of horns and passing shouts of pedestrians and the Nepali music whining out of the jeep's stereo system, it was impossible to hear anything Violetta was feeding King.

So he turned his attention to the outside world.

What initially had seemed like chaos started to make sense the longer he focused on it. Sure, it was bedlam compared to the First World, but Slater had spent enough time on operations in undesirable locations to understand that most people back home, even those close to the poverty line, had luxuries that those here could only dream about.

But the people here were happy all the same. They laughed and joked and smiled as they trudged down dust-choked sidewalks and hefted hessian sacks full of groceries over their heads and ran across roads at breakneck speed to avoid getting wiped out by a dozen different vehicles. They were at ease in the madness, because it was all they had ever known.

Slater compared that to his own life, and half-smiled.

It was the same thing, all across the world.

You get used to your environment.

That's what allowed him and King to train like they did every day back home. They needed unbelievable conditioning to do what they did day in and day out, and that took a work ethic that most on the planet would find sick. Certainly, a faction of psychologists would probably diagnose them both with some sort of obsessive disorder.

But that's who they had to be, and that's what they had to do.

To them, it was normal.

To them, it would be sick not to put their talents to use.

When King finally got off the phone, Slater said, 'Update?'

King shrugged. 'Not as much as I'd hoped to hear. But it's all she had.'

'Then that's why they need us. Because they're in the dark.'

'The girl is Raya Parker,' King said, recapping what they already knew. 'She's missing, along with Oscar Perry and the porter. She doubts the guide or porter are involved, because no one out here knows who or what Aidan Parker really does, least of all the trekking company. He had the bodyguards along with him, but anyone who's paranoid and has a bit of disposable income can get protection. Violetta says they knew nothing about how truly important he is.'

'How important *is* he? What does he do?'

'That's where it gets vague.'

Slater raised an eyebrow.

King said, 'Violetta doesn't know all the details.'

'Bullshit.'

'I believe her.'

'You would.'

'Are we going to start down this road again?' King said. 'Let's not fight over everything. We're not toddlers.'

Slater held up both hands in protest. 'I'm not trying to start anything. Relax. I'm just saying — don't you think there's the possibility you're wearing rose-tinted glasses?'

'Why would she withhold that?'

Slater paused, and said, 'I don't know. But nothing would surprise me anymore.'

'We haven't exactly had the best history with handlers, I know.'

'Lars, then Ramsay. What is it about power-hungry pieces-of-shit?'

'Isla was a good handler,' King said.

'And look where that got her.'

Killed in Dubai. Shot in the head.

That's where it got her.

King said, 'The waters are murky. Think about how little we know about the inner workings of our government. You think Violetta knows *everything*?'

'She knows people who *would*.'

'Parker himself stays very secretive. Apparently he's always been a private man. He used to coordinate Black Force operations, but now that division doesn't exist anymore. He's been keeping busy, but on what exactly ... it's darts at a dartboard. Some say he's pioneering new divisions. Some say he's still working on the same backend stuff. No-one knows for sure.'

'Does that make you suspicious?'

'Everything makes me suspicious.'

'I'm sure he'll enlighten us on the details when we get to Phaplu.'

'He'd better,' King said.

Slater paused. 'You really think he could have done something like this?'

'I think anyone is capable of anything,' King said. 'I assume you feel the same. Given what we've both been through.'

'I'm going to get whatever Parker knows out of him.'

'Gently, at first. We don't want to strong-arm him and then find out he's got nothing to do with it.'

'I'm not good at being gentle.'

'Maybe I can take the reins at first,' King said. 'I'd say I'm a little more...'

'Controlled?'

'Let's go with that.'

Slater shrugged. 'You are. I'm not about to deny the truth.'

'Are we good?'

'Yeah, we're good.'

King reached forward and tapped Utsav twice on the shoulder.

He slipped the headphones off.

'You take care of business?' the guide said.

They both nodded.

The jeep lapsed into silence as Kathmandu fell away, replaced by twisting winding mountain roads. They passed the beginnings of rural villages, and half-destroyed abandoned buildings, and in the strangest twist of all, a dormant water park sprawled across the bottom of a valley.

Then they reached the edge of the outskirts themselves, and there was nothing but endless mountains, rising and falling, with the odd villages or terraces skewered into the hillsides.

Slater watched the undulating landscape until his eyes grew weary and he drifted into a trance-like state — half-awake, half-not.

He thought about nothing, which was a reprieve.

His head pounded from the night before, but pain didn't mean a thing to him.

He could deal with that forever.

K
ing ran through the important details in his head.

Raya Parker, Oscar Perry, and the porter were all unaccounted for. Violetta and her colleagues were doing what they could to get accurate information from trekkers along the trail, but details were sparse, and even though they'd put the feelers out, so far there were no confirmed sightings.

The stretch of trail that Aidan Parker and his team had been trekking along was far quieter than the trail leading to Everest Base Camp. Most hikers flew into the village of Lukla, home to the world's most dangerous airport, and then trekked up through Namche Bazaar on the road to Everest and Gokyo Ri. Parker had opted to begin from Phaplu instead — roughly four days' walk from Lukla — probably with the hopes of conditioning himself to the trail before the altitude symptoms had the potential to interfere.

That had ended disastrously, because the desolate nature of the trail had given *someone* the perfect opportunity to snatch his daughter.

Who that might have been, King wasn't yet sure.

All signs pointed to Perry. According to Violetta, the bodyguard had worked with Parker for five years. Even though Parker had clear instructions to never discuss his work outside the office, it could be imagined that over a five-year stretch certain crucial details would slip out. Parker was no doubt a cautious man, but Perry would have absolutely understood the man's importance. That's all the leverage he would have needed to snatch Raya, determining that mounting a rescue mission in the mountains would be a logistical nightmare.

And it was.

Hence King and Slater's presence.

They didn't play by the book.

They were six hours into the journey, and the jeep had been climbing for what felt like the whole time. Right now they were at an elevation of roughly eight thousand feet. King wore a digital smartwatch that he'd picked up at the airport en route — it tracked the altitude as accurately as possible.

That was one of the only factors that truly worried him.

Altitude sickness was impartial, uncaring. It didn't matter how fit you were, or how young you were — it struck without bias, often sending even those in the best shape into near uselessness. If it struck you, you almost definitely had to get helicoptered out. It came with crippling headaches and nausea and an ache so deep in your bones it felt like you were made of lead.

So King was paying close attention to his watch. The last thing he wanted was to be inhibited that badly in the midst of a live operation.

And if Perry was behind this, the bodyguard would use it to his advantage, especially if he had previous experience at altitude and knew it wouldn't faze him. He'd head further up the trail with Raya and the porter in tow. He'd use his tactical awareness as a trained combatant to make it as difficult as possible for a rescue to be attempted. That meant altitude. It was difficult enough to pull sick trekkers off the trail via helicopter — if King and Slater got themselves dropped closer to Gokyo Ri in an attempt to intercept the party coming *down,* word would spread quick, and Perry would disappear.

No, they needed to do it this way — posing as legitimate hikers, fooling the eyes that could very well be on them at any moment.

So that was the plan, but it could change at any moment. They still hadn't met Parker, and King wanted to have a long chat to him about—

The jeep slowed and branched off onto a narrow path, tearing King away from his thoughts. His situational awareness heightened, and he glanced across to see Slater similarly concerned.

The sun disappeared behind the low cloud passing over the mountain.

Everything turned grey.

King realised, with sudden clarity, that they were in the cloud.

And the cold intensified.

He shrugged on a jacket as the jeep slowed at the mouth of a small cluster of buildings. Some were half-finished, mere construction projects in progress, but most were intact, made of stone and wood and surrounded by fields teeming with crops. It was a tiny commune in the mountains, but King couldn't see a soul in sight, which made the whole place feel like a museum exhibit. Mostly because of the ethereal fog drifting through the village, obscuring their vision to only a few dozen feet in front of them. Driving in the cloud would be a nightmare.

The jeep pulled to a halt in the grey fog and the driver killed the engine.

In the sudden quiet, King said, 'What are we doing here?'

Utsav peered over his shoulder. 'Lunch.'

'Right,' Slater said, but he was similarly tense.

Utsav laughed. 'You two are serious men. You relax, hey? We eat here. Then we go.'

'We have to be serious,' King said. 'It's our job.'

'Now it is job to eat.'

With another hollow laugh, Utsav pushed the passenger door open and dropped out into the dewy grass.

The driver followed a step behind. He missed his door handle on the first go, and reached for it again. In the interim, he threw a glance over his shoulder with a half-smile of indifference.

When his hand clasped the door handle again, it was shaking.

King sat deathly still.

Watching.

Analysing.

Weighing it all up.

He said, 'You got something to tell us?'

It was loud in the sudden silence of the cabin. The driver looked over his shoulder, flashed a sheepish grin, and shrugged.

'No English,' Slater said.

The driver pointed to him, and half-nodded.

King muttered, 'Right. No English.'

The driver flashed a thumbs up.

He was definitely nervous.

Could be a coincidence. Could be because of the presence of American operatives, who weren't your ordinary run-of-the-mill trekkers. They were cold hard men with cold hard gazes, and they meant business. Maybe that was enough to throw the guy off. Maybe he could subliminally sense that he was no longer in the civilian sphere.

Or maybe not.

King had survived half his career based on "maybe not."

The driver's instincts seemed to kick in, and he paused with his palm on the handle, looking expectantly over his shoulder. He seemed to think it might be courteous for his guests to get out first.

King gestured to the driver's door. 'Please. After you.'

The driver got out. He opened the door and pivoted and stepped down into the fog. He stretched his limbs. He nodded to Utsav.

Nothing happened.

King and Slater sat there, saying nothing, listening to everything.

Finally Slater said, 'You okay?'

'Just a hunch.'

'We do need to eat…'

'Where is everybody?'

'I don't know.'

'It's too rundown. Too … empty.'

'Have you looked out the window at all over the last six hours?'

King hesitated, then relented. 'Just keep your guard up.'

'You don't need to tell me to do that.'

King popped the door and slid out of the jeep. The grass squelched underfoot, and the chill bit into his chest. He shivered involuntarily. On the other side of the car, he heard Slater mirroring his actions.

Utsav watched them from a distance. He said, 'Okay?'

King nodded. 'Okay.'

'This way. Time to eat. Dal bhat sound good.'

Dal bhat. The dish of rice, lentils and vegetables favoured by all the Nepali guides and porters. They called it "twenty-four-hour-power," and ate it for practically every meal on the trail. It hit all the nutritional requirements they needed.

King remembered those details from a brief conversation the night before.

He started to wonder if he really *was* paranoid after all.

Utsav and the driver led them past the rundown houses draped in fog. They didn't see a soul. Up the back of the village, they found a long low building, mostly intact, with an empty shopfront skewered into one side. There were Cokes and Sprites and Mars bars and packets of crisps on display.

Trail food.

King said, 'Where is everybody?'

'Inside,' Utsav said. 'Cold out here.'

Sure enough, soft yellow light glowed in a couple of the windows. The building had the same aura as a mess hall, and King thought he could smell food.

He nodded. 'Okay.'

Utsav ushered him toward an open doorway. There was no light emanating from that particular entrance. It was a dark gaping maw.

King said, 'You first.'

Beside him, Slater rolled his eyes.

'Relax, would you?' Slater said. 'We won't get anywhere if you spend the whole trek like this.'

'We haven't started trekking yet.'

'You know what I mean.'

Utsav smiled and gestured to Slater. 'Please. It is customary for guest to go first.'

Slater nodded and turned to King. 'See?'

Then he strode forward and disappeared inside the building.

Ustav followed.

Then it was just King and the driver, alone outside.

It was murky, and cold, and silent.

King said, 'You first. I insist.'

The driver shrugged, and turned, and made for the entrance.

Then he paused, too quickly, too suspiciously, and looked left.

King followed the trajectory and saw the flicker of a silhouette against the corner of the building.

He took off at a sprint.

S later stepped into a musty hallway with a total
absence of natural light.

Except for the soft glow of a dining room at the
end of the tunnel.

He peered through the doorway and noticed the familiar
polished wooden tables and carpeted benches reminiscent
of the traditional Nepali teahouses. They'd be staying at
similar spots all the way along the trail. Violetta had told
them that much, at least.

There was the soft aroma of warm food, but no-one in
sight. No guests. No owner. No-one to greet them.

But it was overcast and foggy and moody, and the
owners probably figured there'd be nobody stopping by for
the rest of the day.

So then why do you smell food?

Instinct told him, *Bait.*

To make it feel legitimate.

But he'd sent King a message by going first, and he
wasn't yet ready to stoop to that level of paranoia. Now it
was there, though. The doubt. Festering in the back of his

mind. Creeping up on him, making him reconsider everything.

If it's not Perry who snatched Raya, it's the porter.

And if it's the porter, then the whole trekking company can't be trusted.

Had Violetta used the same company as Parker? Could she have been that stupid?

Slater doubted it.

But even if she hadn't, he figured the staff knew each other. They probably communicated back and forth every now and then. They would have each other's line.

To organise.

To coordinate.

To bribe.

Slater spun in the shadows just as Utsav backed off a few steps.

Separating himself from... *what?*

Slater sensed movement to his left. He wasn't sure how, because there was nothing but an open doorway leading into dark musty living quarters, but there was something *darker* in there. A shadow. A silhouette.

When the guy lunged at him, Slater was ready.

He caught the knife hand as it protruded from the doorway and twisted at the hips and used the attacker's momentum to hurl him on past. The hallway was tight, and the guy crashed into the opposite wall at full speed, which seems mildly disorienting in the movies but in reality can break bone with a single awkward impact. So the guy winced and froze up for a second as he crashed off the wood, his shoulder and elbow probably cracked, and Slater took the opportunity to throw his own elbow like a World Series pitcher swinging for the fences.

It connected with the force of a bat, and the accuracy of ... well, an elbow.

Right on the jaw.

All that carnage took an eternity to process in Slater's mind, but in reality it played out in a second and a half. There was the throw, the bounce, and the elbow, and suddenly the guy was out cold on the teahouse floor with a broken jaw, violently twitching in unconsciousness. He was small but strong, with a weathered face and light brown skin. Probably Nepali.

Slater twisted on the spot and pointed down and said, 'Who the fuck is that, Utsav?'

The guide kept backing up, horror spread across his face.

But he couldn't take his eyes off the unconscious guy.

So it wasn't the horror of being ambushed.

It was the horror of the planned ambush failing.

Slater took a step forward, and Utsav turned and ran into the darkness. The guide cried out something in Nepali as he fled, his voice shaking.

Outside, Slater heard the faint commotion of a brawl.

King.

But he couldn't concentrate on that any longer, because there was a cacophony of movement behind him.

Coming from the dining area.

Coming from the light.

So he spun and saw three men roughly the same size materialise in the doorway, backlit by the yellow glow. They were small like the first guy, and they were armed. All three had knives. Same as the first. Little sharp switchblades, like box cutters, capable of severing an artery with the slightest flick of the wrist.

Probably real hard to get your hands on a firearm all the way out here.

Slater's heart rate shot through the roof, and he thought, *Forwards, or backwards?*

Easy answer.

He charged.

14

K ing had his hands on the guy before either he or the driver could react.

The silhouette turned out to be a man, maybe five-foot-five and a hundred pounds lighter than King, but he had a knife. He swung hard, narrowly missing King's abdomen, sending King's pulse skyrocketing.

King smashed the bones in the guy's knife hand to pieces with a stabbing front kick, then bundled him up like he weighed nothing and bounced his skull off the wooden corner of the building with a double-handed shove. Like the sound of a coconut hitting concrete as his skull rattled, the guy went down in a crippled heap.

King twisted on the spot and pointed down and said, 'Who is that?'

The driver didn't respond.

'No English, right?' King said.

The guy stood there sporting a guilty half-smile. Like there was something up his sleeve. Like he honestly didn't expect to fail. He was being confronted by a six-foot-three two-hundred-and-twenty pound hulk of a man who'd just smashed one of his friends into unconsciousness, but he still seemed barely fazed.

Then sharp headlight beams lit up the fog, coming in off the main trail. Two, then four, then six.

Three sets.

Three cars.

They surged down the uneven road between the husks of long-abandoned buildings in the ghost town King suddenly realised they'd been led to like flies to shit. They were big vehicles, built to handle the trail, and they must have been keeping a respectable distance the whole time. Then again, the driver had spent half the journey on the phone, babbling in Nepali, and any number of those calls could have been to the backup crew, coordinating logistics, working out where the best place would be to silence their unwanted guests.

Evidently, it was here.

King hovered by the corner of the building, keenly aware that he wasn't armed, debating whether or not to run for—

Then the SUVs arrived, one by one, and three men got out of each truck. Nine total. Six had knives. Three had their fists.

Probably real hard to get your hands on a firearm all the way out here.

King wondered if, inside, Slater was thinking the same thing.

As soon as he realised he wouldn't have to dodge bullets, he bent down and snatched the switchblade off the guy he'd already smashed unconscious, and then he got up and charged for the closest vehicle. Instead of adopting any sort of tactical awareness, the trio of SUVs had pulled up maybe a dozen feet apart, so now all three were equidistant to one another, giving King more than enough time to make his way from one to the next.

They didn't know that, though.

They thought they were dealing with a pair of nosy Americans.

The reality was something a little more visceral to behold.

King made it to the first truck and switched off the merciful part of his brain, like flicking a light switch. It wouldn't do him any good, not in an environment like this. He wasn't about to spare anyone that surrendered. They'd come here to kill him, and that, ultimately, was that.

So King got his hands on the first attacker — unarmed — and bundled him up against the side of the vehicle and thrust the blade up through the underneath of his chin. It skewered his brain and killed him on impact. King dropped his corpse and pivoted and found the second guy baring the switchblade, so King rammed a leg kick into the guy's calf, nearly snapping the bone clean in two, sending him tumbling off his feet and the knife spilling from his grip as he reached for his leg...

So King forgot about him for half a second, just enough time to lunge past and stab the switchblade down so it plunged into the third guy's chest, who moaned and went pale and crumpled.

King left the knife in his chest and pivoted back and stomped down on the second guy's head, knocking him clean out, maybe killing him. No way to know for sure without a detailed analysis. And there wasn't time for that.

King bent down and picked up the second guy's knife and noticed the other six combatants realising what was unfolding, shrugging off their hesitation, preparing themselves to charge all at once.

King couldn't let that happen.

Instead of meeting them head-on in battle, he leapt up into the SUV's open driver's door and threw it into gear and accelerated and twisted the wheel.

He spotted the shocked look on the original driver's face, but King wasn't aiming for him. That guy was useless, a pathetic spineless goon relying on his friends to do the dirty work. He wouldn't know how to swing a fist in anger to save his life. So King spun away from him and aimed for one of the armed knife-wielders by the second car.

The hood crushed the guy before he could get out of the way.

King twisted the wheel again and crushed the second knife-wielder against the side of the second SUV.

Then he leapt out, barely registering the jarring impact above the guttural roar of adrenaline, and intercepted the third man with a flying crash-tackle.

The third guy wasn't armed, so when they spilled to the ground in a tangle of limbs King stabbed him twice in the chest, *thwack-thwack,* and rolled to his feet.

Six down.

An uneasy silence stretched out as the final three men hovered by their vehicle, unsure how to interpret the shocking ballet of violence that had played out before them.

King turned to the original driver, and half-smiled back.

The driver's own smile vanished, replaced by shock and awe.

'Watch this,' King said.

He advanced.

15

Slater kept sprinting flat out, barrelling toward the trio silhouetted in the doorway like a freight train.

Which, despite the fact he was unarmed, can be wholly terrifying when you're not expecting it.

Two of them backed off. Only a few steps, but enough to show they were hesitant. They'd expected their target to waltz into the dining room, oblivious, and stab him in the back before he had the chance to react. Now one of their own was lying broken and unconscious on the hallway floor, and their target was running directly at them, apparently without a care in the world.

So of course two of them backed up.

They probably wanted the openness of the dining area to work with. They didn't like the hallway. It was dark and cramped and favoured the guy who was outnumbered.

Like a miniaturised version of the Spartans at Thermopylae.

If all three of them had backed up, it would have been a brilliant strategic manoeuvre.

But one of them stayed right where he was, his teeth bared and his knife at the ready.

Brave.

No doubt about that.

But exactly what Slater wanted.

He slowed right down, leaving a few feet of space to work with, so he didn't just sprint straight into a knife to the gut. When he slowed, the attacker swung the blade, as Slater expected him to.

It missed.

Not by much.

But it missed.

Slater heard the air *whoosh,* and the realisation struck him that the knife would have gutted him like a pig if it struck home. But then the blade carried on past, opening up a glorious half-second of opportunity. Slater kicked the guy squarely in the balls — an age-old guarantee of incapacitation — and when he buckled, Slater used the same leg to bend into a knee and drive upwards, impacting kneecap to forehead. It made a horrific noise as it slammed home.

The guy pitched forward and crumpled to the floor.

Slater stepped over him.

Picked up the knife.

Weighed up the distances, and the angles.

Figured he could take the risk.

He threw the switchblade like a fastball, making sure it struck blade-first. It was a small square blade, not a machete, so it didn't embed itself in the enemy's throat and stick there. Instead it grazed past his neck, cutting him deep along the way, failing to sever an artery but giving him something to seriously worry about. The guy felt the warm blood flowing down his neck and instinctively reached for his throat, shocked by the sudden pain.

Before he could recover, Slater was right there in his face.

Stomped down with the sole of his boot on the guy's kneecap, shattering it, then simply muscled the knife out of his hands and used it to cut his throat properly, finishing the job.

The third guy put his hands up in surrender.

Slater stepped forward and opened up his hips and pivoted and swung his shin in a tight curve, landing it on the guy's neck, and his eyes rolled back into his head and he went down awkwardly and hit the back of his skull on the edge of the nearest table on the way down.

He'd be out for a while.

Maybe even permanently affected.

Slater found it hard to care when the man had been ready to slit his throat seconds earlier.

Three bodies thunked to the floor. The thuds were hollow in the now-empty teahouse, and Slater realised with sudden clarity that there hadn't been staff here in a long time. The driver and the guide had used this empty ghost town as a staging ground for an assassination attempt.

On that note...

Slater turned on his heel and went straight back the way he'd come.

To find Utsav.

16

—————

King came in fast and hard, because that scared the shit out of combatants unaccustomed to violence.

Sure, they might be tough men with hard lives in the mountains. No doubt they'd been given some training in how to most effectively kill someone with a blade. But that was all theory and practice on target dummies. Not real, visceral, up-close madness.

King lived in that madness.

It was like his second home.

The closest guy recoiled — partly because he'd just seen six of his comrades die and figured his chances weren't any better, but mostly because there was a two-hundred-and-twenty pound brute right there in his face. Instead of swinging with the knife he brought his hands up in an awkward defence, so King ducked low and plunged his own blade into the guy's stomach. It happened so fast that he barely saw it himself.

Shlock.

In and out.

The guy went down.

But before he went all the way down King kicked him so hard in the chest that he plummeted back into the SUV, but not before catching one of the other thugs along the way. Both of them careened into the chassis and bounced off, and on the rebound King cut through the air with his right elbow, slicing it vertically upwards, catching the second guy in the nose with the elbow and in the forehead with his forearm. The impact rattled King's shoulder, but rattled the guy's brain harder. Both of them went down, one clutching his blood-stained gut, the other unconscious.

King stepped over them, and then it was like clockwork.

The last armed man was scared as hell. He dropped the knife and put his hands up. A natural human impulse when you think you have the advantage, then lose it all in a rapid frenzy of violence. He was probably friends with some of the men King had just killed. And although he had a weapon, he'd just seen eight of his colleagues meet the same fate, no matter how talented they were with a knife.

So he surrendered.

King wasn't about to waste time tying him up.

He strode over, grabbed the guy by the head with two open palms, and drove his skull into the side of the SUV.

Lights out.

The village went quiet. It slipped straight back into its usual monotony, broken only by the occasional chilling howl of the wind. The cloud still lingered, draped over the half-demolished buildings like spiderwebs. King caught his breath, feeling every beat of his heart in his chest, and waited for the adrenaline to dissipate.

He didn't need to rush.

The original driver wasn't going anywhere in a hurry.

He was the only one left outside who was both alive and conscious.

King walked right up to him, kicked him in the side of the leg, and pressed a heavy hand down on his shoulder when he sank to his knees.

He lowered the knife into the guy's field of view.

He said, 'Still no English?'

The driver, pale and shaking, tried to keep his composure. He shrugged, as nonchalantly as he could manage. 'Little bit of English.'

'I think your English is more than acceptable. Shame you didn't tell us sooner.'

'You kill me?'

'Maybe. I'm still considering it.'

'You man of honour. You no kill unarmed man.'

'I've done it before. Many times.'

'That no good.'

'And this is?' King said, sweeping an arm around the village.

Nine men lay dead or unconscious.

'You scary man,' the driver said. 'I don't know what I get myself into. I no like this. We paid money.'

'By who?'

'Can't say.'

'Yes, you can.'

'No. Can't say. Don't know. Utsav organise.'

'Where is Utsav?'

'Inside.'

'With my friend?'

'Yes. But maybe Utsav not alive anymore. If your friend like you.'

'He's a lot like me.'

'Then no good for Utsav.'

'You're right about that.'

'You still going to kill me?'

'Maybe.'

'I have family.'

'So do I. Didn't deter you.'

'What that mean? Deter?'

King squatted down, so he could look the man in the eyes. He pointed an accusatory finger toward his nine incapacitated buddies.

'*They* didn't care about *my* family. Why should I care about yours?'

'Because I don't know what I'm doing. I just follow orders.'

'I've heard that before.'

King got to his feet and said, 'I still haven't decided. So, until then...'

He kicked the driver in the side of the head, hard enough to put him out cold. Then he straightened up and adjusted his jacket and exhaled a cloud of breath into the chilly mountain air.

Silence.

Dead silence.

The village was like an anthropological exhibit.

And already King's bones were heavy, wracked with tiredness, plagued by the intensity of that sort of exertion. He listened for the sounds of struggle inside the teahouse, but he didn't hear a thing. Either Slater had already dealt with his own threats, or it was far too late to help. Either way, there was no need to rush.

But King wanted to know all the same.

Because the alternative would be ... disastrous.

To both Slater's wellbeing, and his own mental health.

As much as they might have fought, King realised with

sudden clarity that he didn't have anyone he was closer to in the whole world. Anyone who understood him like Slater, who shared the same mutually traumatising past.

They were brothers.

So King powered straight into the building, no matter the consequences.

He plunged into darkness, went to the end of the corridor, and listened hard.

He thought he heard a creak to his left.

He turned that way, surged forward a few steps, and threw the door open.

He came face to face with Utsav.

17

The guide was suspended from the wooden rafters by his belt, his face dark blue.

His body swung gently in the muddy light.

King paused in the doorway, watching, thinking.

On the outside, as stoic as always.

On the inside, strangely hollow.

He'd seen so much death in his life. He'd caused most of it himself. What was one more body to add to the count?

But something about this one set his nerves on edge, made him shiver involuntarily. He quietly stepped back and closed the door and put his hands on his hips and turned—

Slater almost walked straight into him.

Their switchblades came up in mutual anticipation, but as soon as they recognised each other in the semi-darkness they relaxed.

Slater said, 'You okay?'

'Yeah. I'm not hurt.'

'No, I mean ... you look like you're about to throw up.'

'I might.'

'Why?'

King jerked a thumb toward the closed door. 'Our guide's in there.'

'Did you kill him?'

'Didn't have to.'

Slater let the words sink in.

He stood there, chewing his bottom lip, figuring out how to respond.

Eventually, he said, 'How'd he do it?'

'His belt.'

'Damn.'

'Are you genuinely disappointed?'

'Only because I wanted answers.'

'Me too, buddy.'

'How many did you handle?'

'Ten. Plus the driver.'

'Jesus Christ.'

'You?'

'Four. Plus the guide. But he handled himself, I guess.'

'That's a sizeable force.'

'They were amateurs.'

'Doesn't matter what they were. They tried to kill us all the same.'

'Who are they?'

'If I had to guess ... they're the desperate. I'm not about to feel sorry for them, but I doubt there's much motivation in their heads besides instant gratification. It's the same everywhere, not just here. All you need to do is find those with nothing left to live for. Who think they're just a cog in a machine and that life is passing them by. Offer them a life-changing sum of money to stick a knife in someone's back and they'll do it without blinking.'

'Did you leave any of yours alive?'

'A few. They'll be concussed, though.'

'We could quiz them.'

'They won't speak English.'

'You sure about that?'

'On the off chance they do, we won't get any information out of them. You think they know details?'

Slater turned on his heel and walked away.

King watched him leave, flabbergasted.

'What are you—?'

'Follow me,' Slater said.

They made it to the dining area, now seemingly brighter as the murkiness outside intensified. Under the artificial glow they stared down at the three men Slater had incapacitated.

One was dead, the other was bleeding out, and the third was still twitching in unconsciousness.

Slater said, 'Look closely at them.'

King looked closely.

It only confirmed his prior suspicions.

All three were small men, almost certainly Nepali, with slim builds and old faded clothes. They wore a mixture of plaid shirts and sweaters made of thin scratchy wool, and pants made of coarse fabric. They were locals.

Slater said, 'You really think Parker's bodyguard is behind this?'

'Why would this exclude Perry?'

'The connections. Seems he has a grip on every trekking company in Kathmandu if he's the mastermind.'

'Not really,' King said. 'You ever thought about how many trekking companies there are in that city? We need to speak to Violetta. Maybe she went through the same organisation that Parker did.'

'She wouldn't have. Unless she's stupid.'

King didn't bite. He was too deep in thought.

He said, 'It does make it less likely, though. I'll give you that.'

'What do we do now?'

'Keep driving.'

'You think that's the best idea, given...?'

He didn't finish the sentence. He just gestured to the hostiles he'd mauled.

King thought harder.

Then he said, 'I don't see why not. If it's the porter, then we're either wrapped up in something larger than we thought and not safe anywhere, or we're in the clear. There's a fair chance that was the entirety of the forces he had available. Might be smooth sailing from here on out.'

'I doubt that very much.'

'Based on what?'

'Almost every operation we've ever been on.'

'Correlation isn't causation—'

'Yeah, yeah,' Slater said. 'I know. But honestly, when has it ever been smooth sailing?'

'Noted.'

'I think we should wait to see what Violetta has to say.'

'Are you getting cold feet?'

'If we make it to Phaplu, we might as well paint a target on our backs. Utsav and the driver both knew where they were taking us. They'll have *something* in place for contingencies.'

'Or they planned on overwhelming us with fourteen men right here,' King said. 'They didn't know who we were, exactly. They just knew we were trouble.'

Slater said, 'Your call.'

'We keep going.'

'Because of a hunch?'

'Because of the girl,' King said. 'She's still missing. No matter who's behind it. Clock's ticking.'

Slater nodded. 'I guess that's all it comes down to, right?'

'What do we do with these guys?'

'Leave them. Let them fend for themselves. The survivors won't follow us. Not after what we did to them. Not after the headaches they'll wake up with.'

King nodded. 'Okay. Guess that covers it. Let's go.'

As calm as if they'd just finished lunch, they left the teahouse, walked past the dead or semi-conscious attackers dotted across the grass, and climbed back into the original jeep. King got behind the wheel, and Slater took the passenger seat. They slammed their doors and King threw it in reverse and crept back down the road. They stayed quiet the whole way out of the village, keeping their eyes peeled for any sign of a second assault.

There was nothing.

Desolation.

Silence.

Wind.

Cloud.

King spun the jeep around and mounted the same steadily ascending trail, leaving the village behind.

'Guess we're on our own for the rest of the drive,' Slater said. 'Hope there aren't an abundance of forks in the road.'

King said, 'I doubt that. But just to be sure...'

He reached back with one hand and fished the satellite phone out of the seat pocket, and thumbed a few buttons on the interface. Then he held it to his ear.

After a few beats, Violetta said, 'Everything okay?'

'Now it is,' King said. 'But we've got a few things we need to discuss.'

_____

18

S he didn't interrupt as he filled her in.

When he finally trailed off, she said, 'Christ.'

'Tell me you didn't use the same trekking company as Parker.'

'Of course not,' she snapped. 'How dumb do you think I am?'

'Had to be sure.'

'I'll start investigating exactly what happened and who we hired and how they might have been ... compromised.'

'Did you even consider doing this without the help of civilians? You know how easy it is for them to be—'

'*Enough,*' she snapped. 'We didn't have a choice. In case you didn't realise this operation is incredibly time-sensitive. And we didn't have anyone we were connected to in Kathmandu who knew Nepal like the locals. Fact of the matter is, we wouldn't have got you to Phaplu in time if we didn't use one of the already-established companies.'

'And look where that got us.'

'You're still alive. It's in your job description to deal with any problems that might crop up. We just didn't know it was going to come from civilians.'

'They were amateurs,' King said. 'Fourteen amateurs. Whoever wants us shut down is acting fast. They're working with what they can get their hands on — just like us.'

Violetta said, 'I know.'

'You still think it's Oscar Perry?'

'That's ... less likely.'

'Unless he's interrogated the porter for all his contacts in Kathmandu. Which would be simple, if you think about it.'

'Also a possibility.'

'There's a lot of possibilities.'

'Which isn't your concern,' Violetta said. 'Your concern is getting Raya back alive. That's priority number one. If you find out that Perry's innocent and have the opportunity to get him back, great. But Raya Parker is who you came to Nepal for.'

'Understood.'

'How's Will?'

'He's fine.'

Slater raised his eyebrows in mock surprise. 'Did she ask about me?'

King shot daggers sideways.

Violetta said, 'Nothing's changed. You only needed the guide and the driver to get to Phaplu, but you're over halfway there. I can feed you the rest of the route, and your destination when you get there. Is that enough?'

'Seems to be,' King said.

'You okay with the drive?'

'I just had ten men try to cut me to pieces. I think I can handle a few bumpy stretches of road.'

'If you can't, it'd look pretty bad in your file. "Jason King:

killed by his own reckless driving after an impressive military career."'

He fought back a smile. 'That sounds an awful lot like banter.'

'It is.'

'Thought we were keeping things professional.'

She sighed. 'You know ... if I lose you, it's not just a note in the case files. It's more than that. I can't pretend that doesn't exist.'

'Should we be talking about that right now?'

'I guess not.'

'Stay safe, Jason.'

'Doing my best.'

'Sure sounds like it.'

'Your sarcasm isn't exactly subtle.'

'I care about you.'

'I know.'

The silence drew out, with the understanding that he wouldn't let the facade slip. He took compartmentalisation seriously. There would be no *I love you* or *I care about you too* until he was back on American soil.

Until then...

'I'll let you go,' she said.

'Okay.'

'Take care.'

'You too.'

He ended the call, wanting to say a thousand things, but opting not to.

Slater shifted uncomfortably in the passenger seat. He racked the seat back and rested one foot on the dashboard, then rolled his pants up and winced as he noticed a shallow lump swelling on his shin. A hematoma, most likely. King studied it briefly, but didn't dare take his eyes off the road for any longer than he needed to.

'How'd you get that?' he said.

'Think it happened when I kicked one of them in the head.'

'Then the other guy probably feels a lot worse.'

Slater dropped the pant leg back down. 'Are you two surviving?'

'Who?'

'You know who.'

'Yeah,' King said. 'We'll be fine. There's worse problems in life.'

'She cares about you.'

King didn't respond. He wondered if this was the setup for some cruel insult. Ever since Slater had ramped up the drinking, his truly genuine moments had been few and far between.

But now King looked over and saw the clarity, the seriousness in the man's eyes. He hadn't had a drink yet today. He probably had a splitting headache, but he was keeping his mouth shut about it. Because Will Slater, although he was many things, was not one to complain.

King said, 'I know she does.'

'I'm just saying ... maybe you shouldn't be so cold.'

'I have to be.'

'Part of the agreement?'

He nodded. 'She wanted to break it. She tried to. But if I die over here ... it'd be so much harder for her to move on.'

'It's going to be hard regardless. You might as well let her know what she means to you. At least while you have the chance to.'

King was genuinely taken aback. He hadn't heard anything like this from Slater since New York. Then he realised. It was more than likely the aftermath of the adrenaline rush — with Slater's stress chemicals heightened, he'd probably be more prone to social acuity.

But that didn't mean it wasn't real.

King said, 'Thanks, brother. I'll talk to her when we get to Phaplu.'

'I would have done the same,' Slater said. 'With Ruby.'

Silence.

Slater said, 'No matter what the agreement would have been.'

'She would have done the same for you. You meant something to her.'

'I hope so.'

'You did.'

'I hope she was proud of what she was. In those final moments. I hope she found peace.'

'Did Shien ever tell you what they spoke about?'

'No. But I got the sense it was positive. For both of them.'

'Then she was at peace.'

'Is that what will happen in our final moments? Or will it just be a bullet to the brain, or a knife to the throat?'

'We won't know until it happens. Until then, there's no use speculating.'

'You think it's Perry, or the porter?'

King reeled at the subject change. 'I don't know. But I do know one thing.'

'And that is?'

'We're going to be having a serious chat to Aidan Parker when we get there.'

19

R aya Parker came to in more pain than she'd felt in quite some time.

Part of it was leftover remnants of the trekking, the effects of covering great distances every day. But most of it was new, in the form of bumps and bruises and swelling, all thanks to the wonders of blunt force trauma. She'd had a blindfold tied over her eyes for a long time. She didn't know exactly how long it had been. Days, or weeks, or months. All she'd known was the same murky darkness, coupled with the swimming vision and the constant swaying as someone carried her up a series of mountains and occasionally crammed food into her mouth and made her drink from a lukewarm water bottle. Her hands had been tied behind her back the whole time, and her feet had been bound together with something that cut into the skin around her ankles.

Before that, she couldn't remember anything at all.

Just the remnants of her final night of freedom, falling asleep across from her father and then...

This.

Now she awoke in something resembling a basement, but she couldn't be certain. Her first instinct was to panic. She opened her eyes and saw something other than the blindfold for the first time since she'd been snatched, and instantly she wanted to scream and shout and plead for help.

But the two men across from her made sure she didn't.

First she recognised Oscar Perry, with his blonde curly hair and white teeth and blue eyes. She'd always thought he looked more like a surfer than a bodyguard, but he wasn't flashing his trademark grin today. He had nicks and scratches all over his face, and he sat opposite her with his hands bound behind him and a rope stretched over his torso, looping around the wooden support column against his back.

Next to him was the porter. Raya couldn't remember the man's name. He was small and squared away, and he'd been intensely shy on the trek. She didn't think he spoke a word of English. He had a horrific injury — one of his eyes had swelled completely shut. It looked like it had been painted black and blue. Like a golf ball had been shoved under his eyelid. He sat there with his head bowed, looking awfully sorry for himself, and Raya felt a pang of empathy for him despite her own condition.

Perry was the first to notice her wake up.

He said, 'Raya. Don't scream. Please.'

She looked around.

They were in a dingy room with rock walls. Weak natural light filtered in through narrow cracks in the ceiling, but that only served to elongate the shadows and make everything a whole lot creepier. Raya tried to move, but her hands were stuck behind her back, tied tight to a heavy object. Constricting her movement. There wasn't anything quite like it. She'd never been restrained before. There was something horrifying about it at an instinctive level. She tried to move — couldn't. Absolutely helpless. At the mercy of whoever had put her here.

They could do *anything* they wanted to her like this.

She shivered.

It took her a moment to realise she was resting against a column — same as Perry, same as the porter.

She breathed. In and out.

Slowly.

Calmly.

She'd been practicing meditation through an app on her phone for the last six months, and she'd need every ounce of what it had taught her to prevent herself succumbing to a panic attack.

She kept breathing.

Watching her intently, Perry nodded his approval.

'That's good,' he said. 'Keep doing that.'

'Where are we?' she said, keeping her voice low.

'I don't know. They blindfolded me, too.'

She nodded at the porter. 'What about him?'

The porter was watching them talk through his one good eye. The other hung grotesquely in the lowlight. His expression was mostly placid, but there was something resembling genuine sadness under the surface.

At their situation, most likely.

Perry shook his head, exasperated. 'Haven't been able to get a word out of him.'

'Does he speak English?'

'I'd wager he doesn't.'

Raya sensed the sarcasm. 'Sorry. I'm not thinking straight. What do we... fuck... what do we do, Oscar?'

Perry looked at her for a long time. With the tension in the air, it felt like hours. 'I don't know.'

'You're the bodyguard,' she said, sensing panic building in her chest. 'You must be able to think of something.'

'While I'm tied up like this, there's nothing I can feasibly—'

An enormous *crash* sounded to their left, and Raya nearly jumped out of their skin. She tore her gaze to the left and saw a wood-panelled door ricochet off the adjacent wall. Thrown open hard by someone behind it.

A pair of Nepali men walked into the room.

There was nothing impressive about them — at least, not compared to Perry's brawn. They looked like cold cruel men, but they were small in stature and build, clad in faded khakis and black military-style boots. But they weren't the army. If Raya had to guess, she put them as some sort of rogue paramilitary force — her father, when he was home, often discussed the problem of well-trained combatants banding together outside an official government structure as one of the greatest threats in today's day and age.

Just Aidan Parker's idea of good dinner conversation, she thought.

Then one of the men strode forward and backhanded her across the face, and she stopped thinking anything other than, *Ouch.*

'No talking,' the man hissed in accented English. 'All of you, shut up.'

The porter suddenly babbled something in Nepali. It sounded hostile. Neither Raya nor Perry could be sure what the small man said, but venom flared in the soldier's eyes as he turned to the hostage.

'Don't hurt him,' Raya said, but she practically whispered it under her breath, and it fell on deaf ears.

The soldier stepped over and kicked the porter in the chest.

Raya cried out.

She'd never seen violence like that before. Not in the flesh. Movies and books were one thing, but watching the sole of a boot ram into a sternum with enough force to rattle the wooden column behind it made her sick to her stomach. She fought the urge to vomit.

The porter dropped his head, pain drenching his face, and winced as he faced the floor.

He was in a world of misery.

The soldier turned to Perry, and raised an eyebrow.

The bodyguard didn't say a word.

Nodding and smiling sadistically, the soldier barked to his comrade, who handed over a trio of coarse black cloths. The man wrung them out tight, making them thin, and forced them between Perry's lips, followed quickly by the porter. With both of them gagged, he wrapped blindfolds over their eyes.

Then he turned to Raya.

She didn't kick or flail or scream. There was no point. It'd only intensify the panic once she lost the ability to speak and her world went dark.

Instead, she stared daggers at the soldier as he forced the dry rancid-tasting cloth between her lips, binding it tight against the corners of her mouth. She found herself thinking, *My dad knows people.*

They're coming.

For you, and your friend, and whoever else is behind this.

Then the blindfold went over her eyes and she saw nothing but the dark material pressing tight.

But it didn't end there.

There was a pause as the soldier got to his feet, and then

he barked a sharp command. Raya sat still, assuming he was just talking to his buddy.

But then there was movement directly across the room.

She wasn't able to pinpoint where it came from — the left, or the right. But she knew what it meant, and her heart dropped, and her walls came up, and she vowed to never utter another word to anyone until she was safe. It wasn't so much the fact that it had happened. This was an extreme situation, and she hadn't expected everything to unfold perfectly. It was the betrayal that cut her soul.

Because either Oscar Perry or the unnamed porter had just shrugged off their bindings and got to their feet.

One of them had been faking it.

Pretending to be held against their will.

Footsteps crept across the room, quietly, so Raya didn't know whether it was the heavier Perry or the lighter porter. But the liar joined his soldier comrades and shook their hands — Raya heard palms clasping softly — and then the three of them left the room.

Raya yelled against her gag, but all that came out was a jumbled gargle.

She went quiet, waiting for a response from whoever was left across the room.

But their gag must have been locked tight, because all she heard was kicking feet and the thumping of a body squirming.

She couldn't tell if it was coming from the left, or the right.

Perry and the porter had been seated too close together.

Raya went quiet, and took a deep rattling breath through the gag, and cried into her blindfold.

20

P haplu was overcast and moody as they pulled in later that afternoon. It was a small village skewered into the Nepali mountains, offering a reprieve before the trek to Everest officially got underway.

They mounted a road running between a row of identical wooden teahouses and a tiny airport. The accommodation tried to lure in the arriving tourists coming off the planes. The runway to their left was impressively short, just a small strip of tarmac slapped horizontally onto the side of the hill, separated from the muddy trail by a cheap wire fence.

Slater watched King alternate his gaze between the phone screen and the murky surroundings outside, searching for their destination. They found it near the very end of the trail — a smaller teahouse, complete with the same wooden exterior, tucked into the shadows. The whole building seemed derelict, especially compared to the newer establishments aiming to trap tourists closer to the airport.

King parked the jeep, and they got out in the late afternoon gloom.

Slater's breath steamed in front of his face. He had endless doubts about the mission still festering in his head, but now they were here in the middle of it, and there was no longer an opportunity for Violetta to reconsider.

So we might as well get it done fast, then.

He said, 'This the place?'

King stared up at the forlorn structure. 'As far as I can tell.'

'Parker's the only one here?'

'I think his guide is still with him.'

'Is that wise?'

'It's only unwise if we have reason to suspect the guide's involved.'

'I don't trust anyone.'

'Nor do I.'

'Does the guide speak English?'

'We'll find out.'

'I can take him,' Slater said. 'You take Parker.'

'You sure?'

'I'm a little less ... accommodating. And I think the guide's more likely to know something than Parker is.'

'I wouldn't assume anything.'

'Then we can switch halfway through,' Slater said. 'Good cop, bad cop.'

King nodded slowly. 'That might work.'

'Then let's get this over and done with.'

They retrieved their all-weather duffel bags from the small storage compartment on the roof of the jeep, and trudged through the wet gravel toward the teahouse.

Ten feet from the entrance, the door swung open in their faces.

A white guy stood there, maybe fifty years old, carrying maybe thirty more pounds than he needed to. He must have been an athlete in the past — he still had the stocky, broad-shouldered build and overall poise of someone who knew how to move their body around. But there was a little too much fat under the stubble coating his jaw, and his hair had receded a decade ago. Nevertheless, his eyes were kind underneath the bloodshot surface.

He'd been crying a hell of a lot, it seemed.

Aidan Parker said, 'Thank God you two are here.'

Slater paused to scrutinise, to assess, to look for suspiciousness, but King didn't miss a beat. He strode forward and offered a hand and said, 'I'm Jason King. This is my partner, Will Slater. We're here to help.'

'Thank you,' Parker said. 'Honestly, thank you so much. This place isn't exactly around the corner.'

Slater watched King half-smile and shuffle past as Parker stepped aside to let him through.

Slater stepped up.

'Hey,' he said. 'I'm Will.'

'Hey, Will,' Parker said. 'Thanks again for coming.'

'Don't worry about it. Where's your guide?'

'Sorry?'

'Your guide. The man who brought you back here to wait for us.'

'Oh — Sejun?'

'I'd say so.'

'He's right through here. Do you need to speak to him?'

'We'll need to speak to everyone who was there. This is an ongoing investigation.'

Parker hesitated. 'Am I under suspicion?'

'Everyone's under suspicion.'

From within the teahouse, King said, 'We're just trying to get to the bottom of it. I'm sure you can appreciate that.'

'Of course,' Parker said, but a look of befuddlement

spread across his face, as if he were silently asking, *Me?*
'Come in out of the cold, Will.'

Slater moved straight past. He wasn't courteous about it.
In fact he made sure to brush by aggressively. When he was
inside, he nodded quietly to King, telling him, *We're on.*

If he had to play the bad guy, he'd do a damn good job
at it.

There was no entranceway or corridor past the front
door — instead, the entrance opened straight into this
particular teahouse's dining room. There were a cluster of
European tourists in the far corner, hunched around a
polished table, babbling back and forth. On the opposite
wall, a couple of solo travellers hunched over their masala
and ginger teas, stoic in their silence. It seemed they were
preparing themselves for the trek to come.

There was a Nepali couple — a middle-aged man and
woman — behind the wooden desk, but they must have
been briefed that King and Slater were en route. They just
nodded politely to the newcomers, and went back to
perusing the books.

No one paid them much attention at all.

Good.

On cue, King said, 'Aidan, if you'd like to come with me,
so we can speak somewhere more private.'

'Of course.'

'And we'll get Sejun along the way. Will would like to
speak with him.'

Parker seemed relieved. Which made sense. Better if the
guide had to deal with the angry one rather than himself.
Slater kept shooting him daggers all the way across the
room, until he and King disappeared into one of the hallways leading to the sleeping quarters.

King put a hand on Parker's shoulder from behind, and

guided him out of the main room. Then he turned and looked over his shoulder and nodded knowingly.

Slater nodded back.

A few moments later, Sejun appeared.

21

K ing quietly scrutinised Aidan Parker as they stepped into a small private dining room up the back of the teahouse.

There were a couple of tables and a smattering of chairs, but everything was coated in a thin layer of dust, and there were supply crates stacked across one wall. A bulb hanging from the ceiling shone bright enough to illuminate all the nooks and crannies, but overall the space had the air of disuse about it. King had asked if there was somewhere to speak privately, and Parker had led him here.

The man had been here for three days now, and obviously knew the building inside and out.

Parker squashed himself into one of the benches and put his elbows on the surface of the table. King sat down across from him, in one of the thin chairs. It seemed it could barely hold his weight, and it creaked as he lowered himself into it.

One of the staff — a young woman in her twenties — appeared in the doorway, shooting Parker an enquiring glance.

'Masala tea,' Parker said.

'Two,' King said.

She nodded graciously and vanished.

Parker lowered his head into his hands. King didn't react. He still didn't have a measure on the guy, and didn't know whether he was doing it for dramatic effect or out of genuine misery.

King said, 'This must be tough.'

Parker didn't look up. He nodded, staring at the table, pressing his palms into the side of his head.

King said, 'I'm going to need to ask you some questions about exactly what happened. What you saw...'

'I already told you everything,' the man muttered.

'You told someone. That someone wasn't me. If it's not too hard for you, I'd like to run through it again.'

'I really don't want to talk about it.'

'I can imagine. But in this case, you're going to have to.'

He said it politely, but there was something undercutting his tone that Parker noticed. Which was ideal, because King had made sure to inject a certain ... something into his voice.

Just to let Aidan Parker know he wasn't a pushover.

Parker lifted his gaze and said, 'Okay. Sorry. I haven't been myself lately. I don't mean to antagonise.'

King held up both hands. 'I wasn't assuming anything, Aidan. I'm simply telling you we need to work together on this.'

'I know, I know. Okay — what do you need to know?'

'Walk me through it. Play by play.'

'Raya and I were in the same room. When I went to sleep, she was there. When I woke up, she wasn't.'

'Did you hear her leave at any point during—?'

'No. I slept all the way through the night. Didn't wake up once. Didn't hear a thing.'

'Are you usually a deep sleeper?'

'Not really. Job stress and what not. In fact, back home I'm something of an insomniac. But I'd never exerted myself like that before. I wasn't prepared for how hard the trekking would be. It sapped all the energy out of me. I slept like a log every night on the trail.'

'So you're assuming she got up to go to the bathroom and was snatched outside?'

'I'm not assuming anything,' Parker said, and for a moment King's guard fell away. The guy had serious pain in his eyes — he was either a world-class actor, or honestly affected. 'I can't tell you what happened, or your superiors who contacted me earlier. If I knew anything, or even suspected anything, I'd tell you — I swear to God. But I don't have the faintest clue. I don't want to assume a thing, because what if...?'

He trailed off, but King knew where he was headed. 'What if you blame Perry but he turns out to be innocent?'

Parker paused to ruminate, then nodded. 'I understand he's the prime suspect. But I just can't bring myself to think it's him. He's been so loyal...'

'You'd be surprised,' King said, thinking back to all the betrayals he'd been privy to over the years. 'Sometimes it's the ones you least expect. Or, in this case, the one you most suspect...'

'I don't suspect him.'

'You should.'

'He couldn't kill Winston like that.'

'I mean, I'm sure he was physically capable. Whether he wanted to or not — that's another thing.'

'It's not him.'

'You're certain?'

Parker paused, and rubbed his brow, and finally said, 'No. I'm not certain.'

'There we go.'

'But it's unlikely.'

'Most of my career is based on "unlikely."'

'So what are you going to do?' Parker said.

'Slater and I will set off on the same route you were heading along until we get further intelligence. Trust me — every asset we have available is scouring Nepal for signs of your daughter.'

'That's good to hear.'

'You don't sound relieved.'

'I'm not an idiot,' Parker said. 'I know how most kidnap cases involving the government and private security often end up. I didn't get where I am today by being a giddy optimist.'

'And where exactly are you today? That seems … unclear.'

'You know how it is,' Parker said. 'It's black operations. There's no official ruleset for anything we do.'

'If you had to narrow it down to a single sentence.'

Parker sat still. Thinking hard. Then he said, 'It's tough.'

'Why?'

'If I told you, it'd be exposing something I've been trying to keep secret for a few months now.'

'You're going to have to tell me if you want the best chance of finding your daughter.'

'Why?'

'Because it sounds juicy,' King said. 'And if it's juicy, then there's the chance it's leaked. And if it's leaked, then there'll be people wanting to make some money off it.'

Parker winced. 'Maybe you're right.'

'What do you do, Aidan?'

Parker took a deep breath.

'I'm planning a move into politics.'

King said nothing.

Parker said, 'The highest level of politics.'

'What — you're just going to come out of nowhere and make a run for President? You're not even in public office.'

'I have connections. I've spent my whole life doing work behind the scenes. There's people in high places who appreciate that.'

King bowed his head. 'That's dynamite leverage to the right person.'

Parker seemed to know what he was going to say. 'Perry didn't know.'

'You sure?'

'I didn't tell him anything.'

'That doesn't mean he didn't know.'

King said, 'I'm guessing a move into politics at the level you're talking about comes with a bunch of big political donors.'

Parker paused, then gave a reluctant nod.

'So if Perry found out, he knows you're now swimming up to your eyeballs in cash.'

'I'm not.'

'But you could be. If you phrased it nicely to the donors.'

Another pause.

Another reluctant nod.

King said, 'It's the bodyguard.'

'I don't think so.'

'You're not looking at it objectively, then.'

Parker bowed his head again, and took his face in his hands, and a guttural sob wracked him from head to toe.

King watched closely.

And a lightbulb went off in his head.

In an instant, he knew Aidan Parker was faking it.

22

———

Slater knew within a couple of minutes that he wouldn't get the information he needed.

He sat Sejun down at one of the tables in the communal area. The guide was shy and reserved, but accommodating. He seemed to know only a smattering of English, but he didn't look down or look away to accentuate the language barrier. He kept his attention squarely focused on Slater, and clasped his hands together in his lap, and sat up straight, and waited for the first question.

Slater played the bad guy, but almost immediately realised he wouldn't need to keep up the shtick for long.

'Sejun, right?'

The guide nodded. 'Yes. That is my name.'

'Tell me about the missing porter.'

'Of course, sir. His name Mukta. He with company for three year, but he take other job sometimes.'

'Is that normal?'

'Yes. Porters work for different company. They take any job they offered. Not much money, you know? Need to keep getting...'

He trailed off, snapping his fingers together, scrunching up his face, searching for the right word.

'Consistent work?' Slater said.

Sejun nodded excitely. 'Yes. That's it. Consistent. They need work all the time, to make enough. Very difficult work.'

'Don't you do the same thing?'

Sejun half-smiled and shrugged his shoulders. 'I no carry pack. That's hard part of job.'

'What did you think of Raya?'

Sejun hesitated. 'Of girl who was taken?'

'Yes.'

'Very nice. I sometimes hear her and father ... arguing.'

Slater raised an eyebrow. 'Is that so?'

Sejun waved his dirty palms. 'Yes, but not father who do this. I know that for sure. They argue about ... father not being home. Not make father want to get rid of her, you know?'

'Her father is always at work? That was her problem?'

'Yes. She not happy. She want to see her dad.'

Slater nodded. 'Understandable.'

'Yes. I think so too. I have little girl. I away a lot, on trek. But this is what I must do. You know? I must provide.'

Slater gave another nod.

Sejun said, 'Do you think I have part in this?'

Slater thought about how to respond, and then ultimately said, 'No. I don't.'

'Why?'

'Because if you were guilty you wouldn't be here. You have no reason to be here, other than caring for your client's wellbeing. You could have disappeared along with the rest of them and put your head down until this all blew over. But you didn't.'

'But maybe I stay to take suspicion away...'

Slater half-smiled. 'I don't think so, Sejun. And you don't either.'

The guide shrugged. 'You and your friend — you go find her?'

'We're going to do our best.'

'I wish I help more than this. Do you want me come with you? No worry about payment. I hope she safe. Want her to be safe.'

'That's very kind of you, but we'll be okay.'

'You know route?'

'Not well.'

'I do.'

'I don't want to offend you, but we're probably going to have to set a pace that'll be hard to match.'

Sejun raised a suspicious eyebrow. 'I hear this before. Sometimes tourists think they can go fast. But these mountains ... hard to go fast.'

'We're not most tourists.'

'Yes, I see. Okay. You need something from me?'

'Tell me what you think of Parker.'

'He is good man.'

'You're sure?'

'I spend time with him here. Three days. Whole time, he no seem bad. He care about daughter. He want her to be safe.'

'Has he done anything that's made you suspicious?'

'No. No suspicious. He is telling truth with what he says.'

Slater nodded, somewhat relieved. 'Thank you, Sejun. I trust you.'

'I'm glad. I don't like to be suspected. I not bad person. I try to do right thing.'

'You have,' Slater said, and offered a hand. 'Thank you

for staying here with him. It sounds like he needed the support.'

'Of course.'

Slater slid out of his chair. 'I'll be right back. Need to check in with my friend.'

'Good luck.'

He patted Sejun reassuringly on the shoulder on the way past.

He found them in a back room. Parker had his head on the table, seemingly wracked with emotion, and King was sitting across from him, bolt upright, watching and calculating.

When Slater appeared in the doorway, King looked up.

Parker didn't.

King said, 'Glad you showed up. I need you here.'

Slater said, 'Why?'

'Because he's overacting.'

Parker's head bolted off the table, shocked.

23

Before Parker could utter a word, King said, 'Shut up.'

He added a certain aggressiveness to it.

Parker obliged.

King ushered Slater over, who took the seat beside him. Together they stared daggers at the greying, slightly-overweight man across from them. Parker didn't know where to look. He stayed quiet, tears in his eyes, alternating between gazing into space and glancing briefly at each of them. But he couldn't hold eye contact. Their gazes were withering. He paled in the face of it. It was fairly obvious he'd never been more uncomfortable.

Parker finally said, 'What are you talking about?'

King said, 'You're overacting.'

'What do you mean?'

'What do you think I mean?'

He shrugged and held both hands out, apparently flabbergasted. 'I don't know—'

Slater leant forward and said, 'He means you're trying to sell it too hard. He means that you'd better start explaining exactly what you're doing, and why, or it's going to look very suspicious very quickly. So do you have a reason *why* you're pretending to be sadder than you are?'

'What makes you assume that—?'

King said, 'Because I've seen it before. And I know. You might be distraught but you're overdoing it. It had better be because we're here and you feel the need to perform. There'd better not be anything more sinister behind it.'

Parker didn't immediately respond. He sat there, rubbing his hands together. There were still tears in his eyes, but he wasn't burying his head in his hands anymore.

The knot in King's stomach untwisted. He'd instantly assumed the worst, but these were trying times. There were any number of reasons for Parker to sell an image that wasn't accurate. Sure, one of them could be covering up the fact that he was involved, but it was seeming less and less likely as time went on.

He hadn't run out of the room.

He just sat there, looking awkward.

Slater said, 'Speak.'

Parker said, 'I'm confused, okay? I've spent years operating in the same world as you both. Maybe not on the frontline, but it still requires a serious grip on your emotions. You need to be calm, level-headed, even in the face of the worst case scenario. But I didn't know if the pair of you would understand. I thought you might show up here and see me calm and quiet and rational and suspect that I had something to do with it. So I panicked, and figured I'd break down in tears a few times to sell the truth. I didn't realise you'd figure me out. I swear that's all there is to it.'

Slater stared.

King stared.

Parker stared back.

No longer awkward.

No longer a blubbering wreck.

King said, 'I believe you.'

'I wouldn't blame you if you didn't,' Parker said.

Slater said, 'I do, too. You pass the test.'

Despite himself, Parker showed relief.

Slater turned to King and said, 'Any updates I missed?'

'One.'

'Important?'

'Very.'

Slater raised his eyebrows. 'How important?'

King pointed at Parker. 'He's planning a presidential campaign.'

Slater furrowed a brow. 'But no one knows who he is.'

'He has connections in high places. And if I had to guess, I'd say it's a long process. Maybe five years, even.'

'I'm right here, guys,' Parker said.

'We know,' Slater said.

Parker said, 'Yes, it's a long process. And I already told your friend here that no-one knows about it besides you two and a handful of people I trust with my life.'

'Was Oscar Perry in that handful?' Slater said.

'No.'

'You sure?'

'You think I'd cover that up?'

'I think you might. If it makes you look like an idiot.'

'You think I'd rather let my daughter die than look like an idiot?'

Slater shrugged. 'Nothing would surprise me anymore.'

'I'm not the monster you think I am.'

'We don't think you're a monster,' King said, almost rolling his eyes. 'We're just taking precautions. Instantly clearing people of suspicion has got us in plenty of trouble in the past.'

Parker looked first at King, then at Slater. 'You know … I've heard about you two.'

'Let me guess,' Slater said. 'You coordinated some of our past operations behind the scenes?'

'Yes.'

'What does that look like, if you don't mind me asking?'

Parker stared at him. 'You know I can't tell you that.'

'Be a good sport.'

'I'm always a good sport. Unless it involves NDAs handed down to me from the highest levels. Then I keep my mouth shut.'

'You really can't tell us a thing?'

'It's best that way. Separates the bureaucracy from the active operators. But I'm sure you've heard that speech before.'

King and Slater both nodded.

The trio sat there, more comfortable in the silence. They'd broken the ice. They seemed to understand each other a little better.

King was satisfied.

He didn't know about Slater.

Parker said, 'So — what exactly is the plan?'

'We're waiting on intel,' King said. 'When it comes, we'll—'

The satellite phone barked in his pocket.

Slater said, 'And there it is.'

24

K ing stepped outside and shut the door behind him and put the phone to his ear and said, 'Yes?'

Violetta said, 'We've got something.'

'Enough to let us get started?'

'More than that. We spoke directly to a couple of Swiss backpackers who saw all three of them on the trail to Gokyo Ri.'

King paused, deep in thought. 'Can you trust the witnesses?'

'They have no idea how serious this is. They're not involved in any way. They responded when we put the feelers out that we were looking for information.'

'I just don't understand why the kidnappers would be following the same path.'

'To get to a higher altitude, maybe. That would fuck with anyone trying to make a rescue attempt.'

'Which would explain the porter being behind it.'

'Yeah, it would ... except Oscar Perry was leading the three of them.'

King paused. 'Against their will?'

'He didn't seem to be. The backpackers only gave the group a passing glance, but they remembered them because one of the porter's eyes was swollen completely shut. They said it looked like he had a golf ball under his eyelid. He was bringing up the rear. Raya was in the middle.'

'Did she seem hurt?'

'Not that they can remember. They were fixated on the porter's eye, mostly.'

'Could be an act.'

'Maybe.'

'No way to know for sure until we catch them.'

'That's the main thing. We know where they are, so you have a target to aim at. They just passed Namche Bazaar, so they're making good time, but it's not great.'

'That puts them on the main trail toward Everest and Gokyo Ri, doesn't it? No wonder they've been spotted. There'd be a hundred times the amount of hikers on the trail than below Namche.'

'Yes, which is why you need to leave first thing tomorrow morning and cover as much ground as humanly possible.'

King remembered the map of the region he'd scoured. 'Most hikers fly into Lukla Airport, right? The one right near Namche Bazaar.'

'Yes.'

'So we're in Phaplu. There's an airport here. Just arrange a flight for us so we don't have to spend unnecessary time on the lesser-known trails.'

She sighed. 'We can't do that, because there's a catch.'

'And that is?'

'With the help of a translator, we got in contact with the owners of the teahouse Raya was snatched from. They found something on the trail just outside that doesn't belong to them.'

'What?'

'A briefcase.'

'Locked?'

'Yes.'

'Whose?'

'Probably Parker's. Ask him.'

'Surely he'd remember if he left a briefcase there.'

'Not if it's his, and he thinks they took it, and he hasn't told us it's missing.'

'Oh.'

'He might not be the man you think he is, King.'

'I trust him.'

'Why?'

'We've spoken.'

'Surely not enough to get a read on the situation.'

'It's just a hunch. And my hunches are usually right.'

'Maybe not this time. Ask him about it.'

'And then?'

'Then you and Slater get a good night's sleep and put your head down and trek all the way to Kharikhola tomorrow. You'll stay at the same teahouse Raya was snatched from, and see if anything new has turned up, and get the briefcase open.'

'Where did you say they found it?'

'On the trail.'

'Discarded? If Perry took it, he probably got it open and then closed it again.'

'No way to know for sure unless you're there in person.'

'Right. Kharikhola — how far is that?'

'About eighteen miles.'

'We can do that.'

'It's steep terrain. And you'll need to move fast to cover

that much ground before dark. Most seasoned trekkers do it over two full days.'

'We can manage.'

'I hope so.'

'Is that doubt I hear?'

'This is a different ball game, Jason.'

'This is why we train the way we do,' he said. 'We'll make it.'

'Stay in touch. I'll let you know if I hear anything else. And find out about that briefcase.'

'On it.'

He hung up, and stepped back into the room.

Parker looked up.

Slater looked up.

King said, 'Aidan, we need to talk.'

25

S later watched silently, assessing King's demeanour.

Immediately he knew King was pissed.

Slater sat back, judging whether to interfere or not. He could adopt the role of the bad guy when needed, but King seemed to be handling that all on his own.

Slater said, 'Do you need me here?'

King met his gaze with an icy look. 'Yes. Seems our friend here hasn't been fully honest.'

Slater raised an eyebrow. 'Again?'

Parker didn't say a word, but his hands started to tremble.

King pulled the chair out, sat down hard, placed both calloused hands flat on the surface of the table and waited for Parker to speak first.

Finally, Parker said, 'Come on, guys. What is it this time?'

'Is there something you're not telling us?'

'No. I've—'

'Something that might make you suspect Oscar Perry over the porter?'

'No.'

'You sure about that?'

'What are you getting at?'

'Are you missing a briefcase?'

A pause, and then, 'No.'

But the pause said it all.

King said, 'Don't make me hit you.'

'Okay, fuck. Yes. Yes, I'm missing a briefcase.'

Slater mumbled, 'He's not taking this seriously.'

'I know that,' King said. 'I'm trying to figure out why.'

'Look,' Parker said, and leant forward and put his elbows on the table and rubbed his forehead. This time, he wasn't faking the discomfort. This time, he was feeling every ounce of it, and they could both tell. 'There's certain things I'm hesitant to tell you both. Just the nature of my job. Please don't hold it against me. I'm wired this way. I've spent my whole career being secretive and to open up to you both in the most stressful—'

He stopped mid-sentence, and scrunched up his face, clearly irritated.

King and Slater waited and watched.

Parker said, 'Fuck's sake. Okay, yes, the briefcase is gone. It had my work laptop in it. But that doesn't automatically mean it's Perry. I left it beside my bed. The porter could have assumed it was valuable and taken it.'

'Why didn't you tell anyone it was gone?'

'Because...'

They didn't say a word.

Parker scrunched up his face again. '*Shit.*'

He seemed genuinely horrified that the truth had come out.

'Because I'm a moron,' he said. 'That night ... I was transferring sensitive information out of a cloud we use with military-grade encryption. We do that nowadays so stealing the actual hardware itself doesn't mean anything. They might be able to get into the laptop, but to get into our servers is a different matter entirely.'

Slater held up a hand, cutting him off. 'If you're about to tell us that you pulled sensitive information out of the cloud, didn't put it back in, went to sleep, woke up and found the briefcase missing, I'm going to reach across this table and slap you in the fucking face.'

Parker didn't say a word.

King said, 'That puts more suspicion on you, buddy. Whether you want it to or not.'

Parker said, 'Hence why I didn't say anything.'

Slater said, 'So you didn't say anything about your little presidential campaign, and then you didn't say anything about your briefcase, and now you're expecting us to believe this is one crazy coincidence that you couldn't possibly have anything to do with?'

Parker didn't blink. He leant forward, eyes fixed on Slater, and hissed, 'Why the fuck would I kidnap my own daughter?'

Slater didn't say anything.

Good point, he thought.

King said, 'What was the information?'

Parker didn't respond.

King said, 'Aidan.'

The man looked up.

'What was the information?'

'The locations of a dozen of our temporary HQs back on U.S. soil.'

'Whose HQs?'

'Black ops. Anything the government can't officially disclose. The workforce that operates behind the scenes has secret locations they set up in, but it's on a cycle. We all pack up and move shop every few months. I was arranging a future move, but I started nodding off in bed and I closed the laptop and packed it away and figured I'd wake up early and finish it in the morning.'

'That's idiotic for someone at your level.'

'I know. Another reason I didn't say anything. I'm terrified it will ruin any credibility I'd built up with the connections I've made. It'll ruin everything I've been planning for years. I want to do great things for our country, but I can't if this fucking laptop gets compromised. I made one mistake, and...'

He trailed off.

King thought about it.

Weighed it up.

And, strangely, believed him again.

'What are you thinking?' Parker said.

'I think you made a couple of moronic decisions in a row and then the worst-case scenarios for each of them wound up happening. You kicked your protection detail out to spend more time with your daughter, and then you made a lapse in judgment with information you'd been handling with confidence for decades. So, no, I don't think you're malicious — I just think you're an idiot.'

Parker shrugged. 'That's fair enough.'

No-one said anything.

Parker said, 'Where was the briefcase found?'

'Discarded on the trail right outside the teahouse.'

The man breathed an audible sigh of relief. 'If they couldn't get into it, maybe they threw it aside...'

'Did Perry know the code?'

'Yes.'

'So if he's behind it, we'll get there tomorrow night and the briefcase will be empty.'

'The porter could have got it out of him.'

'How big was the porter?'

'Tiny. Barely over five feet.'

'How big is Perry?'

'Big.'

'Think about that, Aidan.'

Parker looked at them like they were stupid. 'You ever seen someone held at gunpoint?'

'Too many times to count.'

'Then *you* think about that. I stand by my opinion that it's not Oscar Perry. Of course, that doesn't mean it's the porter, either. There could have been a—'

'It's one of them,' King said. 'That's for sure.'

'And what makes you so certain?' Parker said.

'Because they were spotted on the trail earlier today with your daughter.'

Slater said, 'What?'

Parker said, 'What?'

King said, 'Perry was leading the pack. Raya was in the middle, unhurt. And the porter was bringing up the rear with the mother-of-all black eyes. The witnesses said it looked like a golf ball under his eyelid.'

Parker went quiet, and Slater said, 'Shit.'

King stood up. 'Aidan, I think you need to reconsider your stance that it's not Oscar Perry. Might make it easier when the truth comes out.'

He left the room to coordinate the rest of the details with Violetta in privacy.

26

S later didn't feel the urge to sit around shooting the shit with Aidan Parker — partly because he had little in common with the budding politician, but mostly because until the case was closed they weren't ruling out anyone, and it wasn't wise to befriend potential suspects.

So he went to his assigned room, trudging through the creaking upper level of the teahouse, and shut the door behind him. King had the room next door, so for now he was by himself. He breathed in the quiet and savoured it. He still liked being alone. He didn't think that sensation would ever leave. He shed a couple of outer layers and spread out on the bed, then went through the same routine physical check-up he'd conducted on himself after every fight he'd ever been in. He was sore as hell, and anyone unaccustomed to the gruelling nature of physical combat would probably assume they'd broken a dozen different bones in the aftermath of a fistfight. His joints ached from the max-effort rattle of punches and elbows ricocheting off bone. He closed his eyes and visualised a soothing river flowing downstream, working its way from his head to his toes, dissipating the traumatised muscle tissue and rattled joints.

That's what the movies didn't show.

Punch someone in the jaw as hard as Slater could, and your fist is going to ache for a week.

Thankfully, he was used to it.

But he didn't know how it would bode for the following morning.

They had a lot of ground to cover. There were endless questions and muddied motivations and no clear answer. No gameplan either. Whoever was behind Raya's kidnapping was doing the right thing — climbing higher and higher, reaching altitudes that had the potential to neutralise even the fittest, hardest, toughest men on earth. Altitude sickness was a cruel bitch.

That reminded him...

He rolled over, fished through his pack, and popped a couple of Diamox. The altitude sickness tablets would at least do something to prevent any issues that might crop up when they trekked above thirteen thousand feet.

He lay on his back, staring up at the wood-panelled ceiling, and found himself thinking...

...nothing at all.

Was that odd? Here he was, about to undertake a monumental physical task in the hopes of finding a kid who didn't deserve what had happened to her. There'd be sweat and blood and toil and relentless exertion. Maybe in the past that might have frightened him, producing multiple sleepless nights before the pain struck in its fullest intensity, but now there was nothing but calmness and stoicism. He didn't know whether that was good or bad.

It just *was.*

He was sure King felt the same. Together they'd been

through enough war and suffering to fill the lives of dozens of elite soldiers. Nothing would surprise them on the trail, and Slater wasn't sure whether to be wary of that or take it in his stride. The last thing he wanted was to take his skillset for granted and drop his guard when the fear didn't arise. It only took a half-second of carelessness in the heat of battle to lose your life.

He wasn't about to let that happen.

Someone knocked on the door. He swivelled off the bed and opened it to find King standing there, pensive, the satellite phone lowered in one hand.

King swept a hand over his short hair. 'You doing okay?'

'Yeah,' Slater said.

Neither of them said anything.

Slater folded his arms over his chest. 'You babysitting me now?'

'I think this might be more intense than we think.'

'We'll adapt to it. We always do.'

'Violetta didn't seem confident that we'd be able to make the time she wants. It's going to be a hell of a lot of miles tomorrow.'

'I'm in shape. You are too. This is what we train for.'

'That's what I told her.'

'And yet you still have your doubts?'

'What if the altitude gets us? What if we grind ourselves into the dirt to catch up to Raya, and then we're crippled by headaches and nausea the moment we come into contact with the enemy.'

'Then we'll fight through it.'

King didn't respond.

Slater said, 'Really? *Really?* You're having doubts? What do you want me to say?'

'Nothing. Neither of us are babysitting each other. We're

big boys. I just think we should both be prepared if this is harder than we think.'

'Can it really be worse than what we've been through?' Slater said.

King took a step back, and nodded. 'It can always be worse.'

Then he set off down the hallway.

Slater called after him, 'Any updates from Violetta?'

King turned back. 'Yeah.'

'What'd she say?'

'To get a good night's sleep.'

'Noted.'

'We'll need it.'

'I don't doubt that.'

'You can order dinner downstairs whenever you want. I'm told it'll take about an hour to cook.'

'I'll be right there.'

'Did you take your Diamox?'

'Yes Dad.'

'Are you hurt from earlier today?'

Slater flexed his shoulders and arms and wrists, rolling out the aches and pains. 'The usual.'

King half-smiled. 'It's a strange life we live.'

'Always has been.'

'I'll see you downstairs.'

He disappeared into his own room down the hall.

27

The next morning, they both rose at the crack of dawn.

King's alarm ruptured the pre-dawn silence, and he growled as he stabbed a finger down on the touch-screen, cancelling it. He swung out of bed and stretched out and went through a gruelling twenty-minute series of yoga vinyasas, opening his hips and his shoulders, contributing to the ongoing fight to make his body as supple and limber as possible. He credited the endless stretching and the fight to maintain positions as the main reason he was able to live this sort of lifestyle and avoid serious career-ending injury. But as he wiped fog off the window and stared out at Phaplu and the ominous towering mountains in the distance, he wondered if this operation would push him further than he'd ever gone before.

Something in the back of his head told him it might.

He dressed in a long-sleeved compression top and leggings, then threw a pair of athletic shorts and a loose hiking shirt over the top and stuffed his sleeping bag back into his pack. He slung the whole thing over one shoulder

— it was heavy, but he'd trained his whole life to make hard tasks easy — and went downstairs.

Slater was already there, gorging on momos and vegetable fried rice. King ordered the same. The communal area was quiet at this hour — there were a couple of Germans across the room, but they kept to themselves, allowing King and Slater to talk in private.

Slater said, 'You been in touch with Violetta since we last spoke?'

'No.'

'So same plan?'

'Yeah.'

'Why can't we take the plane again?'

'Briefcase in Kharikhola.'

'Right. That little thing.'

'Could be a big thing if it's empty.'

Slater stared at him as if he was stupid. 'It'll be empty.'

'You seem sure of that.'

'Either Perry got it open himself, or the porter put a gun to Raya's head when he refused to open it. Either way, the laptop's gone. The fact that it's locked doesn't mean a thing.'

'So Parker's career is probably over.'

'I don't care. What I care about is getting Raya back.'

'I know. I'm in the same boat.'

'Speak of the devil...' Slater muttered under his breath.

Aidan Parker materialised in the doorway. He had dark bags under his eyes and his thinning hair was skewered out at all angles. He spotted King and Slater, nodded brusquely to them, and joined them at their table.

'Gentlemen,' he said, 'how are we?'

'About the same as usual,' Slater said.

'When are you heading off?'

'Right now.'

'Oh. Well...'

'You don't need to wish us good luck,' King said. 'We'll get your daughter back. I promise.'

Parker didn't immediately respond. He soaked the words in. They seemed to mean a lot to him.

Then he said, 'Thank you. Thank you both. Truth is, I've never been through this much turmoil before.'

Slater nodded his understanding. 'Now, Aidan, if you don't mind...'

'Right, yes, of course,' Parker said, getting to his feet. 'I'll leave you both to it. I wouldn't want to throw you off this close to the action.'

He said it like he'd never experienced it first-hand. There was no weight behind the word *action,* no under-standing of what exactly that might entail. King knew immediately that Parker had never seen violence up close, never heard a bone crack or a head bounce off concrete or a bullet spray out the back of a man's head through the exit wound.

King said, 'Lay low here. We'll see you when we get back.'

Parker nodded, but seemed to recognise the underlying tension in King's tone. He turned on his heel and left them to themselves.

Slater muttered, 'What do you think?'

'I think he's fine,' King said. 'Just not the sort of person I want to be talking to right now.'

'Me either.'

'What's the time?'

'Nearly six.'

'Let's get moving.'

It should have been more grandiose. It should have been the part where the music swelled at the beginning of their grand adventure, as they slung their packs over their shoulders and took the first step out the door and saw the long and winding road spiralling into the lush green valleys and snow-capped mountains.

But in reality it was the same as it had always been. Nothing magnificent. Nothing idyllic. Nothing romantic. There was the scuff of their boots on the gravel and the sound of measured breathing as they found a solid pace, striding it out at a speed just under a jog. They were out of Phaplu within a couple of minutes, and then there was nothing but the road and the pace and the burn in their legs and the thudding of their hearts in their chests.

They kept it up, and neither of them spoke.

They each sunk into something close to a meditative trance as the scenery enveloped them and they powered through Nepal toward Kharikhola.

few hours later, they were making good time.

Slater grimaced as he picked up too much momentum on the way down the side of a small mountain, and ended up uncontrollably jogging a stretch of the trail. The declines were just as severe as the inclines, and there were no flat stretches in sight. They'd alternated between battling their way up incredible rises, followed swiftly by long downward stretches that ruined any elevation they'd managed to rack up along the way.

Because their destination, Kharikhola, was still low in altitude, resting in the foothills below Lukla and the main trail to Everest and Gokyo Ri.

They wouldn't be getting to tricky heights for a few days, at least.

Slater stumbled to a halt as the trail levelled out and caught his breath. He wiped sweat off his forehead, sucked greedily at his water bottle packed with branched-chain amino acids, and checked his smartwatch.

Ten miles covered.

He was feeling it in his feet, his ankles, his calves, his

knees, his sternum, even his arms. They weren't running the trail, but even striding it out at a fast pace tested their cardiovascular capacity. When you had to ascend nearly two hundred feet on every incline, it was practically the same as running up a craggy, uneven staircase. They reached the top of every ascent with their heart rate through the roof, and then they had to deal with the pounding impacts of the descent on their knees.

Overall, it was tough, relentless work.

But that was the norm in their profession.

King caught up. He was considerably slower — sure, he had longer legs and could make greater strides, but the extra muscle he was carrying didn't lend him any favours. He couldn't maintain the consistent pace that Slater could. He stumbled to the end of the descent, rasping for breath, and checked his watch too.

'We're making good time,' Slater said, echoing his earlier thoughts.

King nodded. Perspiration dripped off his nose. 'I know.'

'We'll get there before dark.'

'I know.'

'You okay?'

'Fine. Just ... the pace is high.'

'You warned me. Should have warned yourself.'

'I knew you'd be better than me at this. You're—'

'Twenty pounds lighter. I know. Is this the part where I puff you up by saying you could probably throw a punch harder than I could?'

King half-smiled, and wiped his face on his shirt. 'I took out ten men in that village yesterday, remember? You only had to handle four.'

Slater rolled his eyes. 'I'm sure that's why you're slower.'

'I'll adapt.'

'However fast you're adapting, I am too. My pace is only going to increase. You ready for that?'

'Shut up and walk.'

Slater set off, his shirt drenched in sweat, his heart throbbing, his legs heavy and burning. But the endorphins were flowing and the sun was shining and the scenery, although unchanging, was spectacular. They were nowhere near the snowy plains of Gokyo — right now they were deep in green valleys, with the dusty ochre trail underfoot and the sun beating down on the backs of their necks without mercy. There wasn't a cloud in the sky.

It wasn't what they'd anticipated from Nepal.

But it made them feel alive all the same.

Hours passed in a blur. Slater gave endless thanks for the efforts he'd put into daily meditation. Physically exert yourself for eleven hours straight and you're prone to over-think, your brain churning endlessly to come up with any excuse to justify stopping. But if you can shut that voice up and empty everything from your mind and focus entirely on the breath, you're capable of so much more than you think you are. He'd learned that years ago, and now he put it to use. He put one foot in front of the other and thought about nothing and stared straight ahead and controlled his breathing and extended his stride, and before he knew it they'd arrived in a sweaty heap at the top of a sharp ascent and the town of Kharikhola spilled out before them.

In reality, it was a handful of teahouses skewered into the craggy hillside shoulder to shoulder, but they were relieved to see it all the same.

As long as there was a bed, they'd be happy.

It was five in the evening. They'd stopped once for lunch at a random teahouse, and paused briefly in a couple of villages to refill their water bottles, drop in purification tablets, and mask the acrid taste with more BCAA powder.

So they arrived hydrated, but utterly spent.

King bent over and put his hands on his knees and tried his best to hide a wince.

Slater said, 'You don't have to play the tough guy around me. You've got nothing to prove.'

So King winced.

'Christ,' he said. 'I'll be your weight by the time we're done here.'

'And I'll be twenty pounds lighter than I am right now.'

King glanced over at Slater's frame — packed with dense muscle, but lean. There wasn't a shred of body fat on him. Granted, King didn't have any either, but his body was working overdrive to pump oxygen through the additional muscle.

King said, 'That'd be something to behold.'

'Are you worried about that?' Slater said.

'About what?'

'Your musculature at altitude.'

King didn't say anything. Just winced again. 'We'll deal with that when we get to those heights. We're in shape. We'll be fine.'

'That's not how altitude sickness works.'

'I know,' King snarled. 'It's random. Indiscriminate. So there's no use worrying about it then, is there?'

Slater could tell he'd struck a nerve. They'd both pushed themselves to their limits to cover that much ground in a single day, especially over such difficult terrain, and the possibility that they'd repeat that performance over the next week just to get to the top of Gokyo Ri and fall apart from headaches and nausea was too much to process right now.

Slater said, 'These teahouses aren't the ones we're

looking for. Raya got abducted further down the hill. Shouldn't be too far of a walk.'

King simply nodded.

Didn't say a word.

Caught his breath, stood up straight, and pressed onward without a word of complaint.

Slater had to admire it. He was deep in his own head, struggling with his own demons as his body screamed for relief. He couldn't imagine having to work with another twenty pounds on his shoulders. King was a goddamn work-horse, and Slater respected it.

The sun was gone now, giving way to a rapidly dark-ening sky, and they came to the teahouse that matched the coordinates as dusk settled over the hillside. They pulled up in front of it and King double-checked the info on his smart-watch and nodded once.

'Here we are,' he said.

They stumbled inside.

29

Y ou only realise how exhausted you are when you
stop.

King already knew that from a couple of
decades' experience, but the point hammered home when
he dropped onto one of the benches and his energy reserves
hissed away. He rested against the wall behind him and
closed his eyes and exhaled. His knees and calves and
ankles throbbed, his hip flexors were tight as hell, his chest
ached from maintaining a high heart rate for the better part
of eleven hours with only a brief stop for lunch, and every
muscle in his body felt twice as heavy. His shoulders
slumped and his frame drooped as he fought to get a morsel
of energy back. But he didn't let it show — masking weakness had been drilled into him for as long as he could
remember by endless trainers. It made all the difference in a
field like his, because momentum is everything. So he took
the wince off his face and sealed his mouth in a hard line
and opened his eyes.

Instantly he could see Slater was going through the
same thing, but practicing the same mental fortitude.

They sat side by side, breathing long and slow, expelling the momentum of the day's trek and gearing up to recharge for the next morning.

Then the curtains leading to the kitchen parted and a Nepali woman stepped in. She was small and plump and elderly, but she had a warm smile, and they returned it.

'Hello,' she said. 'Small English for me. You are Americans?'

'Yes,' King said.

Slater nodded.

She nodded back, and maintained the same glowing smile, and toddled back through the curtains. King exchanged a glance with Slater, but there was no way to read into the conversation. She hadn't revealed a thing.

'Where'd she go?' Slater whispered.

'I don't know. I know that if she comes back with a gun, I probably won't be able to raise my hands in self-defence.'

She *did* return quickly, this time carrying a sealed brief-case made of something reinforced with a combination lock by the handle. She swung it back and forth as she crossed the room, and placed it gently on the table.

'You take,' she said. 'I find on road.'

'Could you show me where?' King said.

She smiled and shuffled outside.

King tried to get to his feet to follow, but it took him a moment. Already his muscles and joints had set in place, winding down for the day in a method that came with minor swelling and impediment of movement as his legs set to work gearing up for the next day. So he hobbled a few steps, cursing himself all the way, lambasting his body for uncontrollably showing weakness even though there was no-one around to see it. Then his muscles warmed up and he found some momentum and worked his way up to something resembling a normal gait.

Slater said, 'Are you hurt?'

'No,' he grumbled. 'Just sore.'

He stepped outside and saw the woman down below the concrete patio, already on the trail. She was standing over a cluster of weeds a foot away from the dusty gravel, perhaps thirty feet from the door.

'Here,' she called out.

King judged the distance between the living quarters, and the location of the discarded briefcase. It was plausible.

He said, 'Thank you.'

They returned inside.

She motioned to the briefcase and said, 'You keep.'

Slater nodded his appreciation.

Without prompting, she continued, 'I no like it.'

'Why's that?'

'It remind me of bad times. I have to clean room where man died. Blood — so much. I never forget.'

King nodded solemnly. 'Where's the body?'

'Cart back down mountain. Wrapped up. This place for tourist. No place for body.'

Slater muttered to King, 'You should check with Violetta if Winston's body is getting flown back home. I'm sure his family would appreciate that.'

'Will do.'

The woman said, 'You two look very tired. You eat and drink? What you want?'

'Please,' King said.

Slater handed over their two empty hiking bottles and said, 'Water, thank you. We'll purify it ourselves.'

'Tea?' she said.

They both nodded.

'Masala,' King said.

'Ginger,' Slater said.

She sauntered off to the kitchen.

Neither of them moved. The stress of the day's travels was still at the forefront of both their minds. King savoured the silence and let the transition to a resting state happen naturally. There would be no confrontation tonight. They were the teahouse's sole guests. If struggle and battle and conflict would come, it would come way down the line. Briefly he wondered how he'd manage to put up a fight at this level of physical depletion, but that was a problem to be dealt with later. There was no use stressing over it now.

Slater said, 'You going to do the honours?'

King fished the satellite phone out and called Parker.

He picked up on the first ring.

Must have been nervously anticipating the call, King thought.

Parker said, 'Yes?'

'Give me the code.'

'You've got it?'

'It's right here in front of me.'

'3057.'

King reached out and fidgeted with the combination lock until it displayed the correct four digits.

Then he popped the case open.

It was empty.

30

S later heard King relay the news, and then the tinny
discharge of cursing from the other end of the line.

Parker droned on for half a minute, and then
King said, 'Understood.'

He hung up the phone.

Slater clasped his hands together and said, 'Where the
hell does this put us?'

'Nothing's changed,' King said. 'Parker admitted this was
all his own fault, thankfully. He said he'll get in touch with
the relevant parties and let them know exactly what's now
out in the open.'

'Does that mean ten HQs are going to have to relocate?'

'Probably. It's not our problem.'

'It is if they can't pack up in time before they're
compromised.'

King slammed a palm on the table, taking Slater aback.
When he looked up, there was intensity in King's eyes.

'I know that,' King said through gritted teeth. 'You think
this is any easier for me? I've always hated this shit. Now
that we know the laptop's missing, I'd rather be back on

home soil protecting the hundreds of people that are probably now in danger. But we're out here, doing this, and we have to stick to it because those are the orders. So let's go get Raya and then get back home before everything falls apart.'

'It's not the end of the world,' Slater said. 'Not yet. We don't know how bad it is. For all we know, the file didn't even save. And even if the laptop's password-protected, I doubt whoever has it has the software and hardware to get into it out here on the trail. If I had to guess, they've got it in their possession, but they're waiting until they've dealt with Raya to crack it. Or sell it to someone who can.'

'That's just a theory.'

'So is the suggestion that they've got into it. They're all theories. We don't know for sure. So we focus on the trail, and forget about everything else.'

King hunched over the open briefcase, staring at the indent where the laptop used to rest. He almost put his head in his hands, but seemed to think better of it.

Slater said, 'This changes nothing.'

'There's too much happening,' King said. 'It's hard to keep track of all of it at once.'

'Get the girl back,' Slater said. 'That's what matters.'

'It's all well and good to tell ourselves that, but there's more at play here. I'm sure of it. If Parker has nothing to do with it, I'm convinced he's still keeping something back from us. None of this makes sense.'

'You're tired,' Slater said. 'Don't get me wrong — so am I. But now's not the time to be dissecting all this new info. We'll talk about it in the morning.'

'And now?'

'Now we eat, and rest.'

'I don't rest well.'

'I know. Neither do I. It's hard not to overthink this. But it's what we need.'

The elderly woman returned with mugs of tea, and placed them in front of King and Slater respectively. She smiled and nodded, the universal gesture of goodwill, and they smiled and nodded back.

Then a Nepali man stepped inside, emerging from the dark.

If Slater had to guess, he figured the man was a porter. Small, and serious, with dirt caked into the lines on his forehead. Slater put him at close to fifty, but he could have been thirty. Age and appearance didn't always correlate out here. Some had harder lives than others. He had a strange complexion, with mottled skin and eyes that bulged out of their sockets. He didn't blink. He surveyed the scene, and then turned to the host.

He barked something in Nepali at the woman, who barked back. They were both equally hostile, snapping at each other in tones that no doubt contained thinly veiled insults.

Then the guy scowled and walked straight back out into the night.

But before he disappeared, he gave Slater and King a long stare with those unwavering, bulging eyes.

Then he was gone.

Slater turned to the woman. 'What did he want?'

'He sometimes come through village. He work for himself. Try to get job on trail. No company to organise. I always say, does not work. But he still try.'

'Tries to get jobs?'

'He always alone,' she said. 'He try to find job carry bag. If he get job, no need to give cut to trek company. But no-one trust him with their bag. So he never get job. He only harass … my customer.'

Slater and King nodded their understanding in unison.

But, deep down, Slater couldn't shake the overbearing feeling that something was off.

He remembered the way the man's gaze had lingered.

He looked at King.

Who looked back.

'Same deal,' King said. 'We don't know. So there's no use worrying.'

They ordered their food, and half an hour later the woman returned with heaped plates of fried rice and dal bhat. They ate in the echoing silence of the teahouse, stewing over where they were, what they were doing, what might happen in the future.

At least, Slater was.

He couldn't see inside King's head.

The night enshrouded the building, and it got completely dark, and the clock ticked onward.

He and Slater tried to make small talk, but it wasn't their forte.

The host came to collect the plates, and Slater caught the woman's eye and said, 'Excuse me, ma'am. Would you happen to have a knife in the kitchen?'

She paused. 'What?'

'A knife,' Slater said. 'I'd like to keep one overnight. Just in case.'

King nudged him in the ribs, but Slater persevered. Sure, they had a couple of switchblades in their packs from the hostiles they'd encountered the previous day, but there was a world of difference between an enormous kitchen knife and a rusting box cutter.

The woman seemed to have got the message that they

were here to investigate the murder. Ordinarily she might have scoffed, but now she shuffled off and came back a moment later with a serrated butcher's knife made of thick steel. She placed it on the table in front of Slater and raised an enquiring eyebrow.

He nodded, and took it by the hilt.

'You're being ridiculous,' King muttered.

'Am I?' Slater said.

She showed them to their rooms.

31

In the middle of the night, King tossed and turned in his sleeping bag.

Wide awake.

Coated in sweat.

He'd drifted off for a spell, but it wasn't *obscenely* cold yet and the bag was designed for sub-zero Celsius temperatures, so the result was an abundance of body heat trapped within, heating him up until the perspiration ruptured from his pores. He stuck his arms out and stretched them behind his head, clasping his hands together. He stared up at the ceiling.

There were a thousand thoughts churning, and he figured the constant state of war-readiness in his mind had changed him permanently. Something about that wide-eyed porter set him on edge. In all likelihood, the guy was exactly how the owner had described — an awkward drifter searching for any work he could get on the trail.

But King's brain never stopped whirring, so the bugging eyes and intense stare had lodged there, leaving him to mull over the memory.

He tried to cool down and listened to the roof creaking above his head. Wind battered the side of the building, and he wondered if he was staying in the room Winston had died in.

The room Oscar Perry had probably strangled him in...

Don't assume.

The wind suddenly intensified, swelling to a crescendo and rattling the pane beside his head.

King looked across the room. Sure enough, the other bed was empty. He and Slater had opted to take separate rooms this early in the trek. Later on, they'd huddle together in closer quarters for maximum efficiency but right now it'd only draw attention. A pair of grown men sharing a room when every bed in the teahouse was available would stand out from the norm. And until they got close enough to Raya to act, they had roles to play. They were ordinary hikers. Friends tackling a gruelling trek together.

So King had his gear sprawled across the other mattress, and Slater had the room next door.

Weak flickers of light spilled in through the window, emanating from white bulbs stationed at intervals along the patio outside. They stayed on all night evidently. King sat up and watched the trail fade away into darkness. Eventually he got sick of it and tried his best to get back to sleep.

Then he heard a footstep.

Instinct kicked in. He couldn't exactly pinpoint where it came from, and there was an overwhelming possibility he was just paranoid, but he leapt out of bed all the same. Dressed in a pair of athletic shorts and nothing else, he padded across the room with bare feet and pressed one ear to the door.

It burst open in his face.

The door actually smacked him square in the forehead,

coming scarily close to concussing him. As his neck snapped back and he put a foot down to find his balance, the sleek black barrel of an automatic rifle slipped through the newly-opened gap in the doorway. It had been locked, but whoever was on the other side had snapped the weak thing apart with a single charge. King had blocked most of the initial trajectory with his own skull, so even though there were glowing spots in his vision he managed to throw his weight back into the door, hitting it shoulder-first, trapping the gun between the frame and the door.

Then he calculated angles and figured, *Yeah, go for it.*

He threw the door back open and snatched the rifle — a Kalashnikov AK-47 — by the lower handguard and wrenched it, along with its owner, into the room. He was firing on all cylinders, with sheer *survival* energy coursing through him, and that always translated into uncanny strength, so the guy holding the weapon ended up catapulting forward uncontrollably.

The man tripped over the threshold and tumbled into the room with shock spreading across his face.

Amidst the blur of adrenaline, King just managed to recognise that the guy was wearing faded military fatigues before he stabbed down with the ball of his foot an inch above the guy's ear. He might as well have hit the guy with a steel bat. All the technique and power and nervous energy translated into the mother-of-all impacts, and if the man wasn't dead he was close to it.

King snatched up the AK and turned it toward the door and caught two more mercenaries shoulder-to-shoulder, in the process of muscling their way into the room. They had fearsome-looking curved knives in their hands, ready for use in case their comrade with the rifle failed.

And he'd failed spectacularly.

But they were out of range. It'd take them a couple of steps to get into the room and another second to swing the blade, and that was time they simply didn't have because now King had the Kalashnikov aimed squarely at their faces.

He didn't hesitate.

He shot the closer man through the forehead, then put three rounds into the chest of the second man.

Two corpses toppled backward out of the doorway, and the echo of the gunshots roared down the mountainside.

32

S later vaulted out of bed before his brain even woke up.

It was instinct — he heard the *blam-blam-blam-blam* of four unsuppressed reports, which carried the same shock to his system as if someone had hit him in the face with a flaming two-by-four. All thanks to spending half his life behind enemy lines, in places he didn't belong, in situations where discovery by the enemy meant certain death.

He'd been wired to treat unexpected gunshots like the end of the world, so he was halfway across the room before he shook off the tendrils of sleep and thought, *Oh shit, this is happening.*

The kitchen knife was in his hand. The same instinct had made him yank it out from underneath the pillow when he burst off the mattress. He made it to the bedroom door and threw it open and came face-to-face with three guys crowded in the small space in front of him. It was an alcove in the side of the building, the missing wall exposing the space to the elements. The other two sides were home to another bedroom and a communal toilet.

The three men were dressed in faded military fatigues and wore shiny black boots on their feet and carried an assortment of weapons — one had a Kalashnikov rifle, the other a pistol, and the third had his hands curled into fists and his teeth bared.

So, naturally, Slater slit the throat of the man with the rifle and shot a stabbing front kick into the nose of the guy with the pistol. The rifleman dropped, blood spurting from arteries in his neck, and the guy with the pistol staggered back, bleeding from both nostrils, his nose skewered at an odd angle, blinded by the pain. The pistol was still in his hands, so Slater charged him and slammed him against the opposite door and thrust the knife between his ribs, aiming for the heart.

He thought he found it, because the guy's eyes rolled into the back of his head and he dropped the gun. Slater went to pull the knife out, but was met with resistance. The blade was lodged, probably between a pair of ribs.

Slater abandoned it the moment he saw the last guy swinging for his unprotected head.

He ducked away and barely avoided a right hook that seemed like it might have taken his head clean off his shoulders if it connected. The soldier clearly had some sort of formal boxing training, because he threw with enough technique to impress Slater. He pivoted at the waist and used the entire kinetic chain of motion, but that only made it worse when the punch missed in such a confined space. He connected with the wall and probably broke a few fingers, judging by the wince that spread across his face.

Slater kicked him on the outside of the knee, putting his shin into it like a battering ram.

The guy went down awkwardly into a half-squat, and before he righted himself Slater hit him with a picture-perfect uppercut that cracked off his chin and snapped his head back.

Somehow, he stayed on his feet, so Slater opened up his hips and swung through with the same shin and connected with the same spot on the outside of the same knee, tearing muscle and ligament.

Now the guy went down in a heap, and Slater stomped down on his head.

Crack.

Silence.

A meticulous dismantling.

He took a deep breath, snatched up the AK-47, and went to check on King.

33

K ing let the echo of the gunshots fade before he
made his next move.

The bodies came to rest sprawled across the
alcove floor, bleeding from multiple orifices. It was never a
pretty sight. He didn't think he'd ever get used to the sight of
life sapping from a human being for as long as he lived.
That wasn't something that ever became normalised. It hit
you like a gut punch every single time.

He breathed hard, in and out, controlling his impulses,
listening for sounds of turmoil elsewhere.

He heard them immediately.

There were muffled grunts and then a dull *thud*, and
something faint and distant that sounded awfully like the
slash of a blade against skin.

Slater.

Fighting for his life.

King burst out of the doorway with no regard for his
own life.

Because that was the way he'd always operated.

Protect those you're closest to.

At all costs.

He leapt out of the alcove and down the two steps, exposing himself to the long stretch of patio. The space was barely lit by the weak bulbs, dull in the night, and the wind swept across the slab of concrete incessantly, howling and twisting and writhing in the darkness. King landed and swept the AK-47 in a full revolution, but the patio was empty.

Until it wasn't.

Suddenly there were arms around his waist, and it took him by such surprise that he nearly leapt out of his skin. They came from behind, looping around his mid-section, and calloused hands locked together against his abdomen. He tried to manoeuvre the rifle around to fire behind him but it was far too late. Whoever was holding him was small — at least a full foot shorter than King — but their grip strength was astonishing.

King resorted to desperation, and tried to wrench the guy off him, but it was futile.

He was already off-balance, and sometimes that's all it takes. The next thing he knew he was stumbling toward the edge of the patio, careening out of control.

Heart in his throat.

He felt it pounding in his ears.

He squeezed the trigger of the AK-47, firing a volley of shots into the concrete, hoping the racket of the gunshots would deter his attacker.

It didn't.

The hostile held tight and kept muscling him toward the edge, pushing him further off-balance, and then when the guy realised they were close enough to the end of the concrete slab he put all his weight into it and threw them both off.

It wasn't much of a drop — five feet at most to the trail — but that never matters.

What matters is how you land.

King didn't land well.

He fell forward, face-first, and had to put his hands in front of his face to break his fall, but that meant dropping the rifle.

Which he wasn't prepared to do.

So the result was a last-second panic and fumble, which gave the guy tackling him the momentum needed to drive harder and stronger, tilting King further forward, and he came down awkwardly on his side on the dusty gravel.

Thwack.

His head bounced off the ground, disorienting him just enough to delay the pain recognition. So when he came back to reality with swimming vision and a throbbing headache it took him longer than normal to realise he'd landed badly on his ankle. He could already feel it swelling, only a couple of seconds after impact.

That is not *fucking good.*

Finally he got a good look at his attacker, who was currently scrabbling through the dirt to try and get his hands on King.

Should have known.

He'd recognise those bulging eyes anywhere.

The stray porter was unarmed, clearly expecting that six handpicked combatants with automatic weapons would have got the job done without his involvement. Now the small bull-like man was making his last stand, realising that his plans had failed spectacularly and that he'd need to finish the job himself.

But even though the porter was a freak of nature

strength-wise, most of his initial success had come down to catching King by surprise.

At least, that's what King told himself.

The porter got to his knees and pounced forward, hands outstretched, reaching for King's throat.

Immediately King knew the guy was an idiot.

He batted the hands away like they weighed nothing, drove an elbow upwards from his back, and caught the porter in the nose. He heard a *crack* but he didn't stop there — when the porter froze up to comprehend his broken septum, King grabbed him and slammed him into the gravel. At the same time he righted himself and put a knee on the guy's stomach, pinning him in place. Then he dropped another elbow, this time with the assistance of gravity to add an extra something.

Bang.

Elbow against skull.

Skull against dirt.

Goodnight.

King clambered off the body and tried to put some weight on his tender ankle.

It lit up like someone had actively torched his nerve endings.

He gasped, sat down hard, and wiped beads of sweat off his brow.

Then a silhouette materialised at the edge of the patio, backlit by the white lights.

Wielding an AK-47.

King's pulse skyrocketed and he prepared to launch himself down the hillside to avoid a string of gunfire lacing his torso.

But the silhouette said, 'Relax. It's me.'

King breathed out.

He didn't move.

Slater seemed to recognise it. 'Can you get up?'

'I don't think so.'

'Are you hurt?'

'Ankle.'

A pause.

Slater said, 'How'd you get down there?'

'I fell.'

'All on your own?'

King jerked a thumb toward the unconscious porter. 'Our friend here tackled me.'

Slater took his time assessing the porter. King could sense him lingering on the fact that the guy was about five-foot-two and a hundred and twenty pounds.

Slater said, '*He* tackled you?'

'He caught me off-guard. Now shut up and help me up.'

Slater leapt down off the patio.

34

For obvious reasons, they didn't sleep that night.

A couple of hours after the ambush, King sat in the dining area with his leg elevated on the bench and an ice-pack pressed to his swollen ankle. He was uncharacteristically quiet, even by his own standards. He couldn't take his mind off the injury, and no amount of meditation would stop him overthinking. He sat still as a statue with his eyes glazed over, running through the hypotheticals, getting increasingly restless.

Slater stepped inside as the faint beginnings of daylight appeared on the horizon. He was sweating profusely.

'Bodies are gathered in the storage room,' he muttered, wiping his hands on his pants. 'Just liked she asked.'

'This must be hard on her,' King said.

As if on cue, the teahouse owner waddled out of the kitchen, a look of dejection on her face.

Slater smiled at her, doing his best to keep her spirits up. 'They're out of sight.'

She tried to smile back, but didn't seem to have it in her. 'Thank you. I clean blood soon.'

'We're very sorry we brought this conflict here,' King said. 'We didn't want this to happen.'

'Not your fault. Is man's fault. I always knew he trouble.'

'He sold us out,' Slater said. 'Which means someone is looking for us. Which makes us responsible for what happened here. Again, we're sorry.'

'Not much damage,' she said with a shrug. 'You two okay. Maybe small hole in wall, small blood. That okay. Can clean.'

Slater put his hands in his pockets and nodded his understanding. Then he said, 'Do you have any idea who those men were who attacked us?'

'Yes,' she said. 'But my English ... not good. I don't know how to say.'

They thought about that for a spell, and then King slid the satellite phone out of his pocket and dialled a number.

'Hold on,' he said to her.

Parker came on the line a couple of seconds later. 'Have you found her?!'

'No,' King said. 'Put Sejun on the line, please.'

'Why?'

'Because I asked you to.'

'I want to know why.'

'Because he has better English than the woman we're with, so he's going to listen to what she has to say and then translate it to you. You'll tell us the end result, okay?'

'Okay.'

There was a shuffling at the other end of the line, and King ushered the elderly woman over and handed her the phone.

'Tell him what you know,' he said.

A long conversation played out in Nepali, and King sat back and let her speak. He exchanged occasional glances with Slater, but the pair of them stayed quiet. Neither wanted to acknowledge the truth — it didn't matter how much they knew about their opposition if King couldn't walk. Which was exactly what Perry or the porter were going for by continuing the trek toward Gokyo Ri. They must have figured that, between the harsh terrain and constant assaults from hired mercenaries, even the toughest super-soldiers on the planet were bound to cop some wear-and-tear.

And they were right.

King tried not to think about his damaged ankle. He stared out the window as the sun snaked its way into view, turning the landscape golden. The wind had subsided, giving way to another clear cool morning.

Maybe he was wearing rose-tinted glasses, but he had hope.

Whatever obstacle landed in front of them, they'd find a way over it.

Or through it.

Finally the woman nodded and handed the phone back to King. Before she walked away, she said, 'Breakfast?'

'Please.'

'What you want?'

Slater hurried over and they perused the menu before ordering stacks of pancakes and eggs and huge bowls of soup, with teas on the side for tradition's sake. They weren't worried about overloading on carbs — it didn't matter when you were burning three thousand calories a day. She took their orders and headed straight for the kitchen, and King felt a deep respect as he watched her leave.

She should have kicked them out for bringing such chaos to her establishment. But she seemed to understand they had noble intentions. So she was persevering — even though it made her uncomfortable, even though she wanted to be dealing with anything but bloodstains.

She was an incredible human being.

When she was gone, King pressed the phone to his ear. 'What have you got?'

Parker said, 'It's not good.'

'I didn't think it would be.'

'They're a Maoist splinter group. Like an extremist version of the typical communist guerrillas. Apparently there's hordes of them up in the isolated regions of the mountains. They win the rural villages over by offering security and education that the government can't provide. Their goal is to be celebrated as "freedom fighters," when really all they're after is control. They do that by promising radical change, and it works. Most of those villagers live terribly hard lives, and the communists offer them hope. The violence has been ramping up lately, Sejun tells me. The rebellion is alive and thriving.'

'Which means there'll be plenty of them looking to line their pockets with a little extra cash.'

'That's right.'

'So whoever's behind this has all the guerrillas on their payroll?'

'I doubt it. They must know the area well if they're managing to coax Maoists into doing their dirty work. They must have connections.'

King paused, reading between the lines. 'You're trying to tell me it's not Perry.'

'Do you think it's likely that Perry knows how to contact and coordinate guerrillas?'

'Anything sounds likely right now. If it's the porter trying to raise funds for the communists by kidnapping your daughter, then what does he want with the laptop?'

'I don't know. Any update on that?'

'None so far. We're about to set off. I'll keep you posted on any new developments.'

Across the room, Slater looked up.

He gave King's ankle a worrying stare.

King mouthed, *I'll be fine.*

Slater didn't look like he believed him.

King said, 'Thanks for getting that sorted. It's good to know who we're dealing with.'

'Sejun says to be careful if it's the insurgents. They don't usually go anywhere near the tourist trails, but they must have made an exception for the right price. They need to fund their revolution, after all. So if someone wanted to take advantage of well-trained militants, they could. There might be an army heading your way.'

'We'll keep an eye out.'

'How many men have you killed?'

'Seven so far. Around the same amount before we met you, too.'

'Jesus Christ.'

'Just another day at the office, Aidan.'

King ended the call, then turned to Slater and said, 'Did you collect the—?'

Slater nodded.

He produced the two handguns he'd found on the rebels' bodies. They were Sig-Sauer P320s. Serious fire-power. Full-size models, chambered with .45 ACP rounds. State-of-the-art, put into production only a few years ago, manufactured by the U.S. branch of Sig Sauer.

Just one of the many reasons to suspect Oscar Perry's involvement.

Who was arming rural guerrillas with state-of-the-art American-made weaponry?

For now, they didn't talk about that.

The handguns would be more than satisfactory for the rest of their travels. The Kalashnikovs were reliable, but they were big and cumbersome and impossible to hide on the trail. It was fundamentally useless to carry assault rifles with them when they could be more precise and more discreet with the P320s.

Slater handed over one of the handguns and said, 'I found eight spare magazines. We'll split them four apiece.'

King nodded, and hid the gun from view as the owner came back into the dining room.

He said, 'I have a request.'

35

Slater stood at the mouth of the trail, duffel bag on his back, dressed in hiking gear.

He winced at King's stupidity.

King hobbled down off the patio, his ankle strapped up with nearly an entire roll of duct tape. The teahouse owner had fished the tape out of a storage room and given it to them for free, somewhat hesitant to see King try and continue. But he'd quashed both their protests and Slater had watched him yank the tape around the swollen joint over and over again.

'What the hell are you doing?' Slater had said.

'Compression.'

Now King let out a subdued grunt with every second step, but he was making progress all the same. He shuffled ten feet along the dusty gravel, and then seemed to catch a wave of momentum. Each step from then on grew progressively larger, until he was striding it out at close to the same pace they'd maintained yesterday.

Slater caught up to him, shaking his head in disbelief.

'You shouldn't be doing this. You might be causing permanent damage.'

King turned back, his face white, the corners of his forehead beading with sweat. He said, 'I told you I just needed
to warm up. It's not broken.'

'I know it's not broken, but—'

King held up a hand, cutting him off. 'There's a fourteen-year-old kid in the possession of some madman right
now, and you're worried about my ankle?'

'Yes. If it ruins your ability to operate down the line.'

'Let's worry about that when we get to it. For now, we
walk.'

Slater didn't say another word.

Partly because he knew King wouldn't listen.

But mostly because he understood.

Pain was nothing to them. It's everything to most people,
who shy away when it crops up in their lives. But both he
and King had made a career out of going directly toward the
pain, toward the suffering, in hopes of a better result when it
came time to perform. It was eerily similar to what elite
athletes go through before competition, only with more dire
physical consequences. If they didn't perform in the field,
they didn't get a participation trophy. They died. That translated to a sickening work ethic, and a pain tolerance practically unrivalled anywhere else on the planet.

It meant that when one of them badly sprained their
ankle, they taped it back up and kept soldiering on, no
matter what it did to them mentally.

Because all pain comes to an end.

It can't last forever.

King knew that. Soon he'd be back on U.S. soil, back in
his New York City penthouse, back in luxury. For now, he

had to suffer. He wasn't about to complain about it. He would never complain.

True to his word, he warmed up fast. Slater set the pace, but King valiantly kept up for most of the morning. In truth, Slater had little time to pay attention to his own nagging injuries. His right knee hurt on the descents, probably from the jarring impact when he'd kicked one of the paramilitary soldiers in the face. But all the slight grievances he felt paled in comparison to King, who slaved away at the trail like a man possessed. Slater asked him a handful of times if he was okay, and King didn't respond. Just stared at the ground and put one foot in front of the other and dripped sweat into the dirt.

When they stopped for lunch, King refused to sit down. He paced back and forth slowly across the dining hall until the food came out, and then he wolfed it down, cradling the plate in one hand and a fork in the other.

Slater said, 'What are you doing? You need to rest.'

'If I sit down, it'll swell more. I need to keep it warm.'

Slater shook his head. He couldn't imagine what sort of discomfort the injury entailed. There were certain thresholds that even *he* considered his limits, and it seemed King was pushing past all of them.

They got moving again. The sun beat down on the backs of their necks, scorching it. There was no escape from the heat. The temperature wasn't even that bad — it was the sun exposure coupled with intense physical exertion that did the trick. They sucked down purified water flavoured with BCAAs and kept striding forward.

Toward Phakding.

The town was only ten miles from Kharikhola, but the terrain was brutal, and their various ailments didn't help. Slater went down awkwardly on his bad knee when he leapt onto a rock, and fear speared through him. Not because of the pain, but because of the consequences.

King noticed, and froze.

'You okay?'

Slater swore and slapped the side of his thigh in frustration. Toward himself — the fact that his ignorance might have let himself get injured. He took a step forward and skewered his foot into the next rock, testing his weight on it, wincing in anticipation of any horrific *twang*s.

But there was nothing.

He was fine.

He nodded back to King. 'We're good.'

King breathed a sigh of relief.

Slater fidgeted with his knee for a spell, probing the soft tissue around the joint for any signs of inflammation. He couldn't find anything. The seconds dragged out as he stood in place, fixated on his bad leg.

When King said, 'Mules,' Slater thought nothing of it.

They'd passed dozens of similar convoys over the last day and a half. There were often fifteen or twenty of the animals in a group, all wearing harnesses laden with supplies. Mostly gas bottles or crates of foodstuffs. It was the only reasonable way to get necessary supplies through such hostile terrain. The teahouses along the trail relied on the mules and their guides to keep the kitchens stocked with the right ingredients. That meant sharing the same trails as the hikers, and led to surprises when one of them poked you in the back on the way past.

King and Slater had been told the rules.

When you see them coming, step to the inside of the trail. Enough people have died after being knocked off the trail by a wandering mule to justify being cautious.

So they went through the motions. They stepped to the

inside of the trail. The mules stumbled on past, snorting and bumping into each other. The gas bottles attached to their harnesses clanked and clanged against each other. One of them sauntered a little too close for comfort, so Slater put a hand on its side and guided it back into the midst of the group. They were placid animals. Slater didn't want to think about it, but the recklessness had probably been beaten out of them.

Then the guide came past, bringing up the rear. He shouted and screamed and barked commands intermittently at the pack, trying to keep the mules at the front on the right trajectory. It was simple enough for one of the animals to take a wrong turn and saunter away, never to be found again. It required constant due diligence.

But the guides were friendly enough to passing tourists.

Slater met the man's gaze and said, '*Namaste.*'

The guide half-nodded, a sweat-soaked rag held low in his left hand, and he opened his mouth to respond.

Then he paused, and looked over at King.

Then back at Slater.

Then he was lunging like a wild dog, and the knife was suddenly in his right hand, and his teeth were bared, and he was determined to *kill.*

It took Slater by such surprise that he didn't have time to get out of the way.

36

King saw the knife materialise in the man's palm.

He wondered if he was seeing things.

Then the guy seemed to teleport across the trail, leaping over rocks like they weren't even there, and then the blade was scything downward and Slater was pulling back but it was too late—

The tip of the knife drew a line down Slater's forearm, slashing it wide open.

King watched him reel away, mouth agape in shock, his good hand flying to the wound. The Nepali guy slashed again but the blade sailed on harmlessly by, missing Slater's throat by inches.

Adrenaline surged in King's brain, wiping out any regard for his injury.

He couldn't feel his bad ankle anymore.

He reached for the Sig Sauer in his waistband but the front of his shirt was slick with sweat and he couldn't get a proper grip on—

No time.

Go.

He launched himself down the descent, landing in a heap on top of the guide, sending them both sprawling into the gravel with enough force to break a bone or gash skin completely open. Thankfully King landed on top of the guy, using him to cushion his own fall, and when he rolled off the body out of fear of a stab wound he instantly recognised the man had gone limp.

Lying on his back, panting, he looked over.

And immediately looked away.

He'd seen enough.

The guy was dead. No question about it. The back of his skull had met a particularly sharp rock, and then all two hundred and twenty pounds of King had come down on top of him.

Not good for your health.

King got to his feet and stared up and down the trail. As if sensing the absence of their guide, most of the mules up the back of the pack had come to a standstill. They stood in place on the rocky incline, emotionless, staring at the ground. They knew nothing but the trail.

King barked a sharp unintelligible command and they set off up the mountainside.

Then he put two hands on the body, gave it a short heave, and rolled it off the edge of the path. Limp as a rag doll, the corpse plunged into the thick undergrowth and rolled into invisibility, disappearing down the hillside. King kicked dirt over the grotesque bloodstain on the rock and rubbed it in with the sole of his boot.

With the evidence wiped away, he deemed it acceptable to check on Slater.

Slater was sitting on a smooth rock in the shadow of the mountain, his eyes wide and unblinking, staring straight ahead, refusing to look at the damage. He was using his good hand to hold two folds of skin together along his forearm. Blood seeped out of the wound.

King scrutinised it.

He said, 'Fuck.'

But it wasn't the end of the world. Blood wasn't fountaining out of the cut. There was just a steady trickle — Slater was doing an excellent job of mitigating the blood loss by gripping the wound tight.

Slater kept staring forward and said, 'How bad?'

'You'll be okay.'

'It hurts.'

'I don't doubt that.'

'Get the medkit.'

King shrugged the duffel bag off his back and dropped it to his feet. He unzipped it, fished around, and came up with a clear plastic carry bag about the size of a handbag. It was large by commercial first-aid standards, but they'd brought a few extra goods in case of emergency. They'd been expecting bloodshed, after all.

King pulled a spare water bottle out of his pack, already loaded with iodine tablets to kill germs. He unscrewed the lid, gripped Slater's arm, and poured it all over the wound.

Slater clenched his teeth, closed his eyes, and let out a long and turbulent groan.

When they looked up, there was a Caucasian couple frozen in place beside them, staring in horror at the injury. Behind them, a small Nepali guide carrying their packs tried to peer through to get a look at the wound.

'Oh my God,' the woman said. She was probably sixty, with long hair tied back and tanned, weathered skin. Her accent was Australian. 'What happened?'

Still gripping Slater's arm, King gave a ludicrous smile

and said, 'It's fine. He just ran into a low-hanging branch. Terrible luck. We'll get it cleaned up.'

Trying to stay conscious, Slater half-smiled and half-nodded.

Looking queasy, the Australian man said, 'That, uh... that doesn't look too good.'

'Don't worry,' King said. 'I'm a qualified medical practitioner. I'll sort this out and get him to the next teahouse as fast as possible.'

'Is there anything we can do to—'

'No,' King and Slater said in unison.

A little too enthusiastically.

The couple hovered, unsure how to react. Eventually they turned away from the grisly injury and shook their heads in disbelief.

'If you say so,' the woman muttered.

They set off down the trail.

King waited in silence until they were out of earshot, then said, 'You know what I need to do, right?'

'Yeah,' Slater said through clenched teeth. 'Don't drag it out any longer. Just do it.'

'It's going to hurt.'

Slater stared daggers at him. 'No shit.'

'Just warning you.'

'It hurts right now. Can't get much worse than this.'

'Yes,' King said with a sigh, 'it can.'

He pulled something out of the medkit.

Something thin and metal, with a small trigger.

A medical gun.

Loaded with reusable stainless steel surgical staples.

37

With his right arm bound from wrist to elbow in heavy-duty bandages, Slater staggered along the trail toward Phakding.

This time, King led the way.

Somehow, he'd escaped further injuring his ankle when he'd crash-tackled the assassin into the dirt. He must have come down on his good side, preventing his foot from bouncing off the dirt. Even slightly disrupting the joint might have inflamed it beyond comprehension, and there was a point where no amount of mental toughness would let you walk on a brutalised limb.

So he was in high spirits, setting a cracking pace. Slater tried to keep up, but under the hot sun it felt like he was walking through a fever dream. His arm hurt like hell, but he knew the injury wasn't catastrophic. He could flex his fingers, so his movement hadn't been impeded. There was no nerve damage. It just tested his pain threshold, like most operations did. All it required was steeling his mind, focusing on each step, and absolutely *nothing* else. He couldn't afford to think about how much it hurt, or how far they had to go. That would freeze him in his tracks, flood him with dejection.

After they spent an hour covering solid ground, King seemed to figure it was time for conversation.

He backed up a few steps so they could stride side by side and said, 'Update?'

'I'm fine.'

'No you're not.'

'Is there any point admitting I'm in pain?'

King thought about it, and said, 'That's true, actually. But I need to know if you're on the verge of collapse.'

'No.'

'Good. Then I don't need to know anything else.'

Because he understood. Slater had seen King deal with the ankle with a sealed mouth and a relentless mindset, and now he was attempting to do the same. The less they talked, the better. But now King wasn't so focused on his ankle, and Slater could see his attention turning to the matters of immediate concern.

'Who was that guy?' he said to nobody in particular.

'Just a civilian,' Slater said. 'But there must be word spreading down the pipeline of our presence. Someone wants us out of the equation fast. I'm assuming there's a price on our heads.'

'And you think Oscar Perry is really coordinating this with a network of rebels?'

'Yes, actually,' Slater said.

King didn't respond.

Slater said, 'Think about it. The only thing you're taking into consideration is the language barrier, as if that somehow prevents Perry from being able to do this. But he can work his way around that fairly easily. I'd have to say that the only way this could be the porter is if it was a spurof-the-moment kidnapping. The guy would have sensed an opportunity and gathered together some of his buddies and gone for it. But someone like that isn't going to have connections with an entire guerrilla insurgency. Who do you think is more likely to have the smarts to coordinate with a Maoist splinter group — a bodyguard in the world of black operations, or a porter working for less than minimum wage?'

'You might have a point.'

'I *do* have a point.'

'Do we know how well-trained Perry is?'

'If I had to guess, I'd say he's pretty good. You have to be to reach this level.'

King grimaced. 'Actually, that's making more and more sense. Perry has the knowledge of how this works. He'd be able to put out a hit with the right connections, even if he had to get past the language barrier.'

'Let's try not to debate it,' Slater said. 'Truth is, it could be one or the other.'

'We should be prepared for it to be Perry.'

'I agree.'

'But you don't have an arm, and I don't have a foot.'

'Nothing's broken. They're mostly superficial injuries. It shouldn't impede us in the heat of combat. Adrenaline is a wonder drug.'

'Let's hope so,' King said.

Looking down at his foot.

Slater froze. 'What's wrong?'

'It's getting worse.'

Slater suppressed a curse, and looked at his watch. 'I'd say we've got an hour to go. We make it to Phakding and you can sleep twelve hours straight. Okay?'

'Yeah,' King said, but his voice was barely above a whisper.

He kept moving.

But each step brought a wince to the surface, creasing his features, contorting his mouth and eyes.

Slater worried about himself, but couldn't help concern creeping in about his comrade and closest friend.

38

They crossed a gargantuan suspension bridge swaying over a glacial blue river with caution and reached the town of Phakding at three-thirty in the afternoon.

Utterly exhausted, yet determined to persevere, King trudged into the first teahouse they spotted in a trance-like state. It was a few dozen feet off the main trail, tucked away in the shadows of Phakding's laneways, and they both wordlessly seemed to agree that it was better suited to their needs than the commercial enterprises right out in the open.

They were up past Lukla now, and there were hordes more foreign hikers on the trail that had flown in to start their expeditions, all heading toward Namche Bazaar and then up to Everest or Gokyo Ri or the Cho-La Pass. Phakding was incredibly popular amongst trekkers, a world away from the rural trails they'd been slaving their way along for the better part of two days.

As they pulled to a halt inside the teahouse's entrance, King struggled to comprehend how much distance they'd covered in total. Roughly twenty-eight miles, he figured.

An endurance feat to be rivalled, especially with the sort of terrain they'd dealt with. It was either straight up or straight down, with an almost entire absence of flat stretches. Besides the injuries sustained along the way, everything ached. His legs, his chest, even his shoulders from carrying all their gear on their backs. It was gruelling, back-breaking work — but someone had to do it.

King limped into the main area and found a thirty-something Nepali man practically standing at attention. It seemed they were the only customers in the building — they'd come after the lunch rush, but before most of the trekkers made it to Phakding in the late afternoon.

King stared straight at the guy and said, 'Do you speak English?'

'Yes, of course.'

'Do you have a room for us?'

'Just the two of you?'

'Yes.'

'Of course.'

'Are we going to have any problems?'

'I'm sorry, sir?'

'You heard me.'

'Why would we have a problem?'

King jabbed a finger at Slater, and then back at himself. 'The two of us are on someone's shit list. That means there are people around here actively trying to hurt us. Would you know anything about that?'

The Nepali man shook his head sincerely. 'I don't concern myself with gossip. Whatever problems you have, you're safe here for the night. As long as you pay for the room, of course.'

'What if someone else offers to pay you more?'

'Then I will politely decline and tell them to go harass someone else.'

'How's that likely to work out for you?'

'It might cause me some problems. But I am loyal to a fault. You were here first, so you get my loyalty.'

'I appreciate that. I'll be very angry if you go back on your word.'

'That is not something I have ever done, sir.'

Frankly, King didn't have the capacity to press the issue any further. He didn't have the energy to try and be intimidating. The circumstances of the trek were less than ideal — he was hurting everywhere, his bones and muscles and brain were drained, and his ankle blazed with fiery intensity. He threw a look over his shoulder to see if Slater was faring any better, and immediately gave him a pass. He wouldn't be able to keep up any sort of intimidating act either. He was sweaty and shaky, and the bandages around his forearm were riddled with a mixture of leftover blood and perspiration. He met King's gaze with wide unblinking eyes and ever so slowly shook his head.

I need rest, his eyes said.

King nodded, and turned back to the teahouse owner. 'We'll give you a generous tip for your hospitality.'

The man waved a hand. 'That won't be necessary, sir.'

'Well, we're giving it to you regardless.'

'Much appreciated.'

'Now if you could lead us to our room…'

'Of course.'

This time, they didn't take separate rooms. Each room was the same — the ceiling and walls and floor made of cheap wood, the rickety single-bed frames pressed to each wall, the thin mattresses on top, a spare blanket folded neatly at the foot of each bed. Understanding their condition, the owner gave the space a quick once-over and then left them alone.

'Should we eat dinner before we crash?' Slater mumbled.

'I could use a nap,' King said. 'I'll set an alarm for later this evening.'

'Works for me.' Then he thought hard, despite his compromised state, and added, 'Let's take it in shifts, though. We'll be most vulnerable over these next few days. And I don't trust that guy at the front desk any more than anyone else.'

'You go first,' King said. 'Looks like you need it more.'

Without another word, Slater gently lowered himself to the mattress. He fished the sleeping bag out of his pack and, rather than clambering into it, draped it across his prone body and closed his eyes. Within seconds, he was asleep.

King sat on the opposite mattress, vigilant as ever, deep in his own head. He was exhausted, sore and cold. He scooted to the top of the bed, propped the pillow up against the wall for support, and elevated his swollen ankle onto the mattress. Working quietly, he started to peel off the duct tape to get a better look at the state of the injury.

Halfway through the process, his satellite phone barked.

He noticed Slater peel one eye open, curious enough to emerge from his nap.

He answered.

Violetta said, 'You need to see something. We've received a video. I have to warn you — it's not good.'

39

S later hadn't been asleep for more than a few minutes, but the room was awfully quiet and he heard every faint word from Violetta's end.

He sat up immediately. 'Ask her how they got it.'

King mirrored the enquiry, and thumbed a button to put her on speaker.

She said, 'It's from the kidnappers — whoever they are. They uploaded it to the dark web using tags they knew we'd be searching for. We found it eight minutes after it was uploaded. It's... well, see for yourself.'

'You'll send it to this phone?'

'Yes — it's secure.'

'Okay. Whenever you're ready.'

He ended the call and tossed the phone to Slater, who fidgeted with the display. The satellite phone was blocky and archaic compared to the sleekness of commercial devices, but it was technologically state-of-the-art and could receive video files without issue. The screen was smaller and the quality less impressive than a typical smartphone, but

Slater didn't imagine they'd have to scrutinise the footage too hard to get the picture.

He was right.

The device vibrated in his hands, and he opened the MP4 file sent anonymously from a blocked number. Its thumbnail appeared on the screen, and both he and King took in the scene. Raya Parker, Oscar Perry, and the porter, Mukta, had their hands bound behind their backs, and their ankles strapped together, and grimy gags in their mouths. They were propped up in seated positions in front of a cheap plasterboard wall with no easily identifiable features. The lighting was weak, and all three of them were in rough condition.

Sure enough, Mukta had a horrifically swollen eye.

Perry had superficial cuts and scrapes, but nothing drastic.

Raya just looked exhausted.

'You already know what this is going to be, right?' King said.

Slater looked at him. 'I could assume. I'm trying to be more optimistic, though.'

'You shouldn't be. Hit play.'

Slater took a deep breath.

Steeled himself for what was to come.

Hit play.

The trio came to life, transforming from a freeze frame into living, breathing people. They shook in the cold, and their teeth rattled against the gags, and Raya's eyes seemingly went everywhere at once, fixating on multiple targets behind the camera.

Then two men who looked like the same Maoist rebels who'd ambushed them in Kharikhola stepped into frame.

They wore the same shiny boots and cheap camouflage fatigues, and they had the same soulless black eyes. That was all Slater could make out, because they were clad in cheap black balaclavas. They stared into the camera for a few beats, one on each side of the seated hostages, flanking the trio. Then one of them squatted down so he could speak into the camera.

His English was broken, but passable.

'We know there are two soldier your government send on trail. This is good for us. It prove to us that you take this seriously, so we can make high demand. They are good soldier. They do lot of damage to us, but not enough. We have many men.'

He turned and looked at Raya, who stared defiantly back.

The guy reached out and touched her cheek.

Then returned his gaze to the camera.

'She valuable,' he said. 'She very, very valuable. You send your best. This is mistake on your part. But this is why we take her on this trail. Because it obvious if you send people to get her back. We do not want this, though. This bad for business. We do punishment now.'

Over Slater's shoulder, King cursed.

'Shut up,' Slater said.

He couldn't take his eyes off the video.

The soldier took a knife out of a sheath on his belt. It had already been sharpened, and the blade glinted even in the lowlight. He turned it over and over again in the shadows, almost admiring it before he put it to use.

Then he turned to Raya.

The hairs on the back of Slater's neck bristled.

'Jesus Christ,' King muttered.

The soldier seized the restraints around her wrists, and her face turned white with fear. Her hands shook, bound together as tightly as possible. Slowly, the man lowered her hands to the floor, and spread the fingers on her left hand out. He took the pinky finger and pressed it down against the sawdust, pinning it in place.

Then he rolled the blade over the knuckle with expert precision.

It happened so fast, and so smoothly, that at first Slater thought he'd faked it. Then the soldier picked up the severed finger and displayed it to the camera.

Sweating, shaking, groaning against the gag, Raya's eyes nearly rolled into the back of her head.

'This today's punishment. Every day your soldiers spend on trail, more punishment. Tomorrow, twice as bad. Trust me. Pull your soldiers out, and then we negotiate.'

Neither Slater nor King said a word, but they both bristled with rage.

'And we have demand. We know girl have special risks insurance. So you get back to us on this website, and you tell us how we can speak to professional crisis responder. Then we sort payment. This way, things go smooth. Or you keep your soldier on trail heading toward us, and things no more smooth. Things very messy. Do not make messy. Last warning.'

He reached toward the camera, and the video ended abruptly.

Slater sat in silence.

King sat in silence.

They stared at the final thumbnail — saw the intensity in the soldier's eyes, saw the pain in Raya's, saw the discomfort in Mukta and Perry. Both men seemed genuinely horrified by what had happened. Their eyes were bloodshot and wracked with terror.

It wasn't an emotion you could easily fake.

'Maybe we've got it wrong this whole time,' King said. 'Maybe it's neither of them.'

Slater said, 'Maybe…'

The phone rang in their hands.

40

Violetta again.

King took the phone back, and answered.

'You've seen it?' she said.

'We've seen it.'

'I want you to know I'm seriously considering pulling you out.'

'No way.'

Slater added, 'Not a chance.'

She said, 'This isn't the situation we imagined. Your presence has made it unimaginably worse. We didn't understand that they'd have eyes everywhere. We still don't know how—'

'We were ambushed last night,' King said. 'Everything's been so chaotic that we haven't had the chance to debrief you. We stayed at the teahouse in Kharikhola and woke up to a midnight assault. The owner relayed information to Parker's guide who confirmed it's Maoist paramilitary mercenaries who've been hired to deal with us. Seems like they're committing the cardinal sin of coming down into tourist-heavy areas to take us out, so there must be a pretty spectacular price on our heads.'

She didn't immediately respond, and he could practically hear her processing the information and trying to sort out the next move.

Then she said, 'Okay — I'm pulling you out.'

'No.'

'No?'

'Have there been any more sightings since the Swedish backpackers saw them along the trail?'

'No. We're moving heaven and earth to try and get accurate intelligence, but there's basically nothing. Which means they're probably spreading the hostages out between different groups of these Maoist troops so that no-one ever sees them all together when they're walking during the day. And it's fairly straightforward to cover your face when you're passing by other hikers. They're practically ghosts.'

'But that makes for slow progress,' King insisted. 'There's no way they're keeping a pace like ours. Not with three resisting hostages spread out across multiple groups. Raya's only fourteen, and she'll be in bad shape with a missing finger. They admitted themselves how valuable she is, so they're going to make damn sure she doesn't drop dead on the trail.'

'What are you saying?' Violetta said.

King paused, ruminating.

'We can be up past Namche Bazaar by mid-morning tomorrow. Then we'll keep hiking for as long as it takes to catch them. Logistically, if they were spotted near Namche yesterday, then we'll almost certainly get them tomorrow.'

'That's a massive effort.'

'It's what we have to do.'

'Are either of you hurt?'

'No,' King said.

Slater raised an eyebrow, and gave his bandaged forearm a glance.

King stared at his own swollen ankle.

Then met Slater's gaze and shook his head.

She can't know.

She'll pull us out.

Slater nodded his understanding.

Violetta said, 'I'd need guarantees from both of you that you're in good enough condition to close the gap tomorrow. Because that's all the time we have before this thing escalates out of control. And that's my head on the chopping block if I keep you in the field against my superiors' orders.'

'We'll get it done.'

'How are your bodies holding up? You've probably covered close to thirty miles of extreme terrain.'

'I'm fine,' King said.

'And Slater?'

'I'm fine, too,' Slater said.

'If either of you are lying to me...'

'Do you want this kid back or not?' King snarled. 'If we drop out, she's as good as dead. And what was all that about a "professional crisis responder"? Who the hell do they want to talk to?'

Violetta sighed. 'You know the basics of the kidnap insurance industry, right?'

'Guess I haven't done my research. Enlighten me.'

'Obviously there are certain sections of the planet where kidnapping is more rampant than others. Modern solutions are required, and these days everyone has something to sell. Insert "special risks insurance." These firms offer insurance and protection for wealthy clients if they're going to be venturing into dangerous parts of the world. They have professional negotiators on standby in case everything goes to hell, and they'll also cover any of the ransom costs that might ensue.'

'That sounds like a messy industry to try and maintain control of.'

'It is. And it's usually the richest of the rich that they market these policies to, so they can charge as much as they damn well want. The more paranoid their clients, the better. But it works — they have incredible success rates at negotiating with terrorists and kidnappers. Of course, those success rates are often unofficial because most kidnappings aren't actually reported, especially if they're quietly resolved. So, yes, it's a murky industry to say the least.'

'These rebel soldiers ... they think Parker has special risks insurance?'

'It's fairly well-known amongst kidnappers that the industry exists. Which makes it an even stranger industry, because if kidnappers know that they'll have access to professional negotiators, then they'll know that the process will be smooth and resolved easily...'

'Which encourages more kidnappings,' King said.

'Exactly.'

'I don't like it.'

'There's pros and cons to it. I can't spend all day debating it. Maybe when you get back...'

'I should know as much as possible right now if it affects the operation.'

'It's not important right now,' she said. 'Tomorrow is important. If I decide to let you do this, you need to promise me you'll catch up to them tomorrow. No matter what.'

'We promise.'

'I can stall the professional negotiations for a day or two, and they won't freak out. But any longer than that, and it's anyone's guess...'

'We won't fail.'

'You can't.'

King paused for thought, and said, 'One more thing.'

'Yes?'

'What happens when these special risks insurers have to pay out too many ransoms? Surely if kidnappers know about it, they'd exploit it for everything it's worth. If they know there's firms out there who *have* to make the negotiations smoother, they'd milk the hell out of it. At least, I would if I was in their shoes and had that sort of moral compass.'

'That's the *really* murky part of the industry,' Violetta said. 'None of this is official, of course, but these firms often have middlemen that are actually in contact with the most prominent bands of kidnappers in certain regions. That way, they can come to agreements so everyone profits. If the kidnappers don't go above certain quotas, they can still make consistent profit off the ransoms whilst staying under the firm's targets. Then the insurance money trumps the ransom payouts, and everyone makes money. Except the clients, of course.'

'That's the least ethical thing I've heard in a long time.'

Violetta said, 'Welcome to the modern world.'

He didn't respond.

She said, 'Is there anything else you need?'

'No.'

'Good — then I won't overload you with more talk. You know what you need to do tomorrow. Get some rest.'

King hung up, fished around in his duffel bag, came out with the first-aid kit, and took a massive dose of ibuprofen — four tablets worth. Then he adjusted his foot, draped his sleeping bag over his legs just as Slater had done, and settled back against the wall.

Slater watched him the whole time. 'Your ankle's bad, isn't it?'

'It'll be fine by the morning.'

'King...'

'The more I think about it, the worse it'll get.'

'There's no use covering an obscene amount of distance tomorrow just to fall in a heap at the feet of the rebels.'

'What are you saying?'

'You're too tough for your own good sometimes. So am I. Maybe we're being too hotheaded about this. Maybe that video was actually a positive sign.'

'And what the hell makes you say that?'

'Because they asked to speak to a professional crisis responder. They know what they're doing. They want to go through the due process. Maybe this can be resolved peacefully.'

'No,' King said.

'Why not?'

'Because if it's resolved peacefully, they'll get away with it.'

He rolled over and faced the opposite wall and closed his eyes.

Before he fell asleep, he said, 'I've set an alarm for dinner. Bolt the door, and we can both rest. We need all we can manage for tomorrow.'

Then he drifted off.

41

As much as he tried, Slater couldn't doze off.

Not anymore.

He sat with his knees pulled up to his chest, staring at the locked door, imagining what sort of horrors might come through it. His imagination ran wild, probably intensified by exhaustive delirium. His muscles throbbed and ached and protested the suffering he'd put them through for the last two days, but he savoured every minute of it. Pain meant healing, and healing meant improvement.

So he rocked back and forth in something close to a trance until it got dark outside and the sounds of newcomers rustling around downstairs drifted up through the thin wood.

Dinner time.

He woke King with a pat on the shoulder.

The man rolled over, alert in an instant. 'What is it?'

'Time for food.'

'Uh...'

Slater immediately knew something was awry. He didn't often see hesitation on King's face, but the man was struggling with something. He watched King sit up and peel the sleeping bag off his frame and peek through what little duct tape was left taped around his ankle.

The skin was black and blue.

'Can't walk?' Slater said.

'Not right now. It just needs rest, that's all.'

'One night's rest is enough?'

'Yes.'

'You sure?'

'It has to be.'

'You want to pull out?'

'That's not an option.'

Slater nodded once. 'I won't argue. I'd be just as stubborn in your position. You want me to bring food up?'

'That'd be great. And ice.'

'You're something else, you know that?'

'I had to staple your forearm together today. Don't kid yourself — we're cut from the same cloth.'

With a shiver, Slater said, 'Don't talk about what we're cut from.'

It reminded him of the blade slicing through his flesh, separating his skin folds.

The staples pounding up his forearm...

He went downstairs, already plagued by memories he'd much rather forget.

There was a considerable wait to order food. The dining hall was packed with groups of trekkers, separated into their individual packs, huddled around tables riddled with huge mugs of tea — either masala or ginger. Their scents blended together and filled Slater's nostrils with a pleasant aroma. He opted to drop into a chair rather than stand around drawing attention to himself. As soon as he found an empty table, the nearest group noticed his arm.

'My God,' a plump man with a thick German accent said. 'Are you okay?'

Slater held up the bloody, sweat-stained bandages and managed an innocent smile.

'It's nothing,' he said. 'Just scraped it on a branch.'

The man winced, and so did his friends. 'Have you seen a doctor about that?'

'Yes.'

'What'd he say?'

'Just to rest. I'll be fine.'

None of them seemed like they believed him, but they didn't want to stare, so they transitioned back into uneasy conversation amongst themselves. Slater lowered his damaged forearm underneath the table so no-one else could press him on it.

Then he sat there thinking.

About bodyguards, and porters, and black-operations coordinators, and secret presidential campaigns, and Maoist splinter groups, and special risks insurers, and professional negotiators, and severed fingers, and swollen eyelids, and slashed forearms, and twisted ankles, and sweat, and blood, and toil.

It all tied together — somehow, some way.

He was dull and unfocused. He could admit that. The mind and the body had their limits. There was only so much willpower to go around. Right now all he could focus on was his compromised physical condition, and his efforts to downplay them. There wasn't a whole lot of mental processing power left over to connect the dots. If he was back home in a warm bed, uninjured, full of energy and vigour, he'd solve the puzzle in a heartbeat. But he was here, hanging onto his sanity by a thread in the mountains of Nepal, wondering how King was even going to get out of bed in the morning.

If he can walk tomorrow, then we have a chance.

If not...

He'd never backed out of an operation, and although they'd never explicitly discussed it, he figured King was in the same boat. It'd disrupt their identity, ruin the momentum they'd spent their whole lives building up. You put doubts in someone's head one time, and it festers like an infection. It spreads fast, and Slater had no doubt that if he quit out here, soon enough he'd be finding all sorts of excuses to get out of future operations.

No, it was all or nothing in this game.

And tomorrow, it would be all or nothing too.

The food came out, mostly fried rice and eggs and toast, heaped high on plates. Slater accepted it with a smile and carted it upstairs. King was in the same position, unwavering, staring at his inflamed ankle, willing it better.

Slater said, 'Has the ibuprofen kicked in?'

King didn't react.

Slater said, 'King.'

The man looked up.

Discomfort creased his features.

'It's not doing much,' King said.

Slater couldn't be sure, but he thought he saw a flicker of doubt on his comrade's face.

He handed him the plate of food and said, 'Eat. Try not to think about it. We'll assess it in the morning.'

'How's your arm?'

'I'm trying not to think about it.'

It hurt.

A lot.

They ate on their beds, and then Slater went downstairs

and refilled their water bottles. He came back up and dropped iodine tablets into them, and when the twenty-minute wait was over he added BCAAs and they both sucked the fluids down with greed.

Then they settled onto their beds and lay in mutual silence.

Trying not to think.

Trying not to worry.

Both more exhausted than they even thought possible.

'We have a lot of ground to cover tomorrow,' King said softly.

'We do.'

'You think they'll come for us tonight?'

'I don't know why, but I trust the owner.'

'So do I. Still... he might not have a say in it.'

'We were discreet enough. There weren't exactly a whole lot of witnesses when we first walked in here. I think we'll be okay.'

'You'd hope so. Seems like neither of us could mount a resistance even if we wanted to.'

'Maybe we should concede this time.'

King looked over, and Slater could see his pupils were hazy and unfocused. 'You think?'

'Let's sleep on it,' Slater said. 'We'll figure it out in the morning. I can't think straight right now.'

'They know we're on the trail,' King said. 'So what's the point of walking anymore? Violetta can fly reinforcements over and send them in by chopper.'

'Can she?' Slater said.

Silence.

Slater said, 'Anything they try now will be too late. Kidnaps don't drag out for weeks, *especially* not in an environment like this. It's us, or nothing. They think by heading further up the mountain they'll exhaust us, and they're right. But it's one more day. We can do anything for one day. And then we'll be right there, and we can get her back.'

'Her, and Perry or the porter if they're innocent.'

'The girl is the priority.'

'I know.'

They settled back into the quiet, but before they drifted off Slater said, 'I guess it doesn't matter if we get ambushed tonight, does it?'

'And why's that?' King mumbled.

Slater lifted the P320 out of his waistband.

He said, 'Because for the first night since we touched down in this country, we have guns.'

42

K ing cracked an eyelid open.
Light filtered in through the open curtains.
It was morning.

He swung his legs out of bed, still desensitised by the numbing effects of deep sleep. He'd drifted off somewhere around eight in the evening, and now it was a touch before six in the morning. He found his smartphone and cancelled the impending alarm, set to go off in a few minutes' time. Across the room, Slater slept undisturbed.

King took a deep breath, steeled himself, and touched his bad foot to the wooden floorboards.

Twang.

Painful, for sure.

But manageable.

He nearly sighed with relief. Then he shrugged it off, recognising that this was no victory. The real test would be what happened later in the day, when he racked up the miles and wore down his body. His stride would get less controlled, sloppier, more prone to error. He could picture himself putting his foot down on a sharp descent and *feel* his ankle exploding, which would happen if...

If.

The key word.

No amount of hypotheticals really mattered, because right now he *could* get out of bed.

He roused Slater, who opened his eyes calmly, as if he'd been faking sleep all along. That was the reality of a combatant accustomed to black operations — you had to be completely alert in a heartbeat. There was no time to stretch and yawn and shuffle around under the covers. Everything had to happen *now*.

'How is it?' Slater said.

'I can walk.'

'Then let's get this done.'

They took turns in the shower, opting not to go through the hassle of paying for hot water. King let the ice-cold stream numb him from head to toe, and he let the jet pour onto his ankle for close to a minute. Then he stepped out, taped it up, put clean clothes on, laced up his hiking boots, and went to check on Slater.

Who was also dressed. Also laced up.

They were ready.

It was the same deal as every morning in Nepal. There was no fanfare, no celebration that they were up and moving. Just quiet acceptance of what was to come, and then they put their heads down and got to work. They paid cash for the room and the food, and were the first of the guests of the day to leave the teahouse. They had their duffel bags over their shoulders and were putting one foot in front of the other before either of them had the chance to comprehend what they were getting themselves into.

And then everything settled into monotony.

Suffer for long enough, and it all becomes the same. King already knew that, but he took advantage of it by keeping as much of the trek as monotonous as possible. He put his right foot down and winced, and then covered more ground with the next stride on his good leg. It hurt for the first half-hour, then he warmed up and settled into a rhythm. Of course, it still ached, but he'd repeated the process so many times that it no longer mattered.

They trekked up toward Namche Bazaar, and the air grew cold as they climbed above ten thousand feet in altitude. The wind packed extra bite, aided by the heavy cloud. It was overcast as they kept treading through the dirt, and although the trees around them were still lush green in colour they could see the rising prominence of snow-capped mountains, both ahead and off to each side. They strode over bridges crossing pale blue glacial streams, and let droves of mules past, ever paranoid of another assault.

They were an hour out from Namche when it happened.

King was the first to spot the pack of mules heading their way, descending the slope they were in the process of climbing. He whistled to Slater and they stepped to the right, pressing themselves against the cliff wall. The other side was home to a sheer drop, and neither of them wanted to spend their whole lives completing the most dangerous operations imaginable just to succumb to a careless mule knocking them off the edge of a mountain.

So the pack sauntered past, laden with gas bottles, and King's guard wavered as he studied the Nepali man bringing up the rear. The guy was tall and wiry with rippling corded muscle packed onto a skinny frame. He nodded to each of them, and started to carry on past...

And then his hand scythed through the air.

A sudden movement.

King had his hands around the guy's throat before he could blink. In one smooth motion he shoved him forcefully toward the edge of the cliff, pushing him off-balance so the guy teetered toward the drop and—

Slater screamed, '*No!*'

King froze, holding the guy in place. The man's feet were inches from the ledge.

Then he noticed the panic in the guy's eyes, and the absence of weapons in his hands.

Oh.

He gently took his hands off the man's throat.

Slater muttered, 'He was going to strike the mule. Not you.'

Sure enough, the mule at the back of the group was frozen in place — something both he and Slater had witnessed dozens of times before. Often they needed a slap on the rear to get going, which was precisely what the guy had made to do.

King said, 'I'm sorry.'

The man massaged his sore neck, and stared at both of them in anger. He clearly wasn't a weakling — he had a tough life, and a strong build, and would ordinarily have thrown a punch in retaliation for such a brazen act. But he must have felt King's grip strength and assumed the man he was dealing with was a different breed of human, because all he did was snort with derision and stride off down the trail after his mules.

Slater said, 'You can't let that happen again.'

King put a hand out and pressed it against the rock wall, steadying himself. For some reason, the wind felt colder than usual. A chill ran down his spine, and he shivered.

He said, 'I'm exhausted.'

'So am I. But you came *that* close to killing an innocent man.'

'I know.'

'Don't let it happen again. If we need to rest, that's what we do. I don't want your mental health jeopardised by this. I can't let you get paranoid.'

'I'm not paranoid.'

'I would be. In fact, I *am*.'

'Then that could happen to you, too.'

'The end of the day,' Slater said. 'That's it. That's when we're done. It's close to midday now. There's a half-day left. Then we're out of here. All we need is absolute focus for twelve hours. Understand? Until then, neither of us can drop our guard.'

'Roger that.'

'Let's go.'

They walked onward.

43

S later was the first to reach Namche Bazaar.

The town was constructed in the shape of an amphitheatre — the buildings were laid out in a tiered "U" shape around a hill on the mountainside. He strode through the entrance archway symbolising their arrival in the town, and bent over momentarily to catch his breath.

They were making fantastic time.

And neither of them had hit a mental or physical wall yet.

King pulled up beside him, and they stared up at the sea of brightly coloured roofs — stark reds and blues and greens set against the backdrop of the enormous mountain they rested on. Up above Namche, they could see the terrain become increasingly barren. They were close to twelve thousand feet, and soon the altitude might start to have an effect.

Might.

That was the problem. Neither of them knew how their bodies would react. They'd never been this high before, and there was no way to train for it down at sea level. Even if there was, they wouldn't have had the time. They stared at the looming backdrop, both uncomfortable, both questioning themselves.

Slater said, 'Any symptoms yet?'

'No,' King said. 'But it'll be hard to tell until it hits us properly. I'm so focused on my ankle ... everything else is taking a back seat.'

'Same with me and my arm,' Slater said.

But it wasn't really his arm. It was his heart. Maintaining such an extreme pace over this terrain with less and less oxygen to work with was gruelling, and the smartwatch on his wrist told him he'd been averaging 175 beats per minute for the entire morning. He'd been ignoring it as much as he could, but it was finally starting to take a toll, especially as the oxygen decreased with each passing hour.

And it was only going to get worse.

He tried to force it out of his mind, but it was difficult.

How was he supposed to rescue Raya from a horde of Maoist rebels if he could barely use his muscles when he got there?

That turned his attention to something else, and as they strode up through Namche, he said, 'What exactly *is* the plan when we get there?'

'I'm waiting on word from Violetta,' King said. 'If there's no more intelligence to work with, we're just going to have to keep our eyes peeled. I'd say it's a comprehensive operation to move Raya and any other hostages from teahouse to teahouse along a populated trail. We'll be able to spot anything suspicious if we're looking for it, and then we follow it to its conclusion. But we need daylight to do that, so...'

'We need to keep moving,' Slater finished.

King nodded, his face ghost-white. 'We keep moving.'

They paused for a few minutes in one of the bakeries to load up on carbohydrates, ordering nearly everything in the window and chowing it down between swigs of water. They didn't even take a table. Then they swung their packs back over their shoulders and continued up to the peak of Namche Bazaar, passing open-air markets and endless teahouses and, surprisingly, an Irish pub.

The buildings fell away after that, replaced by barren plains dotted with handfuls of trees. This landscape was a world away from the forests they'd hiked through earlier in the morning. Slater took his mind off his throbbing arm and managed the odd look over his shoulder to admire the astonishing view of Namche and the endless mountains and valleys behind it.

'We're just a couple of dots,' King said at one point, awed by the scenery. 'We're nothing.'

Slater couldn't help but agree. It made them insignificant, their goals wholly unimportant, their grievances not the slightest bit concerning compared to their gargantuan surroundings. Somehow, it gave him strength. He treated the pain as nothing, the discomfort as miniscule. He kept walking, and didn't stop, and didn't even consider taking a break.

Neither did King.

Together they pushed all the way up to thirteen thousand feet, and when they finally reached the peak of the next mountain they stared out at a plummeting descent of nearly fifteen hundred feet, spiralling its way down into a forested valley.

They stood at the edge of a small settlement, sporting a single teahouse and little else. Slater's pulse pounded in his ears, his breath wheezed in his throat, but overall he was okay.

Mentally, he was prepared for the final stand.

One last battle.

But does it ever go the way you think it's going to?

He said, 'Have you seen anything?'

Wordlessly, King shook his head. 'We've only passed trekkers. I'm sure of it.'

'Same.'

'Then they must be ahead.'

'They were spotted just above Namche yesterday. Which means they can't be more than a day's journey ahead. What we could effectively cover in half a day. What's the time?'

King checked his watch. 'Nearly five p.m.'

'Shit.'

Neither of them said a word.

They knew what it meant.

They weren't going to catch them before the sun went down.

44

K ing sat down hard on the nearest rock and pulled the satellite phone from an easily accessible compartment in his duffel bag.

Violetta answered quickly enough. 'You got her?'

'No.'

'You found her?'

'No.'

'Where are you?'

'The map says we're at the settlement of Long-Ma. It'll be dark in an hour. I need to know if you want us to push through in the dark.'

'How tired are you?'

'We're fine.'

'You sound like you're barely staying awake. I've never heard you talk this slow.'

'We're okay.'

'I don't believe you. The answer is no, I don't want you to push through in the dark.'

'Violetta, this is our—'

'You've made incredible progress, Jason. You and Will

have covered more miles in three days than I thought humanly possible. But you can't fight them in the dark in their own backyard. They'll see you coming from a mile away — there's no chance you're trekking through the night without using your headlamps. You'll be sitting ducks.'

'It's the only way…'

'No, it's not. The only way you pull this off is to get as much sleep as you can and reach them by the middle of the day tomorrow.'

'How are you so sure?'

'Because they were spotted at lunchtime.'

King sat up, ramrod straight. 'Where?'

'Well, Raya was. At the Phorste Thanga guest house, which is—'

King stared down the mountainside and added, 'Just down there.'

'Yes.'

'Who spotted her?'

'A couple of civilian American hikers we managed to get in contact with by posing as their trekking company. We tried not to let on that she was a person of interest, but they figured it out. They saw her around the back of the guest house. The guy went out to take a piss because he didn't want to use the drop toilet, and caught a glimpse of her face in the tree line. He thought he'd been sprung, so he went back inside and didn't tell anyone about it until we forced it out of him. It's only when we spoke to him that he realised she might have been tied up.'

'And the rebels?'

'He said the guest house was teeming with Nepali people — dozens, he claimed — and he joked that he thought there was an international porters' conference being hosted there. Which doesn't sound like they were clad in military fatigues, or more people would have noticed.'

'So they're hiding in plain sight.'

'It's relatively easy to do out there. Everyone's focused on themselves and their condition, and it's an alien environment for the average trekker anyway. They're not going to notice anything out of the ordinary, because everything's out of the ordinary.'

'When was this?'

'Four hours ago. Lunchtime.'

King stared into the valley. 'So there's probably a handful of the rebels lingering around, expecting us.'

'I'd say so. Are you armed?'

'We are now.'

'With what?'

'A couple of Sig Sauer P320s we lifted off our attackers. You wouldn't know whether Perry would have access to...?'

'Just because they're American-made doesn't mean it's Perry arming them. Do you have ammunition?'

'Four magazines each.'

'Use them wisely. And aim steady.'

'Will do.'

'We uploaded an audio clip to the same part of the dark web where the rebels dumped the video. We had a team of psychologists who concocted the clip, but it seems the kidnappers bought it hook, line and sinker. We used a voice actor to sound abhorrently stressed, claiming he was doing everything in his power to get in touch with the right negotiator. He told them three of the best special risks insurers in the world were equally desperate to make sure this went off without a hitch. You know what that means, right?'

'You made Raya seem more valuable, so they wouldn't be so quick to hurt her.'

'Yes.'

'Which means, if Slater and I fail, everything's going to escalate significantly, and she's probably going to die.'

'Yes.'

King paused to rub his brow. 'Shit.'

'I just put my career on the line because I have faith in the pair of you,' she said. 'Don't fuck it up.'

'We'll try not to.'

'It's all of our heads if this doesn't work. If the two of you lose yours, then mine's on the chopping block for wasting such important assets.'

'We won't let you down, ma'am.'

'Christ, don't call me ma'am. Enough of that. I fucking care about you, alright? Come home safe.'

He paused, taking it in, and felt the weight of her words.

He said, 'I will.'

He hung up the phone.

Hunched forward, put his elbows on his knees, and caught his breath.

He was tired.

He couldn't mask it.

Slater said, 'How fucked are we?'

King said, 'Not as bad as I thought. They were at a teahouse down in that valley four hours ago. We won't catch them tonight, but we'll do it in the morning.'

'She won't make it until morning.'

'Yes, she will. Violetta bought us time.'

'How?'

Fighting extreme lethargy, King pushed himself to his feet. 'By upping the stakes.'

He set off down the mountain.

45

They reached the Phorste Thanga guest house just as the sun dropped below the horizon.

Slater made it there first. The descent suited his healthy ankles better than King's, and the pain in his arm had become so consistent and monotonous that it no longer had an effect on his stride. The guest house rested at the bottom of a declining slope, nestled into a dip in the trail. Past it, the path rose, continuing on the long journey to Everest and Gokyo Ri. The building itself was three storeys, made of brick, with green wooden window frames set at regular intervals across the levels. Beside it rested a cobble-stone courtyard where trekkers could stop for lunch or a tea break.

Slater made it up three of the rough stone steps before a short Nepali man burst out of the building's front door.

He was waving his arms hard, practically frothing at the mouth with nervous energy.

Shooing them away.

He pulled to a halt at the top of the stairs and shook his head.

Slater got the first word in, 'Look…'

'*No!*' the man hissed. 'Both of you get out of here, right now.'

King trundled to a halt beside Slater and caught his breath. He lifted his bad leg up a step, to take some weight off it. His face was pale — almost green, in fact. He wasn't in good shape.

'We have nowhere else to stay,' Slater said. 'We—'

The owner cut him off. 'They are still in hills. From early today. I cannot refuse service, or they make life bad for me. Very bad. Before they leave they tell me what you two look like. They say if I take you in, they kill me and all the guests. I cannot have this happen. My family future at stake. If you seen here… there will be nothing left for them. No one will ever come here. I will be dead. Tourists, hikers … they die. All because of you.'

King said, 'The rebels aren't here. They're gone.'

The owner sighed and bowed his head, as if contemplating what he could share.

Then he lifted his gaze again. 'Just ahead. Few miles down trail. Many men stay back. They expect you to come. They wait and they ambush. You die. They know this terrain. You do not.'

'We'll manage,' Slater said. 'Can you feed us, at least?'

'No.'

Slater pulled the Sig Sauer out of his waistband and aimed the barrel at the owner's stomach. He kept it low, below the line of sight of anyone peering out the guest house's windows. But he raised an eyebrow, asking the age-old question: *Do you get the message?*

'Bring us food,' Slater said. 'Or you die right here.'

'You will not do that,' the owner said, keeping his voice low. 'I know what you trying to do. They have girl. They try to keep it from me, but I see her. You're good man, trying to help her. You will not shoot me.'

'We're good men who will collapse tonight if we don't get food,' Slater said. 'We respect you, so we're doing what you ask. We won't force ourselves into your property. But we need to eat.'

There was no movement. The owner didn't respond. He was still as a statue.

Which left Slater in a tricky situation.

He said, 'Am I going to have to lead you inside at gunpoint and have you make us food with a barrel to your head?'

'That would not be good for our guests,' the owner said. 'They are tired from day walking the trail. They do not need this fright.'

'We're tired, too.'

'Okay. I will help you. Will you wait out here?'

'Of course.'

'I will be honest. You are good men. I need to tell you truth.'

King said, 'Okay.'

'After I make you food, I must call number and tell them you here. So you must eat, then you must go. If I no tell them, and word gets to them that I help, then me and my family die. I cannot risk this.'

Slater thought about it. After all, he had the leverage. But ultimately he said, 'Okay.'

'Do you hate me?'

'No,' Slater said. 'This is life. Sometimes it's messy.'

'Yes,' the man said, and gazed down the mountainside. 'Sometimes messy.'

'Thank you for helping us.'

'You need water?'

'Yes,' they both said in unison.

The owner nodded curtly, said, 'Wait here,' and trudged back into the guest house.

Sometimes Slater didn't like what he had to do.

But he wasn't about to ruin a hard-working innocent man's life over refusing to shelter them. Not under these circumstances, anyway. And he knew King felt the same.

They sat down on the lower steps, and watched the dull twilight settle over the mountain range.

Beside Slater, King started to shiver.

Slater said, 'So do we walk all the way back up to Long-Ma, or do we give up and bed down in the woods?'

'I can't make it back up that hill tonight,' King admitted in a rare moment of honesty. 'There's only so much longer I can tough this out for.'

'How's your ankle?'

'Bad. But resting helps. Our sleeping bags are good enough. We can bed down anywhere and cover ourselves in layers, and we'll be okay.'

'We might not get the best sleep.'

'You got a better idea?'

'No,' Slater said. 'I really don't.'

'Then we press forward maybe a few hundred feet and bunker down in the woods.'

'You heard what that guy said. Some of the rebels stayed back to intercept us. They knew this would happen. They knew how far we'd make it, and they knew this place would turn us away.'

'They probably projected it based on how much ground they already knew we'd covered. That doesn't mean anything.'

Slater stared. 'Doesn't it? Or does it mean they're getting help?'

'If you're implying it's Parker feeding them information, then you're wrong. He has no idea where we are.'

Paranoid, Slater patted down the outside of his pack. 'Unless he's tracking us...'

King reached over and put a calloused hand on Slater's wrist. 'Stop.'

Slater sat back, and adjusted himself. 'I don't know... I just can't work this out. We should have figured out who's behind this by now.'

'We won't until we get there.'

They lapsed into silence, and twenty minutes later the owner returned with a handful of plates sporting steamed momos, mountains of vegetable fried rice, and a half-dozen fried eggs. Slater and King accepted the food graciously as the daylight receded and devoured the meals within a couple of minutes. The owner waited for them to finish with his hands behind his back, observing the darkening sky, watching for any sign of the rebels returning.

When they handed the plates back, the owner handed over sealed plastic bottles filled with clean water.

They drank, and drank, and drank, and then tucked what was left over into their packs.

'Please go,' the owner said. 'And good luck.'

'One last thing,' Slater said. 'Did you notice a blond American with the group yesterday?'

The owner didn't answer.

Slater said, 'Please.'

'Yes,' the owner said. 'He was here.'

46

King bristled until the man followed up with, 'They had him tied up.'

'And you saw that?'

'I saw them do it,' the owner said. 'They had gun pointed at his back, whole way down. I saw them coming from long way away. They try to conceal gun, but I can tell by the way they walk. It was ... not normal.'

'So he was unrestrained until he got here?'

'Yes. So was girl. They came in separately, with rebel walking behind each of them. Then when they get here the rebel take them round back and tie them up. I cannot say anything. They can kill me if I speak.'

King said, 'Did they tie up a small Nepali guy, too?'

The owner shrugged. 'Not that I saw. But I stay busy in kitchen to feed them all. I no see much.'

'You saw,' Slater said. 'You're perceptive, and you have good info on the girl and the blond guy. Was there a Nepali guy tied up at any point they were here?'

A pause.

And then, 'No.'

Slater didn't answer.

King didn't answer.

They just stood in stunned silence.

'You must go,' the owner said. 'I don't know what this means — what I just told you — but you are both shocked. You must get out of here. Too risky.'

They didn't protest. They just nodded their thanks for the food and drink, and set off trudging down the trail into the dark.

There was the faint remnants of light leftover in the sky, barely perceptible, but it was enough for them to make out the dirt underfoot. They watched for potholes, steep drop-offs — anything that could compromise them. Each step set off a fiery ache in King's ankle, but it wasn't as severe as early the previous day. He could handle it. His mind was bulletproof.

As they strode away from the guest house's exterior lights and plunged into shadow, Slater said, 'It's got to be the porter.'

'We don't know anything,' King said. 'Not until we catch them.'

'You think we can?'

'We just need to survive the night.'

A twig snapped, perhaps a hundred feet ahead.

The remnants of the sound echoed in the semi-darkness.

They both froze.

And waited.

The seconds drew out, becoming long minutes. King kept his hand on his weapon, and he knew Slater would be mirroring his actions. They didn't look at each other — tactical awareness took over, and they became statues against the dark backdrop of the mountain. The wind seemed to pick up, but it was probably an invention of the mind.

Sounds amplified — creaks, rustles, whispers in the dark.

'We need to get off the trail,' King muttered.

'Here?'

'Just as good as anywhere else.'

They stepped off the hard-packed dirt and up into the tree line. King tested his ankle against the forest floor and found the surface springier then the trail. Relief flooded him — it might not have to be a long and painful night after all.

Or so you think.

He didn't have to remind himself of the man's warning.

There are still rebels in these hills.

Out of nowhere, Slater whispered, 'Make sure you keep your headlamp off.'

Explaining the obvious.

'No shit,' King said.

The twilight turned to night. King had only ventured ten feet into the tree line before he could no longer make out the sight of his hand in front of his face. He waved his palm a couple of times to test, but came away with no visual stimuli.

They were literally walking blind.

'I can't do this,' he whispered, his voice barely audible. 'Let's just bed down here. I'll turn an ankle if we go any further.'

'Suits me.'

King heard the rustling of a pack, and then the soft muted *thump* of Slater's rear end hitting the forest floor.

'That's a relief,' Slater whispered. 'Feels good to rest.'

King sat, too, and his eyes began to adjust to the dark. He

made out the faint silhouettes of the trees in front of him, and then the short stretch of trail, and then a plummeting drop that swept across the mountain ranges. As soon as they stopped, the main issue became clear. King started shivering in the evening chill, and beside him he heard Slater's teeth chattering.

They were still close to thirteen thousand feet in altitude.

Out here, the weather was as hostile as the men they were chasing.

He fumbled blindly for his pack, finding the zip after a solid minute of searching. He paused to make sure there were no foreign sounds nearby, and then ran the zipper along its tracks.

It grated in the silence.

King winced.

But then his pack was open, and he found his balled-up sleeping bag in its cover and undid the clasps and rolled it out. His ankle was somewhere in the dark, stretched out in the soft undergrowth, and when he lifted it up it burned hot like an invisible molten orb. With a wince he slipped it into the sleeping bag, followed by the rest of his lower body. He pulled the bag up to his waist, and packed on a couple of extra jackets he found at the bottom of his bag.

Then there was nothing to do but rest and recover.

And watch for signs of insurgents.

For reassurance, he tested the weight of the P320 in his palm.

Slater's soft voice trickled through the darkness. 'Have you got easy access to your gun?'

'Yeah. You?'

'Yeah.'

'So now we wait?'

'Now we wait.'

'We should take this in shifts.'

'I'm not in too much pain. I can tell you are. I'll take first watch.'

'You sure?'

'Yeah.'

'Don't slip up.'

'I can't afford to.'

'Alright.'

King rolled onto his side, nestled down into the sleeping bag liner, and drifted away in seconds.

47

S later didn't waver for close to an hour, and then everything steadily went downhill.

It started with a numb ache in his muscles. Not specific regions in particular, but *all* of it at once. His entire frame, throbbing and lethargic and heavy. It came out of nowhere, and he almost didn't realise what was happening until it seized him completely. He adjusted his position, convinced he was cramping from sitting at an awkward angle.

Then it got worse.

The heaviness swamped him, like his muscles were made of lead, and his heart rate skyrocketed as soon as he moved an inch. It thudded against his chest wall, spearing up into his throat, drawing all his attention

He put it together in an instant.

His heart was working overtime to oxygenate his muscles. That was the crippling downside of having the physique of an Olympic sprinter at high altitudes. It meant there was a whole lot of oxygen required to satiate his body, and at thirteen thousand feet there simply wasn't enough in the air.

The beginnings of altitude sickness were setting in.

He tried not to panic. There was little to do but sit in the dark, regulate his breathing, and conserve his energy. As he adjusted to the new baseline, he realised it wasn't as bad as he initially thought. There'd been a lot of initial anxiety to overcome, but it wasn't anything worse than a dull ache all over. He felt slightly more lethargic than normal, but that wasn't much different from the rest of the trip. And if he could silence the worry over his elevated heart rate, he'd be in the clear.

But to put that into practice proved a lot harder than he thought.

He focused on breathing deeper, a vain attempt to inhale more oxygen, but it didn't help. He ended up practically hyperventilating, and struggled to suppress the sound of laboured breathing. The rasping would carry through the night if he allowed it.

Then something else carried through the night.

Another twig snapping.

Clunk.

Slater had heard it before, so even though he froze up he didn't assume the worst.

Then, at the very edge of his hearing, he picked up the faint muttering of a curse in a foreign language.

In the distance someone lit up a torch, and the white beam played across the trail.

Slater sat very, very still.

His heart thudded faster.

Faster...

Faster...

Dangerously fast.

He couldn't take his mind off it. His muscles were screaming for oxygen, and to amplify the problem his adrenaline reserves kicked in. His vision narrowed to a tunnel and he fixated on the beam of light, only for his body to silently protest.

'King,' Slater mouthed.

He only allowed a sliver of sound to escape his lips.

No response.

'King.'

Silence.

The beam of light drifted closer. Then a second one materialised right beside it, and together the beams swept through the trees further up the trail. Slater narrowed his gaze and thought he could make out a cluster of silhouettes behind the light, hunched over, barely illuminated.

Coming down the mountain.

Getting closer.

'King.'

A little louder this time.

He had to risk it.

Beside him, King stirred.

And murmured, 'Huh?'

Too loud.

Far too loud.

The beam swept towards them, and Slater heard grunts of curiosity.

He waited a beat longer so he could be sure he wasn't about to massacre civilians who'd wandered astray.

Someone racked a handgun slide a half-second later.

Slater raised the P320, steadied his aim, and emptied the whole magazine.

Ten .45 ACP rounds ripped through the trees and riddled the group. The silhouettes jerked and twisted in the lowlight, and the torch beams twisted and spiralled away. One torch fell off the mountainside, and its glow emanated all the way down the slope. The other dropped to the trail and rolled back in the direction of the insurgents, illuminating their corpses laced with bullets. Slater had caught one man in the neck, two in the head, and another in his exposed chest. There were four bodies in the dirt.

Ten unsuppressed rounds on a quiet windy mountainside sounds like fireworks from a mile away.

To the person holding the gun, it's a nightmare.

Slater couldn't hear a thing. Tinnitus whined in his eardrums, preventing him from communicating with King. He was temporarily deaf as he shuffled out of his sleeping bag. He rose to his knees and his head swam. His head pounded and his heart throbbed and his muscles protested.

You're in bad shape, he told himself. *Real bad shape.*

But that didn't achieve anything, so he quashed that voice and focused on reloading the Sig.

When his hearing came back, King was yelling.

It gave him the fright of his life.

'What?' he said, still compromised. 'What did you say?'

He was talking to thin air. The better his hearing returned, the more he could assess where he was in the woods. Without sight, all he had to rely on was his hearing, so the temporary deafness had tested his mettle. Fumbling based on touch alone proved horrifying, and now he realised King was a dozen feet further into the forest, and moving fast.

'Follow me!' King screamed, seeming to recognise that his comrade was compromised. 'There's more.'

Fuck.

Slater got up, kicked the sleeping bag away, and sprinted blind up the hill into the trees.

48

W ell-trained combatants think there's a way to adapt to any situation.

And usually there is.

But sometimes the stimuli becomes too much.

Sometimes you get overwhelmed.

Sometimes...

...it all falls apart.

King quickly realised that moving blind was a whole lot more debilitating than he thought. He put his bad foot down and it went straight into a pothole, which caused the heel to strike at an awkward angle, and suddenly his swollen ankle was on fire. He fought that aside and threw himself forward on his good leg, limping up the hillside into the brush.

Behind him, a cacophony of voices rose up the mountainside.

They were fucked. Completely, totally, utterly fucked.

No point downplaying it.

If you survive this, he found himself thinking, *you can survive anything.*

He yelled for Slater to move.

There was no response.

Then, a few moments later, a soft voice floated up the hill. 'What? What did you say?'

King saw torch beams light up the trail like a series of beacons.

And then the first of the bullets whisked through the trees, a dozen feet to his left.

They know you're here.

So he threw caution to the wind and screamed, 'Follow me! There's more.'

Slater seemed to get the message. There was a brief pause, and then someone whisked past King — a silhouette racing up the mountain.

King said, 'Was that you?'

'Yeah,' Slater called from above, and ground to a halt.

It was impossible to coordinate in the dark.

They set up position between a pair of wide trunks spaced a few feet apart, leaving them a slim gap to fire potshots at the approaching cavalry.

King got down on one knee, taking weight off his ankle, and narrowed his focus. He found two beams heading into the tree line. He raised the P320, took careful aim, and pumped the trigger.

Once, twice, three times.

The light went out, struck by a bullet, and a guttural scream rose up the mountainside.

The other torchlight instantly shut off.

'Oh, shit,' King whispered under his breath.

One by one, the torches died.

Leaving utter darkness in its place.

Slater cursed too.

King dropped the volume of his voice back to less than a whisper and said, 'How do we play this?'

'I don't know.'

The alpine wind rustled the treetops, and some of the undergrowth around them caught in the breeze. There were sounds all around them now. Shaking and rattling and, between it all, the odd scuffing of boots.

The rebels were in the forest.

Something primal took over, and he started gnashing his teeth together. Unable to control his impulses, he crouched lower and pressed his back to the tree trunk, losing clarity of the situation as adrenaline swamped him. He knew what was happening.

Desperation mode.

There would be no firefight out here — not in the dark, on an isolated mountainside, without night-vision goggles or a similar enhancement. And he highly doubted that rural Nepali Maoist insurgents had access to that sort of tech.

So there'd be close-quarters fumbling — running around in the dark until two parties stumbled into each other — and then it would all come down to reflexes. Who could get the first shot off, who could capitalise after the initial shock.

Which, of course, favoured King and Slater.

But that was a dangerous game to play, no matter your reaction speed.

So he whistled softly to Slater, and breathed, 'Go left.'

Slater understood.

If they separated into different sides of the forest, they'd minimise the risk of running into each other and accidentally killing their only comrade.

King heard the rustle of khakis in the undergrowth heading in the other direction, and then Slater was gone.

He breathed in, and out.

Alone in the wilderness.

Then he peeled off to the right, taking his back off the tree.

Exposing himself to the unknown.

He kept quiet as a mouse. All those years of training came to the forefront, and he crept through the night without making so much as a peep. There were low-hanging branches on his face, and brushing against his shoulders, and his knees slithered through the plants on the forest floor.

And then a silhouette reared up out of the gloom, only inches away.

They both recognised each other's presence in unison.

But King was faster. That was guaranteed. His old black-ops division had recruited him for a reason, and most of it came down to otherworldly reflexes. Due to genetic blessing, his brain computed data at a faster rate than most on this planet.

So before the insurgent even knew what he was dealing with, King had darted into range and fired two shots through his heart. A death rattle escaped the man's throat and he collapsed forward, which was King's intention all along. King caught him by the lapels and allowed the corpse to fall over his shoulder, which would protect him if—

Every insurgent in the area reacted to the unsuppressed Sig Sauer by pointing their weapons in that direction and emptying their clips.

At the same time, King used his own muzzle flares to identify two more Maoists at close range, and as the gunfight erupted he sized up his targets carefully and fired a double-tap into each of their faces.

So they sprayed and prayed, and a stray bullet clipped

the body draped over King's shoulder, but thankfully there was enough bone and internal organs to make it ricochet off its trajectory, which meant it spilled out of the exit wound away from King.

Whereas King fired with precision.

And blew all four rounds out the back of his target's heads.

The staccato of gunfire faded, and the muzzle flares disappeared, and all returned to darkness and silence.

King controlled his breathing, and ticked off three tally marks in his head.

His ears whined, and his hearing dulled, and he dropped the body off his shoulder and kept low as he waited for it to return.

When it did, he heard screams to his left.

Will Slater.

Breaking bones.

He looked over and thought he saw two figures tussling, their outlines barely visible.

A moment later, one of them pushed the other to his knees and fired an execution shot.

King's breath caught in his throat.

49

Slater started out at a slightly faster pace than his counterpart.

Call it recklessness. Call it a burning desire to get this nightmare of a situation over and done with.

Call it anything, really.

But it happened. He kept low and kept a tight grip on the Sig Sauer and ran into the first hostile only a few seconds after he set off.

Literally.

He crouch-walked straight into the guy's hip, but the soft *bump* of the impact was drowned out by a particularly vicious gust of wind. So no-one heard it. Slater decided, then and there, to wait before he fired a shot.

So in one smooth motion — before the insurgent could even respond to the knock on his hip — Slater bolted upright and seized the guy in a crushing bear hug, pinning both his arms to his sides, preventing him from aiming the weapon that was more than likely resting in his own hand.

If the guy pulled the trigger, he'd probably shoot himself in the foot.

So he hesitated, and Slater headbutted him once as a test. His forehead smacked into the soft flesh above the guy's ear, and he used the stimuli to work out which way the guy was facing, and then he spun him round and headbutted him so hard in the nose that the *crack* sounded like a miniature gunshot.

The guy yelled out in pain.

When he did, Slater headbutted him in the mouth, knocking a few teeth loose.

Then, satisfied that he'd stunned the man enough to create a split second of hesitation, he released the bear hug and stepped back and smashed the Sig Sauer's stock into the guy's forehead.

Rattling his brain.

Putting him out.

Slater caught the unconscious man, lowered him to the forest floor, and quietly smashed the stock three consecutive times into his throat.

Caving in his windpipe.

He didn't want the man getting up to ambush him from behind.

He crept onward.

Then, far to his right, King fired a pair of shots, lighting up the forest with a strobe-like effect.

'Shit,' Slater whispered.

Gunshots exploded from everywhere at once, a vicious cacophony of death and destruction, and Slater narrowed his gaze to try and make out what was happening. He saw King crouched low, carrying a body over one shoulder, aiming with confidence. Then the two silhouettes closest to King jerked and spun away, lit up by the muzzle flares. Ejections of blood arced out the backs of their heads, and then the world plunged back into night.

Someone tried to seize Slater from behind.

He felt the light touch of arms about to wrap around his chest, and he jerked away like he'd been shot. Which was a good decision considering the *swoosh* of a machete slicing through the air where his throat had been a second earlier. He spotted the silhouette looming over him, trying to recover from the missed swing, and Slater stomped his heel into the guy's kneecap, hyperextending it, shattering bone and tearing ligaments. The guy screamed as he went down and slashed with the machete again.

Again, it missed Slater by inches as he jerked away.

But that's where his reaction speed came into play. He kicked the guy in the elbow, neutralising that joint too. Then he heard the distinctive sound of the guy changing hands with the knife, refusing to quit.

So be it.

Slater raised the P320 and pressed it down on the top of the guy's skull and fired once through his brain before he could swing the blade again.

Then he hit the deck.

A moment later gunfire roared, and bullets whisked over his head, shredding the undergrowth inches above him to pieces.

He thought his heart might explode from the stress.

King, he thought, *it's now or never.*

50

K ing was ready.

He knew it was Slater who fired the execution shot when the insurgents recognised the gunshot wasn't one of their own, and responded accordingly. They laced the trees with bullets, but the surviving silhouette was no longer there. The guy had seemingly vanished, but King knew the truth.

No-one else could react that fast.

Which gave him confirmation that anyone still standing wasn't Will Slater.

So he ejected the magazine that had one round left, chambered a fresh one, and let loose.

He aimed and fired, aimed and fired, aimed and fired, aimed and fired.

Four separate times in the tiny window provided by the muzzle flares.

His own bullets shredded the insurgents to pieces, dropping a trio of them where they stood. He saw blood spray and bodies collapse and then the picture cut out like someone yanking a TV cord from the socket.

Back to darkness.

King stayed low, and breathed, and tried not to focus on how badly his ankle hurt.

He stayed where he was, crouched so low his nose was almost touching the dirt, and waited for retaliatory fire.

None came.

Steadily, inch by inch, he rose.

And there was a small silhouette right there in his face, maybe 5'9 in height.

Definitely not Slater.

King panicked and fired twice into the darkness and missed.

He lined up a better aim and pumped the trigger once more.

Nothing.

Ten rounds in the clip.

He was empty.

The figure raised its own weapon. King had just managed to make out a snarling wide-eyed face in the brief flash of his final gunshot.

Animalistic.

Then again, this was an animalistic game.

King battered the gun aside, probably breaking a couple of the guy's fingers in the process, using his raw strength to his advantage. He figured a hurricane of violence was necessary to ensure he didn't catch a bullet to the face, so he thundered an uppercut into the guy's stomach and cocked his other arm at a right-angle and used the elbow as a whip to cut a line across the guy's forehead. Blood spurted immediately from the wound, blinding the man, and King used the opportunity to stand up and snatch hold of the arm holding the gun with both hands and bring it down on his knee, shattering the bone.

The guy grunted and dropped to his knees, overwhelmed by the pain.

King nearly took the man's head off his shoulders with a follow-up uppercut.

It probably killed him.

He dropped low and reloaded. But he fumbled with the fresh magazine. His knuckles were aching from the two consecutive uppercuts, and he might have broken a finger in the carnage. So, in a rare moment of weakness, his fingers slipped and he had to lunge to catch it again.

Which gave him away.

The next thing he knew, there were voices all around him, whispering frantically in a foreign language. His hearing was dulled from the repetitive gunshots, but he could make out that much.

He spun and found a silhouette and slammed the fresh magazine home and fired...

Killed one man, but another one shot at him and missed.

Just.

It came horrifically close, and King instinctively spun away as he felt displaced air against the side of his neck. When he put his foot down to steady himself, his swollen ankle screamed for relief.

Sweat beaded across his forehead, and he fought the urge to gasp.

He raised his Sig and took aim at the man who'd shot at him but he found himself reeling, his aim thrown off by the extenuating circumstances, his focus wavering.

He fired twice and missed both times.

In the light of the muzzle flares he saw the twisted grotesque expression on the insurgent's face, and saw the guy take careful aim, and King found himself staring right down the barrel of the weapon and his heart rate surged through the roof and panic seized him in its cold grip and he fought the urge to cry out in desperation—

And the guy's head exploded.

The gunshot came from over King's shoulder and he nearly lost his balance again, but then Will Slater was right beside him, looping a hand around his underarm and wrenching him to his feet.

He got a firm grip on the soil underneath his boots, and regained his composure in an instant.

Then they stood side-by-side and realised in unison that they'd memorised the positions of the remaining insurgents from the last muzzle flash.

So they raised their Sigs and fired simultaneously, and their weapons blared with rage, and—

The final insurgents fell dead into the undergrowth, arteries severed, bleeding from several bullet wounds each.

King dropped to his knees as a final precaution, and heard Slater do the same.

He'd lost count of the number of men he'd killed.

They stayed vigilant, waiting for their hearing to return as the seconds ticked by.

Minutes elapsed.

There was nothing.

Slater muttered, 'How bad's your ankle?'

'Not the best it's ever been.'

'Wait here.'

He turned, and his silhouette disappeared. King wasn't in a hurry — he settled back into the undergrowth, placed his back against the nearest tree, and got his breathing under control. The adrenaline wore off. The stress chemicals dissipated. When Slater finally returned with a headlamp in his palm, King was back to normal.

'You ready?' Slater said. 'In case this kicks everything off again?'

King clutched the Sig Sauer tight in his hand and nodded wordlessly.

'Here goes,' Slater said.

He flicked on the torchlight.

The white LED flared, brilliant in the night. It evaporated the darkness, and Slater swung the beam left and right. King tracked it with his weapon, keeping his back to the tree. When everything in a hundred-and-eighty degree radius had been cleared, they shimmied around the trunk and cleared the other side.

No sign of hostility.

A whole lot of corpses.

But no live bodies.

'Well,' Slater said, 'that's sorted.'

King exhaled properly for the first time and squeezed his eyes shut in relief.

51

S later knew King was back in the same catastrophic routine.

Walk all day, maintain momentum, and then freeze up at night as the swelling intensifies. King wasn't going anywhere in a hurry, and the man needed a good night's sleep if he wanted to be in any way functional tomorrow. So Slater told him to stay where he was, and went to retrieve their belongings.

He gathered both duffel bags and both sleeping bags and carted all the gear up the hillside. Then he dropped it at King's feet.

'We sleep here,' Slater said.

'Surrounded by bodies?'

'I'm not letting you walk anywhere. You need these next eight hours to get the swelling down.'

King sighed, but seemed to accept it. He slumped further down the trunk and stretched his bad leg out. The only light came from Slater's headlamp, so he didn't see the wince plastered across his friend's face, but he knew it was there.

Slater said, 'How are you feeling?'

'I'm only going to tell you this one more time,' King said, staring up at him. 'Stop asking me that. It only makes it worse.'

'Sorry. I'm concerned, that's all.'

'Give me the rest of the night to hibernate, and I'll be okay by morning.'

'You should call Violetta.'

King said, 'Good point. I'll do that, and you get me ice.'

'Where from?'

'The guest house.'

'He won't do it.'

'Ask nicely.'

'That won't make a difference.'

'Then ask sternly.'

'King...'

'If you want me to be able to walk tomorrow, I need ice. There's no other way around it.'

'I don't want to get caught hanging around there again. It'll put him and his family at risk.'

'Then use your training, for Christ's sake.'

Slater stared into space for a beat, then shrugged and nodded. 'Okay. You owe me.'

'I've always owed you.'

'You'll be okay here?'

'We just killed a dozen men. I'm sure we've bought ourselves at least an hour, don't you think?'

Slater left the duffels and the sleeping bags with King and set off toward the trail. His arm throbbed with each step, but it was manageable. He made sure to take care where he placed his feet, especially moving downhill, but he was adjusting to the dark with each passing minute. After a spell, he got careless.

Then he tripped on a body.

He plummeted forward and threw his shoulder down and rolled with it, careening through the undergrowth, and loose dirt showered over him. Then he twisted on the spot and brought the Sig Sauer up to aim and found himself face-to-face with a pale corpse. It startled him that he could make out the bullet hole in the centre of the insurgent's forehead, but then he turned his face to the sky and found the moon had crawled out of its hiding place behind thick cloud.

He used the weak ethereal light to guide him the rest of the way to the guest house.

He approached low, aiming for a side door that led to what he believed to be the kitchen, but it opened even before he could knock.

The owner stared at him, wholly disappointed.

Slater tucked the Sig into his waistband before the man could lay eyes on the pistol.

'What do you want?' the man said.

'An ice pack.'

'Go away.'

'Please.'

'I told you stakes before.'

'We've been busy,' Slater said.

'What do you mean?'

'There's no-one left to witness this.'

The owner's face paled, and he steadied himself. Then his expression hardened. 'For now. There'll be more.'

'But not yet.'

Silence.

Slater said, 'I don't want to make you fetch me it at gunpoint.'

The owner growled to himself. 'There only so many

times you can threaten me before it become obvious you not going to do it.'

'I'll do it if I have to.'

The man shook his head in disappointment and retreated into the corridor. Slater didn't follow him. He waited patiently, and rubbed his hands together as warmth spilled out of the guest house.

The owner returned promptly with a trio of ice packs. He passed them over, one by one.

Slater said, 'You didn't have to do that. I only asked for—'

'I no want to help. For what it might do to my family. But if you are here, and I must help, then I help as much as I can.'

'Thank you.'

The guy waved a hand dismissively. 'Worse for you than for me. Your friend … he have trouble walking.'

'Swollen ankle. He might be hurt real bad. We don't know yet.'

'So he need this.'

'Yes.'

'Then wish him good luck. From me.'

'Thank you. I will.'

The owner paused there, scrutinising Slater.

Slater allowed it.

Eventually the man said, 'You have no quit in you.'

'Sorry?'

'Every day, I see guest come into this place. All very tired. All weary from trail. It is tough, especially when cover great distances. I give them food and drink and some-times bed. But I always look at their eyes. So I can see if they have quit. And usually I right. Sometimes altitude affect them, sometimes their bodies break down. But I know if they going to stop. You will not stop. I can see in eyes.'

Slater soaked it in, and said, 'I appreciate that.'

Then the owner narrowed his gaze. 'See, you are definitely feeling altitude. You are heavy. But no quit.'

Slater didn't want to address that.

It felt like his bones were made of lead. Like there was a two-hundred-pound weight resting squarely on his shoulders.

He said, 'No. I don't think I will.'

'Your friend, either.'

'No,' Slater said. 'He certainly won't.'

'Then you will get girl back. I know.'

'Do you?'

'Just guess. But usually, my guess good.'

Slater offered a hand, and the man shook it.

'That means more than you know,' Slater said.

The corners of the man's mouth tilted upward, and he said, 'I know.'

Slater tucked the icepacks under his arm and turned away, trudging back toward the tree line.

Suddenly reassured.

Because, unbeknownst to the owner, for the first time in his life he'd felt like quitting.

52

W hen Slater left, King fished the satellite phone out and kept one hand over the display's glow, just in case there were any insurgents in the vicinity.

He dialled, and pressed the device to his ear with a heavy hand.

Violetta immediately said, 'Are you okay?'

'Yes. They ambushed us. We took care of it.'

'At the guest house?'

'No. The owner didn't let us stay. His family were threatened.'

'I see.'

He could hear every slight waver in her tone as she struggled to suppress her emotions.

It gnawed at his willpower.

Screamed at him to let the emotion out.

But he couldn't.

Not this close to victory.

They were compartmentalising for a reason.

He said, 'We're sleeping outdoors. We'll be okay.'

'How many ambushed you?'

'A dozen, maybe.'

'Jason...'

'We'll catch them tomorrow. You know we will.'

'You have to survive until then.'

'They don't have endless forces. That was their best effort, and we quashed it. They're counting on getting as far up the trail as possible before they begin negotiations, right?'

'They want to begin now, but we're holding them off. We might be able to squeeze another day out of it.'

'Then that's another day they need to keep moving. I'm sure Raya and Perry are dead tired. That's not even mentioning the logistical problems. We'll catch them tomorrow.'

'They'll be heading for Gokyo — the village below Gokyo Ri. I'm sure of it.'

'Then we'll find them there.'

'You'll have to go in dark,' Violetta said, her tone hesitant. 'There's no-one willing to communicate with us in the village — we've already been checking like clockwork. Everyone's turned into a steel trap — the teahouse owners, the locals, the tourists. It's like someone got there first and told everyone to keep their mouths shut.'

King had an idea. 'Can you get us a helicopter there?'

'No.'

'I didn't want to reveal this, but my ankle is bad.'

He heard her lower her forehead to the table in front of her. 'I knew it.'

'I don't know if I'll be able to make the final trek tomorrow.'

'The helicopter companies are already uncooperative, and we know why. There'll be external pressure on them from the insurgents. And if we force them to fly you the final stretch, they'll radio it straight to the Maoists, even if we make them land at a secluded location. You'll be fish in a barrel when you touch down. You need to walk it.'

'Okay.'

'Can you?'

'You said it yourself — I have to.'

'You don't have to do anything. You can pull out if you can't continue.'

'No,' King said, 'I can't.'

'Yes, you—'

'That's never been an option. Not once throughout my career. I'm not about to start making it one.'

'Is it broken?'

'I don't think so. It's just damaged. Swollen like a pumpkin.'

'Do whatever you need to do to get it under control.'

'I'm working on that.'

'Take painkillers if you have to. In the first-aid kit there's some serious—'

'I can't.'

'Why not?'

'They'll dull my senses. I can't afford that.'

Violetta paused for thought, and said, 'You might just be the strongest person I know.'

'Slater would have something to say about that.'

'Yeah, well, I'm not dating Will Slater.'

Despite himself, King smiled. 'I need to rest.'

'I'm sure you do.'

'Anything else you got for me?'

'You should probably know that — statistically — it's likely the kidnappers will turn violent if this drags out any longer.'

'They cut her finger off, Violetta. I'd say we already crossed that line.'

'That's just the start. The fact that they know about special risks insurers and professional negotiators is unnerving. That means they know what they're doing, and it's endlessly more dangerous when they know what they're doing.'

'You think they've been doing this for some time now?'

'It's hard to say. Like I said, kidnap statistics are messy. The vast majority aren't reported. For all we know, they've been hitting trekkers for months now and making sure it all gets swept under the rug. If nothing's officially reported, then they could be experts at this by now.'

'It's a good thing we're here to clean it up, then.'

'Yeah...'

King let the silence drag out.

She said, 'Be careful, okay?'

'One last question,' King said. 'Did Parker tell you about the briefcase?'

'No... Christ, I haven't even been thinking about that. Was there something important in it?'

'His laptop. He said he left a document open with the locations of ten temporary black-ops HQs on home soil. Has anyone in your department heard about that?'

'No... not a word... wait, why on earth would he do that?'

'Fatigue, he claims.'

'That's something we needed to know about the moment it went missing.'

'Get in touch with him, then.'

'I will. He's still in Phaplu, waiting on word from the trail. Shouldn't be too hard to reach him.'

'I don't completely trust him.'

'You shouldn't completely trust anyone.'

'Besides you.'

He thought he heard her smile. 'I'm flattered.'

'We're compartmentalising, remember?'

'I remember. Get some rest.'

'On it.'

He hung up before he said anything he might regret.

Then he lapsed into the same familiar trance-like state, letting his guard down in the process. But there was no need to stay alert any longer. They'd decimated the hostile force, and the bodies all around him proved it. For now, they'd bought themselves time. He closed his eyes and drifted into an uneasy half-sleep, plagued by remnants of pain trickling up his leg.

When he opened his eyes again, his ankle had stopped throbbing.

He breathed a sigh of relief, and then Slater crashed through the trees nearby.

'Christ,' King said. 'You scared me.'

'Good,' Slater said, and handed over three icepacks. 'Means you're paying attention.'

'I won't be for much longer.'

'That's okay. If we bed down here in total darkness, there'll be more than enough time to react if we see more torchlights. Sleep in shifts?'

'I'll need first shift,' King said. 'Sorry.'

'That's okay. I'm fine.'

'How's the arm?'

'It hurts like hell.'

'Nothing out of the ordinary, then.'

'Not long left.'

King arranged the three icepacks in a giant ring around his ankle and taped them into place. Then he rolled over, savoured the numbness that crept through the joint, and went straight to sleep.

53

S later didn't waver.

He sat bolt upright and meditated, figuring he'd make use of the time. Hours passed, bringing nothing but the wind and the rustling of the trees and the distant howling of dogs. The environment might have unnerved a more timid soul, but he'd been through so much since touching down in Nepal that it barely fazed him. He wrapped himself in several layers of all-weather clothing and draped the sleeping bag over his shoulders and stared straight ahead, barely blinking.

He became the night.

And the stillness helped him in other ways. His heavy muscles relaxed, and his heart pumped at a reasonable rate, and he could swear he was staving off the effects of the altitude on his oxygen requirements.

But there was still another trek to be completed in the morning.

To Gokyo.

He knew precious little about the village — then again, he knew precious little about the route in general. That hadn't hindered them so far, and now they were confirmed to be closing in on the enemy party. That gave him strength, despite the pain.

Four hours into the deep meditation, he shook himself out of it and tapped King on the shoulder.

The man sat up in an instant.

'My turn?' he said.

'Yeah. I assume the ice melted?'

'A while ago. But I can't feel my foot. It's brilliant.'

Slater almost scoffed at the masochism. 'Glad to hear.'

He lay down, breathed in and out twice, and was asleep in seconds.

54

King had never been the meditative type.

Then he'd spent enough time with Will Slater for the man's Eastern philosophies to rub off on him, and he'd been a converted disciple ever since.

He employed the same tactics Slater had taught him a hundred times over.

Sit up straight. Focus on the breath — in, out, in, out — and repeat ad infinitum. Don't get mad at yourself if thoughts float into your head — instead, detach from them and let them drift on harmlessly by. Try to separate yourself from the concept of "I" — get rid of the ego, and recognise that you are the same physical matter as the rest of the world around you. It's all consciousness. It's all one and the same. And then, when you reach this inner stillness, do nothing but sit and exist.

Those were the basics. When Slater laid them out, King dismissed them as wishy-washy bullshit, but then after much reluctant practice he'd managed to achieve a full hour of silence, and it changed everything. He came out of it thinking he was capable of literally anything. There was something about the process of blending into his surroundings that flipped a switch in his brain. Suddenly the pain and suffering of training wasn't part of him — it was something separate, something controllable. He found he could push his body harder in the gym every day, just by making his mind quieter.

Now he detached completely, and settled into a gentle rhythm as the multiple layers of clothing kept him warm. Feeling returned to his ankle, but there was less pain. Halfway through his shift, he took the opportunity to probe the joint with two fingers, and found the swelling had reduced.

Maybe it'd all be okay after all.

A couple more hours passed without incident, and then it was four in the morning, and he woke Slater with a tap on the side.

Slater cracked an eyelid open and said, 'You need more sleep?'

'Let me get another hour and I'll be fine.'

'You sure?'

'I know my body.'

'Go for it.'

King stretched out on the forest floor, draped himself in more layers, and with his mind quieter than it had been in weeks, went out like a light.

55

S later woke King at five on the dot, and together they packed up their gear and scouted the trail for signs of life in the pre-dawn light.

There was nothing.

Not a soul around.

The birds came to life as light bled into the sky, and Slater used the opportunity to skirt up and down the hillside, patting down corpses that had long ago gone cold. He found several with identical Sig Sauer P320s and fetched every spare magazine he could find. He came back to King with another eight fresh magazines in total, and again they split them four apiece. With their guns fully loaded, they donned their gear with the newfound expertise of seasoned trekkers and set off before they could convince themselves otherwise.

'You hungry?' King said.

'Somewhat,' Slater said. 'I don't want to bother that guy again, and there's a greater chance he'll be spotted interacting with us in broad daylight. Besides, there's bound to be somewhere to eat further up the trail.'

'Agreed on all counts.'

They didn't talk much, and there was no wonder. The calmness of the morning quickly wore off after the first major ascent, which left them gasping for breath at the top of a long and winding climb. Then they pushed harder, weaving along rock formations and over bridges that crossed glacial streams nearly frozen over. Snow cropped up with increasing frequency, powdering the sides of the trails until they suddenly found themselves surrounded by the stuff. There was no need to shrug on another layer — the intensity of the trekking kept them warm the whole way.

They stumbled into Machhermo — resting at roughly fifteen thousand feet — just after ten in the morning. The small village was situated in a flat basin, surrounded on three sides by stunning snow-capped peaks spearing toward the heavens. The giant mountains weren't in the distance anymore. They were right there in their faces.

But Slater wasn't exactly paying attention to the scenery.

He was in terminator mode, all his focus concerned with keeping up a measured pace so he didn't drop from exhaustion. The number of miles they were racking up each day had finally caught up to him, and when he stopped to assess his condition in the warmth of a random teahouse's foyer, he realised he was in worse shape than he thought.

King, it seemed, was in a similar boat.

They both doubled over to catch their breath, and when they met each other's gaze they found a certain hollow emptiness in each other's eyes.

King said, 'Shit.'

'Yeah.'

'Let's eat and drink and see how we're feeling.'

'Yeah.'

There was little left to be said. They zombie-walked into the dining hall, catching the attention of a handful of trekkers treating themselves to a late breakfast after a sleep-in.

One of the Nepali guides regarded the newcomers warily. 'Where you walk from?'

'Phorste Thanga,' Slater said.

His eyes widened. 'It's ten in the morning.'

'Yeah.'

They thumped down into the seats and dropped their foreheads to the crooks of their elbows in unison. A young Nepali woman approached them as they tried their best to recover.

She said, 'What can I get you?'

'Food,' they muttered together.

It didn't take long. They were the only trekkers the kitchen was cooking for when the last of the breakfast hangers-on trickled out to get their journey started. Gokyo was the only destination worth reaching further up the mountain. Machhermo seemed to exist solely as a pitstop before the final push to Gokyo, and beyond to Everest, so it was no wonder the village was made up entirely of teahouses, supply shops, and, at the edge of the village, a small doctor's office.

Neither Slater nor King needed a doctor.

They had no desire to be loaded with pain pills — not when the culmination of their trip was likely to require all their fine motor skills and then some.

So they sat and recuperated in mutual silence, and popped a couple more altitude sickness tablets in the meantime.

Not that the Diamox was helping Slater in the slightest.

He didn't have headaches, and he didn't have nausea, but the full force of his aching muscles hit him as soon as he stopped moving and killed the momentum. The breath rattled in his throat as he desperately fought to move oxygen to his cramping musculature. It didn't work. When the Nepali woman returned with the usual momos, fried rice and eggs, Slater could barely lift his fork to shovel the steaming food into his mouth.

King noticed. 'What's wrong?'

Slater shook his head — he could barely manage the gesture. 'Nothing — I'm fine.'

'No, you're really not.'

'I don't think I'm getting enough oxygen.'

'You going to vomit?'

'It's not that. It's ... my muscles.'

'They're cramping?'

'I feel a hundred pounds heavier.'

'Can you make it to Gokyo?'

'How far?'

'Four hours, probably.'

He clamped his jaw and clenched his teeth and said, 'Yeah. Should be fine.'

'You need to tell me if you're going to collapse.'

'I'm not. Not yet. I've been through worse.'

'I need you on your A game,' King said. 'If you want the truth, we're probably going to run into them en route to Gokyo. Violetta's been sending intel dumps. Calculating average speeds, based on the sightings. We're either going to reach Gokyo just after them, or at the same time.'

Slater chewed slowly on a mouthful of rice. It took all the effort in his system to simply open and close his mouth.

Then he nodded.

'Sounds good.'

He could feel King's eyes on him.

Slater mumbled, 'How's your ankle?'

'Better.'

'Great. At least one of us is managing.'

King slapped him on the back. 'You'll be fine. Finish your food, and let's go.'

56

As soon as King stepped outside he bore the brunt of the weather.

It's hard to tell whether the temperature's plummeting or not when your body's permanently warm and your heart rate's constantly elevated. Now they'd had the time to cool down, they ventured out into the Mach-hermo air and King started shivering immediately.

Slater trudged behind him.

King couldn't deny he was concerned.

'How are you planning to get through this?' he said. 'We have close to another thousand feet of elevation to go. You sure you don't want to stay here?'

Slater stared at him through half-closed eyes. 'I'm not letting you do this alone.'

'You're no use like this. You have to admit that.'

Slater said, 'All I need is to see them. Then adrenaline will take over. You know that just as well as I do.'

'Sure, but that will only prop you up for so long.'

'Then we'll have to get it done quickly.'

Refusing to listen to another word, Slater brushed past King and began the trek up the hillside.

King bristled, but didn't protest.

The truth was...

...he needed Will Slater.

He was far from a hundred percent, and he knew he couldn't get it done alone. Not in this sort of compromised position. Sure, they'd decimated everyone they'd come into contact with, but exhaustion was creeping up on them. The silent killer. The more fatigued they became, the faster their reaction speed would plummet, and they'd lose the main advantage they carried over their competition.

Against trained insurgents, they'd fail spectacularly if they were doing it solo.

No, they needed each other, as much as their tender egos might hate to admit it.

King admitted it to himself. That was good enough.

They climbed out of Machhermo, weaving their way up sharp ascents until the rising elevation gave way to flat plains covered in snow and riddled with boulders. King likened it to a fantasy landscape — it was hard to believe the sweeping scenery was even real. He chalked half of it up to the terrain's beauty, and half to his own delirium. Then it became a mad game of concentration as he struggled to balance the trekking itself with the constant need to watch for enemies.

He could see Slater struggling with it, too.

They passed handfuls of trekkers with recurring frequency, and each time King's hand imperceptibly wandered to the Sig Sauer tucked under his jacket. He wouldn't put it past the insurgents to disguise themselves amongst ordinary civilians, and each group they passed found themselves at the receiving end of paranoid stares from King and Slater. Frankly, they didn't have the energy to be subtle.

They made it past all three of the Gokyo Lakes without so much as a glance of confirmation that they were on the insurgents' heels.

It was somewhat demoralising.

And Slater clearly wasn't happy with the nature of the terrain.

'They could have one sniper out here and that'd be that,' he said. 'I don't like this at all.'

'Have you seen their arms?' King said. 'It's all the same shit. P320s and AK-47s. Nothing else. I think they got a couple of shipments — one with the AKs, and one with the Sigs that fell off the back of one of our military's trucks — and they're working with that.'

'It wouldn't be hard to get a long-range rifle.'

'Even so, they don't know what we look like. We've got buffs covering our faces, glasses on our eyes — they're not going to kill every pair of men walking together until they hit us. They're not going to risk that kind of collateral — it'd kill their tourism industry and ruin the economy.'

He could almost see the gears turning over in Slater's head, using what little brainpower he had left to compute the possibilities. Then he said, 'Fair enough.'

'We're not far now.'

King watched Slater's hand instinctively go to the gun at his waist. Just for reassurances sake. Slater said, 'Then there'll be a fight.'

'Yes, there will.'

'I should be ready for a fight.'

'You said it yourself, remember? Adrenaline will kick in. You'll be okay.'

Slater's footsteps seemed to become heavier. 'Yeah... it'll be okay.'

King didn't linger on his friend's condition. There was no other way to put it — Slater's body was shutting down.

But you only need to make it to Gokyo.

Figure out who's behind this, fire a few shots, grab the girl, get the fuck out of Nepal.

Simple as that.

He knew it wouldn't be.

Nothing ever goes according to plan.

They passed the final lake, frozen over from the arctic temperatures, and then it was a simple flat path all the way to the base of the village. They saw Gokyo from a mile out, resting in the snowy plains, dwarfed by the enormous peak behind it. Gokyo Ri was a gargantuan piece of nature, rising up into the clouds, its peak invisible in the late-afternoon gloom. Trekkers summited it in the morning, often getting up at four a.m. so they had the best chance of a cloudless photo at the peak.

King saw it, and bristled.

Slater saw it too.

The cold seemed to intensify.

'Be on guard now,' King warned him. 'They'll see us coming from the village. Keep the buff over your nose and mouth, and don't adjust your glasses. And get ready to fight.'

'Mmm...'

King spun around and seized him by the shoulders, fear rippling through him. Not toward the insurgents they would almost certainly encounter, but toward Slater's health. He'd never seen his friend like this. Snowy wind whipped and lashed against them, but they both steeled themselves.

'Hey,' King snapped, speaking over the snowstorm. 'You hear me? Get it together. You might not have anything left in the tank, but you need to find some sort of reserves. You're simply not going to survive if you walk into Gokyo like this.'

'I'm trying.'

'I know. Try harder.'

'Okay.'

'This is it,' King said. 'A few more hired thugs, and either Perry or the porter, and then it's all over.'

Slater was sluggish as he nodded his understanding. 'I'll perform. Don't worry.'

'You ever felt anything like this before?'

'No.'

'Then how do you know you'll be able to?'

Slater shrugged off King's grip and started trudging through the snow again. 'Because otherwise I'm dead.'

King wanted to say a million things, but elected not to.

He followed Will Slater into Gokyo.

57

I t hurt to breathe.

Slater considered himself something of an expert in human willpower. He'd spent most of his career pushing his own limits, and been rewarded handsomely for it.

This, though...

This was a different beast.

His heart was working overtime to keep his body moving. There'd been a *click* inside his head halfway between Machhermo and Gokyo. He'd ignored it, just as he was ignoring all the discomfort rippling through him, but he knew what it meant. He was operating on full survival mechanisms now — when he stopped, he would crash. The fight or flight response was keeping him moving, but when he came to rest his body would likely shut down.

He couldn't afford to think about it. Each step forward took a Herculean effort, and it was only going to get worse the longer they spent at this altitude. He'd been telling himself the adrenaline would override his exhaustion when it came time to fight for Raya, but as time passed he found himself doubting that more and more.

You don't know who's behind it.

You don't know what you're walking into.

You don't know anything.

The right move would be to call it in. Accept they were compromised, inform Violetta they were pulling out, and leave it to the professional negotiators to sort out the mess they left behind.

A few hundred feet from the mouth of Gokyo, he voiced his concerns.

King said, 'No.'

'Why not?'

'Now that we're this close to it, I'm pushing ahead. If you need to stop here, then stop. But something about this whole thing is fishy as hell, and you know just as well as I do that the negotiators won't get to the bottom of it. I have an awful feeling if we pull out, no one will ever work out what happened here.'

Slater wasn't going to argue with any of that. He shut his eyes, screamed at his body to respond, and quickened his pace.

It worked.

Even though his muscles protested, he sped up. King matched his pace and suddenly they were moving fast underneath a snow-covered archway. It symbolised their official entrance into Gokyo. They exchanged a glance, tucked their buffs a little further up the bridges of their noses, and pushed on.

'Door to door?' Slater said.

'Yeah,' King said. 'Door to door.'

'We're going to get ourselves killed.'

'No,' King said. 'Somehow, I don't think we are.'

Slater could see the man's demeanour shifting. It was more obvious because his own body was refusing to respond — in past confrontations they'd shared, their adrenaline tended to peak in unison, narrowing their focus, giving them tunnel vision. Now Slater could see King going through the transformation. King straightened up, and his breathing intensified, and he seemed to expand across the shoulders as his muscles linked together in a cohesive chain. He was ready for a fight to the death.

Slater wasn't.

He could move faster than before, but the cocktail of stress chemicals that his brain ordinarily released like clock-work was still buried deep down inside. Inaccessible for now.

He told King.

There was no use hiding it.

'Let me take the lead,' King said. 'There's only a handful of teahouses here. We'll have what we need to know within minutes.'

'You hit the first one,' Slater said. 'I'll wait out front.'

'Try to make yourself invisible.'

'Always.'

Then it was game time.

No build-up, no unnecessary machismo, no mutual chest-puffing.

Just a simple nod to each other, and then they went into operational mode.

As promised, King took the lead. He shielded himself from any vantage points in the windows of buildings they were approaching and transferred the Sig Sauer from his waistband to his jacket pocket. Then he kept both hands in his pockets, turned back to face the town, and made a beeline for the closest teahouse.

Slater followed.

It was a two-storey lodge-style building surrounded by snowy slopes, complete with smoke billowing from a chimney atop the roof. There was a dry room just inside the entrance to hang any outerwear before venturing further into the warmth of the hallways. A few fogged-up windows faced them as they made their approach, but there was no-one looking out. They were invisible for now.

King hustled into the entrance and dusted snow off his jacket and pants. He stamped his feet a few times and gestured to a thin wooden bench running the length of the dry room.

'Wait there,' he said.

Slater actually appreciated the coddling. He couldn't think straight. He sat himself down on the bench, put his back to the wall, made the same transfer with his Sig from waistband to jacket pocket, and widened his gaze to encompass the entire room. If anyone stepped in with hostile intentions, he'd have the wherewithal to blow a hole through their forehead before they could try anything.

Then he slumped down and tried to recharge.

King hovered across the room. 'You're not going to drop dead on me, are you?'

'Not if I can help it.'

'I'll be right back.'

He ducked into the hallway and vanished from sight.

Slater took in a deep rattling breath, held it for a few seconds, and released it.

He was hurting.

And then, piece by piece, the lack of oxygen caught up to him.

Minute by minute, he started getting worse.

58

K ing stepped into the dining room and found at least twenty trekkers spread across the tables.

One by one, they turned in their seats to check him out.

He didn't do anything out of the ordinary. He hunched over as if the day's journey had sapped all the energy out of him, which didn't require too much of a performance. He kept his hands in his pockets and trundled over to the service desk skewered into the far wall, manned by an older Nepali guy in his fifties. The P320's stock in his right palm gave him reassurance, and he kept a tight grip on it the whole way across the room.

He could almost taste the tension.

They were here. Raya, and Perry, and the porter, and a small army of rebels. They were probably spread across the teahouses to minimise scrutiny, but they were here all the same. There was simply no alternative. Camping away from settlements wasn't conducive to survival, so they'd have to stay in a village. And Gokyo was the only option, based on where they'd been spotted along the trail.

So this was it.

The culmination of the journey.

He stepped up to the desk, met the worker's gaze, and paid very close attention for signs of suspicion.

And he found them immediately.

He said, 'Can I get a room?'

The man wasn't a good actor. He stared at King for a few beats, registering the newcomer's appearance. Then he said, 'Just you?'

Then and there, King knew the man had been given their description.

String him along. Find out what you can.

He said, 'I have someone with me.'

'Who?'

The guy was too curious. His ears practically perked up at the announcement of another traveller. So the word was out. Maybe every teahouse in the village had been told to look out for King and Slater, and to contact the necessary parties if they arrived.

The gears were now in motion. The cat was out of the bag. There was no going back.

King said, 'My wife.'

'Your wife?'

Palpable confusion.

Not part of the game plan.

King said, 'Yes. Is there a problem?'

'Where is your wife?'

'Downstairs.'

Hesitation.

More confusion.

The guy was unsure how to proceed. He had limited English as it was, and wasn't particularly nuanced in manipulation.

He said, 'Sir, could you bring wife up here, please?'

'No.'

'I need to see who is getting room.'

King allowed rage to settle over his features, and said, 'She's very tired. That would be incredibly rude if you made her come all the way up here. She needs to rest.'

'Yes, sir, but—'

King glared at him. 'Would you like me to take my business elsewhere?'

It wasn't so much the prospect of losing money as it was going against his instincts. The Nepali were overwhelmingly kind and polite people, and even though this man might have been instructed at gunpoint to identify King and Slater together, he wasn't about to offend anyone in his establishment. So he held up both hands and offered a placid look of acceptance and said, 'No, sorry, sir. I give you room, and you pay when you check out. Okay?'

There was little else to say. King wasn't in the mood to loiter with his back turned to the rest of the room, so he nodded his thanks and held his hand out for the key.

The man handed it over.

'Downstairs,' he said. 'Corridor 1. It is labelled. Room 105.'

'Thank you.'

An awkward silence elapsed, and King immediately knew they would find no refuge here. The guy didn't want to make small talk — he no doubt had direct orders to inform someone as soon as he identified the persons-of-interest. Even though Slater wasn't up here with King, enough suspicion had been aroused to proceed.

King turned and walked away. He felt eyes drilling into him, but didn't meet any of the trekkers' gazes. There wasn't likely to be anything hostile in them, but he wasn't in the mood for a chat with anyone.

Tension laced the air.

He sensed the worker's eyes boring into the back of his skull. Thinking, *Are you the man everyone's looking for?*

Yes, King thought. *Yes, I am.*

And we both know it.

He wondered how long it would take for the cavalry to arrive.

Was the guy dialling the phone already?

King didn't look back. He figured if he acted oblivious it might buy more time. They could slow down and formulate a game plan if they thought neither King nor Slater were wise to their presence.

They.

Whoever "they" were.

And that was what made him truly uncomfortable. He and Slater knew *nothing,* and now the owner was alert to who they were.

But there had to be principles in place. Rules and customs that could not be violated. The owner wouldn't have agreed to anything if it ran the risk of ruining his business. A shootout in the hallways of a popular tourist destination wouldn't do anyone any favours in the long-term, so the job would have to be carried out quietly.

That, at least, gave them something.

King made it back to the dry room.

The satellite phone in his pocket shrieked.

And he found Slater half-conscious.

59

H e answered with one hand, and used the other to haul Slater to his feet.

He already knew it was Violetta.

'Please tell me you have something,' he said. 'We're quickly running out of options. I think our cover's blown already.'

'Are you in Gokyo?'

King took almost all of Slater's weight and helped him limp across the dry room into the corridor, plunging them both into shadow. The whole time, he kept the phone pressed to his ear. Slater murmured something. King said, 'Wait one,' and leant over.

'What?' he said to Slater.

'Not ... doing well.'

'No shit.'

'Need rest. Not for long. Just got to ... gather myself.'

'You need a fucking hospital.'

He kept dragging Slater toward room 105.

Then he leant back into the receiver and said, 'Yeah, we're in Gokyo.'

'Were you talking to Will just then?'

'Yeah.'

'He's not doing well, then.'

'I think his body's having trouble circulating oxygen.'

'Headaches? Nausea?'

King relayed the questions.

Slater shook his head. 'No. Just ... heavy.'

'You need to get him to a lower altitude,' Violetta said.

'We can't do that right now.'

'Jason, you're going to have to push on alone.'

'Why?'

'We have another video.'

'Oh, Christ. Can you hold on?'

'Yes.'

They reached a cheap door at the end of the hallway with "105" scratched into the wood. King shoved the key into the lock, twisted, and pushed it open. The whole time he fought the knot in his stomach.

Another video.

He wasn't sure if he wanted to watch.

Slater mumbled, 'What did she say?'

King didn't respond. He helped him into the room and lowered him to one of the thin mattresses. It was freezing, practically the same temperature as outside. King peered out the window, his breath clouding in front of his face. He saw nothing but the outlines of distant buildings obscured by the snowstorm. He drew the blinds shut and helped Slater adjust his position in bed. Then he picked up the phone again.

'How bad is it?' he said.

'Raya's not in it.'

King paused. 'Who is?'

'Oscar Perry.'

60

King took his time to respond.

Then finally he said, 'Just let me watch it.'

'I'll send it through now.'

'I'll call you back.'

He hung up, sat down on the other single bed, and put his elbows on his knees.

Slater said, 'Why the long face?'

'There's another video.'

A pause.

Slater said, 'What did they do to her?'

'Nothing. Violetta said Perry's in it.'

'Show me.'

'It hasn't come through yet, but—'

The phone beeped in his palm.

King opened the file and scrutinised the thumbnail. It showed Oscar Perry, all six-foot-two of him, all his muscle, all that curly blond hair. He still had the same superficial cuts and scratches dotted across his cheeks and jawline, but there was a certain vitality in his eyes that hadn't been there before. He was sitting on a chair in a bare concrete room.

There was a piece of lined paper in his hands.

He was reading from it.

'Hope the pair of you are tired,' he said, his voice stilted as he vocalised the written message. 'You've done well to make it to Gokyo. We thought you'd turn back, but you haven't, so now we're somewhat impressed. We agree to meet with you. Maybe you can be the negotiators for your government instead. But you know what that means. If something happens to Raya, you're the ones responsible. That's a lot of weight on your shoulders. That's a heavy burden to carry.'

Oscar Perry took a deep breath before continuing.

'We are already at a pre-established encampment a short hike down the other side of Gokyo Ri. Don't worry — it's well hidden. We made the climb today. Raya, to her credit, persevered well. The pair of you can meet us there tomorrow at nine a.m., and not a minute later. This is the only opportunity we will give you to resolve this peacefully. Hiking up to this elevation should sap every last bit of energy from you, especially after what you've managed to cover in three days. That's exactly how we want you when we meet face-to-face. We are looking forward to it. Please bring your best negotiation tactics, and don't even think about bringing backup. The benefit of our position is an unobstructed view of *anyone* coming up to the peak. You even think about using a helicopter, we'll know. And we won't be here when you arrive. We know this terrain better than you or anyone in your government.'

Perry gulped, wiped sweat off his brow, and hunched over a little more.

Clearly uncomfortable.

'So,' he continued. 'Those are the conditions. Nine a.m. tomorrow. As you watch this video, we probably know where you are staying. But we will hold back. We will not attack you tonight. We want you tired, but not dead. Raya Parker is clearly worth a lot of money, and we're not about to waste that opportunity. So you can sleep comfortably, knowing that we place value in your lives, and we will see you tomorrow. Do not try to figure out who is behind this. There's no point. Good luck.'

Perry looked up, meeting the gaze of someone behind the camera, and nodded once.

All done.

There was a grunt of approval, and the feed cut out.

King played it back one more time, took in every word that left Perry's mouth, and then when it came to its conclusion for the second time he said, 'It's him.'

Slater said, 'We don't know that.'

King gave him a look, as if to say, *Really?*

'What?'

'You think a Nepali porter wrote that? You think his English is that good?'

'I don't know,' Slater admitted. 'I have no fucking idea what's going on. Care to enlighten me?'

'I'm just as much in the dark as you. I don't know why Perry's doing it, or how he's working with all these people, but it's him. I think he needed to string the porter along as a guide with knowledge of the region until he could meet with the Maoists and wave money in their faces.'

'That doesn't make any sense if you think about it for longer than five minutes.'

'None of this makes any sense,' King sighed.

'Are you going to do it?'

'I think so.'

'You'll die.'

'That's always been a risk. Figured nothing would change on this trip either.'

'I'm telling you not to.'

'And I'm refusing to listen to you. What other chance are we going to get to resolve this?'

'You're being boneheaded,' Slater said. 'You're really going to do exactly what they ask?'

'I have to. And I have to do it alone. You can't even get out of bed.'

'And I'm not going to try to. You know why? Because I can accept when shit's hit the fan. You can't seem to.'

'They don't know who we are.'

'What?'

'They know we're operatives, and I'm sure they're assuming we're elite. But they don't know the details. Even if it's Perry — he's still just a bodyguard. He wouldn't know about any of it — the history of Black Force, the genetic reflexes, what we've collectively been through. I can still get the jump on them. I'm sure of it.'

Slater practically rolled his eyes. 'Call your girlfriend, then. Tell her what you just told me. See how she reacts.'

'I'm going to do it regardless of what she says.'

'Leave now, then. Take them by surprise.'

'No,' King hissed. 'Don't you understand why this needs to play out the way they want?'

'Maybe I'm slipping,' Slater muttered, adjusting himself in bed. 'Maybe I'm missing the point. To me it all sounds insane.'

'They're telling the truth about having the terrain advantage. It'd only take a couple of sentries scattered about to see me coming from miles away. That's the advantage of a peak. There's only one way to get to it. If neither of us do this, they'll get angry, and she'll probably die. I need to play along and hope like hell that my reflexes hold up to the test when it's time to go for the draw.'

'And if they strip you of all weapons before they let you meet with whoever's orchestrating this?'

'Then I'll just have to shoot it out when they try to take my gun off me.'

'Let's see how I am in the morning,' Slater mumbled. 'I might be able to join you.'

King stared at him. 'No. You won't.'

Slater made to respond, but didn't.

He just quietly nodded his agreement.

Then he drifted into an uneasy sleep.

King stayed perched on the edge of the bed, struggling to muster the courage to call Violetta back.

Then she called.

He stepped outside, picked it up and said, 'I'm going tomorrow morning. I don't care what my orders are. That's what I'm doing.'

61

Slater didn't dream.

He entered a sleep so deep and undisturbed that when he finally came out of it he thought, *That's what it might feel like to die.* It took him minutes to worm his way out of the fogginess. He rolled onto his side — painfully, laboriously.

King was watching him.

Clearly concerned.

Slater mumbled, 'What time is it?'

'Nearly midnight.'

'Have you slept?'

'Not yet.'

'You need to.'

'You need it more.'

Slater figured he'd give himself a test. He sat up, and his muscles throbbed. It took everything he had just to lever his torso off the mattress. He put his feet on the floor, rocked back and forth a couple of times, and stood up.

His heart rate shot through the roof.

He could feel it smashing against his chest wall,

pumping two times a second, then three. Somewhere close to 180bpm.

At his age, practically his max heart rate.

He sat back down, collapsing on the bed. Lowered his head back to the pillow and tried to breathe as deeply as possible. When his heart settled, he said, 'I hate to break it to you, but I'm not going anywhere.'

'I can see that,' King said.

'My chest...'

'I know. I was watching the vein in your neck. Counting the beats per minute. You're not in good shape.'

'To say the least.'

'You'll be okay,' King said. 'Your muscles aren't getting enough oxygen. You just need to stop moving for a day or so, and then get to a lower altitude.'

'You're twenty pounds heavier than me. Why aren't you in this state too?'

'It's genetic. Can happen to anyone. Be grateful you don't have any of the other altitude symptoms.'

'So you're still going through with this?'

'I have to. It's the only way it ends.'

'It could end with you helping me back down the mountain. It could end with us both living to fight another day.'

'There's no difference between that outcome and giving up.'

'It wouldn't be giving up. It would be making the tactical decision.'

'The right tactical decision is to make that climb. Sure, they want me tired, but don't think they're not feeling it too. They could go anywhere from here if we retreat. It wouldn't take much for them to bunker down somewhere along the Cho-La Pass. Then they can negotiate for as long as they want. No-one's mounting an effective rescue operation at that altitude. They know we're down here, so they came up with a plan to get us where they want us, but it's not smart for them. This is my chance to capitalise on that.'

'It's not smart.'

'Nothing in this game is.'

'And what do I do when you're gone? Lie here and hope I don't get shot?'

'Point your weapon at that door for eight hours and wait for me to come back. You don't even have to move.'

'You don't get it,' Slater said. 'I *can't* move. Even if my life depended on it. My heart would explode if I tried to muscle my way out of here. If you leave, I'm a sitting duck.'

'They promised they wouldn't come for us. I believe them. They think we're valuable. They think we're their chance to negotiate.'

'And what will happen when they see you heading up Gokyo Ri alone?'

King didn't answer.

'Well?' Slater said.

'Then you need to be ready.'

'No shit.'

'I'll help you switch rooms tomorrow morning,' King said. 'The owner knows we're in 105. That'll delay them, at least.'

'Not for long.'

'You can play hide and seek for eight hours,' King said. 'It's possible.'

'And if I'm caught?'

'Then shoot them.'

Slater raised his arms in disbelief — it took all the effort he could muster. He said, 'What can I honestly do like this?'

King said, 'You need to do this for me. It's our only chance to pull this off.'

'*Your* only chance.'

'We operated alone for the majority of our careers,' King said. 'It can't be that hard to do it again.'

'For you, maybe. In case you didn't notice, I can't move.'

'We're going around in circles,' King said. 'Sit in bed, point your gun at the door, and don't move until I get back.'

Slater lay still.

King said, 'I need sleep.'

'Go for it.'

King rolled over, nestled into his sleeping bag, and fell quiet.

In the darkness, Slater muttered, 'And what if you don't come back?'

62

Morning arrived unceremoniously.

There hadn't been a peep of hostility overnight. King woke up at four in the morning as his alarm went off, and within seconds he was fully alert. He sat up and rubbed his ankle — the swelling had reduced. He didn't know whether to take that as a positive or not.

In all likelihood, it would only mean he'd arrive at death's door faster.

There was no natural light coming in through the windows. The landscape outside was dark and silent. Most trekkers rose at five a.m. to get the ascent started — King was up and moving well before they'd stirred from their slumber.

He dressed in fresh hiking gear, double-checked that his P320 had a full clip, and inserted the magazine back into the weapon. Then he gave himself the once-over.

This is it, he thought.

When he turned around, Slater was wide awake, watching him.

King said, 'Are you any better?'

'No.'

'Let's get you up. I'll find you an empty room.'

'Don't bother,' Slater said. 'It's pointless.'

'Why?'

'Didn't you see the rooms when we arrived yesterday? The empty ones are bolted shut. You'd need to rob the owner at gunpoint, and then he'd know which key he was giving you anyway. It's futile.'

King thought about it. 'I could put you in the—'

'Anywhere else you put me inflates the risk of civilian casualties,' Slater interrupted. 'That's not what we came here to do.'

King chewed his bottom lip in consideration, but he was exhausted. He had few alternatives to offer. He knew he wasn't at the same level as Slater, but their mammoth journey had fatigued him all the same. His body was weary, his mind was considerably dull, and he couldn't think of a better idea.

He said, 'You sure?'

'No. But I doubt you're sure about hiking up Gokyo Ri either. This was never going to be ideal for either of us.'

King said, 'This better not be the last time I see you.'

'Don't worry about me. You said it yourself — all I've got to do is point my gun at the door. Your part's a little trickier.'

'So if this is the last time we see each other...?'

'Then that's the job.'

King nodded. 'That's the job.'

'Go get it done.'

'I need you in somewhat decent condition if I make it back with Raya.'

'"*If?*" You will.'

'Maybe.'

'When have you failed?'

'Plenty of times.'

'But when has it killed you?'

'There's a first time for everything.'

Neither of them knew what to say. One thing was for sure — they hadn't anticipated this level of suffering. They thought they'd known exhaustion, until *true* exhaustion hit them in the face. King shrugged off his own worries and anxieties and managed a nod of farewell.

There was nothing left to say. They each knew what they had to do. It wouldn't be easy for either of them. King had an uneasy suspicion that the insurgents would come for Slater as soon as he was spotted on his own at the base of Gokyo Ri. Wipe out one of the American operatives, and force the other into negotiations.

All the better if they got him alive, too.

More bargaining power.

King stepped out of room 105 and made his way outside. The stars were incredible, a glittering canopy that gave the landscape a touch of silvery illumination. He saw the vast mass of Gokyo Ri literally dwarfing the village, and checked he had all the supplies he needed in the rucksack slung over one shoulder — a full water bottle, anti-flash glasses, and four spare magazines for the Sig Sauer. The P320 was at his waist, ready for instant use.

Other than that, it was up to the three pounds of grey matter between his ears to get the job done.

Which is what it always came down to. Thankfully, he'd been honing his brain for most of his life.

So he got started. He used a manmade path of rocks to traverse a glacial stream, and then it was a long flat slog to the base of Gokyo Ri. He reached the foot of the climb, took one deep breath to steel himself for what was to come, and hardened his mind as he took the first step.

Then he began to ascend.

It proved monotonous enough. It was steeper than anything he and Slater had covered so far in Nepal, and the storm from the previous day had left a thin coating of snow over the trail, leading to a muddy, sloshy journey, but he managed well enough. He wasn't so much concentrating on the climb as he was on what he'd find when he reached the top. It wasn't difficult to keep his pace consistent and his breathing measured, and all he had to focus on was making sure not to burn himself out before he reached the peak.

He quickly realised it would be a long, gruelling climb.

He had five hundred metres to ascend vertically. Nearly a quarter of the way through the climb, blue daylight crept into the edges of the surrounding mountain ranges, giving him a better view of what was underfoot. He'd slipped a couple of times, but his ankle was sturdier by the day, and it was holding up.

He paused to fetch his bottle and take a few gulps of water, and when he craned his neck to stare up at the peak, he thought he saw something.

Hundreds of feet above.

The barely visible outline of a silhouette, already at the top of Gokyo Ri, staring down.

Observing.

King watched it for a few seconds, trying to take in as many details as he could.

It was futile.

A moment later, the silhouette vanished from sight.

Overwhelmed by dread, he continued onward.

63

There was a flurry of activity in the rooms at five a.m., almost an hour after King left.

Slater heard a faint cacophony of alarms go off within the same minute, as each smartphone struck five on the dot. There were the sounds of feet shuffling, and zips gliding up jackets, and trekking poles touching the ground. Then doors opened and hikers grumbled quiet greetings to each other as they bled out into the main corridor, heading to the other building for breakfast and tea before the day's climb.

He listened without moving, keeping the Sig Sauer in a tight grip. When the last of the Gokyo Ri trekkers vacated the premises, the building returned to silence.

Slater kept his eyes fixed on the door, and did his best to focus on recovery.

He wasn't sure exactly what he was trying to achieve. He knew descending the mountain was all that would help. It would take weeks for his body to adapt to this altitude, and he had mere hours before shit was bound to hit the fan one way or the other.

Either King wouldn't return and he'd be left to fend for himself, or King would return with Raya in tow and a pissed-off Maoist splinter group hot on his heels.

The cold never let up, leeching through the thin walls and chilling him to the bone. He dragged the sleeping bag over himself, but didn't dare get inside. Even though his body was on the verge of total shutdown, he knew there'd be some final morsel of energy locked away that he could access when his life depended on it. He didn't want to use it up struggling to get out of a sleeping bag.

So he lay there and shivered and focused on his breathing and watched the door and tried not to get tired.

Minutes blurred into hours, and he lost all sense of time. He refused to check his phone — it would only make the time pass slower. Light steadily bled in through the frosted window pane as the sun rose behind the distant mountains. Now he could see the breath clouding in front of his face on each exhale, which somehow only made him colder. It was the inevitability of hyperintention — draw your attention to something, and it only makes it worse. He could see the physical effect of the cold in his breath, and it only served to chill him to the core.

His teeth started chattering when there was a knock at the door.

He nearly leapt out of his skin.

He listened hard. He hadn't heard anyone approaching. Whoever was out there was making a deliberate effort to keep quiet. But it couldn't be the insurgents. Not if they wanted him dead. They'd simply kick the door in and come through the window simultaneously. Hit the room from all angles, and there's no way he'd survive the onslaught.

Slater angled the Sig toward the door, squaring up the barrel with its centre. He kept the sleeping bag draped over his mid-section, but the material wouldn't affect the bullet's trajectory at all.

He said, 'Come in.'

He'd left the door unlocked. It'd take all his effort just to cross the room, so he'd elected to allow ease of access in case someone showed up to enquire about anything banal.

The door swung open.

It was the man who'd checked them in the previous day.

His hands were bare.

But Slater kept the gun angled at his chest all the same.

The guy couldn't see it, obviously. The gun was covered by the sleeping bag. But if he tried anything hostile at all, Slater would put a bullet in his heart.

Slater said, 'What do you want?'

The man looked sheepish. 'You are still here.'

'Yes. I'm sick.'

'Your friend...?'

'He went on ahead.'

A pause, and then, 'To where?'

'You know where.'

The owner bowed his head. 'I cannot pretend I do not know. You could tell ... when I checked you both in.'

'Yeah.'

'They said they would kill my family.'

'I know. You're not the first person they threatened.'

'I had to do what they say.'

'I know.'

'I am sorry.'

'Are you here to kill me?'

The owner shook his head.

'Are you here to talk?'

'I saw your friend leave an hour ago. I thought you stay. Had to make sure.'

'What are you going to do now?'

'Give you option to kill me.'

Slater paused. 'What?'

'They tell me to call and give them information when you or your friend leave. I have delayed long enough. If I do not tell them, they carry out their promise. I know these people. Very bad people. They hurt my children if I do not do what they say.'

'Then why are you here?'

'To give you warning. To tell you to run. I do not want you to die.'

'I can't run,' Slater said. 'I can't even move. So it looks like I'm staying right here.'

'They hurt me and my family if I do not call.'

'Then call.'

'You can kill me,' the owner said. 'If you want. I have ... dishonoured you. You are guest here, and I put your life in danger. This is not something you forgive.'

'It's fine,' Slater said. 'Call them.'

'I know you have gun under there. You shoot me?'

'No.'

'Why not?'

'Because this isn't your fault, and you're backed up against a wall with no way out. I don't blame you. Make the call.'

The owner thought about it for a long time. He said, 'I respect you.'

'Thank you.'

Then the man thought about it some more. 'Give me your key.'

'Why?'

'I give you one for empty room, and replace it. Then I tell them you staying in that room. It look like I'm telling truth because that is only key I give out. You understand?'

Slater half-smiled. 'Yeah, I understand. You'd do that?'

The owner fished a key out of his pocket and threw it over.

The digits *108* were inscribed into it.

'Maybe this buy you some time,' the owner said. 'Maybe this mean you live.'

'Maybe.'

'Do you hate me?'

'No.'

'Good luck, sir,' the man said. 'I am sorry.'

'It's okay.'

'I leave you now.'

'Okay.'

'Can I bring you food and drink? Before ... everything happen?'

Slater thought about it. 'Sure.'

He tossed the *105* key over, leaving his life in the owner's hands.

64

I t took King two hours to summit Gokyo Ri.

He covered the last half like a walking zombie, dragging his feet with every step. He'd underestimated the severity of the slope. It was steeper than any terrain he'd covered before. If he was in good shape at the bottom, he would have breezed through it, but the miles he'd clocked up over the last few days were finally taking their toll. He reached the archway of multi-coloured prayer flags at the peak in a sweaty, breathless heap.

Despite everything, he took time to admire the view. He was the first trekker on the peak, and a single glance down the mountain showed the next group behind him were at least an hour from the top. He checked briefly for any sign of hostiles, but there was little point. If they wanted him dead, they'd potshot him from a distance. He was putting blind faith in them to stick to their word, at least until he could meet with them face-to-face.

So there was no harm in soaking in one of the most incredible views he'd ever laid eyes on.

He spotted Everest to the east. It was further away than

most of the mountains in sight, but it still dwarfed them. It was something to behold. Below he could make out the village of Gokyo, just a speck in front of a glacier that was at least twenty miles in length. To the south-west he saw the Renjo-La Pass in all its beauty, consisting of endless snowy mountains twisting and turning in every direction. There wasn't a cloud in the sky, and by now the sun had risen over the mountain ranges, coating everything in a golden hue.

Still spectacular, despite the circumstances.

He knew the kidnappers and their rebel buddies were residing somewhere to the north. It was the only side of Gokyo Ri that wasn't home to a sheer descent down the mountainside. Instead, the peak declined maybe fifty feet into a natural bowl in the landscape, covered entirely in snow and surrounded by peaks. The terrain was visibly treacherous and there was no clear path leading down there. Gokyo Ri was meant to be climbed and descended via the one path. There was no room to be trekking around the unstable north side that led further into the mountains.

King would have to figure out his own way down.

He knew they were watching him. He could feel eyes on him from *somewhere* — there were endless vantage points down in that rocky maze. They'd be peering out from all of them. They'd leave nothing to chance.

'Well,' he said under his breath, 'here goes nothing.'

He could sense the lack of oxygen in the air as he set off again. Each breath seemed to come up short — no matter how much air he sucked in, his system pined for more. He deliberately exacerbated his breathing as he set a measured pace down the north side of the peak, sucking in giant lung-fuls of air.

His muscles were aching, but he didn't panic. It could

still be chalked up to general exhaustion rather than the crippling effects of altitude.

If he succumbed to the same fate as Slater, then he'd never make it back down.

But he wasn't there yet.

And, if that was the way it was going to go, he'd fight it until his last breath.

He made it a few dozen feet through the knee-high snow before he sensed the first sign of movement. It came from a cluster of boulders to his right, and he picked it up in his peripheral vision.

But he didn't overreact.

A man stepped out from behind one of the rocks.

Clad in faded camouflage fatigues.

Wearing black shiny boots.

Pointing an AK-47 at his face.

'Hey,' King said, hunched over against the wind chill.

The guy didn't budge. His aim didn't waver. He wasn't going to slip up — not with this much on the line, not with the potential for unimaginable riches dangling in front of his face.

'Don't accidentally shoot me,' King said. 'You know why I'm here.'

No response. No movement.

King said, 'You want to pat me down for weapons?'

'No. Walk.'

Smart man, King thought.

If the guy got into range, King could batter the cumbersome Kalashnikov away with a single swipe. Then he'd break the man's neck for having the gall to point a loaded weapon at him. But the insurgent clearly recognised these risks — King's frame was intimidating to anyone — and he kept his distance, skewering himself into the snow, looking through the AK-47s sights, unblinking.

King said, 'Walk where?'

'Keep going. Down there.'

'Where?'

'Walk or I shoot.'

'No you won't. You don't want to upset your boss. The girl is worth a lot of money. I'm the guy who will get you that money. You understand how that works?'

'Walk.'

Stalemate.

Call it delirium, call it recklessness, call it idiocy. King didn't know which label to assign to it, but he decided not to draw his weapon. It would be relatively simple, and the odds were in his favour. A single jerky movement to the left and then a dive to the right, throwing the rebel's aim off for the split second it would take to get the Sig Sauer in his hand and the bullet through the guy's forehead. The sun would help him, reflecting off all the snow, compromising the man's aim. King had the reflexes, the training, and the track record to pull it off.

But he didn't do it.

Instead he said, 'Okay,' and trudged down the slope through the snow.

The insurgent followed, keeping at least a dozen feet between them at all times.

King could sense the barrel aimed at his back. So he went slow, which was easy considering the circumstances. He was dead tired and it was hard to breathe. The wind died off as they sunk lower into the natural valley between the peaks, and then they were surrounded by clusters of rocks and boulders, all coated in powdery snow.

Obscured from the sight of any trekkers' who happened to reach the top of Gokyo Ri behind them.

King could feel how alone he was. It was palpable, and it'd get to him if he let it. It'd transform into doubt, plaguing him with the knowledge that even if he got wounded and survived, no one would ever find him.

Behind him, the rebel growled, 'Here.'

King looked around.

And then he saw it.

The mouth of a shallow cave. It was hard to spot amidst the maze of rocks, but the shadows caught his eye and he realised every answer he'd been seeking rested in that gaping maw.

'Inside?' he said.

'Yes.'

King only had to take a couple of steps forward before he saw them.

Two silhouettes, maybe twenty feet inside the cave.

A small woman, and a large man.

The man was holding her out in front, and had a handgun pressed into the side of her head.

King trudged the final few steps through the snow and stepped into the mouth of the cave.

There was just enough sunlight to make out the curly blond hair.

King said, 'You could have just told us at the start. It wouldn't have changed anything. You'll still get your money.'

Oscar Perry kept his mouth shut. His eyes were rabid, almost animalistic. The shadows were deep, but the sun was at the appropriate angle to illuminate him. His clothes were dirty, ripped in a few places. He had a tight grip on the handgun — another Sig Sauer P320 (probably the same shipment) — and his finger inside the trigger guard.

Raya looked okay, all things considered. She was tall for her age, pale and lean. Probably paler than usual due to the bloody bandage wrapped around her hand. The shock of losing a finger would take some time to wear off. She wore hiking gear and had deep bags under her eyes. Her hair was slick with sweat and grease. She was shaking.

King took another step forward. 'You wanted me here to talk. So let's talk.'

Perry still didn't speak.

He didn't take his eyes off King.

Didn't blink.

Didn't make a sound.

Just watched.

King took a final half-step forward, and behind him the rebel said, 'Hey.'

King looked over his shoulder casually, both eyebrows raised. Like, *What's the problem?*

The rebel opened his mouth to say something.

King blew his forehead apart with a single round.

He'd drawn his own P320 with half his body facing away from the insurgent, so the guy had never seen it coming. The body hit the cave floor with a wet *smack,* but King didn't see it because at lightning speed he whirled around and had the gun pointed between Perry's eyes before anyone could even blink.

Reflexes, he thought.

They've saved me more times than I can count.

Perry barely reacted. He still didn't say a word.

'Now let's talk,' King said.

'Not to me,' Perry said.

The words came out croaky. Like they were his first of the day.

Like he'd never been prepared to speak.

King said, 'What?'

'He was waiting for you to do that.'

'Who?'

'I'm being told to stand here.'

'Oh.'

'This gun is empty.'

A barrel touched the back of King's neck.

65

S later lowered the empty plate to the carpet next to his bed.

The motion made his heart speed up.

He lay back and tried to focus on digesting the food. There was little else worth paying attention to besides listening out for intruders. There was an invisible ball of lead on his chest, pushing him deeper into the thin mattress, turning his bones to deadweight. He couldn't move. Couldn't concentrate. Could barely breathe.

It had been three hours since King left. By now, he should be at the summit. It was all playing out up there, far out of reach, too far for Slater to offer any kind of assistance — not that he could help anyway. He needed to descend *now* — reach a lower altitude so his body had some hope of recovering — but he couldn't do it alone.

And by now, the insurgents would know he was here.

Alone.

Compromised.

Vulnerable.

They'd want to do it quietly. No point ruining their

country's tourism industry by going into a trekkers' safe haven with all guns blazing. Far easier to slip into the room without disturbing the other patrons and put a suppressed round through the top of Slater's head.

He just had to hope the owner stayed true to his word.

If not, they'd overwhelm him.

Then he heard it, and his pulse quickened. He fought it back down and listened hard, struggling to a seated position in bed. Everything hurt, but he didn't pay attention to it. He focused everything on what he'd heard.

A footstep.

He wouldn't have suspected anything if a civilian had come stomping into the corridor, but this person was making a deliberate effort to stay quiet. Much like the owner had done nearly an hour earlier. Slater had switched to operational mode thirty minutes ago, figuring his next encounter would be with someone brandishing a loaded weapon.

Another footstep.

Then another.

Right outside his door.

He braced himself.

Slipped a finger inside the trigger guard.

Aimed the handgun at the door.

Exhaled.

Ready.

Then there was a rapid flurry of footsteps, and an almighty *crash*, and a door flew open, and a suppressed gunshot coughed and echoed through the rooms.

Not Slater's door.

Not Slater's room.

They'd gone for 108, just down the hall.

Slater breathed out, and the adrenaline hit him in a

wave, as he imagined it would. He knew that was the trigger he needed. He also knew time was finite. Stress chemicals didn't last forever. You could only stay wired to the eyeballs for a narrow window of time.

But for now...

Slater leapt out of bed, good as new. If anyone had been watching him as an observer for the last couple of days, they might have assumed it was a Herculean effort to lunge to his feet, but he knew enough about the primal workings of the human body to take it in his stride. He crossed to the door, opened it softly, and leaned into the hallway.

The doorway to room 108 was across the hall, maybe a dozen feet down.

There was no door there.

Someone had smashed it off its hinges and sent it tumbling into the room.

Slater couldn't see anyone. Whoever had rushed 108 was now inside, probably hurling sheets off mattresses, realising the room was empty, rapidly calculating alternatives.

Slater counted to three.

Then a tall wiry man clad in a balaclava and camouflage fatigues crept back out through the open doorway. His mannerisms were sheepish — he'd created a whole lot of noise and had nothing to show for it. There was an AK-47 in his hands. Serious firepower for an assault on a crippled man. Clearly they didn't underestimate Slater... but the guy didn't get a chance to use the rifle.

He looked up and noticed Slater standing there, and that was the last thing he saw. Slater pumped the trigger once and gore exited the back of the man's skull, and then Slater was on the move. He kicked the guy in the chest before he could collapse and sent the corpse splaying back through the doorway, where it crashed into two more guys on the way out. They didn't fall over, but it took them a beat to lower their dead friend to the carpet and reach for their weapons again.

Slater filled the doorway.

He shot one of them through the top of the head and the other in the face when he jerked upright to greet the new threat.

Reacting to an impulse, Slater pivoted in the doorway and took a step out into the corridor. He aimed down the length of it, levelling the barrel with the glass entrance doors and the snowy embankment beyond.

Fresh insurgents stepped into the entranceway, responding to the blaring gunshots. Their guns were up and they were ready for a war.

They didn't get one.

Slater put a round into each of them.

One.

Two.

Three.

They dropped like dominoes, a couple of them crashing into each other on the way down. The third guy pitched forward and fell straight through the glass door, shattering it. What ordinarily would have been an almighty noise fell on deaf ears.

Slater shrugged off the temporary hearing loss and backpedalled into room 105.

Because now his muscles were leeching, protesting, whining, his heart rate rising, his brain screaming, *The tank's empty. You're done.*

He stumbled through the doorway and barely got it closed before his legs gave out and he slid to the floor.

He tried not to panic, but it was like trying to hold back a tsunami with a dam wall.

Chaos reigned on the other side of the door. The handful of trekkers still in their rooms were now screaming, running, banging into walls and doors as they fled. Under the impression they were now caught in the midst of a deadly mass shooting. When they got out of the building, they might keep running until their legs gave out.

Slater closed his eyes, pressed his back to the door, and tried his best not to pass out.

66

'Drop it, please,' an accented voice said.

King calculated how fast he could pivot, smash the gun away, seize the upper hand.

He couldn't.

He'd been through enough combat to know when the odds were hopeless.

So he dropped it.

He didn't have a choice.

Turned around slowly, so the barrel came to rest against his forehead.

'I know you move fast,' the porter said. 'Don't try it with me. It won't work.'

King believed him. The small man's calloused finger was millimetres off the trigger. He was barely a shade over five feet tall, with skin like leather and an unimposing physique, but he only could have pulled this off if he had an arsenal of experience in this very realm.

And then the opportunity was gone anyway, because the porter backed up a few steps. Now he was out of range, leaving King a sitting duck in the depths of the cave.

'Oscar, put the gun on the floor,' the man said. 'Then all three of you stand in a line.'

Perry complied. King heard him lower the empty handgun to the cave floor, and then sensed the man's size-able bulk in his peripheral vision. Perry stood still as a statue beside him, and Raya joined them. None of them said a word. They couldn't afford to.

Then King decided to test his luck.

'Mukta, isn't it?' he said.

The porter nodded.

King said, 'That's Indian?'

'I was a Naxalite,' Mukta explained, 'for most of my adult life.'

India's Maoist insurgency.

No wonder he was able to recruit Nepal's own rebels so effortlessly.

Their supposed cause was one and the same.

'And now you're here,' King said.

'Now I'm here.'

Mukta whistled low under his breath, and a trickle of insurgents bled into the mouth of the cave. They were all identical, seemingly materialising out of nowhere, dressed in the familiar dark green fatigues and draped in balaclavas. King counted four of them, plus the porter.

The porter.

King said, 'Your job. That was all a front?'

'Yes and no. It's a good cover story. I'm small, and you can tell I've lived a hard life. I don't look any different from them. If I pretend I can't speak English, I'm practically a chameleon.'

King recalled what Violetta had said. *Most kidnappings aren't actually reported.*

He said, 'How many ransoms have you racked up out here?'

Mukta's eyes lit up. 'Enough.'

'How long have you been doing it?'

'You're an inquisitive one, aren't you?'

'I'm here to negotiate.'

Mukta laughed. 'Cute.'

The faint inklings of dread began to creep up King's spine.

Because there was nothing more dangerous than an enemy who didn't care about money.

King said, 'You're in the kidnapping business. Your hostage is worth a lot of cash. I'm the one who can put you in touch with the necessary parties. Isn't that what you want?'

'It *was*,' Mukta said, looking bored. 'Now I figure it's not worth the hassle.'

'Why?'

'Several reasons.'

'Care to enlighten me?'

'What's the point?'

King shrugged. 'Some basic level of respect. I made it up here, didn't I?'

Mukta thought about it. King could see the gears whirring.

Do I make the age-old mistake of talking too much? the man was thinking.

But that's the thing about age-old mistakes.

They keep getting made for a reason.

It's *awfully* tempting to brag.

Finally Mukta said, 'Fine. Here you go. This business is volatile. The girl's not worth the hassle she's created. And besides, I now have two prizes that are much more valuable.'

King stayed quiet.

Mukta said, 'One of them is a laptop.'

Beside King, Perry visibly tensed.

Mukta noticed, and half-smiled. 'Frustrating, isn't it? You see, Oscar here is a terrible liar. I started playing around with the thing on a whim and saw the colour drain from his face. That told me all I needed to know.'

King said nothing.

Mukta said, 'The second prize is you.'

'Is it?'

'I saw how fast you shot my bait. You're a fuckin' freak of nature, aren't you? How much would your government pay to get you back?'

'That's a dangerous game to play.'

'I know. You probably think I'm some dumb henchman. But I can tell when I'm out of my depth. It wasn't in the job description to deal with super-soldiers. So I think I'm deciding, right here and now, to get out of the business. I've done enough of these. I've milked those negotiators for all they're worth. I know they're not happy with me. And I can't be bothered dealing with live hostages anymore, so I'll sell the laptop to the highest bidder and that'll be that.'

He turned to look at his men. 'I think it's time to disappear, don't you?'

One by one, they nodded.

'Cashing out,' Mukta said, bemused. 'Never thought I'd see the day. As for you three...'

A pause.

A long, deadly, ominous pause.

'...well, I guess you're no longer any use to me.'

King sensed what was about to happen and screamed,

'*No!*' to try and throw Mukta off his rhythm, but the man was a professional.

He didn't hesitate.

Didn't even blink.

Just turned and raised his weapon and shot Raya Parker in the head.

PART II

67

Somehow, Slater drifted off.

He didn't intend to. It was the last thing he wanted. In reality it was pure exhaustion, but it sure felt like falling asleep. His vision faded and his brain powered down and he gently slid down the doorway, inch by inch, until the whole thing smashed against his upper back as someone rammed it from the other side.

The jolt woke him up in an instant, and with a shock like a car jumpstarting he rolled away from the door.

The next impact broke straight through the lock.

The door flew open, its trajectory missing Slater's unprotected face by inches. It swung on past and there was a man right there in the doorway, wielding another Kalashnikov. He was hopped up on either natural or artificial chemicals, and ready to kill with his bare hands if it came to that.

But it didn't.

He was expecting Slater to be standing, and maybe half-expecting him to be stretched out on the bed, but he certainly didn't think he'd be lying on the floor. Slater shot upwards from his back twice. One bullet struck the guy in the chest, and the other snapped his head back.

He was dead before he hit the floor.

Slater reached out with one foot, caught the edge of the door, and swung it shut. It didn't close all the way, catching on the corpse's shoulder.

He tried to sit up.

His chest pounded faster and faster.

He sunk back to the floor and grimaced, staring up at the ceiling.

Move! he screamed at himself. *Just move!*

He couldn't.

The adrenaline he'd used to decimate the first wave had depleted him entirely. There was nothing left. He inched across the carpet on his back, dragging himself across the floor, painfully slow. He reached the doorway and extended a weak hand, fingers outstretched. He placed his palm on the corpse's shoulder and pushed. It was like moving a five hundred pound weight. The guy didn't budge.

Slater took a deep breath, then strained with all his might.

His face contorted into a grotesque mask of exertion, but he battled not to make a sound.

The body shifted.

First an inch, then half a foot, and then...

It was clear.

Slater reached for the door, willing his aching muscles to just *hold on,* and gripped the edge.

He closed the door.

And collapsed against the wood.

There wasn't a chance in hell he was putting up any more of a fight. The next wave would kill him. There was a body directly outside his door, and if that didn't signify it as a location of interest then he didn't know what would. Then again, there were half a dozen more corpses scattered through the rest of the hallway.

He had to hope...

Time passed — seconds, or minutes, or hours. No way to know for sure. He was barely holding onto consciousness, let alone managing to keep track of the clock. But eventually there were more footsteps. Boots crunched shards of glass underfoot as a fresh party of rebels made their way into the building. He could sense them sweeping the corridor, searching all vantage points, clearing all corners.

He heard them move right past the door.

And then a pair of footsteps doubled back.

Slater held his breath. His vision had narrowed to a dark tunnel, and he was barely lucid. He raised his gun in a sweaty, shaking palm, but he couldn't find the energy to take it all the way through its trajectory. It came up short, halfway toward pointing at the door, and then his hand dropped as he lost all ability to move.

The footsteps stopped right outside his door.

There was a lengthy pause.

Then a sound eerily similar to scratching.

Fingers against clothing.

His eyes half-open, Slater watched the door and waited to die.

Then he heard a muttered curse, followed by the footsteps pattering away. Slater waited, breathing hard and deep. That was about the only thing he could do. The newcomers swept room 108 — he could tell where the majority of the sound was resonating from — but they didn't seem concerned about the other rooms.

Then what was...?

He put it together. One of the rebels had bent down and

checked the pulse of the corpse out there. Maybe the dead man was a close friend. Whatever the case, the body must have blended into the half-dozen other dead insurgents scattered down the hallway. The door to Slater's room mustn't have stood out enough to investigate.

Slater fought to control his impulses. Every part of him was on the verge of losing control. It wouldn't take much prompting. He was utterly helpless, all his training thrown out the window, praying the second wave of rebels didn't walk in. They might take him alive if they found him in such a state. That would be a whole new world of awful.

Out in the hallway, they muttered to each other in Nepali. They were keeping their voices low, even though every civilian in the building had fled in a panic minutes earlier. They could shout if they wanted. No one was around to hear. No one was around to help.

Slater tried to raise the Sig Sauer one last time.

His shaking hand made it a few inches off the floor.

Then fell straight back to earth.

He lay still and focused on avoiding a heart attack.

And then, all of a sudden, there was silence.

Slater couldn't help himself. He drifted off again. Consciousness fell away as his body entered survival mode, and he didn't know how much time passed before he came out of it. When he cracked an eyelid open, he realised it might as well have been hours.

But he was still alive, and during the time he'd been out cold his body had scraped together a few morsels of… something.

He sat up.

Cradled the Sig in his palm.

He couldn't move fast. But he could move.

And he knew he needed to get the hell out of Gokyo

before the rebels tore every building in the village apart searching for him.

Shaky, weak, faint, he attempted to get to his feet.

Levered up onto his knees, then fully upright.

He wavered.

But he remained standing.

Then he wobbled forward and threw the door open.

68

King fell to his knees.

He couldn't process it properly.

He and Slater had nearly killed themselves to get here, and now their rescue was eradicated with a single piece of lead.

The only salvation he could find was that she never would have known what was coming. It happened so fast, so unexpectedly, that King almost didn't realise himself until her body hit the cave floor.

Then he dropped, all the feeling sapping out of his legs.

He rocked back on his haunches, turning pale, turning wide-eyed, and tears flooded his eyes.

Mukta actually smiled.

'How does that feel?' the porter said. 'How does it feel to fail? I wouldn't know, to be honest. This shit is too easy.'

Oscar Perry barely batted an eyelid, but King knew he was hurting on the inside. He also knew the bodyguard was confused. Elite operations were about compartmentalising your emotions and refusing to let them affect you in the heat of combat, no matter what happened. And here was supposedly the best warrior on the planet, succumbing to an emotional breakdown. What the hell was King thinking?

King didn't blame him for being surprised.

Mukta and the rebels, however, didn't seem to notice anything out of the ordinary.

King bowed his head and sobbed into the cuff of his sleeve.

'Shut up,' Mukta hissed. 'Stop your whining.'

When King sat up, he scooted back half a foot on his rear.

But he timed it well, so both movements aligned, and Mukta didn't notice.

'Get up,' Mukta said. 'You're pathetic. Makes me embarrassed that I gave up on the ransom. Maybe you're not as special as I thought.'

King moved slow, lethargic with his actions. Like all the life had been sapped out of him. Like he'd lost any motivation to continue. Eyes bloodshot and red with tears, he rolled onto his knees, turning his back to the mouth of the cave. He stared into the dark abyss for a moment, contemplating reasons to get to his feet.

'*Up,*' Mukta roared.

King rose. But as he did he reached out for the object he'd blocked with his body.

The empty Sig Sauer P320 given to Perry to use as bait.

He tucked it in close to his body, rose to his feet, and slotted a fresh magazine home, lifting it gently out of his belt.

Then he turned and unloaded the weapon in the space of three seconds.

He blew the brains out of the two rebels with Kalashnikovs, sending them careening off their feet in the mouth of the cave. Then he put three rounds into the guy with the pistol — two in the chest and one in the head, just to make sure his soul was ripped from his body. He put a round into Mukta's left leg, then his right, disintegrating both his kneecaps. The result was grisly — the porter's legs splayed out at unnatural angles and he broke a few bones in his upper and lower legs as the limbs simply folded beneath him. Mukta passed out from the pain, but King didn't notice because he was already putting the last two rounds of the magazine into the unarmed insurgent hovering in the snow outside. The guy took both bullets to the throat and he died before he could even reach for his neck.

The carnage ended, almost before it had begun.

The echo of the gunshots rippled through the cave, and Oscar Perry said, 'Holy shit.'

King didn't hear it. Fury roared in his ears. First he went over to Raya and made sure she was dead, but he quickly realised there was no room for debate. She had a cylindrical hole in the centre of her forehead, and an exit wound out the back of her skull, and her eyes were glazed over. He bent down and put a gentle hand on her shoulder, horrified by what had unfolded, and then he went straight for the porter.

Mukta was still unconscious, so King took a run-up to build momentum and scythed an open palm through the air, slapping the guy so hard on the cheek that it sounded like another gunshot on the cave walls.

Mukta came awake in a world of pain.

King grabbed him by his mop of hair and held him a few inches off the cave floor.

'I'm going to ask you a few questions,' he said.

Pale and shaking, Mukta noticed his broken mangled legs. 'Ohhh...'

King bashed his head against the ground like a bowling ball.

'Just kill me,' the porter mumbled.

'Soon,' King said. 'I'm still trying to piece this together.'

'What... do you want?'

'How long have you been doing this?'

'Two years.'

'How often are you successful?'

'Almost every ... time. Oh, my legs, oh. Please. Just... help me. Get rid of this pain.'

'No,' King said, and smashed his skull into the rock floor again.

Hard enough to hurt like hell.

Not hard enough to knock him unconscious.

'How much money do you think you've made doing this?'

'Tens... of millions ... of U.S. Dollars. This was... my last job.'

'Why hasn't anyone caught you?'

'Because when they pay the ransom... it's easier for everyone if no one speaks about it.'

'And when they don't pay the ransom?'

'They always do.'

'What made you think you could get away with kidnapping an important government official's daughter?'

'I didn't... know how important... she was. Please. The pain.'

King slapped him across his already-swollen cheek. 'How did you know who she was in the first place?'

'I... pay some people who know who's coming into Nepal. There were... certain flags we picked up on... when Aidan Parker came into the country. No one... knew... what he did. So I knew he was important. I made sure... I got the porter job... for his trek. From there it was easy.'

'Did you know about the laptop beforehand?'

'No.'

'How important do you think the laptop is?'

'I know it will sell for millions. Maybe double my fortune... maybe more. I already told... the rest of my forces... to get it.'

'How many are there?'

'Many more.'

'They'll come for us?'

'They are already on their way.'

'Why are you telling me this?'

'Because maybe... you will help me.'

'Sorry to disappoint,' King said.

He put a huge palm on Mukta's throat and squeezed the life out of him.

69

Like moving through a fever dream.

Slater went down the hallway, drenched in shadow, stepping over bodies, surrounded by desolation. There wasn't a soul in sight. He made it to the shattered entrance doors and stepped right through the frame, holding the Sig in front of him as best he could. The cold hit him like a punch to the chest, threatening to sap *more* of his momentum, but he killed that line of thinking and stepped down into the snow.

He was in a snowy laneway between the two buildings — the main dining room, elevated on stilts a few feet above a snowy embankment, and the dormitory-style accommodation behind him. From there the slope descended to the flat plains between the village and Gokyo Ri.

But not before it gave way to a small divot in the hillside, home to a patch of land filled with dirt and rock. The snow had been cleared away earlier that morning for...

For what?

Slater blinked.

Really?

He saw the helicopter perched there, painted red and silver, powered down as it rested on its landing skids. But he couldn't quite believe it wasn't a figment of his imagination.

When the hell did that show up?

When he was passed out, probably. There wasn't anyone inside it. There were any number of explanations for that — the pilot had landed for a routine supply drop, or to evacuate one of the many trekkers who succumbed to altitude sickness each and every week. The visit in itself was nothing out of the ordinary — there were choppers flying in and out of the remote villages all the time — but the sheer dumb luck *was* worth scrutinising.

Slater didn't believe in coincidences.

But right now, he didn't give a shit what he believed in. There was a helicopter there, ripe for the taking, and he wasn't about to debate the semantics.

He didn't move, though. He swept his surroundings, but frankly it was impossible to cover all his bases. There were probably ten buildings in total facing the helicopter, and all of them had multiple vantage points from which to blast his head off his shoulders.

He just had to hope for...

A door swung open in the dining hall to his left. He pivoted and caught a peripheral glance of a woollen balaclava, and that was all he needed to see.

He swung the P320 up and pumped the trigger ten consecutive times.

He had spare magazines, after all, and nothing to lose anyway.

The rounds shredded everyone in the doorway to pieces. Three or four rebels jerked back inside or collapsed over the threshold, bleeding from entry and exit wounds, either dead or soon to be.

Slater didn't need any further encouragement.

He turned and ran.

Flat-out bolted for the helicopter.

Bad move.

Very bad move.

Give an elite athlete with unparalleled genetic reflexes all the combat training in the world and they're still bound to make mistakes when unfamiliar circumstances arise. Slater had never been affected by altitude. The warrior ethos dictated that the solution to all physical problems was just to tough it out, but that wasn't conducive to success out here. He honestly thought he could make it to the chopper at a sprint. But he made it probably five steps in total before his legs gave out and he sprawled forward on the slope, landing face-first in the powder and tumbling head over heels down the hillside. He picked up steam, his body thrashing this way and that, and when he came to rest in a bruised heap at the bottom of the slope he checked himself over for injuries.

But he genuinely couldn't tell.

He could have a broken leg for all he knew, and the leeching ache in his muscles would override it.

He rolled over in the snow drift and aimed up at the windows of the building on stilts, slotting a fresh magazine home. It felt like he was moving through quicksand. The windows were fogged up, and he couldn't see a thing inside.

Then one of them blew out as a bullet shattered it from within. But any contact with a bullet in flight alters its trajectory, even slightly, so the insurgent firing through the window missed his target. The snow right near Slater's head exploded, and the *thwack* of the impact came a millisecond later, but as soon as he realised he wasn't dead he returned with three rounds through the window frame.

And he struck something, because crimson droplets splattered the grimy windows on either side of the gaping hole.

Slater rolled over, got to his feet, and half-limped, half-walked to the motionless chopper.

'Get the fuck down,' a voice with a British accent hissed. 'Are you out of your mind?'

Slater didn't respond, or even search for the source. He was in a trance, but he still had an objective.

Find cover.

He circled around the nose of the chopper and took refuge behind its chassis.

A thirty-something man in decent shape seized him by the collar.

'Are you fucking crazy?!' he hissed. 'Now they'll shoot it to pieces.'

'Who are you?' Slater mumbled.

'What does it matter? You just got us killed, you moron.'

Slater could barely think.

A bullet thudded into the chassis on the other side of the chopper.

'What's your name?' he said.

'Drew.'

His accent was British.

'Nice to meet you, Drew,' Slater said. 'Can you fly this thing?'

'I'm the pilot.'

'I'll take that as a yes.' Slater looked to the heavens. 'Maybe miracles do happen.'

'Have you lost your fucking mind? You look like you've just rolled out of bed.'

Eyes half-closed, Slater mumbled, 'I feel like it, too.'

'Where'd you get that gun?'

'It's mine,' Slater said. 'Get your own.'

'Are you really making jokes right now?'

'I think I'm delirious, Drew.'

'No shit.'

'How about we get the fuck out of here?'

'I got called here to airlift an African-American man to a lower altitude,' Drew said. 'That wouldn't happen to be you, would it?'

Slater scrunched up his face. 'Who the hell called that in?'

'The owner of the teahouse you're staying in, you moron.'

Slater felt like he was on the verge of death, but he still managed a smile.

You are a good man, Slater thought. *Better than I deserve.*

He said, 'I'm your man, Drew.'

He dropped to a prone position in the snow, aimed underneath the body of the chopper, found a sliver of space available to aim at the windows of the building up the hill, and fired several rounds through the open frame.

More blood sprayed against the windows.

'Now,' Slater said.

Drew lurched forward and threw the cockpit door open.

70

King turned to Perry and said, 'I'll be honest. I thought it was you all along.'

'Obviously,' Perry said, his features forlorn. 'That's what they were going for.'

'You knew?'

'I knew what they were painting me as. I knew why they were stringing me along when I wasn't worth shit. I was the scapegoat if it all went to hell. And it did. They felt the need to come all the way up here to lure you out of your comfort zone, so that says it all.'

'Yeah, well, I didn't help much...'

King trailed off. He thought about looking at Raya, but decided not to. He'd faked the first wave of emotion, but now the threats were neutralised he had more time to process what had happened.

And they were still very far from safety.

Perry said, 'They were going to kill her anyway.'

King looked up. 'They were never going to negotiate?'

'You and your partner killed dozens of his men. I saw him

deteriorating before my eyes. He was losing his shit. That first video — it was his knee-jerk response to the chaos. He thought if he made himself look like a prisoner he'd cause confusion, but it achieved nothing. He was flying off the rails with each failed attempt on your lives. I watched him smash his face into the corner of a table to give himself that eye injury. He was doing anything he thought might work.'

'If his goal was to kill Raya, then he succeeded.'

'It wasn't. He knew you and your friend were dangerous as hell, and he knew if he killed her he'd lose his only chance to manipulate you. His only fucking concern was the laptop.'

'What happened?'

'I knew what was on it. That first night ... they put a gun to my head and strangled Winston in front of me and made me watch. Then they tied me up and carried me over their shoulders out of the teahouse. But I saw them take the laptop, and I freaked. Because that compromises everything. They didn't notice at the time. But then Mukta started playing around with it the next night in front of me and I couldn't help it. I went pale. Tried to act like nothing was wrong, but I'm a terrible actor. I can't keep it together when I'm under duress.'

'Great qualities for a—'

'I know,' Perry hissed. 'Let's not conduct a performance review up here, okay? I have my strengths and my weaknesses. Like we all do.'

Then Perry looked around.

'Except you, apparently.'

King looked at Raya.

'We all have weaknesses,' he said. 'We all come up short.'

Perry looked from King to Raya. 'You do this for a living, huh?'

'Yeah.'

'Does it affect you?'

King glanced at Perry, and the man noticed the hurt in his eyes.

King said, 'How could it not?'

Perry said, 'You're a warrior, man. A true warrior.'

'We're in the same field.'

Perry put his hands behind his head and gazed into space. There was a myriad of emotion in his eyes. He said, 'Yeah, but I'm up the shallow end with floaties on. You're way in the deep.'

'Let's get ourselves out of the deep,' King said. 'Ready for a hike down?'

Perry went pale, and gave his head a slight shake. 'We're screwed, man.'

'Why?'

'That was the plan all along. Mukta knew how valuable that laptop was, so he organised a bottleneck in case they ran into trouble up here with you.'

'You mean...?'

'There's a twenty-man party of Maoists disguised as guides and porters on their way up to Gokyo Ri right now. Like a pincer trap. There's nothing but open terrain up here. They'll kill us. We need to wait it out.'

King swore. He almost punched the cave wall, but stopped himself short of breaking his hand.

Perry said, 'What?'

'I can't wait it out.'

'Yes you can. We have to.'

'You know that partner you kept mentioning?'

'Yeah,' Perry said, then trailed off. 'Where is he?'

'Down in Gokyo. He can barely move. The altitude's fucking with his system. His heart's set to burst if he exerts himself too hard. Not enough oxygen.'

'Christ. They'll be sweeping the village for him.'

'I know. So I can't spend all day here.'

Perry went quiet.

King said, 'Actually, if I'm being honest, I can't afford to spend another minute here.'

'They'll kill us,' Perry said. 'Twenty against two on a wide-open slope with civilians in the crossfire. Tell me what's tactical about that.'

King thought hard.

There was one way up, and one way down.

No alternatives.

This time, he did punch the cave wall.

71

King's fist went numb, but he barely felt it.

Panic was doing its best to seize hold of him. He battled it back down.

'Fuck this place,' he said. 'There has to be another way down.'

Perry shook his head. 'There's nothing. Trust me.'

'You've swept the whole mountain?'

'Okay,' Perry conceded. 'You can wade through waist-deep snow on either side of the trekkers' trail if you want. But they'd spot you in seconds. It's a sheer vertical slope. There's no covert way down.'

King mulled it over, and surveyed the bodies. 'We could put their gear on. Use their balaclavas to—'

'Have you seen the size of these guys?' Perry said.

King scanned Perry's six-foot-two frame, and then looked down at himself. 'Maybe not, then.'

'They'd realise before we got within a hundred feet of them. How many of these rebels have you seen that are our height and weight?'

'It was just a suggestion.'

'We need to stay here,' Perry said. 'Or we're dead. I know you think the noble move is to go try and save your friend, but you'll just get us all killed. And then your buddy is *definitely* fucked.'

'How many more rebels are there?' King said.

'He had plenty to work with. They kept me blindfolded for a fair portion of my time in captivity, but I was seeing a fresh face almost every hour. You haven't made a dent in their forces.'

'They can't all be here... can they?'

'Mukta knew how important that laptop was. He sounded the alarm as soon as he figured it out. If they're not all here, then they're on their way.'

A gust of wind ripped through the cave, and King shivered.

He said, 'How *did* you all go so long without getting spotted? You were using public trails packed with hikers, and it seemed no one could remember you passing by.'

Perry stared at him. 'It's easier to fool our intelligence than I thought, then.'

'What do you mean?'

'I assume you asked passersby if they'd seen two Americans — a big blond male and a fourteen-year-old girl?'

'Something like that.'

'They split us up. Put a beanie on my head to cover up the hair, and put sunglasses on Raya and a cloth over her mouth. Then they flanked us on the trail — a man on either side, and one behind. They looked like guides and porters, but in reality they were a convoy. There were three guns on me at all times, inside pockets. Same as Raya. There wasn't a hope in hell I could try anything.'

'Were you going to give it a shot?'

'I figured when we reached our end destination, I'd try

something. I wasn't able to convince myself it was going to work, though.'

'How do you feel now?'

Perry almost glanced back at her corpse, but decided not to. Instead he balled up a fist.

'I've been working for Aidan for five years,' he said, choking back emotion. 'I watched her grow up.'

King grimaced. 'I'm sorry.'

'Nothing we can do about it now.'

'Maybe if I had just—'

'Don't go down that path,' Perry said. 'I know where it leads, and you'll never work your way back out if you spiral down.'

King nodded. 'I've been told the same thing a few times in the past.'

'We can't overthink this shit.'

They stood there, hands on hips, bracing themselves against the wind.

Thinking.

Overthinking.

Finally King said, 'We can't stay here. We both know it — we just don't want to think about the alternative.'

Perry thought about it.

And shrugged.

'You might be right. No food. No water. If we let them bring the fight to this cave, we'll be trapped. We'll run out of ammo. They can just shoot it out with us.'

'This is the worst terrain I can think of for mounting a plan.'

'There is no good plan.' Perry scratched his chin. 'How important is your friend?'

'He's practically my brother. And I won't make it out of here without him.'

'You know this is a death sentence?'

King fished through one of the corpses' pockets and came up with a spare magazine for the P320. He reloaded, going through the motions like they were automatic.

Then he said, 'What else can we do?'

Perry bent down and picked up one of the Kalashnikovs. The AK-47 hadn't fired a shot — its clip was full. He slung it over one shoulder and froze in place, as if reluctant to continue.

'We stay here,' King said, 'we die.'

'We leave,' Perry said, 'we die.'

'Then we go for the option that has the best chance.'

'There's a small army headed for us. Mukta's dead, but the wheels are already in motion. You're not Rambo.'

'I've overcome similar odds in the past.'

'On a mountainside with no cover?'

King paused. 'No. Not exactly.'

'Let me guess — close quarters, claustrophobic, indoors.'

'Yeah. Usually.'

'That's not what this is. We're out of our depth here. We're up to our necks in shit.'

King didn't respond, because there was nothing to say. He knew it was the truth.

The cold harsh world outside the cave meant death.

Staying in here, sheltered from the elements, meant death.

Slater was probably already dead.

He said, 'I didn't think this would be where it all came crashing down.'

'This isn't the movies,' Perry said. 'Killing the big bad guy doesn't magically solve all our problems.'

'Where's the laptop?'

Perry pointed to the body outside the cave. There was something resting in the snow alongside him. It had fallen off his shoulder when he'd gone down.

'In that duffel,' he said.

'Get it.'

'What's the point, man...?'

'Are you giving up on me?'

'No, but—'

'Get the laptop,' King said. 'We're not quitting at the final hurdle, for God's sake.'

He led the way, collecting every spare magazine he could find off the bodies on the way out. The wind assaulted him as he stepped out into the snow, and the sun glare made him squint. He waited for Perry to rummage through the duffel, and saw the man come out with a chunky old-school silver laptop. Like a brick compared to the sleek modern variants.

King said, 'That's what all this is about?'

Perry said, 'Yeah.'

'Then give it here. I'll destroy it.'

Perry went pale. 'Are you out of your mind?'

'If we smash the magnetic platter inside the hard drive, then nothing's recoverable. Why wouldn't we do that?'

Perry chewed his bottom lip. 'I'm not supposed to tell you this...'

'You'd better.'

'It's not just what he left out of the cloud. Parker has documents he needs on this hard drive. He's notoriously terrible at backing them up. I've been in a war with him about it for most of the five years I've worked for him.'

'What documents?'

'I don't know. He doesn't tell me. But I know they're vital for what he does for a living, which makes me think we'll put lives at risk if we wipe them out of existence.'

King stared at the grey brick, cursing its existence, cursing Aidan Parker's ineptitude.

Frankly, he didn't have time to consider alternatives.

He said, 'Fine. Keep it close.'

They started trekking uphill, back to the peak. Neither of them rushed. There was a certain nihilism behind their movements, like they were walking to their deaths. King wasn't in the mood to get to the peak in a hurry. They'd find civilian trekkers happy to have accomplished the climb and, further down the mountain, a convoy of Maoist insurgents coming for their heads.

In what could very well be his last moments, King thought of Slater. If he died up here, his closest friend would lose his final lifeline. No matter how hard he fought, Slater would succumb to the endless waves of rebels storming Gokyo to find him. They knew he was down there. Maybe he'd already been overwhelmed, which, King had to admit, would give him nothing to live for.

So maybe it was a good thing his plans had come crashing down around him.

Raya was dead.

They'd failed their objective.

Slater was probably dead.

So it was almost poetic they'd go down in unison.

It was fate.

King reached the peak first, and greeted two exhausted Europeans resting on one of the flat rocks, admiring the scenery. He couldn't comprehend such a carefree existence. Here they were without a worry in the world, savouring their achievement.

The woman said, 'What were you doing down there?'

King said, 'Just exploring. There's nothing to see. Don't bother.'

He looked around. Noticed Everest, noticed the staggering glacier, noticed the endless mountain ranges.

Not a bad place to die, he thought.

He stole a glance down the south side of Gokyo Ri. Saw a tight cluster of trekkers, perhaps halfway up the mountain. There were at least twenty of them. Perry had lowballed it. Amidst the scattered pairings and trios hiking upwards, the convoy looked like a small army.

Which it was.

King gripped the P320 under his jacket and turned to Perry. 'That's them.'

Perry was pale as he gazed down the mountainside. 'We're fucked.'

'Tell me about it.'

The European woman said, 'What the hell is *that*?'

King winced, thinking she'd overheard too many details and put it all together.

He turned to her to try and explain.

But she wasn't looking at him.

She was staring wide-eyed over his shoulder, as if she couldn't comprehend what was happening.

King pivoted.

Expecting the worst.

The red-and-silver helicopter lurched through the air like it was being piloted by a drunk. Its bulk had been masked from view by the rock formations on the east side of the peak, but now it roared over the peak and came to hover right over their heads. The din of its rotors drowned out the mountaintop wind, and King and Perry and the Europeans craned their necks in mutual shock.

The chopper wobbled, and started to descend.

King could see the underside of its chassis clearly, and he counted dozens of places where bullets had thudded into the thin material. He thought he saw smoke wafting from the tail rotor.

'What the fuck are they doing?' Perry shouted over the din. 'There's nowhere to land.'

King didn't answer.

He ran over to where the Europeans sat on the rock, and said, 'Sorry,' before he wrenched the Sig out from under his jacket and pointed it up at the chopper's windshield.

The man said, 'Hey,' and the woman turned pale.

King realised he might have to shoot a few rebels dead in front of these civilians, and wondered what it might do to their mental health.

But then the helicopter jerked and bobbed and weaved and crashed to earth, one of its landing skids crushed as it impacted a flat rock.

It came to a standstill, the rotors still roaring at full speed, barely keeping balance on the peak.

King aimed his weapon right through the windshield and saw Slater half-conscious in the passenger seat.

'Holy shit,' he breathed.

He seized Perry by the collar and hauled him toward the waiting chopper.

72

S later could barely keep his eyes open, but when he spotted Jason King on the peak he couldn't keep the smile off his face.

What surprised him most was Oscar Perry standing alongside the man, clutching a laptop between his fingers.

It was the fucking porter?!

He heard Drew's muffled voice saying, 'This might be rough.'

'Whatever,' he mumbled.

'Hold on to something.'

He gripped the door handle, and the chopper smashed into the rocks underneath it a couple of seconds later. He lurched forward, thrown against his seat, and what little energy he had left hissed out of his body.

He almost moaned.

'Go,' Drew yelled through the windshield, coaxing King and Perry into motion. 'Go, go, go!'

Slater was so preoccupied with finding King alive that he lost concentration on the Sig Sauer in his hand. The barrel drifted away from the pilot, arcing into the footwell.

Slater mumbled a curse and readjusted his aim.

Drew looked across. 'I could have knocked that thing aside about a dozen times already. Give it a rest.'

Slater paused for thought as outside, King and Perry raced for the chopper.

He said, 'Why didn't you?'

'You seem like a decent guy,' Drew said. 'You just want to help your friend.'

'*Friends*, apparently.'

'Who's the blond guy?'

Slater muttered, 'I know about as much as you do.'

King hurled the rear doors open and ducked low as he launched himself up into the cabin. He scooted across and allowed Perry to crush in behind him. Perry swung the door closed, then reached over and tapped Drew once on the shoulder.

'All good,' he yelled above the roar of the rotors.

Drew lifted off with a stomach-lurching swoop.

And something *thwack*ed against the underside of the chopper.

Slater swore. 'Where's that coming from?'

King said, 'Halfway up Gokyo Ri.'

Slater risked a glance out the window. Sure enough, it was bedlam. Trekkers were scattering to the sides of the trail or hitting the deck, reacting with understandable terror to the unsuppressed gunshots. The gunfire itself was coming from a convoy of more than twenty men bunched together, clad in ordinary hiking gear but wielding extraordinary fire-power. There were rifles and pistols in the mix, and something that looked eerily like a—

'*To the right!*' Slater screamed. '*Now!*'

Drew understood, and worked the cyclic control and the collective control simultaneously. The chopper lurched violently to the right. Slater's head nearly hit the roof, and the whiplash sent pain bolting through his neck. Without their seatbelts fastened, King and Perry smashed into the far door and collapsed back into their seats in a dazed heap.

But the missile streaked past them, missing the helicopter by a dozen feet, and that was all that mattered.

'Holy shit,' Perry shouted, watching the smoky streak whisk past his window. 'Get us out of here.'

Drew complied.

He dropped the nose and worked the controls like an expert and the chopper rocketed to the left and plummeted lower in altitude, almost skimming the slope of Gokyo Ri in the process. Slater heard two distinct clicks — King and Perry getting their harnesses over their shoulders just in time — and the next thing they knew everyone was lurching this way and that, thrown around by the violent manoeuvres.

Slater gave silent thanks that Drew was such a competent pilot.

Then again, anyone who had to work in this region of the world would get good, fast.

They picked up speed and the surroundings outside flashed by, like a surreal dream, snow-capped mountains racing past the windshield and the sun glare nearly blinding them as they plummeted toward Gokyo. Drew pushed the chopper even harder, and it banked to the left like it was manoeuvring on the set of a Hollywood blockbuster. A sharp *thwack* emanated from the back seat and Slater twisted around to see King wide-eyed and pale, staring at a bullet indentation in the rear door, next to his chest. If it had penetrated the chassis, he'd have been a dead man.

Then another bullet shattered the window right by his

head, spraying him with glass, and wind screamed and howled into the cabin.

Slater shielded his eyes from the glass shards whipping around in the centrifuge, and then checked to make sure King hadn't been struck.

The man was unhurt. Riddled with cuts, bruised in a dozen places, on the verge of total exhaustion...

But not shot.

And that was the important thing.

They rocketed past the convoy on the mountainside and left them behind, the threat level now rapidly diminishing. Then they passed over Gokyo and followed the route they'd used to arrive in the village, only in reverse. Soon the town was a speck in the distance and they were surrounded by white valleys and rocky peaks.

Slater said, 'Where are we headed?'

'I'll take you to Lukla,' Drew said. 'There's an airport there you can use to get wherever you need to go. Then I need to go back to Gokyo. I'm sure there were civilians caught in the crossfire. The aftermath might be messy.'

'I think it was clean,' Slater said. 'From what I saw, they all got out.'

'No harm in checking.'

'You're a good man,' Slater said.

'I try to be.'

Slater let the silence settle over the cabin, and then something forced its way into his murky brain and hit him like a bolt of lightning.

He twisted around and said, 'Where the fuck is Raya?'

73

King explained, and then gave him time for it to sink in.

Which meant shutting up and letting Slater compartmentalise.

Because it was bound to hurt.

In truth, it hadn't fully hit King either. He'd seen her die in front of him, but everything since had been a mad scramble for survival in a hostile environment. Now there was breathing room, and he replayed it over and over again in his mind.

The gunshot. Her body falling. Mukta's sick, twisted smile.

'How do people like that exist?' he muttered to himself.

Perry noticed, and figured out what he was talking about. 'I spent nearly a week with him. By the end, I understood.'

King looked across. 'He told you?'

'He let certain details slip.'

'What's his story?'

'In India, he lived with his parents in a small rural village. The village rested on land that had been claimed by a right-wing militia. No one who lived there even knew, so they went on selling their crops and livestock to anyone who wanted them. Then the militia found out they'd sold a small amount of maize to left-wingers. So they burned the buildings to the ground, raped the women, and beheaded the men.'

'Christ...'

'I guess Mukta became a Naxalite out of necessity. Then, after nearly a decade of waging war as a communist insurgent, he realised you can't get anything done without money. So he came here, put together some resources, and started hitting the special risks insurers fast and hard. Because you don't hike to Everest unless you've got money to burn, and he found that a whole lot of hikers had all-inclusive insurance packages. None of it got reported, and he got rich beyond his wildest dreams.'

'But he also got greedy.'

Perry shrugged. 'Can you blame him? He thought he was doing it for a righteous cause.'

'Yes,' King said, thinking of Raya's soul leaving her body. 'I can blame him.'

Perry paused, then said, 'Probably a poor choice of words.'

He cradled the laptop like it was made of twenty-four carat gold. It hadn't suffered so much as a nick or scratch during its time in transit — clearly, Mukta had recognised its importance and assigned great care to its protection.

King exhaled his misery and said, 'Right, so what's the plan? Get to Lukla, figure out if we're still being hunted, and then rendezvous with Aidan in Kathmandu?'

'Seems like our best bet,' Perry said.

'What altitude is Lukla?' Slater mumbled from the front seat.

'Under three thousand metres,' the pilot said.

'Thank fuck.'

'You'll be feeling better in no time,' King said.

'I sure hope so.'

'What happened down in Gokyo?'

'They came for me.'

'Did you hide?'

'Sort of.'

King realised Slater was being vague because of plausible deniability. He pointed to the pilot and said, 'I don't think this guy's going to say a word. You can talk.'

'I'm Drew,' the man said.

'Jason.'

'It's a pleasure, mate.'

Slater said, 'No, I didn't hide. I killed half a dozen of them.' Then he turned to Drew and added, 'In self-defence.'

'Oh,' Drew said, 'of course.'

'They'll have men in Kathmandu,' Perry cut in.

He'd been deep in thought.

King said, 'But now they're leaderless. It'll all fall apart soon enough. They'll realise their boss is dead and they'll scatter.'

'But not yet,' Perry said. 'Right now his corpse is still in that cave. If they have men in Lukla...'

'There's no alternative,' Drew said. 'Your friend here's in terrible shape, and you need the lower altitude. And Lukla's got the only airport for dozens of miles in any direction. It's your only chance for a clean getaway.'

King paused, taking it in, then said, 'Drew, how do you know we're doing the right thing?'

'Just a hunch, mate.'

'I wouldn't base it solely off that.'

'Well, I don't have time to do anything else.'

Silence.

Drew said, 'Are you doing the right thing, lads?'

'Yes,' King said.

'There we go. That's good enough for me.'

'You been in a situation like this before?' King said.

'I'm ex-SAS.'

'Ah.'

No wonder you're so calm.

'How far's Lukla?' King said.

'Ten minutes,' Drew said. 'I'll drop you three in the heli landing zone and then take off again. As soon as you're out, scatter. I can't be bothered explaining myself to anyone who looks half-official. Not until this has all blown over.'

Slater said, 'Do you think there'll be insurgents in Lukla?'

'This is uncharted territory,' Drew said. 'I've never known them to show their faces in front of foreign trekkers, *ever.* You three must have royally pissed them off.'

'We have,' King admitted.

'They'll be watching the airport, then. Planes are the only way to get anywhere undetected, because they're keeping tabs on the helicopters. That schedule isn't exactly private information. You're lucky you ran into me.'

'I assume you're not going to report this,' Slater said.

'Wouldn't dream of it.'

King said, 'Slater, how much carnage did you leave back in Gokyo?'

'My fair share.'

'Enough to close Lukla's airport down?'

'No,' Drew said. 'Not yet. They don't know I was there.

As far as any investigation is aware, the only way for the culprits to get out of Gokyo is on foot.'

Outside, the ground swept up to meet them. They spotted Lukla resting on the hillside, its airport visible from the sky. King noticed the runway — it was possibly the shortest he'd ever seen. Nothing but a small strip of tarmac rolling toward a sheer cliff-face and then dropping away into nothingness. He couldn't believe planes were even capable of taking off in such a limited window.

He said, 'Is that the airport?'

Drew said, 'Most dangerous in the world.'

'Great.' King paused for thought, and then said, 'Wait, why *were* you in Gokyo?'

'I made a friend,' Slater said. 'The teahouse owner called it in.'

Drew said, 'See? Most of us can tell you guys are doing the right thing.'

'But if he called it in,' King said, 'it'll show up on the schedule. And you said the insurgents are watching the schedule.'

Halfway through descending to a flat grassy field on the outskirts of Lukla, Drew said, 'Shit.'

They craned their necks to look down at the landing zone.

Trying to see if anything was awry.

There was activity all over the field. Workers in high-visibility vests wearing hard hats lugged slabs of soda, gallon jugs of water, and crates of foodstuffs from aircraft to building. There were two choppers parked on the dusty dirt — one had just touched down, its rotors still spinning, and the other lay dormant. Everyone seemed to be bustling to and fro. No one was loitering.

It was impossible to tell if anyone was anticipating their arrival.

'They won't know you're coming here,' Drew said. 'So you probably have a narrow window to take advantage of.'

'Then we need to move,' King said. 'Slater, how's the body?'

'Not good.'

King grimaced, then inched forward to speak to Drew. 'How long will it take him to get back to normal?'

'Depends. He might have exhausted himself. If he's too depleted, he'll take days to recover.'

'I'll be fine,' Slater said through gritted teeth.

'You might not be,' King said.

Drew touched down. The mangled landing skids thumped into the dirt and a couple of workers in high-vis vests ran over to greet them. Their hands were bare, and they seemed unassuming enough.

But there was no way to know for sure.

King's head spun. There was too much to handle at once. He looked over at Perry, who was clutching the laptop tight.

'Keep that thing close,' King said.

Perry nodded.

King slipped the P320 under his jacket, but kept a tight grip on it. He checked to make sure Slater had done the same, then pushed the door open and stepped out into Lukla.

74

The first thing Slater noticed was how much warmer it was.

They'd covered over twenty miles since departing Gokyo, and the altitude had plummeted the whole way. Now they were comfortably below three thousand metres, and he could immediately taste it in the air. His body cracked and groaned and protested as he swung himself out of the cabin, but each inhale drew glorious oxygen into his system. He touched down in the dirt on shaky legs and ducked low to avoid the rotors screaming above his head.

One of the workers saw him struggling to stand and reached over with outstretched hands.

Slater darted away from them, almost bouncing off the side of the chopper in his haste to protect himself.

When he realised the guy just wanted to help, he held up his hands in apology and set off hobbling for the edge of the field.

King came over and grabbed him by the arm. 'You okay?'

'Yeah, actually,' Slater said. He could feel the vigour returning, ounce by ounce. 'I just... need time.'

'How much time?'

'Shouldn't be long, right? Just need to... get oxygen in.'

They made it a dozen paces from the chopper before they pulled to a halt. Together they turned and saw Perry skirting around from the other side. The bodyguard flashed a thumbs-up through the windshield and Drew returned the favour from the cockpit.

Slater raised an arm in farewell, and King did the same.

Drew nodded to them all, worked the controls, and the helicopter lifted off and rocketed back toward Gokyo.

Gone.

Just like that.

'Let's get you somewhere safer,' King said, still holding up most of Slater's weight. 'That reminds me — I need to change the bandages on your arm.'

Slater tried to mumble something in return, but he saw stars. He froze on the spot and waited for his vision to return and the light-headedness to dissipate. He knew what it was. His body, now flooding with oxygen, was struggling to process the development. It had just been acclimatising to Gokyo's altitude, and now it was back in favourable conditions.

King said, 'What's wrong?'

When his vision returned, Slater felt half-human.

'Nothing, actually,' he said, suppressing a smile. 'I feel brand new.'

He flexed his hands and feet and breathed audible relief. It was the first time since they'd stumbled into Gokyo that he'd felt a marked improvement in his condition. He was nowhere close to a hundred percent, but he might as well have been.

He might as well have been flooded with superhuman strength.

Because Will Slater at fifty percent was still a force to be reckoned with.

And now he could move without worrying his body would snap.

He ushered Perry over and said, 'Let's get a room somewhere while we figure out what to do next.'

Perry regarded him warily. 'You seem more energetic.'

'It's the air.'

'You had altitude sickness?'

'Of sorts.'

Perry paused for thought and said, 'Let's get to the nearest teahouse, then, and stop standing around in this field.'

King said, 'Can you walk?'

Slater nodded. 'Take the lead.'

King and Perry made a beeline for the corner of the heli field, where a short flight of chipped concrete steps led up to one of Lukla's cobblestone streets. From there it spiralled into the town, weaving through teahouses and general stores all made of the same faded wood. Slater followed in their stride, letting his body warm up before committing to anything drastic. He shook out his legs with each step, each aching muscle relaxing as he kept inhaling deeply and fully. He figured it was vital to pump as much oxygen through his system as possible for the foreseeable future.

But it made him slow, and it allowed King and Perry to gain a considerable lead, so Slater saw everything that happened as if watching it through a wide-lens camera.

He was still shaking out his muscles when he noticed one of the workers staring at the laptop under Perry's arm.

The guy had the same high-vis vest and hard hat, but his

complexion was more cracked and weathered than his colleagues. At first glance it seemed he'd had the hardest life of them all, which you wouldn't chalk up to anything suspicious unless you knew he'd come down from the mountains.

But which mountains?

Slater put two and two together and broke into a sprint in unison with the worker.

It was going to be close.

His body wasn't ready for it. He stumbled and faltered a couple of times as his oxygen-deprived muscles pined and pleaded for him to wait, to let him recover first before trying anything drastic and—

'Perry!' he yelled, realising he wasn't going to make it.

The bodyguard spun around and lunged away, but the worker was right there in his face. The guy didn't bother to throw a strike. He knew he'd probably lose a fight with Perry, and with King right there it was a guarantee. But he was small and fast and strong, so he reached out and snatched the laptop and wrenched it out of Perry's grip before anyone could react.

Then he doubled his pace and ran away like a pro sprinter.

Slater understood the ramifications of shooting an unarmed man dead in front of a dozen potential witnesses, so he didn't draw his gun yet.

But he timed the trajectory to perfection.

He picked his interception point, aimed for it, waited for the right timing, and ran flat-out.

Then lunged.

He wrapped his arms around the worker's mid-section and used his own weight and momentum to crash-tackle the guy into the side of a holding shed. They hit the thin aluminium with a noise akin to a bomb going off, and both of them sprawled into the dirt. Slater rolled over and smacked the worker with an open palm directly in the nose, either breaking it or coming very close. Then he wrestled the laptop off him, taking care not to crush it in the process.

He got to his feet, handed it back to Perry, and watched almost every worker in the field descend on them.

Slater pointed to the guy clutching his face, moaning, rolling back and forth in the dust.

'Thief,' he said.

No one responded.

Out of the corner of his mouth, King muttered, 'Let's get out of here before we get mobbed.'

They hurried up the steps into the village.

75

King couldn't believe how fast Slater had recovered.

Slater was striding it out behind them, tackling the uneven cobblestones underfoot with ease, keeping pace with their stride. In Gokyo he'd been a shell of himself.

Altitude's a bitch.

They weaved their way up through the south-west side of Lukla, passing townspeople who shot them curious looks. There were no foreign trekkers in sight — they were either cooped up in their teahouse rooms recovering, or somewhere along the trail en route to the town.

He kept a hand on his weapon, but held it under his jacket. Each breath seemed to supercharge him with energy, and he realised he'd been feeling the same effects as Slater, only to a much lesser extent. Now he could taste the oxygen, and it was glorious. Maybe if they'd undertaken the trek over a couple of weeks, they'd have had time to acclimatise.

He was in a state of limbo. Raya's death hung thick and oppressive over him, and he stopped himself reaching for his phone to call it in. Then Violetta would know they failed, and Aidan Parker would know they'd lost his daughter. The consequences threatened to suffocate him, weigh him down, dump him in a vat of misery and never let up.

He couldn't let it get to him until he was back on home soil.

Then he could start to digest it.

Perry muttered, 'Jason...'

King looked up. There was a platoon of soldiers coming down the staircase they were ascending. He counted a dozen men in army gear, all moving in sync, all brandishing handguns in holsters at their waist and grey packs over their shoulders.

He froze.

Slater pulled to a halt to his left.

Perry stopped to his right.

Then they merged into single file to let the group past.

Everyone made eye contact. King looked from soldier to soldier, searching for any hint of suspicion. He found none. They nodded politely to him, Slater, and Perry in turn. Five of them hurried on past. They had places to be. Then a few more. Then another.

The last three stopped.

They pulled up alongside them all on the staircase, more inquisitive than their peers. One of them said, 'Where is your guide?'

'We don't have one,' King said.

'How did you get here?'

'We walked.'

The three soldiers exchanged a glance. Then the one that spoke English turned back to them and said, 'Many of our guest houses will not accept you if you do not have a guide.'

'We've managed so far,' King said. 'We'll be fine.'

The man's gaze wandered to the laptop tucked under Perry's arm. 'What is that?'

Perry lifted it up so everyone could see. 'What do you think?'

'Looks valuable. You shouldn't carry it like that. Put it in a bag.'

'Thanks. I'll take that into consideration.'

Everyone stood there, bristling, staring at each other. King didn't have a clue what this was. If it was hostile, then he should act now, getting the jump on them before they could go for their guns. But if it was just a friendly enquiry...

Perry stepped forward, put a hand on the guy's shoulder, and said, 'It's fine.'

The man scrutinised him for a beat, then nodded and turned away. He set off down the staircase. His two comrades followed. No one looked back.

King waited for them to get out of earshot, then raised an eyebrow. 'Are you telepathic or something?'

'They needed prompting,' Perry said. 'We look like tough guys — they probably thought we were here to cause trouble. Best to give them a gentle reminder that we're not here for that. I looked them in the eyes. I stood my ground. They appreciated that.'

Slater muttered, 'Didn't realise social skills were a superpower.'

'Ninety percent of my job is just being courteous,' Perry said. 'You get the hang of it after a while. You learn when to step in, and when not to.'

'What's your magic lamp telling us now?' King said.

'That we should find a room and sort out this mess. And then make our way back to Kathmandu.'

'Good plan.'

They ventured up to the top of Lukla, past the tourist

commotion around the airport, past the popular teahouses. They went down back-alleys and through routes that ordinarily lay dormant. Then they found a simple wooden lodge near the town outskirts, and Parker said, 'Perfect.'

King was grateful they'd reached shelter, because it seemed another rapid turnaround was occurring. Now Slater was in better condition than he was. The man was practically springing from foot to foot, whereas every step that King took felt slow, laborious, weighed down with invisible lead.

What's happening?

Slater noticed. He pulled up alongside King and said, 'Now look at us.'

'We're seesawing back and forth,' King said.

Every word took considerable effort.

King said, 'I think the Gokyo Ri climb is catching up to me.'

'It didn't look like fun.'

King trudged into the teahouse, waited on a hard wooden bench as Perry and Slater acquired a room from the owner, and let the brain fog seize him.

76

When they got into the room, Slater saw King eyeing one of the single beds.

Probably debating whether to collapse onto it or not.

In the end, the man opted not to. He went over to the corner of the small room, put his luggage down, and put his hands on his knees.

Trying to recover.

There was little light filtering through the overcast sky in the first place, but most of it still got caught on the curtains. They were heavy and coarse, made of some cheap beige material. Slater crossed the room and drew them closed, giving them the shadowy atmosphere they needed to discuss clandestine matters.

Perry opened his mouth to speak, but Slater held up a hand. 'Give me the laptop.'

'What?'

'The laptop. Give it to me. I'm going to find this file you keep talking about, put it back in the cloud, and then we can leave the laptop in the bin. It's caused us more trouble than we need. One less thing to worry about as we sort out a way to get out of here.'

'There's more than the one file on there. Aidan has other—'

'Then I'll put it all in the cloud. I'm good with computers. I'll figure it out.'

'Aidan wouldn't want you to mess around with his personal—'

'I don't give a shit what Aidan wants,' Slater said. 'We can't have this risk hanging over our heads any longer.'

'It's a matter of principle,' Perry said. 'It's a private—'

Slater said, 'Are you really going to refuse? Is that where we're going with this?'

Perry didn't answer.

They stood there in a makeshift triangle, King and Slater equidistant from one another, watching the bodyguard closely.

Slater noticed the mounting tension.

Then Perry said, 'Fine,' and handed it over.

He threw his hands up in the air, silently bemoaning their decision, and crossed the room to sit on the other single bed. Muttering something to the effect of, 'He's going to fucking kill me,' the whole time.

Slater understood. It's one of the fundamental rules of black operations. Don't *ever* let anyone mess around with your gear, especially if it contains sensitive information. The fewer eyes on it, the better. There's too much on the line, too much at stake, too many variables to be exploited and—

And none of that mattered.

This was bigger than rules.

That's why black-ops existed in the first place.

To be flexible.

Slater placed the laptop on the small wooden table in

the corner of the room and dragged the whole thing over to the edge of the nearest bed. He sat down on the mattress, opened it, and ushered to King. 'Give me the phone.'

King handed it over without a word of protest.

Slater dialled. It rang, and rang, and rang. The dial tone was tinny and faint, but it seemed to echo in the room.

Then it went to voicemail.

Slater thumbed the END CALL button and stared at Perry.

The bodyguard stared back. 'What?'

'Do you know something we don't?'

Perry scoffed. 'Oh — you think I'm acting suspicious?'

'I don't know what to think.'

'I'm rehearsing what to say to my boss before I hand in my resignation,' he said. 'That laptop was not to be touched by anyone other than Aidan Parker under any circumstances. If you think I look off, it's because I feel off. Take that as you will.'

Slater dialled again.

It rang, and rang, and rang.

And Parker answered.

'Do you have her?' was the first thing he said.

A jolt of unease rippled through Slater. He chewed his bottom lip, deep in thought, wondering when was the right time.

Not now, he concluded.

'Not yet,' Slater said. 'But we're close. We managed to retrieve your laptop.'

'Oh, thank God.'

'I need the password.'

'What?'

'I need to get into it.'

'No you don't.'

'Yes,' Slater said. 'I'm afraid I do. If you refuse, I'll bring the full wrath of our government against you. I don't care how senior you think you are.'

He sensed Parker stiffen on the other end of the line. 'You should be careful who you play those sorts of games with before you—'

Slater said, 'Do you want your daughter back, or not?'

Silence.

'Her life is in our hands.'

'You wouldn't dare...'

'The password, Aidan, or we turn around.'

'You fucking—'

'*Stop,*' Slater hissed. 'We've nearly got ourselves killed a dozen separate times for you. You're going to do this for us, no matter how sensitive you think the data is or how unqualified I am to see it. Frankly, I need to see it, because I need to get it back into your encrypted cloud and then destroy this thing before it costs us any more attempts on our lives.'

'Do you know how to do that?'

'Yes,' Slater lied. 'Violetta's walked me through it.'

'She shouldn't have granted you access to that sort of—'

'Well, she did.'

'W-8-2-U-V-9-3-R-4-T.'

Slater paused, repeated it once in his head, and then once out loud.

'Is that right?' he said.

'Yes,' Parker said. 'But don't go around spewing that out. It's an incredibly important piece of information.'

'I know,' Slater said. 'I'll be in touch.'

He hung up.

King was staring at him.

Perry was staring at him.

He said, 'What?'

King said, 'That's his daughter, Will.'

'I know.'

'She's dead.'

'I know.'

'I don't like that one bit.'

'I need this laptop taken care of,' Slater snarled. 'I'm sorry if I offended either of you, but this thing is going to keep putting us in danger until we get rid of it. I don't have time to sit around all day playing games with Aidan Parker. If you want me to, I'll be the one to tell Parker about Raya. To make up for it.'

No one answered.

King turned away.

Parker kept staring.

It seemed a little odd, but Slater ignored it and fished around in his own duffel bag for the appropriate adapter. He plugged it into a power socket in the wall, and waited for the laptop screen to light up in response. Then he tapped in the ten-digit password and found himself on a dull featureless home screen. He brought his finger to the trackpad and started scrolling through folders, diving into the contents of the hard drive.

The room fell quiet.

77

K ing was the first to notice Perry getting fidgety.

Slater couldn't have been fiddling with the laptop for more than a couple of minutes, but in that time Perry went from picking at his nails, to cracking his neck, to pacing the room.

When Perry shuffled over to the far corner of the room, searching for anything suspicious, King took a subtle step to the right.

Putting himself between Perry and the laptop.

And his heart started to thump in his chest.

Slater squinted, trying to make out the small digital pixels spelling names for folders, documents, files. He said, 'Do you know where Parker left these documents?'

King turned to Perry, who shrugged noncommittally. 'Not sure. My boss's work is none of my business.'

King stayed right where he was.

A silent barrier.

But his bones were starting to ache. Invisible scales had been tipped, and he was declining rapidly. The overbearing sensation suffocated him — the knowledge that he'd pushed his body past its limits and jeopardised his health in the process. He tried to quietly will himself toward regaining energy, but it was useless. The tiredness took hold of him, and he did his best to ride it out.

Meanwhile, Slater hunched further over the laptop.

King sensed Perry bristle.

Not good, he thought.

Slater said, 'I can't find anything.'

'Keep looking.'

'Hold on, there's something here...'

A thought struck King, and he wheeled around. 'You said your boss's work is none of your business, right?'

Perry said, 'Right.'

'But when I met you, you told me that's how Mukta worked out the laptop was valuable. Because you saw him fiddling around with it, and you freaked out.'

'Yeah.'

'Why would you freak out if you didn't know there was compromising information on it? How do you know he left documents out of the cloud?'

Silence.

'You and Winston were in the other room, Perry.'

Silence.

'What made you freak out?'

Perry didn't respond.

He was caught up in too many lies.

He needed time to sort them out.

King knew immediately something was wrong, and went for his gun.

But Perry had been anticipating that.

King had his palm around the P320 when Perry lunged across the room and tackled him in the mid-section. He took his hand off the weapon to make sure he didn't shoot himself in the foot, but the momentum of a pair of two-hundred-pound men falling backwards prevented them from getting off any further strikes. They crashed into the metal bed frame and sprawled across the concrete between the single beds.

King made to leap to his feet, but two things weighed him down.

First, his condition. He was firmly on the decline, and no amount of adrenaline could fight through the fatigue of total exhaustion for very long.

Second, he'd smashed the back of his head on the bed frame.

He didn't even realise in the heat of the moment, but now he got to one knee before his vision jerked to the right, throwing him entirely off-balance. He came down on his rear and scrambled for purchase on the cold hard floor, but he couldn't find anything fast enough.

He got his hands underneath his body and tried to lever to his feet, but Perry kicked him in the face before he got halfway through the motion.

Then Perry spun and ripped his own handgun from his waistband so he could get the drop on Slater, but King saw none of it.

His vision was reeling this way and that. He wasn't unconscious, but he might as well have been. With his equilibrium firmly disrupted and his muscles pleading for mercy, he kicked and flailed on the concrete like a fish out of water.

And he was forced to listen to the horrifying sounds of two men fighting to the death.

78

S later took longer than usual to react.

He saw something on the laptop that *really* shouldn't have been there. He read the file name, blinked, and read it again just to make sure.

Then there was a moment of hesitation as his brain connected the dots.

He thought, *Are you fucking kidding me?*

Then there was an explosion of sudden violent movement — a hurricane of noise — and when he looked up King was on the floor and Perry was halfway through the process of pivoting toward him. One of the bodyguard's hands was on the way down to his waistband.

That was all Slater needed to see.

He tensed up and utilised a surge of adrenaline and literally threw the whole table at Perry. It was a small round circular thing, but it was still made of sturdy wood and heavy enough to pack a punch. The laptop flew off the surface and smashed against the far wall and the three table legs hit Perry in the chest. Something cracked in the man's sternum, and the blunt force of the impact sent him stumbling back across the room.

Slater went for his gun but it wasn't there.

He remembered feeling something tickling his waist back in the chopper, but the whole flight had been a blur of fatigue and exhaustion. If Perry had lifted his weapon off him before even arriving in Lukla, then the bodyguard was more brazen than he thought. It didn't gel with Slater's usual situational awareness, but he recognised that had been thrown out the window when his body shut down. He honestly couldn't remember the last time he remembered feeling the Sig Sauer at his waist.

For all he knew, it was resting in the dirt of the heli field, discreetly discarded when they all slipped out of the chopper.

Then he worked out where it was all at once, because both of Perry's hands flew to his waist.

He had both guns.

Slater didn't hesitate to wonder how, or why, or what. He just flipped a switch in his brain and lunged across the room like a man possessed. He got his hands on Perry at the same moment the bodyguard ripped both P320s from his belt.

But by that point Slater had momentum on his side, and he used another savage burst of intensity to pivot and tense and squeeze and throw.

Perry went airborne, bounced like a rag doll off the concrete wall, and sprawled in a heap onto one of the thin mattresses.

The guns went everywhere, skittering around the room.

Slater thought about lunging for one, but there was no guarantee they were ready to fire. Instead he took advantage of a disorientated enemy and leapt onto Perry, pressing all his weight on top of the bodyguard. As soon as Perry lifted his head to break free of the crushing pressure, Slater would loop an arm around his throat and squeeze the life out of him.

Jiu-jitsu 101.

But Perry didn't do that, because he was obviously a trained combatant himself.

Instead he tucked his chin to his chest and pushed off the mattress and sent them both tumbling to the floor.

Slater landed on top of King, who groaned in protest. He had no time to check on his friend's condition — everything was a fast-paced blur, and concentration was impossible — so he rolled off King and tried to get to his feet.

Perry lunged into range, got both hands around Slater's mid-section, and locked them together.

'Fuck,' Slater snarled.

He smashed an open palm down, catching Perry in the nose. The appendage broke, and blood sprayed. Then Slater used the same arm to drop an elbow into the soft flesh behind the man's ear. It was a brutal strike, like a blunt axe ricocheting off a coconut, but Perry didn't go out. He stumbled, wobbled, but kept his grip tight.

Then he picked Slater up and dumped him down on his head.

Slater tucked his chin to his chest at the last second, and came down on the concrete on the base of his neck. Then all Perry's weight crushed on top of him, driving him harder into the floor. A wave of nausea rippled through him and as he broke free of the man's grasp he fought the urge to vomit. But he simply couldn't afford to, no matter how hurt he was. Anyone who stayed still for longer than a second was going to get beaten to death.

Perry swung with a looping right hook and missed, and Slater thought, *Now.*

He dove on Perry, who'd overcommitted with the punch, and wrestled him down to his knees. Then he interlocked his fingers behind the man's skull and crushed his face with a scything knee.

Thwack.

Right into the broken nose.

Blood sprayed again, this time coating both Slater and King, and Slater followed up with another knee to the same spot. The results were gnarly, and the extent of the damage made Slater hesitate as he figured out exactly how to kill Oscar Perry with his bare hands. Really, it was only half a second of decision-making, unnoticeable to the untrained observer, but Perry noticed.

And he was a *tough* son-of-a-bitch.

Because he ignored his broken nose and shattered face and ducked his head low, breaking free of the Muay Thai clinch. He backed away, still on his knees, and dove for one of the guns.

Slater dove for Perry.

Another impact, just as brutal as the last.

The crash-tackle took them both into the side of the nearest bed frame, and the impact stunned them both. Either man could capitalise on the narrow window, and Slater tried to, but—

He was a few milliseconds too late.

Perry seized the leverage and scrambled on top of Slater, distributing all his weight evenly. Slater tried to gouge an eye but Perry dropped a devastating elbow. It sliced across the top of Slater's forehead, and suddenly all he could see was blood. He tried to fight through the crimson mask, but it was futile. He felt crushing pressure on either side of his head, and realised Perry had seized hold of his skull.

The bodyguard smashed Slater's head into one of the metal legs.

He lost sensation in his hands and feet.

He was on the verge of unconsciousness.

About to slip into a long and dreamless—

Then the hands fell away. Suddenly Perry's weight pressing down on him was nowhere to be found, and Slater took the opportunity to reach up and wipe the blood out of his eyes.

He blinked twice, and saw Perry scrambling for the nearest weapon.

But he didn't get there in time.

Jason King, gun in hand, strode up to Oscar Perry, seized him by his curly blond hair, wrenched him away from the nearest handgun, and placed the barrel against his head.

Perry's face contorted into a grimace and he squeezed his eyes shut. 'No, no, no, please—'

King pulled the trigger.

The gunshot exploded in the confined space.

Then the room went quiet.

Slater lay on his back, panting, bleeding, his head throbbing. There was blood everywhere. On the walls, on the mattress, on the floor. All over King.

King surveyed the scene, unblinking, wide-eyed. Probably in shock.

He let the chaos settle, then turned to Slater and said, 'What just happened?'

79

King caught his breath.

It was difficult, but he managed.

As soon as he'd crawled out of the semi-conscious state, he was free to move. Like a boxer recovering before the ten count, he'd clawed his way back to reality, got to his feet, picked up a gun, and put a bullet through Perry's head.

Now he stumbled over to Slater and helped the man to his feet.

Slater got up on shaky legs, clutching his forehead to stem the bleeding, and sat down on the mattress.

Wordlessly, King went into his duffel bag and retrieved the medkit. He eyed the staple gun, but Slater hissed, '*No.*'

'It might be for the best.'

'It's not that deep. Just tape it up.'

'If you say so.'

King swabbed the cut with rubbing alcohol, then pinched it closed for a long thirty-count, and finished by winding a long unbroken strip of medical tape around

Slater's head several times in a row. When he taped it in place, it looked like a makeshift headband.

Slater said, 'That's fine. It'll do until we're out of here.'

'What *was* that?'

'We probably don't have time to talk about it,' Slater said, getting to his feet.

'Why?'

'Because Perry and whoever else he's working with have at least three soldiers in his back pocket.'

'Wha—?' King started, and then trailed off.

"It's fine," Perry had said.

The troops on the staircase had listened.

He'd given them the all-clear, and they'd let him go.

'What the hell is going on?' King muttered to himself.

'I think I'm putting it together,' Slater said. 'But we just fired an unsuppressed round in a civilian lodge. We need to go — right now.'

Sure enough, they made out distant screams echoing down the corridors. They hadn't been paying attention to them before, but now they were prevalent.

'After you,' King said, throwing the duffel over his shoulder.

Slater picked up his own pack, then the three guns. He passed one to King, and tucked the other two in his own waistband. King eyed the shattered laptop warily, and Slater shook his head.

'We don't need it,' he said.

'Why not? Wouldn't it be evidence?'

'I don't want it to be evidence.'

'Why?'

'Best they think no one knows. Best they think no one's coming for them. But we'll be coming for them. When we get out of here.'

'What are you talking about?'

'I still haven't figured it all out. Let's go. We'll talk when we're safe.'

Both covered in blood, both walking on shaky legs, both disorientated, they stumbled straight out of the room, leaving Perry's body for the cleaners.

'Where do we go?' King said, flashing paranoid glances left and right.

Sure enough, an older Caucasian woman threw her bedroom door open, saw them both striding down the hall, screamed at the top of her lungs, and disappeared back inside her room.

Slater said, 'Airport.'

'We'll be sitting ducks out there.'

'Would you prefer the trail?'

'Probably.'

'We'll get overwhelmed, and you know it. There's a whole lot of places to ambush us out there, and they don't have to pretend to be courteous anymore. The game is over. We need to be back in Kathmandu as fast as humanly possible.'

'Whatever you say.'

'But first, Phaplu.'

King remembered the airport in the village they'd set off from. 'We can fly there if we—'

'Yeah.'

King thought about it. 'You want to get Parker?'

'Yeah.'

'Care to elaborate?'

'Not yet. I'm working it out.'

King was about to press the issue, but they made it to the teahouse's entrance and suddenly there were five or six people in their face, screaming at them. Most of them were Nepali, with the odd weary trekker thrown into the mix. King shouldered his way past all of them and went straight out the front door. Slater followed in his stride.

Then they were jogging down cobblestone streets, steadily descending toward the airport, their eyes peeled for any sign of danger. They passed local after local, who stared at them like they were aliens.

Finally, Slater said, 'Fuck this,' and wrenched the Sig Sauer from his belt.

King followed suit.

They barely noticed civilians scattering, because by that point their visions had constricted to twin tunnels. They ran at breakneck speed through Lukla, weaving left and right in a hopeless attempt to make it to the airport before anyone in the town realised they had a situation on their hands.

King saw Slater wrench the satellite phone free and dial a number.

'What are you doing?' he said, his heart in his throat.

'Making a call,' he said. 'We've still got every insurgent in the mountains looking for us, but I think I can get the army off our backs.'

'How?'

Slater pulled to a halt in the lee of an archway and sucked in the cool mountain air.

King stopped alongside him, patiently waiting.

'Parker,' Slater said into the phone. 'It's Will. We have Raya. We have your daughter. Find somewhere secluded in Phaplu to meet us, and call me back. Somewhere away from civilians. We're going to be coming in hot.'

King inched closer to the receiver, and thought he heard the faint words, *Let me speak to her.*

'Okay,' Slater said, and mimed taking the phone away from his ear. 'Raya, here's—'

He hung up.

He said, 'That should give us the window we need to get out of this place.'

King stared at the phone. 'What if he has nothing to do with this?'

'Huh?'

'What if he's innocent? You just gave him false hope that his daughter's alive.'

'He's not fucking innocent,' Slater snarled.

'Care to enlighten me as to what was on that laptop?'

Slater paused, and bowed his head.

Then he looked up and said, 'A spreadsheet of payments from a dozen special risks insurers, totalling tens of millions of dollars. And it seemed like that was just deposits. Like the real payout would come later.'

King didn't answer.

He wasn't entirely lucid.

He knew that was bad.

He just didn't know why.

He said, 'What does that mean?'

'It means Aidan Parker's in bed with them. It means he knew about Mukta before his daughter was taken.'

King tried to piece it together.

But he couldn't quite connect all the dots.

Then a raucous group of hikers rounded the corner a dozen feet in front of them, gesticulating to each other and speaking rapid Spanish back and forth.

One of them — deeply tanned, in his early thirties, with a full head of straight black hair — stared a little too long.

King and Slater stared back.

Then the guy looked over his shoulder, back into the alleyway they'd just come from, and shouted in broken English, 'Down here! They here! Come quick!'

The trekkers scattered, and King dropped to one knee and took aim with his Sig.

80

S later, on the other hand, wasn't about to wait for the firefight to come to them.

As soon as he registered the Spanish guy yelling, he took off at a sprint for the mouth of the alley. He screeched to a halt on the path and found three men in camouflage fatigues working handguns free from leather holsters on their belts.

More insurgents.

They were already in Lukla.

Already searching for King and Slater.

Slater controlled the initial panic response, exhaled fully, and lined up his aim. Then he pumped the trigger three times.

Thwack-thwack-thwack.

Heads snapped back on shoulders, exit wounds sprayed blood on the cobblestones, and nearby trekkers and locals screamed bloody murder as the ballet of violence unfolded in front of them.

Which was accurate enough.

It was bloody, and it was murder.

Slater yelled, 'Come on!'

King got to his feet and hurried after him. As soon as Slater knew King was on his tail, he broke into a sprint for the airport. Shouts and screams spread through the town like wildfire, and it wouldn't be long before most of the residents realised war had broken out on home soil. Then there would be bedlam, accompanied swiftly by the closure of the airport. There was no way they could get their hands on a plane if everything was locked and the keys were thrown away.

No, they had to run for their lives and hope that—

Slater rounded a corner and saw the tiny airport through its surrounding wire fence. There was a small passenger plane idling in one of the four loading bays, capable of carrying no more than twenty passengers in total, and a thin queue bleeding out of the three-storey building that passed for a terminal. The trekkers had been lining up to board, but the gunshots rippling through the village froze them in their tracks. Now they were staring up the hill, mouths agape, whispering nervously to one another.

A handful of them saw Slater's outline through the fence, gun in hand, and pandemonium erupted.

Everyone scattered — passengers and workers alike.

Slater saw the small plane's propellers powering down.

'*Shit,*' he yelled.

King skidded to a halt beside him. 'What?'

'Over the fence. *Now.*'

King clearly had enough experience in trying times to need no further prompting. He heard the urgency in Slater's tone and moved immediately. He dropped his duffel bag and hauled himself over the wire fence, nearly falling head over heels down the other side in his haste. He landed hard on the thin ledge, narrowly avoiding a two-storey drop to the tarmac. The fence had been erected at the top of a sheer rock wall, and they'd need to traverse it with caution if they wanted to keep their bones intact on the descent.

Slater tossed King's bag over, followed by his own. Then he vaulted over the fence, landed in a similar heap, and picked himself up to observe the scene.

The passengers were scattering in a dozen different directions — some racing back into the safety of the terminal, others opting to flee at breakneck speed across the three empty loading bays. It was understandable — they thought they were under attack.

Then a couple of security guards stuck their heads out of the terminal, far across the tarmac.

Slater thought he saw the glint of gunmetal.

He raised the Sig Sauer and fired three shots over the roof of the building, making sure the bullets sailed harmlessly out of Lukla.

But the security didn't know that.

They disappeared, lurching back behind cover, opting not to get into a firefight with what they assumed were trained combatants.

'Now,' Slater said.

Together, he and King tossed their duffels over the lip of the ledge, where each bag thudded to the tarmac after a second's freefall. If either of them followed that trajectory, they'd probably break both their legs. Instead they used their non-dominant hands to guide them down the rock wall, keeping their guns firmly clenched in their right hands. They probed with the toes of their boots and dropped steadily, foot by foot, down the wall. When Slater deemed he was close enough to the tarmac to avoid serious injury, he let go and plummeted to the runway. Landed, rolled to his feet, and dusted himself off.

King opted not to risk the plunge, given his barely-recovered ankle, and took a few seconds longer to finish the descent.

When he touched down on the runway, Slater handed his duffel over, and together they took off at a run for the plane.

They caught the pilot and co-pilot halfway out of the exit door, racing to get away from what had quickly become an active war zone.

King intercepted them at the bottom of the stairs and held them at gunpoint. They froze, shaking.

He turned to Slater. 'Do we need them?'

Slater studied the plane. It was a Dornier Do 228 — a twin-turboprop with an odd rectangular fuselage. He said, 'No. I can fly it.'

King jerked his gun in the direction of the terminal and stepped aside to let the two men past. 'Go.'

They didn't need any further prompting. The moment they found a gap they both took off at a mad sprint, practically shouldering past King in their desperation to get away. They were halfway to the terminal before either King or Slater had mounted the stairs.

Slater took both bags and hustled up into the fuselage. There were maybe a couple of dozen seats in total for passengers — one on either side of the aisle, running the entire length of the plane. They were a sickly brown colour, made of cheap sticky leather. Slater dumped the duffels on the nearest empty seat and ran for the cockpit. He levered himself into the pilot's seat, soaked in the myriad of controls, and started deciphering what seemed like an impossibly complex puzzle to the untrained eye. But a couple of years in the Air Force during the pre-black-ops days of his career had taught him everything he needed to know, and he figured a twin-turboprop plane shouldn't be too much to handle.

He familiarised himself with the controls, and assumed the aircraft was STOL-capable.

Short Takeoff and Landing.

It had to be.

The runway was the shortest Slater had ever laid eyes on.

He gulped back apprehension, fired both turboprop engines to life, and started backing out of the loading bay.

From the open fuselage door, King screamed, '*Faster!*'

Slater's heart skipped a beat, and he urged the aircraft to speed up.

It groaned in protest, but responded.

Then the first of the gunshots rang out across the tarmac.

81

King was crouched low in the open doorway when he noticed the jeeps roaring around the side of the terminal.

He counted four in total, all open-topped, all packed tight with insurgents brandishing assault rifles and hand-guns. There was a paramilitary army headed their way, and seemingly no one around to stop it. The floor underneath King shifted, and he realised Slater had spurred the plane into motion. The wheels rumbled on the tarmac, backing out of the loading bay...

...right into the path of the first jeep.

'Faster!' he roared, and Slater seemed to get the message.

The plane jerked violently as it reversed, and King snatched at the door frame so he didn't go tumbling out onto the runway.

He steadied himself, then took careful aim and squeezed off a flurry of rounds — six consecutive pumps of the trigger and the driver and passenger died amidst an explosion of shattered glass as the windshield gave out. The jeep veered to the right as the dead driver slumped forward over the steering wheel, and within seconds it had crashed nose-first into the rock wall bordering the rear of the airport. It seemed no one was wearing seatbelts — bodies went everywhere, some still alive as they were hurled from the vehicle.

Slater finished reversing and King heard him talking to himself as he worked the controls. King didn't blame him. It was a logistical nightmare — figuring out how to fly a specific type of plane whilst under attack.

So King focused on taking the heat off them.

He lined up his aim with the second jeep, and unloaded the last five rounds. The plane was bouncing and shaking, throwing his concentration and focus off. Although he didn't hit any of the insurgents, he blew out the two front tyres when his aim drifted low. The jeep dropped forward on its nose and sparks flew off both exposed wheels. It slowed drastically, nearly taking out the vehicle behind it as its speed plummeted.

The two remaining jeeps avoided the collisions narrowly, and surged forward.

King fell back behind the seats as eight gun barrels floated in his direction.

Bullets tore through the open doorway, blowing out some of the windows.

That's fine, King thought. *As long as the engines stay intact.*

He reloaded and threw caution to the wind by crab-crawling back out into the line of fire.

He had to. The longer he spent cowering away, the more time the insurgents had to fire at the turboprop engines.

He tried to line up his aim, but it was chaos. Slater was roaring forward out of the loading bays, and the plane careened out onto the start of the runway. King almost had one of the jeeps in his sights, but then the floor lurched beneath him again, sending him tumbling and rolling several feet down the aisle. When he righted himself, he realised Slater had lined up the nose of the plane with the end of the runway.

'Hold onto something!' Slater roared from the cockpit. 'We only get one shot at this.'

King stared down the length of the aisle, through the cockpit, out the windshield. He saw the runway stretching down the mountainside, uncomfortably short for a standard takeoff, and then he saw it plummet away into nothingness.

Hence the need for a fast start.

If you don't build up enough momentum, you don't generate enough lift to get the plane off the ground before the runway simply ends.

Fuck, King thought.

The end of the runway sent shivers down his spine.

Then more bullets tore through the open doorway, blowing out the opposite porthole windows.

'Do it!' King yelled. 'No time.'

He could already hear the chorus of the turboprop engines rising. Slater was charging them up, building power through the propellers, preparing for—

King saw him slam the controls.

The plane *lurched* off the mark. King nearly went head over heels as the floor shifted underneath him, and then his stomach was dropping and they were racing into the plunge. They gained more and more speed as the nose dipped and they raced downhill, and more bullets hit the fuselage, and King fought and clawed his way to the open door frame and emptied the rest of the P320's magazine at the pursuing jeeps. He could barely keep the contents of his stomach down, let alone control his aim in any meaningful way, and he was pretty sure the entirety of his shots missed. There was no way to tell, though — the wind was roaring in his ears and bringing involuntary tears to his eyes, and when the gun was empty he snatched hold of the nearest seat and held on for dear life.

Then he turned all his attention to the front of the plane.

They were gaining speed faster, the whole fuselage rattling and shaking and groaning. Slater was hunched over the controls like a man possessed, every morsel of his attention seized by the view out front. Wind howled in through the open portholes, deafeningly loud in the fuselage, and King roared, 'Are we going to make it?!'

The end of the runway was impossibly close.

Do we have enough speed?

His heart was in his throat. Slater was by no means an experienced pilot — King knew he'd be relying on the archaic remnants of his brief Air Force career. This was one of the most dangerous airports in the world, and only seasoned STOL-capable pilots made regular flights in and out of Lukla...

The whole plane suddenly bucked violently, the whole fuselage bouncing up and down at once, nearly throwing King head-first into the wall. He went pale and clammy, convinced one of the engines had blown out. By now, there wasn't enough room to stop. If they didn't lift off, they'd plummet to their grisly deaths and—

The view of the runway disappeared, replaced by sky.

King gripped the back of the seat with white knuckles as the floor rose underneath him, nearly taking him off his feet.

The nose had lifted off the tarmac.

But what about—?

The whole plane jerked and bucked and went airborne, and the floor suddenly dropped away, and King thought he'd get flung out the open doorway as his vision rattled and frantic noise screamed in his eardrums and—

They were in the air.

Not falling to their deaths.

The back of the plane had nearly bottomed out as it came off the runway at the very last second, but they'd made it.

King collapsed in relief.

Lukla fell away almost immediately, already a tiny blip through the portholes, and King let his wobbly legs recover before stumbling his way to the front of the plane.

He stopped in the cockpit doorway and said, 'How close was it?'

Slater's hands wouldn't stop shaking.

Which told him everything he needed to know.

'Fuck,' King said. 'Let's never do that again.'

'You read my mind,' Slater mumbled.

Then King noticed the multitude of warning symbols flashing across most of the screens.

As they levelled out above the mountains, Slater said, 'I think we might have a problem.'

82

S later coasted for close to ten minutes.

The controls screamed at him, desperate for manual intervention. They might as well have been hieroglyphs. He could handle a standard flight path, but this...

This was way above his pay grade.

But Phaplu was close. Incredibly close. The airport, as far as he could tell, was less than five minutes away if they maintained their current speed. Slater figured it'd be the longest five minutes of his life, but he was confident the old Dornier could tough it out.

Then the nose dipped violently.

If he hadn't been strapped in, he would have hit the roof. Luckily King had deemed it prudent to find a seat, because he might have been thrown out of the plane entirely. They each jerked against their seatbelts and crashed back down into the seats in twin heaps.

Slater coughed, fought the urge to lose the contents of his stomach, and squinted hard at the controls.

Everything was falling apart. He didn't know what

exactly had caused the chaos — one of the bullets striking something vital, obviously — but now the situation was growing more dire with each passing second. The plane jerked again, and Slater had to fight to prevent it dive-bombing into the peak of the nearest mountain.

Sweat beaded on his forehead, and ran off his nose.

He gritted his teeth and fought for control.

Then he spotted Phaplu. The village was barely visible in the valleys below, but he made out the roofs of buildings and, alongside it, the tiny runway. He dove for it, abandoning all hope of a smooth landing.

Because they were running on borrowed time.

The Dornier whined and shook and rattled in its descent, but it was rapidly approaching the village, and if Slater could touch down in one piece, they'd be at the home stretch—

Then one of the turboprop engines faltered.

There was a pop to their left and the plane jerked brutally to the right.

Slater's brain screamed, *Emergency landing.*

Only option.

But that wasn't even an option. They were screaming toward Phaplu, perhaps a minute out at best, but there was no way he could touch down on a runway that short with the engines in their current state. He swore at the top of his lungs, and heard King unbuckle his seatbelt behind him.

King fought his way into the cockpit doorway.

'Was that an engine?!' he shouted over the roar.

'Sure was.'

'Can you land?'

'I don't think so.'

King went white as a ghost. 'What do we do, then?'

Slater's brain was going haywire as a dozen different

thoughts fought for his attention. He could barely concentrate on the landscape, let alone—

The landscape.

He spotted the bright blue glacial river running parallel to Phaplu, less than half a mile from the village. He thought he recalled a name he'd read on a guide map days earlier, but it was deep in the recesses of his mind.

Solu?

He wasn't sure. It sounded right. It didn't matter either way.

He aimed for it.

Which mattered plenty. He was committing to it. There'd be no room for an alternative plan.

It was this or nothing.

An emergency landing, or a fiery crash.

No Plan B.

King realised too. 'Oh, shit.'

Slater didn't have time to respond. He was zoned into a tunnel, like he'd taken the entire planet's supply of Adderall at once. There was the river, and nothing else. He could see the position of every rock, every trickle, every sliver of dirt on the riverbanks. He got a sense of the depth of the water, the flow of the streams, the rising and falling of the land beneath it.

Then, in the blink of an eye, he realised a landing would be impossible.

And the only feasible option for survival presented itself.

'No,' Slater said. 'No, no, no, no...'

'What?!' King shouted.

Slater steeled himself.

'Leave the bags,' he said, his voice ice, his demeanour

ice. 'We don't need them anymore. Go to the exit and get ready to jump.'

'*What?!*'

'No other option.'

'You can't land?'

'It'll tear the plane apart.'

'Holy shit,' King said to himself, backing out of the doorway. 'Holy shit, holy shit, holy shit.'

Slater heard the cursing fade as King went down the fuselage toward the open doorway, bracing himself against the wind the whole time.

Then he zoned in even harder on the river.

He flew lower.

Lower...

Lower still...

Lower.

Then he pulled up at the last second and the Dornier levelled out perhaps twenty feet above the river. The speed was ludicrous, the wind deafening, the fuselage rattling, the whole plane threatening to shred to pieces at the slightest provocation.

They wouldn't make it thirty more seconds.

Slater employed every ounce of concentration he had available and let impulse take over. He opened his gaze wide, expanding his peripheral vision, and waited for the right moment.

Then he saw it.

A couple of hundred feet ahead, the light blue of the glacial water was a shade darker.

There was enough depth there.

He figured out trajectories *fast,* calculating when to jump and—

NOW.

He twisted in his seat, unclasped the seatbelt, and yelled, '*Jump!*'

King obliged. Anyone else would have hesitated, but both of them were keenly aware of the importance of timing in a world like this. King heard the command and threw himself out the door without a moment's hesitation, his body pummelled by the wind and the G-forces. He whipped out of sight and was gone.

Slater leapt out of the pilot's seat, scrambled out of the cockpit, and flat-out sprinted for the exit door.

Every stray thought in his brain, every instinct, every ounce of common sense — it all banded together and urged him to stop, screamed for him to stop.

He felt the nose of the plane dip with no one behind the controls, and knew the Dornier would impact the water at any moment.

He fought against the wind and clawed his way out of the plane into the open air.

83

He only fell ten feet before hitting the water with horrific intensity.

Still travelling at the same speed as the low-flying plane, he had the sensation of shattering every bone in his body as he broke through the surface. There was a single moment of impact, and then absolute silence.

He floated in the glacial water, barely conscious, barely clinging onto his sanity and his life.

If he passed out now, he'd sink to a watery grave.

He floated gently downward a couple of feet, and his feet touched solid ground.

The bottom of the river.

He hovered there for a spell, in too much pain to function, unsure whether he'd paralysed himself. He couldn't see a thing, and realised he had his eyes closed. At the edges of his hearing, he picked up a dull concussive underwater *boom,* and recognised it as the plane plunging into the river further downstream.

He let the icy water numb his wounds before opening his eyes.

It was surprisingly bright. The water was clear, so cold it had nearly frozen over, and the natural ice bath helped to dull the pain. He pushed off the bottom and ascended to the surface. When he broke it, sunlight flooded his senses, and he blinked hard to adjust to the new conditions.

The Dornier rested in a hundred separate pieces only a short way down the river. Slater found himself floating toward the wreckage, and he swam to shore before he got caught up in the debris. It would have pulverised him if he'd hesitated only a couple of seconds longer. And if they'd jumped from a greater height — well, it wouldn't have been pretty for their internal organs.

The miracle of unnatural reflexes had saved him, once again, from death or permanent disfigurement.

He clambered onto the riverbank and collapsed on his front. His stomach churned restlessly, and he realised he'd swallowed river water when he opened his mouth and vomited a torrent into the mud. Then he rolled onto his back, put his hands behind his head, and tried not to think about what he'd put his body through.

Further up the bank, he heard a groan.

He rolled to one side and squinted against the glare.

King sat on his rear with his knees tucked up to his chest, sporting a thousand-yard stare. One side of his face was already swelling, the skin bruising and turning purple in real time. He looked over and said, 'That was a hard landing.'

He couldn't stop shivering.

Slater managed to jerk a thumb toward the Dornier wreckage. 'Not as hard as that would have been.'

'Touché.'

'Did you land face-first?'

'I... don't know,' King said.

His words were slurred. The byproduct of swollen lips.

Slater said, 'You might be concussed.'

'Maybe.'

'We did it. We're here. The end of the road.'

King patted himself down. 'I assume you lost your gun too.'

Slater lowered a shaking hand to his waist. He prodded and touched. Then he said, 'Yeah. It's gone.'

'We're dead if we walk into that village.'

'No we're not.'

King looked over. 'I don't know about you, but I'm on the verge of collapsing.'

'Yeah.'

'And you expect us to go up against the rest of these insurgents unarmed and half-dead?'

'There won't be any insurgents in Phaplu.'

'You seem to think Aidan Parker has been orchestrating all of this.'

'No,' Slater said. 'Only part of it.'

'If I was feeling better, I might be able to work this out. But right now... I can barely put two and two together.'

'Don't worry. I worked it out myself.'

'You did?'

'Yeah.'

'When?'

'It hit me all at once. When I saw that spreadsheet.'

'Care to explain?'

So Slater did. He laid it all out, every last detail, demonstrating how this complex puzzle of Maoist rebels and ex-Naxalite kidnappers and scheming bodyguards and secret files all came together into a straightforward storyline. King listened, and his eyes progressively widened as Slater told him everything he knew.

When it was over, King said, 'So Parker won't have anyone protecting him?'

'Maybe a couple of soldiers he's paid off,' Slater said. 'But it's unlikely. He'll be scrambling right now. He won't have time.'

A pause.

Slater said, 'And he thinks we have his daughter.'

King placed his hands on the dirt and pushed off the riverbank, getting unsteadily to his feet. His legs shook. Slater could see the pain on his face as he tested his bad ankle. Clearly the impact with the river had disrupted any healing that might have begun on the swollen joint.

But he could stand.

And he could limp.

And he could close a fist.

He helped Slater up and said, 'Let's go get that son of a bitch.'

84

They'd lost the satellite phones, and their bags, and their guns.

They had nothing but the clothes on their backs.

But that was enough.

They limped up the riverbank, traversing the forest-coated hill between the river and the village of Phaplu. The sun went away as they hobbled through the clusters of trees, replaced by the eerie grey of low-hanging cloud. Each step sent bolts of pain through their battered, broken bodies, but they'd managed to avoid any permanent injuries. They could walk, and they could think straight. So even if it took them all day to cover the half-mile of terrain, they'd do it.

Because neither of them had an ounce of quit in them.

King put the majority of his weight on his good leg, dragging his puffy ankle behind him. It hurt like hell, but what didn't? By now it was all blurring together. He looked to the left and saw the staggering snow-capped mountain range far in the distance. Had he really just been there? Had he summited Gokyo Ri earlier that morning? Had he seen Raya die at the peak?

It felt like a lifetime ago.

'How do we find him?' he said. 'You told him to go to a secure location. We have no way of contacting him.'

'It's a tiny village,' Slater said. 'We walk around, and keep our eyes peeled.'

'And if we come up with nothing?'

'Then we don't stop until we get our hands on him.'

'Do you think he suspects anything?'

'I think he's holding out hope that we're actually going to show up with Raya.'

'Surely he imagined—'

'You now know what he is,' Slater said. 'You know what he was willing to do. He had to know this outcome was a possibility. He had to know we might fail.'

They didn't speak as they ascended the steepest part of the hill, and as soon as they reached the top, Phaplu spread out before them. They'd come up on the opposite side of the airport. They looked through the perimeter fence and saw the small runway draped in cloud, and beyond it, the hiking trail. On the other side of the trail was the familiar row of teahouses they'd walked past at the beginning of their journey.

Only days ago.

It felt like ten lifetimes ago.

Slater took the lead, and King followed. They walked the length of the airfield until the fence fell away and they were able to meet the trail. Then they strode into Phaplu.

It was now mid-afternoon, and there was some activity. Guides, porters, and foreign hikers alike moved through the mud, either fresh off planes and brimming with vigour or worn down by a return journey to be reckoned with. The contrast was palpable. King couldn't imagine what everyone thought of him and Slater. There was the exhaustion of days or weeks of trekking, and then there was a whole other level of tired reserved only for those who had pushed their bodies to the brink of death.

King scrutinised first himself, then Slater. He shivered in the chill, dragging one leg behind him, clad in dirty, damp, tattered clothes. He knew his face was lined with dirt and sweat and the remnants of blood that hadn't been washed out by the glacial river water. Then there was Slater. The bandage around the man's head had somehow held tight, but it was yellow with sweat and red with blood and faded and torn by the hell they'd gone through in Lukla. His arm was still wrapped in day-old bandages, but the makeshift cast was falling apart, exposing the grisly knife wound underneath. The staples had done their job, though, and the wound seemed to already be healing. When they got back on home soil, Slater would need to be loaded up with every antibiotic under the sun to prevent infection.

Together, they were a sorry sight.

But they were alive.

Adversity hadn't defeated them.

And that gave them strength.

They moved slowly past every teahouse, glancing through windows, lingering unnecessarily, letting everyone see them. They were a sight for sore eyes, but there were no hostile parties in this village. They'd realised the second they stepped foot onto the trail. There was no tension in the air. No one was squared away or reserved. Just weary travellers finishing their journey, and fresh faces about to start. No insurgents, no soldiers — no trained killers of any kind. It was a quiet, quaint village, and King almost regretted that soon they would have to disrupt that.

Hopefully they could do it in privacy, if Parker had done what they'd asked of him.

They passed the teahouse where they'd spent the first night, where they'd first met Aidan Parker and his guide, Sejun. It lay dormant and silent. They hovered in the entranceway for a beat, scanning the main communal area for any sign of them.

Nothing.

So he *had* relocated.

That was something, at least...

They ventured down the nearest laneway, choosing it at random. The road was potholed and the walls that enclosed the space were damp with mildew. The cloud had drifted into Phaplu, draping a thin veil over everything.

They'd almost reached the back of the village when a side door flew open beside them.

King turned fast, ready for anything, his fists clenched.

Neither he or Slater had access to a weapon, but they would fight to their last breath with their bare hands if it came to that. But they both realised it wouldn't be necessary.

Aidan Parker stood in the doorway, his features dulled by the shadow of the cloud and the darkness of the building. He was unarmed. He suspected nothing. His paunchy belly stuck out over the edge of his weatherproof pants. He wore an expensive windbreaker and had heavy bags under his eyes from lack of sleep. His hair was a mess, its thin wispy tufts sticking out at a dozen different angles.

He had the aura of a good man stressed to the eyeballs, involved in a situation he didn't deserve.

Slater knew better.

He knew it was a facade, carefully crafted to dissipate suspicion.

Parker said, 'I tried calling, but you didn't answer...'

'We ran into a few problems,' Slater said. 'We handled them.'

Parker noticed their condition, and lingered on the extent of their injuries for what felt like forever. Then he noticed the absentee.

'Where is she?' he said.

Slater said, 'Is your guide here?'

Parker hesitated. 'No. I figured from the tone of your voice in the call, it would be best if we were alone.'

'Good,' Slater said.

King stepped up and shoved Parker inside.

Slater followed, and they closed the door behind them.

85

P arker gasped in mock horror, as if it were the most brazen crime on the planet to push an innocent bureaucrat.

After all, he wasn't the one to get involved with the physical side of the business. He sat behind a desk and coordinated logistics and made sure intelligence was conveyed accurately. That made him soft and weak and flabby, which he must have thought put an unconscious barrier between himself and the men and women he sent out into the field to die.

That was all about to change.

Slater grabbed him by the collar and shoved him further into the room.

Into the shadows.

It was a storage room, loaded with crates of Cokes and Sprites and raw ingredients, all stacked neatly up to the ceiling. There were no lightbulbs or lamps of any kind — only a couple of fogged-up windows on the far side of the room that let in twin shafts of silver light. The floor and walls were made of rock, and the space echoed. It was cold. Dark.

The perfect setting for an interrogation.

Parker managed to keep his feet, but King hit him once in the stomach and he went down to his knees like he'd been shot. Slater moved in to follow up with another strike, but King put a hand on his chest and murmured, 'Wait,' under his breath.

Slater hesitated.

Wondered what King was getting at.

Then Parker lunged for one of the crates.

He was slow and unathletic, and he was shaking. He managed to slip his hand through a pair of wooden slats before King pounced on him. King seized him by the shirt, spun him around like he weighed nothing, and threw him toward the opposite wall. Parker bounced off a couple of the crates and collapsed in a sobbing heap.

King reached between the same slats and extracted a fresh, clean Beretta M9.

Loaded.

Ready to fire.

He pinched it between two fingers and held it up for Slater to see, like it was evidence at a crime scene. 'See?'

Slater nodded. 'Now we have a gun.'

'Yes,' King said, turning to Parker. 'We do.'

Parker moaned and said, 'I think you broke my back.'

'No,' King said. 'We threw you around a couple of times. You might have a few bruises. You're not used to pain, are you, Aidan?'

Parker went pale.

Slater stepped forward, boot by boot, placing his feet right near Parker's unprotected face.

He said, 'You sit behind a desk and think you know what people like us go through. It's delusional, sure, but I guess it explains why you made the decisions you made. Because you didn't think about the repercussions.'

'What are you talking about?' Parker said. 'Where's my daughter?'

'We'll get to that later. But whatever happened to her ... you should know it was your fault. You should carry that with you forever.'

Parker looked up, and there were tears in his eyes. 'What are you *saying*? Are you saying she's—?'

'I'm not saying anything. All you know is that she's not here right now. What you should be focusing on is the answers to the questions we're about to ask you.'

'I don't know what you're on about,' he said, talking fast to try and defuse the situation. 'I haven't done anything. You have the wrong information. You—'

'Shhhh,' King hissed.

Parker looked up. 'Please, guys, I'm—'

King raised both hands in innocence. 'Don't look at me. I'm not the one who figured it out. That was all Slater's work. So he's going to ask you the questions.'

King stepped back.

Slater stepped forward, and crouched down by Parker's cowering form. 'If you had to guess, Aidan, how many insurgents do you think we killed over the last few days?'

'I don't know.'

'I told you to guess.'

'I don't know what you're talking about. What insurgents?'

'You know.'

'I told you both already, I'm—'

Slater turned to King. 'How long do you think it's going to take him to realise?'

King shrugged.

'Realise what?' Parker said.

Slater turned back. 'Sooner or later you're going to figure out that your best bet is to be honest with us. We know exactly what you did. We know why you did it. We know how firmly you're going to try to deny it. But no amount of whining or pleading or begging is going to get you out of it, and hours are going to pass, and we're still going to be here in this room with you, and no one will come to help. Eventually you're going to cave in. The only question is whether it's going to be now, or in a few hours, or in a few days. And there's a lot we can do to you in that time.'

The silence was ominous.

Slater said, 'Be honest with us, Aidan. It won't hurt your chances. You're in deep shit regardless.'

Parker's upper lip quivered, but he didn't respond.

He stared a thousand yard stare, directly into the cold concrete beneath him.

Then he raised his gaze and said, 'What happened to my daughter?'

'She died,' Slater said. 'Because you got greedy and thought it would all go off without a hitch. Because you wanted power. Because you put your own child in harm's way to advance your political career.'

What little blood was left in Parker's face drained away completely.

He turned white as a ghost.

Guilt settled over him in a cloud.

When he lifted his eyes again, Slater knew he would confess to everything.

He was broken.

Slater said, 'How many insurgents do you think we killed for you, Aidan?'

'Probably dozens.'

'And that was the plan all along, wasn't it?'

Parker hesitated, realising if he responded it would be his first admittance of guilt.

But the walls were already crashing down around him.

He had nothing left.

Silently, he nodded.

86

S later said, 'Confirm everything I'm about to tell you. And don't even think about trying to cover anything up. If I'm wrong, correct me. If I'm right, tell me. Understand?'

Parker nodded.

He didn't look up.

He couldn't take his eyes off the floor.

Slater said, 'Planning a future push for president as an unknown candidate is going to require at least a couple of billion dollars in campaign spend, right?'

A nod.

'Because nobody knows who you are. You're not a known politician in the public sphere, and you're not a celebrity. So you need to go all out to get the American people on board. Which creates the need for donors.'

A nod.

'Most donors are big businessmen. They have their hands in many different pies. Some of them are, among other things, special risks insurers. They keep a tight grip on the global kidnapping market to make sure everything is running smoothly. Our handler already briefed us on the details of that particular industry. There's middlemen who are in communication with the kidnappers themselves, to make sure no one goes overboard with their ransom demands. That keeps everyone profitable. The kidnappers make money through successful ransom payments, and the insurers make money by receiving more from their clients than they have to pay out.'

A nod.

'But there was a slight problem. Someone in Nepal of all places had figured out how to exploit the system. An Indian man named Mukta, who used to be a Naxalite insurgent, figured out that there was a neat opportunity there. Because negotiations *had* to go smoothly with these firms, or there was no point taking out special risks insurance in the first place. It had to be a guaranteed transaction, which made the firms more likely to actually *make* the payments, and less likely to fret over the details. So, as soon as he figured out the script to get paid every single time, he started snatching foreigners left and right and siphoning huge ransom payments out of these big insurance firms.'

A nod.

'And the middlemen weren't able to contact him. They weren't able to tell him he was way out of line. They couldn't even find out who it was. Someone was ruining their profit margins by going rogue. Disrupting the whole goddamn industry. Everything had been chugging along in perfect harmony for long enough, but now this was threatening to ruin their business.'

A nod.

'So they saw you as a solution. They'd pitch in staggering amounts of money to your future campaign if you used your position in the government to help them quash this little problem for them. You're in black operations. Your connections are unparalleled. They knew if you or your family were in jeopardy, the government would pull out all the stops. They'd send in the best. They'd send in us.'

A nod.

'To them, you were a home run. You were easily influenced because you wanted the presidency. Dollars meant more to you than the average bureaucrat, because you knew what you could do with them. And you also knew how good our government's elite soldiers are. You figured — what's the risk? Sure, you had to leave your kid in the hands of a band of rogue kidnappers for a few days, but they're focused on smooth transactions, aren't they? They wouldn't actually harm their hostage. And besides, you've been coordinating the most feared and respected elite soldiers on earth for years. You know what your black-ops killers can do. You figure, it's the perfect storm. Let us hunt down and neutralise Mukta, shutting down that particular problem, and round up most of your campaign money in the process.'

A nod.

'You'd think the donors wouldn't make enough money from the kidnapping industry alone to justify the cost, but there's two aspects to this. There's the problem of the rogue kidnapper, and there's also the problem of the Maoist insurgency. Mukta's been using the rebels as his own personal militia, but your donors don't like them much either. They're a splinter group, and they're making everything unstable. They're converting rural villagers to communism. They're carrying out violent attacks on infrastructure here in Nepal. They're trying to stir up a rebellion. Which is bad for multinational corporations who have business endeavours over here. They've invested heavily in the developing third world, and they need to keep the peace. So paying you huge sums of money isn't a problem. The elite soldiers who come to your aid will take care of the rogue kidnapper and the insurgents all in one go.'

A nod.

'And then, after you kickstarted the process, you realised you'd fucked up. Mukta or one of his goons lifted your laptop, which had actual evidence you were being paid to coordinate this. You weren't expecting that. You thought they'd just take Raya and either one or both of your body-guards and leave everything else untouched. So, in your panic, you invented some bullshit story about HQ locations to make us prioritise getting the laptop back. You didn't expect us to actually look through it after we retrieved it.'

A final nod.

Slater said, 'You used us as pawns to carry out your dirty work, Aidan, and you got your daughter murdered in the process.'

Parker finally broke down.

He pressed his face to the cold floor of the storage room and wept.

87

W hen Parker finally resurface from his anguish, he moaned, 'I didn't even know they were going to kill Winston. I was promised a smooth process. I didn't know...'

'You did know,' Slater said. 'But you chose to ignore it. You thought ignorance would be bliss. Because if it all went to hell, which was always going to happen, you could just tell yourself it wasn't your fault. Clearly it was the failure of the operatives, or the miscommunication from the donors. Surely it couldn't be your responsibility that you let your own child get shot in the head by a lunatic kidnapper.'

Parker bowed his head.

King said, 'That's what the weakest of the weak do. They blame everyone else. They shirk all responsibility. They do anything and everything to advance their own position in society, and if it all falls apart they throw their hands up in the air and say, "What else could I have done?" You slaughtered your own kid. You'll have to live with that for the rest of your life.'

Slater snatched Parker by the collar and jerked him forward, so he had to look Slater in the eyes.

The man's eyes were bloodshot and teary.

Slater said, 'I want you to know that I blame myself for Raya's death. I'm sure King blames himself, too. Because that's what good men do. They try to find any area they could have improved, and they vow to do just that. If we were a little faster, or a little sharper, or a little more resilient, then a fourteen-year-old girl would be here with us instead of dead at the top of a mountain. But that's not what happened.'

Parker said nothing.

Slater said, 'I want you to see what good men do. So maybe you can realise how pathetic you are before the truth comes out and you get vilified for it.'

'Can you kill me?' Parker said in a voice barely above a whisper.

'No,' Slater said. 'That would make it too easy.'

Silence.

'We should,' King said. 'You know how close your little scheme came to killing both of us? You know what we went through to get back here?'

'That wasn't the plan,' Parker moaned. 'None of this was the plan.'

'That's too bad,' Slater said.

Parker scrunched up his face.

King said, 'Do you actually expect us to feel sorry for you?'

'I guess I expected you to show mercy.'

'That's not what this is,' Slater said. 'Maybe in the movies we might get cut and shot and beaten and exhausted half to death, then come back here and find it in our hearts to forgive you. But that's not how the real world works,

Aidan. You used us as your own personal enforcers. We came within a hair's breadth of death. And your foolishness led to the death of the person you love most.'

Parker sat still, silent and morose.

'Did you really love her?' Slater said. 'Or does everything come second to the pursuit of power?'

'Of course I loved her.'

'Not enough to protect her,' King said. 'Isn't that what a father is supposed to do?'

'I'm sorry.'

'Don't apologise to us. We're grown-ups. We don't need it.'

Silence.

'Apologise to her.'

'I can't...'

'And whose fault is that?'

Slater knew he'd broken through the sociopathic exterior. He'd cut through to the core, and Aidan Parker would never be the same. The budding politician's old life had consisted of numbers, and charts, and projections, and risk analysis. And there was no doubt his assumptions had merit. If Mukta had just stuck to his normal routine, he wouldn't have turned murderous, and Raya would still be alive. But that's the problem with breaking everything down, analysing everything, sitting behind a desk and trying your hardest to work out how to climb to the top...

It just never goes that way in the real world.

Parker now understood that.

It had cost him everything.

Slater said, 'We're not here to babysit you. We operate outside the law, so none of this is our responsibility. We're not going to arrest you, or punish you. But we're going to go back home and tell them everything. Your life is over. I don't know what they'll do with you, but it won't be sunshine and rainbows. You should steel yourself for that before you come back.'

Parker nodded quietly.

Slater said, 'If you think we're going to talk you out of doing anything drastic, we won't. We honestly don't care about you. You almost got us killed. We're ambivalent about what happens next.'

Another soft nod.

'Do you have a second gun?'

Parker nodded. He reached into his puffer jacket, came out with a second Beretta, and handed it over without the slightest hint of hostility.

He was truly broken.

Slater took it, and checked to make sure King had the other Beretta.

Then he said, 'We're leaving now.'

Parker nodded.

'I'd say it's been nice knowing you,' Slater said, 'but it really fucking hasn't.'

King opened the door and shuffled out, and Slater lingered in the doorway for a long moment.

Looking back at the man who had almost destroyed them.

Parker looked up.

'Are you going to shoot me?' he said.

His voice echoed.

Slater said, 'No.'

And tossed the gun on the floor at his feet.

'Do what you think is best,' he said.

He stepped outside and shut the door behind him.

King lingered in the dirt laneway. He noticed Slater

come out without a weapon, and cocked his head to one side.

'What are you doing?' he said.

Slater said, 'Giving him a choice.'

'Don't underestimate his desperation,' King said. 'He's going to open that door and try to shoot us.'

'I don't think so.'

To make sure they were covered for all contingencies, King raised and aimed his Beretta.

The silence drew out. Sounds from the village floated by — the distant rumbling of engines, the faint whine of a plane taking off, the steady *thunk-thunk-thunk* of a local chopping wood.

The door stayed closed.

There was no movement from the other side.

Then a single gunshot rang out, muffled by the rock and the heavy door.

Slater nodded. He took no pleasure in it. It was a horrible situation, and there was no joy to be had in the demise of the man who'd orchestrated it. But still...

...it was some measure of finality.

King said, 'So that's it.'

'That's it.'

They turned and walked away.

88

Washington D.C.
Three days later...

Jay Randwick had spent the past thirty years of his life obsessed with efficiency.

It had led to many outcomes, the large majority of them positive. There was the mansion in a quaint tree-lined street in Spring Valley, one of D.C.'s most exclusive neighbourhoods. There was the Bentley and the Rolls, and the Lamborghini Huracan for weekends. There were the memberships to the most esteemed country clubs, tables at the best restaurants in town, the finest whiskeys, the rarest cigars. There was the trophy wife — number three, which he had to admit had caused some considerable disruption to his career trajectory — but there were no kids. He'd never admitted it to anyone, but he'd done the math and realised how much children would cost him in future earnings. It simply wasn't worth it. So he paid meticulous attention to detail in practicing safe sex, and despite his numerous affairs he'd never been confronted with a positive pregnancy test by any of the call girls or budding socialites he used and discarded with increasing frequency.

Sometimes he wished he found deep satisfaction in the material conquests — houses, cars, girls.

But really, none of it meant anything to him.

What he relished was the hunt.

The game. The process. It's all he ever cared about, and he'd decided decades ago that it would be all he focused on until the day he died. There was something *beautiful* about the art of constructing things and then implementing them — businesses, ideas, routines. He was always coming up with faster and more efficient ways to carry out his days, and it had led to an empire he couldn't fathom. There were so many industries he'd conquered, so many different pies he had his hands in. Because at the end of the day, everything came down to a simple logical process. Do this, do that, repeat until you're profitable. Learn from your mistakes, fix what's broken, don't touch what isn't. Use the profits to keep expanding. Never settle. Never relax. Never rest on your laurels.

Just keep going onward and upward.

He'd mastered the process.

And now there was the next logical step.

He'd made enough money for ten lifetimes. He had more than he knew what to do with. So what does a man who has everything acquire next?

Simple.

Power.

Sure, Aidan Parker was an unorthodox candidate for President, but Randwick had been dissecting what made people successful his whole life, and he knew Parker had the goods for a successful campaign. The man had an incredible knack for breaking down complex matters into simple explanations. That's what the American people needed, and they'd buy his speeches hook, line and sinker. Randwick already knew it. He'd foreseen it.

And above all, Parker had the experience and the connections.

He knew how everything operated behind the scenes.

In a position like the presidency, that was golden.

So Randwick had put it all into a contract, as he did best. He'd laid it all out in simple, clear terms.

Use your resources to take care of a slight problem I have in Nepal, take a personal risk to demonstrate your loyalty, and I will reward you with unlimited funding.

Parker signed on the dotted line.

The last he'd heard, it was all going swimmingly.

So he pulled into his driveway with a certain optimism he didn't usually allow room for. Things were looking up. He killed the Bentley's engine and slipped out from behind the wheel. Which wasn't a regular occurrence, but he'd told his chauffeur to take the day off. There was a certain power you felt when you were in the driver's seat, and he wanted to experience it on the day the Nepal problem was cleared. He'd invested considerable funds in the country's infrastructure, and there was no room for an insurgency when big business was involved.

Not that he had any inkling of what that meant for the soldiers sent in to do his dirty work. He knew the theory, obviously, but his specialty was coordination. He was the ideas man. There was no use getting involved in the gritty details. He simply gave orders, and allowed them to be carried out.

And it had carried him to unparalleled heights.

He went inside and called his wife's name. He was met with silence. She was probably at the gym, slaving her way through the daily pilates class. He didn't really care. He was going to savour his alone time.

He put his laptop bag down in the marble hallway and went to the study. Fixed himself a generous serving of fifty-year-old Glenfiddich in a crystal tumbler, dropped into the armchair, and exhaled the stresses of the day. The oak walls gave off a subtle caramel odour, and he drank it in. Outside, it was getting dark. Twilight settled over Washington as the sky turned purple, then dark blue. There was little light in the mansion, so he reached across and flicked on the standing lamp.

There were two men in the corner of the room.

Randwick froze in his seat, the tumbler halfway to his lips.

But then the efficient part of his brain took over, crafting the best solution to the problem over the top of his skyrocketing pulse.

He said, 'If it's money you want, I can—'

'No,' one man said.

Randwick said, 'What, then?'

They stepped out of the shadows and rounded the leather couch across the room. They sat down in unison, one of them cradling a sleek black handgun. One Caucasian, and the other was African-American. They were both big and built like stone-cold killers. Randwick had been analysing people his whole life, and he immediately knew these men were more dangerous than any he'd ever met. Their muscle was not for show. They didn't have the soft supple frames moulded from commercial fitness routines. Their bodies were hard and corded and their hands were thick and calloused. There were fresh cuts and bruises all over them, which would soon turn to scars. They were built to break people.

And their eyes were ice cold.

The larger man said, 'How's business, Jay?'

Randwick gulped.

89

J ason King had also spent most of his life analysing people.

He could see sheer panic rise up in Randwick's eyes, and he knew it was a foreign sensation. This was a guy who previously thought he was tough, thought he worked harder and longer and more efficiently than anyone else, thought that gave him confidence. But now the mental walls he'd spent his whole life erecting were crashing down in the face of true adversity, and it was tearing him apart from the inside. He'd crafted a whole storyline for himself that had never faltered, never wavered, never been tested by *actual* difficulty.

It was easy to give orders.

It was hard to face their consequences.

King said, 'Do you know who we are?'

'No.'

'You seem like a reasonably intelligent guy. Take a guess.'

Randwick put the whiskey down and bowed his head.

Thought hard.

In the interim, King reached over and picked up the crystal tumbler. He sniffed. Double-checked the bottle to make sure he was correct in his assumption. Then tipped the contents of the glass back and almost purred with satisfaction as it snaked its way down his throat.

Randwick watched him with suspicion.

Slater did too.

King shrugged. 'It goes for thirty-six thousand a bottle.'

Slater raised his eyebrows. 'Well, in that case...'

He reached over, snatched up the bottle, poured himself a generous serving, and tipped it back.

Went through the same reaction.

Randwick said, 'I doubt you two are happy with me, so why don't you get to the point?'

'I asked you to guess who we are,' King said.

'I don't know. Is this because of the Saudis?'

King paused. 'No, it's not. But it's good to hear you've pissed them off, too.'

Randwick shrugged. 'You don't get a life like this without making a few enemies.'

'Well, you made the wrong ones,' King said.

'What'd I do?'

'You sent us in to clean up your issue in Nepal.'

'Oh.'

Slater said, 'We didn't appreciate that.'

'Look, if you honestly think I had malicious intent toward either of you, you're mistaken. I don't know who either of you are.'

'We know,' Slater said. 'But now we know who *you* are.'

'Are you honestly pissed that I sent you to kill a few savages? I assume you're elite operatives, right? Isn't that part of the job description?'

'No,' King said. 'It isn't.'

'We *were* elite operatives,' Slater said. 'We retired.'

Randwick said, 'And yet, here you are.'

'The government asked us to rescue a fourteen-year-old girl. We take odd jobs every now and then, so we agreed.'

'Yeah, well, she was in the hands of a bunch of rogue amateurs, so I'm sure—'

'She's dead.'

'Oh.'

'You got her killed with your little ploy to mask your true intentions. You and Aidan Parker both.'

'Where's Parker?'

'Still in Nepal.'

'I haven't been able to contact him.'

'That's because he shot himself in the head three days ago.'

'Oh.'

King looked around. 'Judging by our surroundings, I assume you're not going to do the same.'

'No, thank you,' Randwick said. 'I'd rather not.'

'You're a different level of corrupt,' Slater said. 'You think this is the first time your business decisions have led to innocent deaths?'

Randwick shrugged. 'It's the first I've heard of it.'

'You're a powerful man,' King said.

'I guess.'

'You seem to have it all figured out.'

'I'd like to think so.'

'Figure this out,' King said, and shot him in the face.

The suppressor didn't suppress much. A vicious cough still echoed through the empty mansion. But King and Slater barely noticed. They rose off the couch and made for the door. King tucked the gun away, and they stepped outside as if nothing had happened at all.

Slater said, 'Three left.'

They split up and disappeared into the night.

90

Upper East Side
Manhattan
One week later...

I t was their first official day back home, and they were expecting company.

They sat across from each other in King's penthouse, resting against the backdrop of Central Park. The view was as astonishing as ever, but with a few months of ownership under their belts it was steadily becoming the norm. They were still surprised they'd been allowed to keep their twin residences, resting side by side at the apex of one of the Upper East Side's most luxurious towers. Especially after what had happened before Nepal. One of the floor-to-ceiling window panes seemed fresher and cleaner than the others — a dramatic reminder of the private war that had played out months earlier between King, Slater, and a horde of hired mercenaries. But the damage had been repaired and the crimes swept under the table as an unsteady allegiance was formed between the U.S. government and two of the best black-ops killers to ever live.

So it irritated them to think that that allegiance might soon fall apart.

It all depended on how the following confrontation unfolded.

Neither of them expected it to go smoothly.

There was a knock at the front door. King got up, took a deep breath, and said, 'You ready?'

Slater said, 'As I'll ever be.'

He went into the entranceway and answered without checking the peep hole. He knew who it was.

They hadn't seen each other since before Nepal.

It was bound to be a shaky reunion.

As soon as he opened the door, Violetta LaFleur burst through. She was as beautiful as ever, but the intensity with which she stared at him overshadowed it all. He admired the blond hair, the piercing blue eyes, the shapely physique. Instinct took over. He loved her, and their bond had been forged through their mutually turbulent pasts and the similarity of their work. They understood each other in a way most couldn't, and it was the only reason they were able to work together in such a demanding field and still maintain a relationship.

But right now, greeting her partner seemed to be the last thing on her mind.

Her eyes flared with anger. 'What the *fuck* have you two been up to?'

He stood over her, unsure how to proceed. 'I'd say it's good to see you, but I'm afraid you'll shoot me...'

'Where's Will?' she snapped.

'He's here.'

Slater's voice floated through the penthouse. 'Hey, Violetta.'

She stormed down the entranceway, and said, 'Follow me.'

King followed.

Didn't say a word.

She strode into the open-plan living area and pointed to a vacant chair. 'Sit.'

King sat.

She said, 'You two are in deep shit.'

'Are we?' Slater said, raising his eyebrows. 'I wonder why...'

Ever the daredevil.

King just crossed his hands over his lap.

Waited for Violetta to speak.

She paced back and forth in front of them, running both hands through her hair, on the verge of tearing it out. 'Do you realise the sorts of favours I'm having to call in just to keep the hounds at bay?'

'Who are the hounds?' King said.

'Everyone above me,' she said. 'You both know the drill. I'm your only point of contact behind the scenes. It creates deniability — if you're taken on enemy soil, you know nothing about the inner workings of clandestine operations. You don't know what goes on behind the scenes, or who's involved, or how it's structured. But that might all be about to change if those in charge call you in.'

'Why would they call us in?' Slater said, feigning innocence.

'You know why.'

'Break it down for us. Just in case there's been a huge misunderstanding.'

Violetta rolled her eyes, but she obliged. 'As soon as you told us exactly what went down in Nepal, we started our own investigation. We put all our resources behind it. Didn't take us long to figure out exactly who was connected to Aidan Parker through shell companies. And guess what?'

'What?'

'We traced it to four separate individuals. All incredibly powerful people. Three men, and one woman. All in their fifties and sixties, all moguls, all guilty as sin of practically every crime under the sun. What they did in Nepal was one thing, but we have a lot of investigative horsepower, and when we put the spotlight on their business dealings we uncovered a treasure trove of seriously shady shit.'

King shrugged. 'They sound like scum.'

She stared daggers at him. '*Why* are they all dead?'

'What?' Slater said, widening his eyes. 'You think we—?'

He wasn't even trying to make a respectable performance of it.

In fact, he was making a mockery of the whole thing.

She nearly hit him. 'You realise I could put you both in a military prison right now and throw away the key?'

'But you won't,' Slater said.

'Will...' King warned.

He turned. 'What? You want to go with her — be my guest. But I'm not going to sit here and listen to this.'

'You'd better watch your mouth,' Violetta said.

Up until that point, Slater had been lounging against the seat back, keeping his voice low. Now he sat up ramrod straight and stared at her with withering intensity.

'Listen,' he said, much louder. 'You can storm in here with your anger and your self-righteousness and pretend like you're going to do something to punish us. But you're

not. You're a small cog in the machine. If you and your superiors were really going to do something about it, you would
have done it already. You all fear us — and you should.
Because I'm not going to apologise one bit for what we did.
Yeah, that's right, I just admitted to it. If you go after us
because of this, then you're just one more piece of the
corrupt system. That system is the reason we took matters
into our own hands in the first place. Because what the hell
would you lot have done about it? You would have gone
around in circles trying to find a way to prosecute them
within the boundaries of the law, and then eventually they
would have paid the right person off and it all would have
quietly gone away. Swept under the rug, like nothing ever
happened at all. That's how it works when you do everything by the book. That's why our careers were forged in the
first place. That's the point of black operations. If you think
for a *second* it would have gone any differently, then you're a
fool.'

Violetta didn't answer.

Slater said, 'What you say next is going to reveal to us
who you are, Violetta. Choose your words carefully.'

She didn't blink.

Instead, she looked at King.

She said, 'Does he speak for you, too?'

King knew what it meant.

He knew their separation of business and pleasure was
on the edge of a precipice.

One slight tip in the wrong direction, and it would all
fall apart.

But he was not a man of compromise. He was a man of
integrity, and he'd been operating with the same moral code
for his entire life. The moment he gave in, even for a

moment, the walls would come tumbling down. If he jumped into bed with the wrong side based entirely on his own personal attachments, that was something he might never come back from.

So, despite the potential consequences for both him and the woman he loved, he said, 'Yes. He does.'

91

No one spoke.

Slater could see Violetta contemplating what to say next.

He got there first.

He said, 'Don't assume we play by the rules.'

'I never—'

'You did. You thought because you're dating King you could walk in here and reprimand us for what we did. We don't work for you or the government. We accept gigs because we want to help, and we agreed to lend our services to you with the understanding that we don't operate within the normal parameters. We've spent our whole lives in this game. We know deep corruption when we see it. We handled it. And now we don't expect anything to result from it if you want to keep this mutual partnership in place.'

She said, 'And you shouldn't assume I play by the rules either.'

Slater said nothing.

She said, 'I could snap my fingers and the two of you no

longer exist. I don't care what personal ties I have to either of you. The personal side of things is a non-factor right now. Sure, you're strong, and you're fast, and you're tough — but you're just two men. I could assemble the resources of our entire government to take you out. It wouldn't take much. Put a sniper in a building across the street and both your heads would go up in clouds when you step outside this tower. That's what I *can* do. Don't think you're the only one showing restraint.'

'That's the route you want to go down?'

'No. But if I punish you for what you did without our permission, then there's nothing you can do to stop me.'

'Oh, but there is,' Slater said. 'It's real easy to give orders. But you're here now, with us. You're comfortable with the knowledge in the back of your mind that you can call for backup. But they're not here yet, are they? You think because we know you we won't hurt you if it comes to that?'

Violetta didn't respond.

Slater said, 'Your boyfriend might hesitate for obvious reasons.'

She stared at him.

Slater said, 'But I won't.'

She said, 'Then let's mutually agree that we have something to lose. If it comes to a war, none of us will make it out alive.'

Finally, King piped up. 'Agreed.'

She looked over. 'A war is not what I want.'

'Nor do we.'

'But you two have to understand that when you accept a job from us, we expect you to—'

'That's your mistake,' King said. 'You shouldn't *expect* anything. It's your choice to hire us. If we do good work, then use us again. It's completely up to you. But we'll never follow orders we don't agree with. And we'll never stop ourselves from following every operation to its natural conclusion. Whatever that entails.'

'*Whatever* that entails,' Slater said.

She didn't say a word.

King said, 'If you don't like what we did, and you think we deserve punishment for it, then that makes us enemies.'

Silence.

Slater said, 'Do you want to make us enemies?'

'No,' Violetta said. 'I don't.'

'Do you understand why we did what we did?'

'Yes. But that doesn't make it right.'

'Nothing is right. This world is dark and murky and corrupt. That's the way it's always going to be. If you don't let us stand against that, then you're no better than they are.'

'You realise you haven't changed a thing, right?'

They raised their eyebrows inquisitively.

She said, 'You think modern empires fall apart just because the person at the top meets an untimely demise? Each and every one of the four people you killed will be replaced. Life will go on.'

'Then let's hope their successors take a closer look at their business practices,' King said. 'I think we delivered a fair warning.'

'And if they don't get the message?'

'Then they'll have us to answer to.'

'You're going to keep tabs on all the corruption in the world?'

'We didn't say that.'

'You're sure acting like it's a possibility.'

Slater shrugged. 'We'll just do what we've always done.'

'And that is?'

'Our best.'

She brooded, still pacing back and forth.

Mulled over what to say next.

The seconds ticked away.

One.

Two.

Three.

She said, 'I — and by extension, the government — would like to maintain this partnership. You've proven yourselves to be morally rock solid time and time again. So we'll let this slide. Thank you for everything you did in Nepal.'

'Are we done?' Slater said.

She nodded.

He got up, brushed past her, and said, 'I'll give you two some alone time. I'm sure you have a lot to talk about.'

He was deep in his own head by the time he made it to the front door, and barely noticed someone following in his wake.

When he turned around with his hand on the doorknob, Violetta was there, staring up at him.

She said, 'You're a good man, Will. I don't want you to forget that.'

'I try to be,' he said. 'It's the only thing I can hold onto after... you know...'

She said, 'Ruby is looking down on you. I'm sure she's proud.'

He nodded.

Tried to stop himself from showing emotion.

She said, 'If you're feeling alone, you know you can talk to someone. We have many respected therapists—'

He looked past her, and saw King hovering at the other end of the hallway.

They exchanged a wordless, knowing look.

Slater said, 'Don't worry. I'm okay. I have all I need.'

I have a brother.

He turned and walked out, and closed the door behind him.

92

They stood at opposite ends of the corridor. The space felt a hundred times larger.

King put his hands in his pockets and bit his lower lip.

Violetta folded her arms over her chest.

He said, 'Does that wrap up the professional side of things?'

She said, 'Hard to move straight on from something like that.'

'We knew what we were getting ourselves into when we agreed to this. We knew it wouldn't be a smooth road.'

'I didn't think it would be this bumpy.'

'That's the life. That's the job.'

A pause.

She said, 'What if that had gone differently? What if it had taken a turn south? Where would we be right now?'

'It didn't.'

'But it could have. You said it yourself. You aligned with Slater.'

'He's my brother.'

'What does that make me?'

'It's different.'

'Is it?'

He said, 'I love you.'

She froze. 'Do you mean that?'

'Yes.'

'But you would have waged a war against me if it came to it.'

'I know.'

'No apology? No explanation?'

'I can't apologise, and I can't explain.'

Silence.

He said, 'It's just who I am. I stand up for what I think is right. I don't waver. If I did, I'd never forgive myself. If I did, I wouldn't be here.'

'What does that say about the future?'

'I don't know. I don't care.'

'You don't?'

'If life's taught me anything, it's to live in the present. I might not be here tomorrow. That's the nature of what I do for a living.'

'And you're at peace with that?'

'As much as I can be.'

'How do you think that makes me feel?'

'I was never going to be the perfect partner, Violetta,' he said. 'I'm just who I am.'

'Do you ever think about quitting?'

'Not anymore.'

'You could. I could. We could go to the Caribbean. Spend the rest of our lives making love in a beach hut.'

'Sounds idyllic.'

'But it's not for you.'

'No. I tried it.'

'And you ended up right back here.'

'I can't escape it.'

'Does that disturb you?'

'Not anymore.'

She said, 'I think I'm stuck doing this forever, too.'

'You don't have to be.'

'But then I'd have to leave you.'

'You could. If you wanted to. You deserve better.'

'But I'm good at what I do. And I'm in love with you. So where does that leave me?'

'Right here. You can't escape either.'

She shrugged and said, 'At least we're both as fucked up as each other.'

He smiled.

'How about dinner?' he said.

93

It was one of the most exclusive Japanese restaurants in New York City, but they waltzed right in.

Violetta was nearly unrecognisable in a gorgeous black off-the-shoulder dress, showing off her pronounced collar bones and tantalising curves. King had gone for a simple button-up shirt tucked into a pair of smart dress slacks. She'd told him in no uncertain terms how his wardrobe selection showed his own physique off in all the right places.

They stepped inside and the shadows draped over them, elongated by the soft romantic lighting.

Before they were greeted by their waiter, she patted him gently on the behind.

'Damn, you look good,' she whispered.

An attentive man in his twenties showed up and wordlessly ushered them to a private booth up the back. When they were seated, he said, 'The usual?'

King nodded. 'Thanks, Jack.'

'Not a problem, sir.'

He bled away into the aisles, and less than a minute later

another waiter brought over a bottle of outrageously expensive saké for the table, and a neat whiskey for King.

He sipped at the blend and smiled. 'I missed this.'

'We never did discuss exactly what happened in Nepal,' she said, pouring herself a generous serving of saké. 'How was it?'

'Brutal.'

'As brutal as usual?'

'Worse.'

She sipped her drink and mulled over it. 'How do you think Slater pulled up?'

'He's fine. He's always fine.'

'You know he's not. And you aren't either. You can't hide from the consequences forever.'

He swept a hand around the restaurant. It was a packed house, but the patrons were accustomed to fine dining, and suitably respectable. There was only the low murmur of private conversation, the soft clinking of glasses, and the distant muffled sizzling of hot plates.

He said, 'Do you see where we are right now?'

'Yes,' she said. 'It's beautiful. It's a fine life. But you're competent enough to do a thousand other things and make the same amount of money. That's not why you do it.'

'You know why I do it.'

'Is it worth the cost?'

He shrugged and said, 'Let's not talk about that. I prefer to enjoy simple moments like this than worry about the future.'

'But you know pain is coming.'

'Pain is always coming. Slater and I are worth eight figures each — Slater more like nine. If we wanted to, we could live the rest of our lives in absolute hedonism. It takes a lot of effort to avoid getting seduced by that. So that's why I like to dip into it when I can. Slater takes that concept... to another level.'

'I'm worried about him.'

'I told you not to be.'

'And yet, I still am.'

'He'll be okay.'

'He wanted to be with Ruby. Forever.'

'I know.'

'That's got to be wearing him down. Thinking about what could have been.'

King nodded, then thought of both his and Violetta's separate histories. He said, 'We both know exactly what that's like.'

'Can't change the past.'

'No,' he said. 'We can't.'

'It led us here, at least.'

They clinked their glasses together, and took sips in unison.

She said, 'You know, this is so nice, I almost forgot you threatened to kill me earlier today.'

'Only by proxy,' King said. 'Slater did the talking.'

She laughed. 'What a life we live.'

Seized by impulse, he leant over the table and kissed her gently on the lips.

Then pulled back, and took her hand in his.

He said, 'It's worth it. The sacrifices we make. It's all worth it.'

'I know,' she said. 'I guess I just can't help stressing about what will come next.'

'Something big, I imagine,' King said. 'We stirred the pot over the last couple of weeks.'

'You pissed off a lot of people.'

'What's new?'

'I might get killed just for associating with you.'

'Is it worth it?' he said.

'Oh, yes,' she said, and stared at him with unrestrained passion. 'Very.'

They ate fast, opting not to waste a second. When the bill came, King handed his card over without looking at it. They waited for the receipt, then slid out of the booth and walked the two blocks back to the tower at breakneck speed. They burst into the private elevator and threw themselves on each other, hands probing, mouths intertwined.

They barely made it to the penthouse.

For round one, then two, then three.

Like bullets roaring out of the chamber.

When it was over in the early hours of the morning, they lay on the floor beside the bed. Naked, short of breath.

Violetta said, 'You should know there'll be more professional conflict. Between us. It's not going to end.'

King kissed her on the forehead.

She smiled. He felt her breathing against his chest, and smiled too.

There would always be carnage. There would always be violence. But what they had between them kept something alive. Some fleeting hope. Something raw and real amidst the suffering.

She said, 'There's no happily ever after. Not with us. Not with this life.'

He said, 'Good. At least that means there'll be some excitement.'

She looked up at him with those deep blue eyes.

He looked back.

Truth was...

...he was already ready for the next war.

He said, 'No one likes a happily ever after.'

KING AND SLATER WILL RETURN...

Visit amazon.com/author/mattrogers23 and press **"Follow"** to be automatically notified of my future releases.

If you enjoyed the hard-hitting adventure, make sure to leave a review! Your feedback means everything to me, and encourages me to deliver more books as soon as I can.

Stay tuned.

BOOKS BY MATT ROGERS

THE JASON KING SERIES

Isolated (Book 1)

Imprisoned (Book 2)

Reloaded (Book 3)

Betrayed (Book 4)

Corrupted (Book 5)

Hunted (Book 6)

THE JASON KING FILES

Cartel (Book 1)

Warrior (Book 2)

Savages (Book 3)

THE WILL SLATER SERIES

Wolf (Book 1)

Lion (Book 2)

Bear (Book 3)

Lynx (Book 4)

Bull (Book 5)

Hawk (Book 6)

THE KING & SLATER SERIES

Weapons (Book 1)

Contracts (Book 2)

BLACK FORCE SHORTS

Join the Reader's Group and get a free 200-page book by Matt Rogers!

Sign up for a free copy of '**HARD IMPACT**'.

Experience King's most dangerous mission — action-packed insanity in the heart of the Amazon Rainforest.

No spam guaranteed.

Just click here.

ABOUT THE AUTHOR

Matt Rogers grew up in Melbourne, Australia as a voracious reader, relentlessly devouring thrillers and mysteries in his spare time. Now, he writes full-time. His novels are action-packed and fast-paced. Dive into the Jason King Series to get started with his collection.

Visit his website:

www.mattrogersbooks.com

Visit his Amazon page:

amazon.com/author/mattrogers23

CPSIA information can be obtained
at www.ICGtesting.com
Printed in the USA
LVHW091439030919
629783LV00001B/153/P

9 781074 672539